D1566670

the siren's cry

jennifer anne kogler

HARPER
TEEN
An Imprint of HarperCollins*Publishers*

HarperTeen is an imprint of HarperCollins Publishers.

The Siren's Cry

www.epicreads.com

Library of Congress Cataloging-in-Publication Data
Kogler, Jennifer Anne.
The siren's cry / Jennifer Anne Kogler. — 1st ed.
p. cm.
Sequel to: Otherworldlies.
Summary: During a trouble-filled school field trip to Washington, D.C., twelve-year-old Fern finds and tries to rescue fellow Unusual Miles Zapo, who is imprisoned at the National Zoological Park, using her abilities with teleportation and telekinesis.
ISBN 978-0-06-199443-2 (trade bdg.)
[1. Supernatural—Fiction. 2. Psychic ability—Fiction. 3. School field trips—Fiction. 4. Twins—Fiction. 5. Brothers and sisters—Fiction. 6. Washington (D.C.)—Fiction.] I. Title.
PZ7.K8215Sir 2011 2010045560
[Fic]—dc22 CIP
AC

Typography by Torborg Davern
11 12 13 14 15 CG/RRDB 10 9 8 7 6 5 4 3 2 1
❖
First Edition

To the girls of Dod Hall

Contents

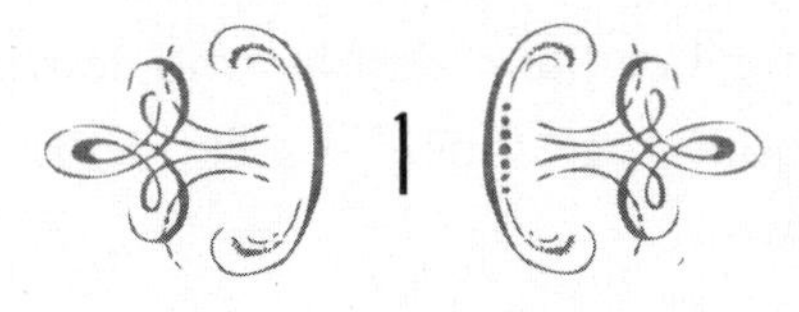

1
the threat at pirate's cove

Haryle Laffar's gray eyes flashed angrily as he stood on the cliffs above the beach at Pirate's Cove, surveying the carnage below. Fern McAllister's unconscious body had washed up onshore, and gentle breakers now rippled peacefully across her lifeless form. Laffar spotted a man huddled and shivering behind a rock partway down the hill and recognized his old friend immediately. When he reached the man, Laffar yanked on his soaked hair, forcing his friend to look up at him.

"What happened here, Flarge?" he asked accusingly. His swift journey down the stairs had caused some windblown sand to catch in his dark beard. Laffar had been late meeting his brother, Vlad, but he did not expect to find such slaughter and destruction on the beach. A large tidal wave had engulfed all of Vlad's followers except Flarge. Yet again, Vlad had failed in his mission.

"The girl," Flarge stammered. "She did this. . . . Vlad tried to destroy her, but it was she who destroyed him."

"What about the stone?" Laffar demanded. "Who has it?"

"It's gone," Flarge said despondently. Laffar watched from their position in the shadows as some of the Rollens who had recently arrived shackled his brother. "What will we do?"

"We won't *do* anything . . . not now," Laffar insisted, adjusting the bandanna he wore over his shoulder-length hair. He helped Flarge up and hoisted his injured friend's arm over his shoulder.

"But what about the plan?" Flarge said as they headed toward the stairs dug into the cliff. "If the girl, Fern McAllister, really is an Unusual . . ."

"The girl won't be a problem," Laffar said, his single silver front tooth gleaming. Haryle Laffar and his friend were nearly at the top of the stairs when they turned and looked back down at the beach. Vlad, shackled and strapped to a board, was being carted off in one direction. Moving in the opposite direction, a man had Fern McAllister's limp body in his arms, no doubt on his way to deliver her to someone who would nurse her back to health. Haryle Laffar's gray eyes blazed in the moonlight as he spoke once more.

"We'll kill Fern McAllister before she has the chance to do any more harm."

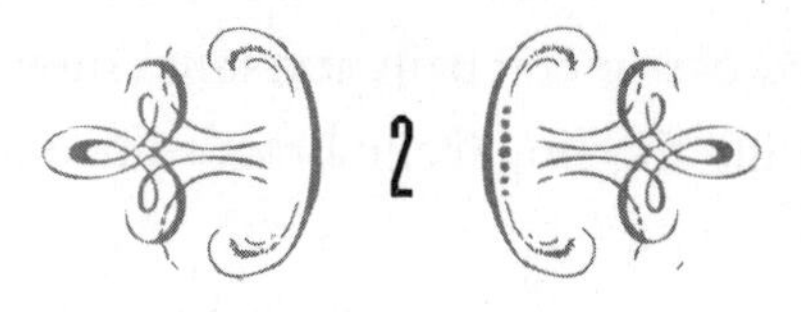

the mystery of miles zapo

Fern was sure she was suffocating.

Each gulp of air she inhaled made her lungs feel as if big handfuls of sand were being dropped down her throat. She gasped, hacking as she rolled over. The flesh on her bare back tingled as it touched the cold concrete floor. She looked up and saw more concrete above—a single flickering orange light crackled directly overhead. Her eyes slowly adjusted as she forced herself to her knees and then teetered to her feet.

The room was about the size of a classroom. Tattered netting hung from the low ceiling, and a half-dozen rusty steel cages were piled in one corner of the room. Some of the cages, large enough to hold several people, had broken bars. Others had doors hanging from loose hinges or no doors at all. Fern noticed a dark patch in another corner of the dingy concrete room—a doorway, she supposed.

Scrambling toward the darkened entrance, she panted as she climbed over metal pails and large shovels. Fern had the creepy, spine-tingling feeling that someone was watching her.

These days, though, Fern McAllister always felt like someone was watching her.

She scrabbled over a large bundle of dry, cracked bamboo stalks. To her left was a crate with oversize block letters stamped on its side. In the faint light, she could barely make out the words: PROPERTY OF NATIONAL ZOOLOGICAL PARK.

Fern took a step back, reevaluating. She seemed to be in a basement, surrounded by rusty cages, bamboo stalks, mops, shovels, and pails.

Where, exactly, was she?

On the other side of the doorway, Fern heard something shuffle. She dashed toward the doorway. Once she was past the threshold, everything was considerably darker—the only light came from the room Fern had just exited. But even in the semidarkness, what she saw was unmistakable. Huddled in the corner, cowering in the back of a medium-size cage, was a small boy, whimpering. There were half-empty boxes of cereal, a few banana peels, and a large pile of rags in the cage with him. The boy's shoes were unlaced and only half on his feet. Using his arms, he clenched his knees to his chest and rocked himself back and forth quickly. A giant padlock hung from the door of the cage. It looked like it would take a workbench full of power tools to break it open. Fern cautiously approached the boy, peering through the vertical steel bars of the cage.

As she got closer, she realized how filthy he was.

"Hello?" Fern asked timidly.

The boy did not respond. He stared straight ahead, almost looking through Fern, his eyes unable to focus.

"Are you okay?" Fern asked, this time louder, as she drew closer. She scanned the room. Except for the boy and the cage, the room was bare with gray walls.

"Where are we?" She questioned. "How did you get here?"

The boy was wearing thick Rivers Cuomo glasses. His jet-black hair was the same color as Fern's. His small frame led Fern to believe he was probably not as tall as she was. She waved her hand in front of his face. The boy didn't flinch. He seemed to be sleeping with his eyes open.

Who was this kid? Who had done this to him, putting him here, alone, in a locked cage?

The strange boy's eyes began to focus on Fern.

"It's—it's you," the boy stammered, wincing as he spoke. Moving his thick-rimmed glasses up his face, he rubbed his eyes vigorously. He inched forward in his cage. "You're her." He smiled weakly at Fern, revealing a set of brilliant white teeth. A strange sense of déjà vu overcame her, but she couldn't place him.

"I'm who?" Fern said. Her eyes traced the walls to the

ceiling. There was a single grate above them, which had been pushed halfway open.

"You made it," the boy said, his eyes slowly glazing over again. "You survived when you were in the water. You're a Tlaloque."

"A what?" Fern said, trying not to show the shock on her face. Was this boy talking about her battle with Vlad on the beach? How could he possibly know about that?

"One of Tlaloc's helpers," the boy said, his voice becoming clearer. "Aunt Chan said you're just like me. And now you're here to help me . . . aren't you?" he asked feebly, with innocent hopefulness. Fern's heart nearly broke as she looked at his handsome face and terror-filled eyes. The boy had clearly been in this place a long time. Judging by the type of lock on his cage, the unknown villain who'd put him here was making sure that he did not escape.

"What's your name?" Fern asked, trying to stick to topics she thought the boy could handle. *And how in the world am I supposed to help you?* she thought.

"Miles . . . Miles Zapo," the boy said.

"Nice to meet you," Fern said, trying to sound cheerful for both their sakes. She stuck her arm through two of the bars but couldn't reach Miles in the back of the cage. She withdrew her hand. Was Fern here because she was supposed to help this Miles Zapo? Or had someone drawn her here because they wanted her in a cage as well? Fern's stomach somersaulted.

"Where are we?"

For Fern, appearing all of a sudden in strange places was not surprising anymore. Ever since she'd discovered that she could teleport—move from one place to another instantaneously—she'd found herself in a whole variety of places, some of them more pleasant than others; some intentional, some not. When Fern had blacked out and wound up on the top of Splash Mountain at Disneyland, with a news crew filming her from a helicopter, she began trying to control her strange power. This dingy place, though, was far more frightening than an amusement park ride, no matter how precarious her mountainside perch had been.

"Who put you in that cage? How long have you been here?" Fern asked when Miles didn't answer her last question. This time, she tried to speak slowly so he would understand.

"He took me from my house," Miles said, his eyes growing wider. "The tall man with the gray eyes and the silver tooth."

"Took you? From where?" Fern grew more insistent, hearing the panic creep into her own voice as she pictured the type of person who would lock Miles in a cage.

"Mound, Minnesota," Miles replied. "Where I live. As soon as he took me, *they* came and made me feel that horrible pain." Miles began to tremble, his body shaking back and forth.

"So you were kidnapped by a group—"

Faint footsteps from above silenced Fern. The noise was

directly overhead. Fern's body tensed with alarm. She pressed her lips together as she and Miles stared at each other, listening intently. The clamor grew louder until it no longer sounded like footsteps but dozens of hands slapping on the ceiling at once, coming from all different directions.

"What's that?" Fern asked, her eyes widening.

"They're coming back! They'll trap you here too! We've got to get out!" Miles gasped, looking up toward the open grate and cowering in the back of his cage. He began pushing himself between two poles in the back of the metal cage's frame. Fern grabbed the two bars on either side of the cage door, hoping to rattle them hard enough to shake the rusty door free of its hinges, but her hands went right through the steel bars as if they weren't there at all. She tried slamming her hand against one of the bars with the same result. It was as if she were a ghost. The rumpus above Miles and Fern grew louder and louder still. Fern again attempted to shake the cage, but it was as if she had no body mass at all.

She was tempted to bolt . . . though she hated the thought of leaving Miles Zapo to fend for himself. Still, one look at how frightened he was at the thought that *they* were coming back convinced her that if she wanted to stay alive and unharmed, she should run as fast as she could away from this place.

Fern eyed the escape route straight overhead, through the grate in the ceiling. She felt woozy and petrified all at once and dropped to her knees. Colorful spots formed under her eyelids. She blinked rapidly, trying to combat the cloud she felt enveloping her brain. She made eye contact with Miles and recoiled at the panic in his eyes. Everything went white. Then black. Then there was nothing.

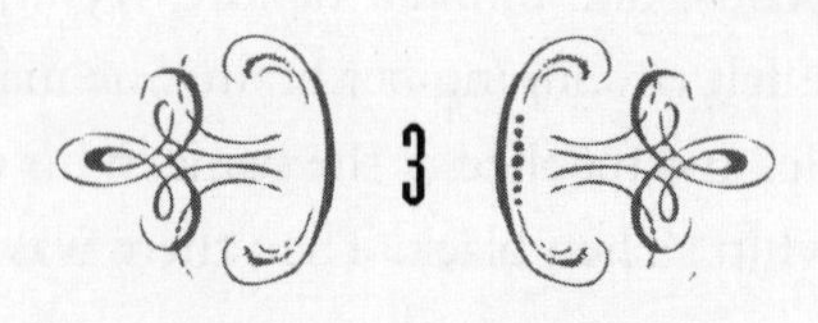

3

the accommodations

"Ahhhhhh!" Fern yelled at the top of her lungs.

Something had a grip on Fern's shoulder and was shaking it firmly. Fern opened her eyes, breathless as she held her hands up and tried to grip Miles Zapo's metal cage again.

But there was nothing there.

"What in the world's *wrong* with you?" Fern's twin brother, Sam McAllister, said, staring at Fern as if she'd gone completely nuts.

Fern looked around, utterly confused. The dingy basement had been replaced with the bright interior of an airplane. Lindsey Lin, her best friend, was on her left, sitting in an aisle seat. Sam, still staring at her, was on her right, sitting by the window.

"At this time, please return all tray tables and seat backs

to their locked and upright position," a female voice blared over the loudspeaker.

Half the main cabin was filled with students from St. Gregory's Episcopal School. Though none of the students were wearing their school uniforms, it was easy to recognize the dozens of seventh and eighth graders and weary chaperones among the other passengers.

Everyone stared at Fern. Visions of her Splash Mountain escapade flashed through her mind. She wondered how loud her scream had been. A flight attendant was rushing to row thirty-six, where Lindsey, Sam, and Fern were sitting. The crew member glared at Fern with a skeptically arched eyebrow.

"Was I yelling out loud?" Fern whispered to Sam.

"Uh, yeah. At the top of your lungs, for like the last ten seconds," Sam whispered back.

"Oh," Fern said.

The flight attendant paused for a moment to ensure that Fern was no longer disturbing the main cabin's tranquility. She cleared her throat, wagged her finger at the row, and made the shush signal. Then she moved on.

Everything came flooding back to Fern all at once. She was on her spring break school trip to Washington, DC.

Five days of activities were planned, including a trip to Arlington National Cemetery, the East Wing tour of the White House, a tour of the Capitol conducted by someone from the office of San Juan Capistrano's representative in the House, and dozens of other scheduled events. The trip used to be an eighth-grade-only annual event, but Headmaster Mooney realized several years ago that it was less work for him to make the journey every other year and open it up to all seventh- and eighth-grade students. Decisions like this, in fact, had led Mrs. McAllister to identify the headmaster's leadership style as "lazy."

This year, half the seventh and eighth graders had signed up for the trip, including, unfortunately, Fern's three least favorite people at St. Gregory's: Lee Phillips, Blythe Conrad, and Headmaster Mooney.

But the one person Fern was unable to get out of her mind was not on the plane at all. Fern was certain that Miles Zapo was somewhere far less comfortable and far less safe. The plane was now over northern Virginia, beginning the descent into Dulles International Airport. The excitement level of the students rose as those with window seats glimpsed the Washington Monument and the snaking Potomac River below.

Fern couldn't erase the image of the terrorized boy with big-framed glasses from her mind. Who exactly was Miles Zapo?

"Bad dream?" Sam asked, turning away from the views of Washington.

"Yeah," Fern muttered.

Ever since Fern's dramatic showdown a month before with the powerful Otherworldly Vlad, she'd been having some very strange and vivid dreams. Her dream about Miles was the fourth of its kind.

In the first dream, Fern was at a picnic near a body of water. The water was clear and dark blue, and everyone was speaking a language she couldn't decipher. A girl her age with dark skin and hair seemed oddly familiar, much as Miles had. Fern felt like she was there—but when she tried to stick a toe in the refreshing, cool water, she awakened.

A week later, Fern had a second dream. She was fairly certain she was in England, standing in the corner of a kitchen looking out at the grounds of a sprawling manor. A tall, lanky boy named Lancaster was being scolded by his British-accented, ruddy-cheeked mother. She was accusing her son of spying on the girls' locker room at school. Fern woke up before she learned more.

The third dream took her to a small, cramped living room above a restaurant in the middle of a bustling city somewhere in Asia. A family of eight gathered around a table, laughing, smoking, and eating strange food Fern had never seen before. She watched silently as a girl, about her age, looked up in her direction, raised both eyebrows, but said nothing. Fern waved at her, and the girl cocked her head to the side. No one seemed to see Fern in the room. It was as if she were invisible to the people she was watching. After her third dream, Fern began to wonder if the vivid dreams meant she was entering the next stage of her transmutation into a full-fledged Otherworldly. She fervently hoped that fangs would not be next.

This most recent dream, though, was different. Miles

Zapo seemed so real. She was sure that it was more than a dream. Fern had spoken to Miles and he'd responded. He was in desperate trouble, he'd asked for her help, and she'd been unable to provide it.

Though Fern couldn't explain why, she felt an undeniable urge to do everything in her power to rescue Miles. But where was he? Somewhere in Minnesota? The crate had a zoological park logo on it. Maybe it was from a zoo in Minnesota—and maybe she could teleport there once she came up with a plan to save Miles.

Fern glanced over at her brother, who was bracing himself for the landing. Sam had hated flying ever since he was a little boy. He pretended that he didn't mind the takeoffs and landings, but when they were about to land, Fern saw him close his eyes and grip the armrests so hard his knuckles turned white.

Fern considered telling Sam right then and there about the dream she'd had about Miles Zapo.

When she had told Sam about her previous dreams, he'd insisted that she start writing everything down.

"What if you're actually seeing the other ten of the Unusual Eleven?" Sam had exclaimed over breakfast. "Maybe you're having visions of them and the dreams are important. Didn't the lightning storm connect you all together? Wasn't that part of the prophecy?"

The prophecy about the Unusual Eleven, the special group of eleven Otherworldlies, all having the ability to teleport as well as distinct individual talents, had been circulating for thousands of years. A little over a decade ago, rumors spread that eleven Otherworldly births, which were exceedingly rare even singly, all occurred on the same day, during a series of electrical storms throughout the world. Soon buzz began anew among Otherworldlies that the prophesied Unusual Eleven had finally arrived. The Unusual Eleven, the most powerful and unique Otherworldlies in existence, were assumed to share a special connection, stronger than any other bond existing between living creatures.

Ever since Fern had been officially confirmed as one of the Unusual Eleven, her life had turned upside down and inside out. In the span of a month, she'd learned that Otherworldlies were the real-life version of vampires from the legends. She'd discovered that she'd been adopted by Mary Lou McAllister, the only woman she'd previously ever known as her mother. Mary Lou had been chosen by her best friend, Fern's now deceased Otherworldly birth mother, to step in to protect Fern from any exploitation resulting from her Unusual status. Fern also learned that she could harness water with fearsome results, teleport to any location she could visualize in her mind, and that she was part of a large Otherworldly secret society divided into two distinct groups: Blouts and Rollens. Blouts had no problem using and destroying their Normal human counterparts. Rollens wanted to live peacefully within Normal society. Fern had been identified as a Rollen when she nearly killed Vlad, one of the most powerful vampires in existence, after Vlad had threatened to harm the rest of the McAllisters if Fern did not join the Blouts.

All Otherworldlies had superhuman abilities. Lindsey Lin, for instance, was an Otherworldly who could, under certain conditions, conjure up a vision of what was happening in any part of the world. Kenneth Quagmire, who was head of the Rollen faction of Otherworldlies, could manipulate and eradicate memories.

The strangest part of Fern's recent past, though, was that because of her confirmed Unusual identity, in the secretive underground Otherworldly community she had become a full-fledged celebrity. Strange visitors appeared at the McAllister doorstep, hoping to catch a glimpse of the girl who'd nearly defeated one of the most powerful and feared Blouts. Eventually Mrs. McAllister, better known as "the Commander" to the McAllister brood (who had given her the nickname because of her military-style parenting), installed a security system, including a closed-circuit camera network that monitored the McAllister house's perimeter twenty-four hours a day.

A few months ago, Fern never would have believed any of it. Neither would her family, for that matter. Not her older brother, Eddie, or her mother, or least of all, Sam. Although Sam was becoming somewhat of an Unusual Eleven-Rollen-Otherworldly geek, constantly trying to discover more about his sister's past. Fern knew, as only a sister could, that Sam, more than anything else, was secretly worried about her and channeled his energy into activities he viewed as helpful.

Fern had almost come to expect that kind of devotion from Sam. Her birth mother, Phoebe Merriam, may have died long ago, Fern realized, but before she did, she'd managed to pick a pretty amazing surrogate family for her daughter. Landing the McAllisters as her adoptive family was, perhaps, the first and only time Fern had been lucky in her life.

Still, Sam McAllister was everything Fern was not: blond, athletic, tan, popular, and, most of all, normal. Though Sam was her closest friend and confidant, Fern could feel the differences growing between them, like a snowball gaining mass as it rolls down a mountain. She was sure that the snowball wedged between them had already started tumbling downhill and there was little she could do to stop it.

She decided to table telling Sam about her latest dream until after the Washington, DC, trip. Most likely Sam would ask her about the dream when they were alone. But they probably wouldn't be alone any time soon. Sam would be off with his friends Preston and Taylor, and Fern would be with Lindsey anyway. There was no reason to get Sam riled up now. After all, Fern wasn't even sure if any of her visions were real, part of her transmutation, revelations of the past or future, or merely bad dreams.

Regardless, it could certainly wait a week.

Sam, white knuckles intact, survived the landing without incident (as did Fern and Lindsey). The students of

St. Gregory's spilled out of the plane and into Dulles International Airport. A few minutes later, though the bags from Flight 187 were starting to stack up on carousel three, there were no students retrieving luggage. Instead, all sixty-four St. Gregory's students were huddled around Headmaster Mooney, excitedly shouting back and forth to one another.

"If you don't quiet down," Headmaster Mooney yelled, "I will *not* read this list." Headmaster Mooney, who Matt McGraw estimated weighed over three hundred pounds, smoothed over his bushy gray and brown mustache with his index finger and thumb. He then moved his hand to his reflective bald head and rested it there.

"I repeat: I can wait as long as it takes, but I will not scream over sixty-four voices."

Because Headmaster Mooney normally wore a suit and tie to school, Fern thought he looked quite strange today in khaki pants and a hooded sweatshirt. She realized it was sort of like seeing Santa Claus in street clothes. That is, if Santa Claus was a fashion idiot.

Mooney was flanked by chaperones. Mrs. McAllister and Lindsey's parents, Mr. and Mrs. Lin, were on one side of him. On his other side stood Lee Phillips's mother and Mr. Billing, the physical sciences teacher at St. Gregory's, who was also the father of one of the students.

"You will each be assigned to a group, named for a famous United States president. A group will be led by one chaperone, and there will be four rooms in each group.

mother holding a large poster-board cutout of George Washington above her head. Though Mrs. Lin was known for her elegance, she looked ridiculous now—like an offbeat chauffeur waiting for her best client, good old George, to arrive from Mount Vernon. Fern wondered why St. Gregory's couldn't just use numbers or different-colored umbrellas like other DC tourist groups. Perhaps Headmaster Mooney wanted credit for beginning the students' historical experience right here in Terminal A.

"Room one in the Washington group will be," Headmaster Mooney continued, "Preston Buss, Taylor Kushner, Greg Daniels, and Sam McAllister." *That's good for Sam*, Fern thought. *He's with Preston and Taylor.* Preston high-fived Sam gleefully. They ran over to Mrs. Lin, who was still valiantly holding George Washington's face above her head.

"Washington group, room two," Headmaster Mooney shouted. Fern noticed his face beginning to turn red from the strain of trying to be heard over sixty-four excited kids, not to mention the other amused passengers jockeying for their luggage. "Mary Eileen Noff, Olivia Bruno, Alexa Freed, and Lindsey Lin."

Guided by instinct, Lindsey grabbed Fern's upper arm. Fern turned a whiter shade of pale as she shook her arm free.

"I thought you put me down!" Fern cried.

"I *did.* I swear," Lindsey said. "Maybe they're not letting seventh graders room with eighth graders. Or someone else must have put you down." Fern looked skeptically at Lindsey. Out of the corner of her eye, she saw Mary Eileen and Olivia celebrating the fact that they were in a room with Lindsey.

Though they were best friends, Lindsey and Fern were newly minted best friends. They had bonded over the fact that they were both Otherworldlies. Lindsey's whole family was Otherworldly, and she'd learned to fit in with Normals like her parents had—which is to say, far better than Fern. Though being friends with the popular and older Lindsey had improved Fern's social standing, she was still regarded as a total freak by most of her schoolmates. In truth, most of the kids at St. Gregory's had decided that Fern was another one of Lindsey's charity projects, and in addition to Fern, Lindsey still had dozens of friends she spent time with. Alexa and Mary Eileen were on the volleyball team with her. Olivia was the secretary of the Associated Student Body. Lindsey, of course, was president. While Lindsey was the sun in Fern's friend solar system, Fern was merely one of many moons in Lindsey's.

Fern saw Sam eyeing them. She could tell her brother was alarmed by the fact that she and Lindsey weren't rooming together.

"Maybe you're with Nancy Greenbaum," Lindsey said, in a hopeful tone. Nancy Greenbaum was one of the nicest girls at St. Gregory's, let alone the seventh grade. She was very quiet and studious, with pretty blond hair and a perfect J. Crew fashion sense. She also didn't get involved in the catty stab-you-in-the-back friend wars the other girls at St. Gregory's relished. She truly was above it all. Nancy Greenbaum would not go out of her way to be mean to Fern. In fact, she would probably even talk to Fern. The rest of the girls in the seventh and eighth grades, though, were likely to torment her.

Perhaps the girls weren't totally to blame. Fern was abnormally abnormal. She had terrible sensitivities to the sun and horrible stomachaches that sent her to the nurse's office on a regular basis; she spent most recesses in the maple tree in the south corner of the soccer field and claimed she could talk to her dog. Almost worse, Fern actually *could* talk to her dog. Until Lindsey offered help in the form of special Otherworldly eyedrops, she also had worn sunglasses to and from class (and sometimes into class) because she couldn't handle the brightness of the morning sun. Fern and Sam had named them her Breakfast Sunglasses. Some seventh graders were branded freaks and had to live with an undeserved label until well into high school. Fern, for better or worse, actually was one.

"You'd better go over to your group," Fern said, eyeing Mary Eileen and Alexa, who had found Olivia in the crowd of students and were waving Lindsey over. Lindsey gave Fern a sympathetic look.

"I'll be fine," Fern said, not wanting her own lowly social status to hold Lindsey back. She remembered what Eddie had told her before they left—her older brother had said that the other kids would come around if she were confident in herself. Of course, as the star of the St. Gregory's football team, it was pretty easy for Eddie to be confident. Fern, though, was a different story. Nevertheless, she continued trying to exude poise. "I mean, it's not like we're going to be on separate trips. We just won't be sleeping in the same room. No big deal."

Confident or not, Fern and Lindsey knew that on a school trip, nighttime—a time when all the authority figures retired to their separate rooms—was also when the fun began for most and the real torment kicked in for Fern. In some ways, nights on school trips resembled the early days of the Wild Wild West before Wyatt Earp had arrived to keep people in line. The Commander called the kind of activities that went on "shenanigans."

Last year, the sixth grade had traveled to Sacramento, the California state capital, on an overnight trip. Fern tried not to fall asleep. She finally did doze off, only to wake up with her head duct taped to the mattress. Getting the tape off meant painfully ripping away some of her skin as well.

Fern looked around the baggage claim area and realized that the other students were avoiding her. Everyone yet to be called was steering clear of her, confirming her worst fears. The groups that had been called were already standing at the baggage carousel, collecting suitcases.

Headmaster Mooney, sweat forming on his brow, had finished calling out the Washington group and was now announcing the Jefferson group. Mr. Billing waved a cutout of Jefferson's head above his own.

"Nancy Greenbaum," the headmaster called out, completing the Jefferson contingent. It was official. All hope was lost for Fern.

After the Madison group was announced, the Lincoln group was next. Headmaster Mooney was naming the presidential groups in chronological order, continuing his Terminal A history lesson. The chaperone for the Lincoln group was Mrs. Phillips, Lee Phillips's mother. Lee was one of the cruelest girls at St. Gregory's. One look at Lee's mother, and Fern was convinced that she must be just as cruel as her daughter. Mrs. Phillips was wearing a fitted olive-colored Diesel leather jacket, a short skirt with black tights, and red Ferragamo heels, and she had bleach-in-a-bottle hair as shiny as a new car.

Fern would have done anything to avoid Mrs. Phillips's group.

Headmaster Mooney started out by calling the names of a group of boys. "Room one: Lance Figgins, Grady O'Keefe, Jimmy Wells, and Mike Sullivan," Headmaster Mooney rattled off. "Room two: Fern McAllister, Candace Tutter . . ."

Fern's heart began trembling inside her chest. She tried to calm herself, though—Candace Tutter wasn't Lindsey, but it could be a lot worse. Candace was a genius. Not the normal kind of genius, who everyone thinks is smart. But a ten-year-old who was too smart for each grade she'd entered, with an IQ off the charts. She knew tidbits about *everything* a person could think of, rattled these tidbits off in rapid succession, was rumored to have a photographic memory, and had already skipped two grades. Most everybody at St. Gregory's ignored her, except when they needed homework answers. Candace, though, did not ignore most everybody in return. In fact, she was constantly following people around, observing them and writing things down in the spiral notebook she'd labeled "A Systematic Study and Survey of the St. Gregory's Student in Its Natural Habitat." Fern worried about keeping her Otherworldly and Unusual status secret from Candace.

She breathed in and out, trying to normalize her heart rate, anxiously waiting for Headmaster Mooney to read the next two names.

"Blythe Conrad," Headmaster Mooney announced as Fern gasped out loud. *Oh no. How could it be?*

"And Lee Phillips," Mooney said, completing the group.

Fern whipped her head around and found Blythe Conrad and Lee Phillips in the dwindling crowd of students. They smiled at each other as if they knew something the rest of the world didn't.

Blythe Conrad and Lee Phillips were best friends who bonded over three things: boys, bands, and bullying Fern.

Together, Blythe and Lee had come up with the nickname "Freaky Fern" and spread it throughout St. Gregory's. They'd attacked her in the bathroom several months ago, lopping off clumps of her hair with scissors, and, as a pair, they were responsible for the majority of the tears Fern had shed in the past two years. Worse still, the two blond girls' hatred for Fern had only grown recently as she gained notoriety and found a friend in Lindsey.

It was as if someone had set out to find the worst three girls in the school for Fern to room with—and they had succeeded in spades. Fern had hit the bad roommate trifecta.

She mournfully shuffled her feet forward, as she forced herself toward her chaperone. Mrs. Phillips was clutching Honest Abe's cardboard head with both hands and brandishing it wildly from side to side as if she were on a street corner advertising an everything-must-go, going-out-of-business sale. Blythe and Lee stood together, their eyes shining with anticipation of the terror they would be able to inflict on Fern over the next week.

The lyrics to "Sloop John B" by the Beach Boys began to play in Fern's head, almost as if someone had paused the song in the perfect spot.

The Beach Boys were Eddie's favorite band, and they were singing about the worst trip they'd ever been on. Fern wished her older brother was here in Washington with her. He might be able to save her from what was sure to be an awful series of nights.

In that moment, the words to "Sloop John B" rang truer to Fern than any lyrics that had ever been sung. This *was* the worst trip she'd ever been on—and she hadn't even collected her luggage from the airport carousel.

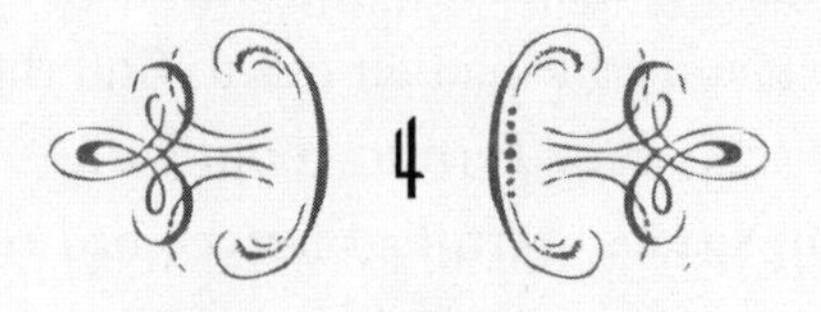

4
the itinerary

The weather in Washington, DC, was bitter cold, and the Lincoln group was shaping up to be Fern's worst nightmare. St. Gregory's had chartered a bus for the entire week, and as the bus driver loaded luggage into the compartment on the bottom of the bus, students scrambled to call dibs on their seats. Fern, who was in the very back of the pack of students, dragged her suitcase behind her. She couldn't find Lindsey or Sam in the crowd. They were probably already on board, enjoying the company of actual friends.

Friends.

Just when Fern thought that Lindsey Lin would be her first lasting friend, their bond was crumbling before her eyes. All it took was a class trip and some bad luck with rooming assignments to obliterate a new friendship. Lindsey had so many other options, after all—everyone loved her. Fern handed her luggage to the bus driver. She looked right, then left. Somehow, she ended up being the only person besides the bus driver who wasn't already on the bus.

"Are you waiting on somebody, sweetheart?" the bus driver questioned. He had a jovial tone to his voice and friendly eyes set deep in his face.

"No . . . no, I guess I'm not," Fern said, hanging her head. She could hear the gleeful shrieks of her classmates spilling out the open bus door. The vehicle looked enormous as it loomed in front of her.

"Someone in there you don't wanna see?" the bus driver asked, bending down to get a better look at Fern.

"Something like that," Fern responded. Unconsciously, she shook her head. She was an Otherworldly. An Unusual. She had single-handedly defeated an evil vampire's plan to steal one of the most powerful objects on Earth only a few weeks ago. Now she was afraid of boarding a bus full of Normal twelve- and thirteen-year-old classmates.

"Well, look here, sweetheart. I'm gonna go start the bus and you take a few breaths. Sometimes a few breaths is all a person needs, eh? Holler if there's anything else I can do for you during the trip. The name's Willie."

Willie put his hand out, and Fern shook it. His hand was cold in hers, but his smile was warm. Even though he didn't really know her, Willie seemed to have taken a liking to Fern. Perhaps it was only kids her own age who hated her, Fern thought.

She was now the lone figure standing outside the bus. She took a deep breath and released it five seconds later. The breath formed a small cloud of steam in front of her. After taking another breath and holding it longer, Fern took the first step into the bus, and then the next. She pivoted and was now facing her classmates, who were hitting, standing, yelling, swaying, singing, and whispering to one another. The commotion reached near-deafening levels.

The five adult chaperones and Headmaster Mooney were seated in the front three rows. All were clutching clipboards, seemingly in the middle of an impromptu meeting, shouting over the pandemonium behind them.

"Feelin' better?" Willie asked.

"Much. Thanks for your help."

"No need," he said, tipping his Washington Nationals baseball cap.

Fern decided she'd better find a seat before someone noticed her. Four rows in, next to Mark Gaber, there was an open seat.

"This seat's taken," Mark said in his loudest voice.

Fern spotted another unoccupied seat next to Samantha Crothers.

"I'm saving that for someone," she said. There was no way that was true, of course, since Fern was the last one to board the bus, but she didn't have the energy to argue.

Fern approached two more open seats and was met with the same response.

Had the whole school schemed against her while she stood outside talking to Willie?

"Fern!"

Fern searched through the snickering crowd to pinpoint the location of Lindsey's voice.

"Over here! In the very back!" Though Lindsey was waving her arms wildly, she blended in with the rest of the hyperactive students.

Lindsey had separated from Olivia, Alexa, and Mary Eileen in order to save a seat for Fern. Overjoyed, Fern trotted to the back of the bus. Just as she gained speed, Blythe Conrad extended her leg into the aisle and snagged Fern's own with her foot. Suddenly Fern was airborne. The left side of her face met the rubber-treaded floor of the aisle with a loud *splat.*

The bus quieted to a whisper as the students erupted from their seats, trying to get a better look at Fern, now splayed in the aisle. Fern rolled over so that she was faceup. She cupped her left eye with her hand. It stung and throbbed all at once. Both of her knees were skinned.

Headmaster Mooney lumbered down the aisle toward her.

Fern felt someone picking her up by the arms, forcing her to her feet.

"She's fine," Lindsey said as she helped Fern to the back of the bus.

"Are you sure you're unharmed?" Headmaster Mooney

asked Fern with feigned concern, mentally reviewing all the different ways St. Gregory's could be sued because of a situation like the one unfolding in front of him. He silently thanked those individuals who'd invented the permission slip, the consent form, and the parental waiver.

"I'm okay. I'll only have a little bruise," Fern said, still seeing stars from her fall.

Lindsey was careful to wave off Mrs. McAllister, who stormed down the aisle behind Headmaster Mooney.

After hovering in the aisle for a minute, Mrs. McAllister repressed the urge to check on her daughter and returned to her seat next to Mrs. Lin in the front of the bus. The trip had barely begun and already her daughter was the focal point of a small spectacle—but the one request Fern had made when the Commander signed on as a chaperone was that her mother not baby her. With that promise firmly in mind, Mary Lou McAllister was doing her best not to start the trip off on the wrong foot. Fern had been more temperamental lately (not that Mary Lou blamed her given all that Fern had gone through), and she didn't want to upset her further. She worried constantly about her daughter, but Mary Lou was trying to give her some of the space she thought every teenager needed, all while still keeping tabs on her.

Lindsey steadied Fern, holding her arm, and guided her into the seat in the back next to her own. Sam and Preston were sitting directly across the aisle.

"You okay?" Sam asked.

“I’m fine,” Fern said, still covering her left eye with one hand.

“What happened?” Lindsey asked.

“Blythe Conrad tripped me. Where did you disappear to?” Fern used her most accusatory tone, though she wasn’t quite sure what she was accusing Lindsey of.

“I was the first one on the bus, to make sure I could save you a seat next to me,” Lindsey replied defensively.

“Oh,” Fern said, relieved. Lindsey hadn’t forgotten about her. The bus lurched forward, heading toward the Marriott, signaling that St. Gregory’s Spring Break Trip was officially underway.

“I’ll bet she’ll have a nasty shiner tomorrow,” Preston said, leaning over Sam from his window seat to get a better look at Fern. Sam shot Preston a dirty look—he didn’t want Preston involved. Preston took the hint and put headphones on.

“I’m going to make Blythe Conrad wish she never came on this trip,” Sam declared, glaring down the aisle at Blythe and Lee.

“Wait. No one’s going to do anything to Blythe or Lee,” Fern said, defeated.

“What? She deliberately tripped you! For no reason,” Lindsey said, airing her own outrage.

“I want to live through this week, and I think it’s probably best if we just leave them alone so that they’ll leave me alone. I’m rooming with both of them.”

“You’re *rooming* with them?” Sam said, having been

too distracted to hear the announcement of Fern's room. "How did *that* happen?"

"Oh, I don't know. I thought it'd be a great week for me to make some new friends, so I put them down as my top choices," Fern said sarcastically.

"This is a disaster," Sam said, putting his head in his hands. "I knew we shouldn't have come."

After all that had happened with Vlad, Fern, and the Otherworldlies, Sam was convinced that the two of them should stay at home over spring break to both hide and lick their wounds. Fern was now someone every Otherworldly on planet Earth was after. In Sam's opinion, it was not the time to go cavorting off to Washington, DC, and expose Fern to all sorts of unknown dangers—his worst fear was that some Blout would kidnap his sister.

In addition, since Fern's sudden disappearance from English class one day and almost immediate reappearance at the beach (her first experience teleporting), the teasing at school had become worse than ever. She'd only further guaranteed her position as the school punching bag, despite Lindsey championing her cause.

For her part, Fern insisted that Sam should go on the trip, at the very least. He'd been looking forward to it all year. Fern hated to think that his concerns about her would keep her twin brother home. She'd already disrupted everyone's life enough.

In the end, the McAllisters worked out a compromise. The Commander would go as a chaperone, along with

Lindsey and her parents for added security. The Lins were senior officials in the Rollen intelligence community, and they assured the McAllisters that there had been no reports of plots to harm Fern. As the first verified Unusual and a partial fulfillment of the centuries-old prophecy, people were very curious about her. But there were no known threats. In addition, Mrs. Lin thought it might be a good thing for Fern to change locations for a little while. Only those in the St. Gregory's community would know exactly where Fern was.

"It's not a disaster. I'm supposedly one of the most powerful Otherworldlies around, remember?" Fern asserted with Eddie-like confidence. "You really think I can't handle a week with Blythe Conrad and her lame evil sidekick, Lee Phillips?"

"Be a little quieter, Fern," Sam said, glancing nervously around the bus. He was more worried about keeping Fern's secret than she seemed to be.

"Students!" Headmaster Mooney bellowed from the front of the bus. "Itineraries for the week are being passed back to you. Please do not lose them. They have all meeting times and locations listed. You'll also find important phone numbers attached, should you need them. I'm not anticipating any problems, of course." Fern was certain Headmaster Mooney was staring directly at her as he emphasized the last sentence of his announcement.

Slowly, stapled copies of the itinerary reached Sam, Lindsey, and Fern in the back of the bus. Fern looked absentmindedly out the window. They were zooming away from Dulles Airport and toward the District of Columbia. The bus was on a four-lane highway—but it was much different from the freeways and highways she was used to in California. There were large trees on both sides of the road and a large green swath of grass in the middle. In Southern California, a sprinkler system would have to be installed if a green parkway was to remain green for very long.

"Here," Lindsey said, shoving Fern's copy of the itinerary in her face. Fern glanced at the schedule.

"They're giving us two whole hours to walk around the National Museum of the American Indian?" Sam complained. "Why do we have to go there?"

"Quit being so culturally insensitive," Lindsey said, reaching across the aisle and punching Sam in the arm. "You stole all their land . . . the least you could do was give them a museum and go visit it every so often."

"'*You*'? Why are you saying it was just me? You're an American too! You're not innocent!"

"My Chinese relatives did not arrive in this country until well after your relatives had mistreated the Indians and taken their land," Lindsey said.

Sam was about to continue the argument when Fern gasped so loudly that the kid sitting in front of her, Garth James, swiveled his head to look at her.

"You okay?" Garth asked.

"She's fine," Lindsey answered, signaling for Garth

to turn back around.

"What is it?" Lindsey whispered to Fern, hoping not to draw any more attention from Garth.

"It's nothing," Fern said. "I thought I saw a spider." Fern was disappointed that she couldn't think of a better excuse.

"A spider? On the bus. Really?" Sam added skeptically.

Fern knew she wouldn't be able to come close to convincingly explaining why she had gasped. Her reaction was to the itinerary for Friday, March 29. After gathering in the lobby of the Marriott, all of the St. Gregory's students were to board the bus so they could spend two hours at the morning's designated location: the National Zoological Park. That had been the name on the crate in her dream about Miles Zapo! Sure, there might be many other places with a similar name, but Fern suspected there was only one *National* Zoological Park. It made sense that it was in Washington, DC.

Was Miles Zapo there now, in some dark corner? Was Fern supposed to find him? Was that why she'd had the dream?

Fern's elevated heart rate caused her normally pale face to turn red. Sam and Lindsey both realized something was wrong with her but knew the back of the bus was not the time to have any kind of substantive conversation about it.

"Where is the National Zoological Park?" Fern asked Lindsey and Sam, trying to sound casual.

"It's in the north part of the city—it's got its own stop on the subway or whatever," Sam responded. "Our hotel is close to it, I think." Though he would never admit to it, he'd brushed up on his capital knowledge over the past few weeks.

"What kind of park is it?" Fern asked.

"It's a zoo. I don't know why it has that name."

"Oh."

After a dinner of pizza, which had been served to the students in one of the Marriott's conference areas, Fern returned to her room and curled up on one of the double beds. She put on her headphones, mostly to block out the incessant chatter of Blythe, Lee, and the ten-year-old genius, Candace Tutter. Her roommates were unpacking their things into the dressers of the Marriott hotel room the four girls were to share for the next week. The Commander had given her an ice pack to soothe her bruised eye, but it languished melting and leaking on the floor next to the bed. Fern didn't want to give Blythe the satisfaction of knowing she had caused her any pain. Besides, Fern thought a black eye might make her look tough. She had abandoned all hope of fitting in and was now focused on cultivating a strong outsider persona—at least that way she would be left alone.

Fern determined pretty quickly that both Blythe and Lee had requested her as a roommate as part of a diabolical scheme. Fern wondered if they'd managed to alienate every other friend they had. When she confronted them in the hotel room, Blythe was forthcoming.

"You know what they say," she'd said, popping a piece of Trident between her front teeth. "Keep your friends close and your enemies closer."

"We are going to have *such* fun together, aren't we, Lee?" Blythe purred. She plopped on the flowered bedspread next to her cohort.

"I wouldn't be surprised if we aren't all *best friends* by the end of the week," Lee responded. The two girls giggled.

"Well, thirty-six percent of people in the United States own a pet and of those, fifty-five percent say their pet is their best friend," Candace Tutter began, talking quickly. "Do any of you own a pet? Because if so, I'd say the probability of us becoming best friends is not in our favor." Candace had already unpacked all of her clothing and had neatly hung her coat in the closet. She was sitting at the table by the window, reading Leo Tolstoy's *War and Peace* (for the second time, she informed Fern later).

"Shut up, Candace," Blythe said, springing up from the bed and taking two steps toward her. "You will SPEAK only when we tell you to . . . get it?"

For a girl so tiny and underage, Candace Tutter didn't scare very easily. She ignored Blythe and continued reading *War and Peace.* The phone rang, and Blythe jumped over Fern to grab the receiver, a wicked smile on her face.

"It's for you," Blythe said, waving the phone in front of Fern. "Probably one of your *freak* friends." Fern removed her Bose headphones. They were huge and cumbersome, but Fern liked the way the music sounded with them on.

"Those headphones are ridiculous, by the way," Blythe said, rolling her eyes. "Do you think you're a DJ?"

"I've got the perfect DJ name for you," Lee said, glowering at Fern. "DJ Ugly Freak."

She and Blythe snickered as Fern picked up the receiver of the telephone.

"Hello?" Fern said, trying her best to ignore the two girls.

"Yeah, um, this is hotel security," a voice said. Fern recognized immediately that the person on the other end of the line was lowering his voice to try to sound older and more authoritative. "If you don't come remove your underwear from the front lawn, like, immediately, we're going to, uh, have to arrest you." Fern heard bursts of laughter in the background—clearly the caller had an audience. Then came a click and a dial tone.

Fern frowned. Lee and Blythe eyed each other mischievously.

"Who was that?" Lee asked, feigning innocence. Fern didn't bother responding. Instead she walked over to the window. The girls had a seventh-floor room on the front side of the hotel, facing Woodley Road and overlooking much of the Woodley Park neighborhood of northwest DC. The hotel had a well-manicured lawn and several vine-wrapped gazebos.

Fern pulled the drapes open and looked down. Spotlights were set on the lawn, shining on the hotel to illuminate the towering redbrick building at night. Almost immediately, Fern noticed a hot pink splash of color resting on one of the spotlights. She noticed a few white blots on the lawn and a spot that seemed to be orange.

Someone had spread her underwear all over the lawn. Fern clenched her teeth and her fists in one movement. Her whole body stiffened as she turned around. Lee and Blythe were covering their mouths with both hands, stifling guffaws.

"What—what—," Lee said, unable to form a complete sentence because she couldn't stop herself from laughing. "What's the matter, Fern? *Lose* something?"

Fern felt the anger pulsing through her veins. She was upset about her underwear, of course, but the idea that Lee and Blythe had searched through her things positively enraged her. What if they'd come across Phoebe's letter or her bag of soil?

She scowled at Lee and Blythe and then shifted her eyes to the bottle of Coke that was open on the nightstand next to Lee and Blythe's bed. Narrowing her eyes so all she could see was the bottle underneath her half-closed lids, she focused on it. Fern imagined the brown liquid streaming from the mouth of the bottle and spraying both Lee and Blythe in the face. She smiled, imagining them shrieking, as Classic Coke coated their designer clothing and turned them into a sticky brown mess.

Lee's and Blythe's screams broke Fern's concentration.

As if she were suddenly awakening from a dream, Fern saw the Coke bottle floating upside down close to the ceiling above where Lee and Blythe were sitting on the bed. It looked as if an invisible hand was suspending the bottle above their heads and pouring the brown liquid directly on them. The air was raining fizzling Coke, but only over Blythe and Lee. Fern blinked and the bottle fell rapidly, bouncing off Lee's head and landing on the bed—its final resting place.

For a moment the four girls stood still, frozen in shock at what had happened seconds earlier.

"You MONSTER!" Lee screamed once she'd regained her power of speech. She ran into the bathroom.

"What did you do?" Blythe asked, boiling with anger.

"What do you mean?" Fern said coolly.

"How did you *do* that?" Lee exclaimed.

"I have no idea what you're talking about," Fern echoed.

"I don't know how you rigged that bottle, but you've ruined my sweater, you freak!" Blythe yelled, following Lee into the bathroom. The door slammed behind them and the lock clicked into place. Fern, still standing by the window, took a long, amazed breath as she stared at the now empty bottle, lying on the Coke-soaked bed.

Candace Tutter's eyes had darted away from *War and Peace* as soon as the plastic bottle of Coke floated off the nightstand up to the ceiling and inverted itself. Now she rose from her chair and cautiously edged toward the bottle on the bed. She extended one finger and touched the bottle quickly, as if it were a recently used frying pan that was still hot. When nothing happened, Candace picked up the bottle with both hands and examined it at eye level. She twisted the bottle, inspecting for strings or anything out of the ordinary. Looking at Fern, she raised an eyebrow.

"How *did* you do that?" Candace said, her voice denoting an element of astonishment.

"What?" Fern responded. In truth, Candace's question was one Fern was asking herself. She'd been able to move water before—it wasn't so long ago that she'd put out the fire in a neighbor's house by directing the water from a swimming pool onto the blaze—but this was something new. She'd moved a *whole bottle.*

"Unless I didn't detect you moving," Candace began, "which itself is highly unlikely, the bottle floated by itself over Lee's and Blythe's heads. Then it turned over. *Telekinesis.* From the Greek words for mind and motion. Moving something with your mind. That's what."

"I was standing right here. I didn't *do* anything," Fern said, trying to sound casual. Internally, she was starting to worry.

"If you did what I think I saw," Candace said, cocking her head to the side and giving Fern an inquisitive look, "then you not only performed telekinesis, but in doing so, you also violated the laws of physics—specifically speaking, the second law of thermodynamics and, in addition, quite possibly the inverse square law."

Candace calmly moved back to her chair. She searched

through her backpack and pulled out the spiral notebook in which she kept the notes on her "Systematic Study" of St. Gregory's students. Setting the empty Coke bottle carefully on the table next to her, she began writing furiously in the notebook.

Fern was sure she was the subject of Candace's latest entry in her "Study." Though she wasn't quite sure what Candace would do with the information, the uneasiness was welling in her stomach and creeping up into her throat.

The bathroom door opened. Lee and Blythe, who had cleaned themselves up to some degree, stepped out of the open doorway with arms crossed and hatred on their faces.

"You are *so* dead," Blythe said flatly. "You'll wish you never met us by the time this week is over." With that, Blythe and Lee opened the door to the room and marched out into the hallway, though it was in violation of Rule Four of the St. Gregory's Spring Break Trip Regulations, which forbade any student from leaving his or her hotel room after the nine o'clock p.m. curfew. The door swung shut automatically. Fern figured they were probably going to the room of the boys they were friends with who'd helped with the underwear prank.

Fern and Candace were now alone in the room. Fern could only imagine the kinds of evil schemes Blythe and Lee were hatching. They could tell Mrs. Phillips what Fern had done. Or worse, they could be gathering forces to help carry out a plot to destroy Fern.

With a sigh, Fern collapsed onto the bed and put her

arms over her face, waiting for Headmaster Mooney or the Commander to storm into the room and punish her. The Commander, Fern knew, was already frustrated with her daughter's recent lack of judgment when it came to using her special powers. As recently as last week, Fern had caused a stream of water to splash in Sam's face at the local Chili's as a practical joke. The Commander gave Fern a stern lecture on the trouble she'd be in if she used her unusual talents unnecessarily and drew attention to herself. Fern imagined a very public scene where the Commander flew off the handle about this latest Coke bottle incident. Fern couldn't totally blame her, though. If Fern herself didn't understand what was happening to her, how could she expect her adoptive mother to? After all, the Commander had no possible point of reference from her own adolescent transmutation.

Fern opened her eyes in order to search for her headphones. Candace was standing over her, still wearing the curious look on her face. It was as if Fern was an exhibit at the zoo and Candace was a few feet away, outside her cage, observing her.

"A true social scientist is not supposed to express an opinion about her subjects," Candace stated matter-of-factly. "But those two girls are horrible. And whatever it is you did to make that Coke dump all over them, I can't help but admit that I'm very happy you did it."

"Uh," Fern said. She let a half smile creep across her face. "That's nice of you to say, Candace."

"I'm not saying it to curry favor with you. I only thought it should be express—"

Before Candace could finish articulating her thought, the phone rang again. Fern popped up. She and Candace looked at each other. Anger stirred in Fern again as she thought of what sort of trick Lee and Blythe had orchestrated this time. Candace saw the angry glint in Fern's eyes and let the growing curiosity show in her own.

Fern got off the bed and took a step toward the phone. It rang twice and then a third time. Fern snatched the receiver from its cradle as she thought about every pair of underwear she'd brought displayed on the Marriott front lawn. Now what? Perhaps her pajamas were already hanging from the flagpole near the hotel's entrance.

Fern gathered all her determination and anger and tried to transfer it into her voice when she spoke.

"What do you want this time, huh?" she said, shoring up her resolve.

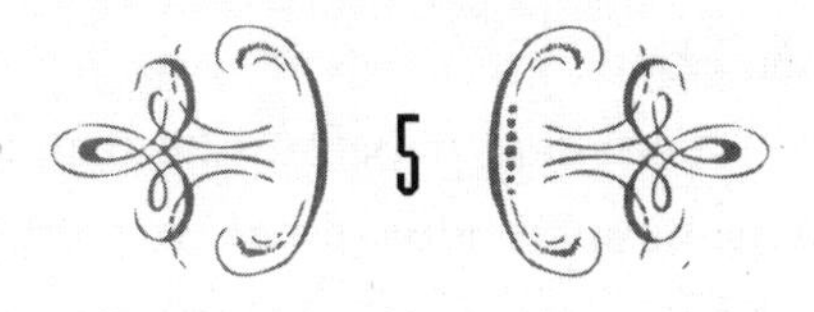

5

the experiment in the exercise room

"Well, what is it?" Fern repeated into the phone after she got no answer.

"Fern?" the voice on the other side questioned. "Is that you?"

Fern exhaled as relief replaced her dread and anger.

"Hi, Sam," she said. Candace, recognizing that no threat was imminent, at least as far as the phone call was concerned, went back to scribbling furiously in her spiral notebook.

"Jeez, Fern. Who died? I didn't even recognize your voice at first."

"It's been a long night," Fern confided.

"It's only nine fifteen!" Sam blurted. There were a few

seconds of silence before Sam spoke again. "Anyway, you can tell me all about it in ten minutes. We're meeting in the Fitness Center."

"Who's *we*?" Fern said it before she realized that she had no reason to be suspicious of her twin brother.

"Um, me and Lindsey. Look, I gotta go. Ten minutes. Fitness Center. Don't be late." Fern hung up the phone and shook her head in amusement. Though she knew Sam, in reality, was a sensitive soul (who sometimes held funerals for birds that had died in the McAllister yard), her twin brother liked to pretend that he was destined for a career in covert ops. He wasn't Navy SEAL material yet, perhaps, but it wasn't for lack of trying. Fern loved that only she knew this about Sam.

Walking toward the window, she looked down at her underwear, still on display on the front lawn. She was surprised a hotel staff member hadn't been sent to remove it, but maybe Fern's underwear wasn't as conspicuous at ground level as it was from seven floors up. Fern looked at Candace from the window and realized she was deeply involved in the latest journal entry she was writing. Quickly and quietly, Fern made her way to her suitcase, cataloging the items she cared about most. She located her bottle of W.A.A.V.E. eyedrops and W.A.A.V.E. lotion—both of which were gifts from Lindsey and offered some protection from the sun's brutal effect on her.

She saved the search for her most important objects for last. Fern's heart began to pound and she could feel beads of sweat form on her forehead as she unzipped the top compartment of her suitcase and then reached deep inside it until she felt the sealed black plastic bag.

Trembling, she peeked within it and found the single envelope and letter, as well as the small Ziploc of soil from the McAllister yard she'd packed and protected within the dark plastic bag. The letter, from Phoebe Merriam to the Commander, was her favorite of the series of letters the two women wrote to each other in their late teens and twenties. The Commander had given Fern a box of them to keep soon after revealing that Phoebe was Fern's actual birth mother. Fern had read all of them dozens of times. In the one Fern carried around with her, Phoebe sounded happy, carefree, and, well, cool. It was exactly the way Fern wanted to remember a mother she had no real memories of.

As for the Ziploc of soil, Fern couldn't sleep without it. She had kept this quirk to herself, until she finally worked up the courage to ask Lindsey if she was somehow weird, even by Otherworldly standards. Lindsey laughed and explained that because Otherworldlies, or vampires, lived such long lives and usually traveled many places, it was important for them to establish a bond with their original homes so they didn't lose their sense of self. Around the time of transmutation, Otherworldlies always fixated on and became very attached to one or two things, called Amulets, that served to remind them of their origins. Otherworldlies became very uneasy if they were ever separated from these hallowed objects.

Some famous Otherworldlies had even become deranged after losing an Amulet.

Fern figured the letter and the soil, representations of both her birth (Phoebe Merriam) and the only home she'd ever known (San Juan Capistrano) had become her Amulets. Which was why she couldn't bear the thought of Blythe and Lee rifling her suitcase and stumbling upon them.

Holding the two items slowed her pulse. Fern's breathing returned to normal. Blythe and Lee must have stolen her underwear by sneaking up to the room when the rest of the students were eating their pizza dinner. She couldn't risk them exploring her suitcase once again and finding her Amulets. So Fern decided that she would carry them with her from now on, stowing them in her jacket for the time being.

The clock read 9:27. Fern had three minutes to get down to the Fitness Center.

"Hey, Candace," Fern said, interrupting Candace's writing binge. "I'm going to go downstairs for a sec and talk to my brother. So if the phone rings, say I'm in the bathroom, okay?"

Fern wasn't exactly comfortable asking Candace to lie for her, but she didn't have any other options. Hopefully, it wouldn't come to that. Lee and Blythe hadn't returned with Mrs. Phillips for the moment, which most likely meant they hadn't ratted her out to the authorities yet.

"But that's in direct contravention of Rule Four of the

St. Gregory's Spring Break Trip Regulations!"

"Say whatever you want, then. I'm not trying to get you into trouble. But I've got to go." With that, Fern walked past both double beds and out the door. She felt a slight twinge of regret for being abrupt with Candace—the young genius was very strange, but she hadn't really done anything to Fern except offer some words of support (even if that support itself was very odd). Aware that there were chaperone rooms on either side of her own, Fern crept quietly down the red-carpeted hallway.

What Fern was not aware of, however, was that not far behind her, Candace crept even more quietly, intent on following Fern's every move. *After all*, Candace thought, *an exceptional social scientist would never let her most interesting subject escape observation at such a pivotal moment.* In the name of science (with a dash of nosiness), Candace Tutter shadowed Fern down to the fourth floor.

Sam aimlessly pushed the pedals on the stationary bike in slow circles. Lindsey Lin sat on a treadmill across from him, and Fern had taken a seat on the only rowing machine in the Marriott Fitness Center. It was a medium-size room with three treadmills, two stair climbers, a stationary bike, a rowing machine, a small television mounted on the wall in the corner, and a water cooler, complete with plastic cups and a stack of white towels on top. Besides Sam, Lindsey, and Fern, the room was deserted.

Although Fern had resolved not to tell Sam about her

dream, seeing National Zoological Park on the itinerary had distressed her enough to realize she'd need Sam and Lindsey's help if she was going to act on the dream. Also, Fern was well aware that there was no way Sam would let the subject drop after he'd witnessed her reaction on the bus.

"You're sure the crate said 'National Zoological Park'?" Sam asked. Having heard Fern's recap of the dream involving Miles Zapo, he was having trouble interpreting it. If his theory was correct and Fern was seeing other Unusuals in the dreams, Sam thought it meant she had a special bond with the ten other Unusuals born at the same time she was during a series of electrical storms. Though, if his speculation was true, then this latest dream about the boy in the cage was all the more upsetting. Fern's previous dreams had been of distant people in exotic places. However, if Miles was at the National Zoo, then he was close by, within walking distance of their hotel. Did it mean that Fern was meant to save him? Did she have some kind of responsibility?

"I know what I saw," Fern said.

"We've got to find out more," Lindsey said, trying to suggest a more practical approach. "Did he say why he was there? Or anything about who took him?"

"No," Fern said. "Other than telling me he was from Mound, Minnesota—it was like he was drugged or something."

"When did the itinerary say we're going to the zoo?" Sam asked.

"Friday morning," Lindsey recited from memory. "Can't we look around then and see if anything appears out of the ordinary? That seems like the most obvious thing to do. . . ."

"Sure," Fern agreed, though she wasn't positive Lindsey's plan was the right one. "If Miles is being hidden somewhere at the zoo, there has got to be some sign of him, right?"

"Fern could teleport there tonight," Sam offered, ignoring Fern's comment.

"What do you mean, Fern could just teleport there tonight?" Lindsey questioned.

"She knows what the place looks like, right?" Sam insisted. He stopped pedaling on the stationary bike, and a serious look came over his face. "Fern's gotten very good at teleporting over the past few months. We've been practicing. She can totally control it."

"Would you two stop talking about me like I'm not here?" Fern growled.

"Sorry," Sam said.

What he had said was true, though. Over the last couple of months, Sam had been the best tutor a girl with supernatural powers could ask for. The first time Fern teleported, she'd disappeared from her English class and appeared, moments later, miles away on the beach. She'd had no idea what was happening. Several times after that, when Fern would get upset, she'd uncontrollably teleport to places without intending to. It was just such an episode that had put her on the evening news when she found herself atop Splash Mountain at Disneyland one afternoon. It was terrifying for Fern, not knowing when or where in the world she'd disappear to.

When Fern regained her strength after battling Vlad, each weekend she and Sam would head out into the backyard to hone her teleportation skills. Now Fern could instantly transport herself almost anywhere and, as the Omphalos prophecy predicted, it was a fearsome power to behold. The week before the Washington trip, Fern had teleported directly to the front of the Arc de Triomphe in Paris, France, staying for five minutes before teleporting back to the McAllister backyard. She would have dallied longer under the majestic arch at the western end of the Champs-Élysées, but she knew Sam would worry if she was gone for too long. When Mrs. McAllister found the picture Fern had taken of herself in front of the Arc, she received another lecture about the inappropriate use of her powers. The Commander reminded Fern that she was still a teenager and couldn't travel alone wherever and whenever she felt like it.

"That's *way* too dangerous!" Lindsey said, getting up from the treadmill. "First of all," she continued, gracefully jumping from one treadmill to the next to get closer to Sam, "we don't even know if Miles Zapo is a real person. Second of all, we have no idea where he is. And even if he *is* real and Fern *can* get there, we need more information before we send her somewhere where some maniac has left a kid in a cage."

"Fern can teleport back instantly if it's too dangerous," Sam said, dismounting the stationary bike and taking a step toward Lindsey.

"We don't even know what kind of danger she'll face when she gets there," Lindsey said, raising her voice.

"You're doing it again," Fern said. "I'm right here, you know." It was becoming increasingly clear that she had little part in controlling the escalating argument.

"We sure won't figure anything out by taking a walk through the Great Ape House on Friday!" Sam yelled back. He and Lindsey were now in the middle of the exercise room, less than a foot away from each other.

Fern honestly thought Lindsey might take a swing at Sam. Both her brother and her best friend had clenched their fists as if the bell for Round One had rung and the fight was about to begin. From her vantage point on the seat of the rowing machine, Fern looked around the room for something that would distract them.

Her gaze fell on the stack of towels on the water cooler in the opposite corner. Fern focused on the top towel. She closed her eyes and imagined the towel floating off the water cooler slowly. It glided across the room, drifting directly above the space between Sam and Lindsey.

"Don't you care at all, Sam, that your sister may be in real dang—"

Lindsey was the first to notice the towel hovering directly above her head. She glanced quickly at Fern, who had her eyes half-open as if she were in a trance. Lindsey looked back up at the towel. Sam followed Lindsey's eyes upward.

"Whoa . . ." Sam, mesmerized by the levitating gym towel, let his voice trail off. He looked over at his sister. "Fern!"

Fern's head snapped forward, and the towel dropped to the floor.

"New development I forgot to mention . . ." Fern began with a mischievous smile. "I can perform telekinesis."

"Tele-what?" Sam asked.

"Telekinesis. Candace says it's Greek for moving something with your mind."

"Candace?" Lindsey questioned. "Candace *Tutter*? You've been talking to Candace Tutter about your powers?"

"Why in the world are you talking to Candace Tutter about *any* of this?" Sam added.

Lindsey and Sam had shifted from facing each other to facing Fern, still lounging on the rowing machine. Though they'd been nearly at each other's throats seconds before, shared outrage over Fern's consultation with Candace united them once more. They made no attempt to hide their absolute disapproval. Of course, had Lindsey or Sam (or Fern, for that matter) known that about a dozen feet away, Candace Tutter sat with her ear pressed to the Fitness Center door, listening and trying to remember every word spoken so she could record them later in her spiral notebook, their outrage would have turned to outright alarm.

"Blythe and Lee rifled my suitcase and had someone spread my underwear all over the lawn of the hotel."

"You're joking," Sam said.

"If you don't believe me, go look at the lawn right now," Fern responded.

"I'm really sorry," Lindsey said. "That's awful."

"Yeah, well, maybe I didn't handle it all that well. But I was so angry; I tried to move the Coke so it would splash in Lee's and Blythe's faces. I didn't realize the entire bottle had moved until it was floating above their heads. Candace saw the whole thing."

"That could be a problem," Lindsey said. "What if Candace tells someone about it?"

"I'm not sure anyone will believe her. She has even fewer friends than I do."

Lindsey looked at Fern sympathetically. "You have us," she said, smiling. "In fact, why don't you spend the night in my room? Olivia, Alexa, Mary Eileen, and I are going to have a Spit card tournament. Alexa says she's never been beaten, but we all know that's not true," Lindsey continued, growing excited. "And then we're going to stay up and watch *Breakfast at Tiffany's.* Olivia brought it and says it's supposed to be a classic."

"That's okay," Fern said, trying to hide the sadness welling up inside her as she thought of a night surrounded by friends, laughing with them until the sky went from black to orange. "Blythe and Lee will report me if I'm gone too long."

Lindsey always had her back, but Fern knew that Lindsey's other eighth-grade friends would not welcome her intrusion. Out of respect for Lindsey, they might not say anything, but Fern had imposed on Lindsey's kindness enough as it was.

Sam, still focused on Fern's recent revelation, took a few quick steps toward the water cooler, grabbed a cup, and filled it with water from the gurgling jug.

"See if you can focus on moving the water in the cup," he commanded Fern.

Fern got up from the rowing machine so she could get a clear view of the water in the cup. She focused on it and imagined the water flowing out of the cup, into the air, and across the room. When she shook her head to snap out of it, she saw Sam standing there, with the cup full of water unmoved from his hand.

"Nothing?" Fern asked, surprised.

Lindsey and Sam shook their heads.

"Try the cup," Sam offered.

Fern took a deep breath and half closed her eyes again. Now she imagined the whole cup rising out of Sam's hand, drifting into the space between them. Fern snapped her focus and saw the cup fall to the floor, splashing water a few feet in front of Sam.

"You can't move liquid, maybe, but you can move things for sure!" Lindsey said. Part of the reason she was so shocked was that everyone in the Otherworldly community, including her, thought Fern was a Poseidon, with special talents surrounding water. The name was taken from the Greek god of the sea, and Otherworldlies who had talents for moving water were referred to as Poseidons.

"It's like your power mutated," Sam said, puzzled. "Maybe when you were submerged in the ocean, and you caused that tidal wave to form, it made something change in you. Near-death experiences can do that, right?"

"It's impossible. Otherworldly powers don't change," Lindsey said.

"She's still in her transmutation stage," Sam said, referring to the point in an Otherworldly's life when special powers begin to emerge. "Maybe that means whatever the source of her powers is . . . it's still changing somehow."

"But that doesn't happen to Otherworldlies!" Lindsey insisted.

"Fern isn't just an Otherworldly. She's an Unusual. No one really knows what the true extent of her power is," Sam said. "The Omphalos prophecy was a guess. And even if part of it turned out to be true . . . that doesn't mean *all* of it is true."

"Sam, no offense, but you don't exactly know what you're talking about. You're a Normal . . . my family's been involved in Otherworldly affairs for hundreds of years."

Sam's cheeks flushed with irritation. "If you're the expert . . . then explain why Fern can do telekinesis now!" he demanded.

Fern moved in between her brother and Lindsey.

"Both of you need to calm down. I can't move water anymore, but I can move things. I showed you so that you'd both know, not so you could fight about it. Besides," she added, "we really don't have time for this."

"I'm sorry, Fern," Lindsey said, talking quickly. "I just don't think we should rush to judgment. Maybe I should talk to my parents. They can consult *The Undead Sea Scroll* and see if there's something we're missing about your transmutation or about Miles Zapo."

Lindsey's parents were among the few Otherworldlies who had access to *The Undead Sea Scroll*. *The Undead Sea Scroll* was a thousand-year-old, large, top-secret volume compiled by high-ranking Otherworldlies and continually updated, detailing many facts relating to the mysteries of their existence. It had entries for nearly everything and functioned like a mysterious encyclopedia of sorts. There were fewer than a hundred copies in existence.

"I'm sorry too, Fern, but I'm sure there's nothing in *The Undead Sea Scroll* that will help us figure any of this out," Sam said.

"How would you know?" Lindsey demanded, picking their fight up once again.

"Both of you, stop!"

Fern rarely raised her voice. But when she did, those who knew her usually listened. Her patience with Sam and Lindsey had run out—they seemed more interested in being right than determining why she was having these dreamlike visions. She decided that if she couldn't ask for input, she'd have to solve this puzzle herself. Though she wasn't certain why she felt she must help Miles Zapo, it was a feeling she couldn't shake. If there was one thing Fern had learned over the past few months, it was to trust her instincts.

"Listen," she said, looking down, proceeding thoughtfully. "I'm going to see if I can teleport to Miles Zapo and find out more about him. I remember exactly what the basement area looked like. When I do it, I won't stay for more than thirty minutes, and when I get back, I'll call each of your rooms, let it ring twice, and then hang up. If that happens, you'll know that I've gotten back safely," she said, turning to Lindsey. "If you don't hear the phone ring within that half hour, then I want you to tell your parents where I went, Lindsey. Sam, try to avoid telling the Commander for as long as you can."

"When are you going?" Lindsey asked, feeling uneasy at the thought of her friend teleporting somewhere with so many unknown dangers.

"Tonight . . . at midnight," Fern said. Though she tried her best to pretend that she wasn't scared beyond words, Sam and Lindsey could see the fear on her face. They weren't the only ones who could tell Fern was putting on a brave front. Fern might not have many friends, and her nights might be spent fending off the torturous pranks of Lee and Blythe, but she was determined to solve the puzzle of Miles Zapo.

Several feet away, from her position pressed up against the door to the Fitness Center, Candace Tutter couldn't see her anxious face, but she could very clearly hear the panic in Fern McAllister's voice.

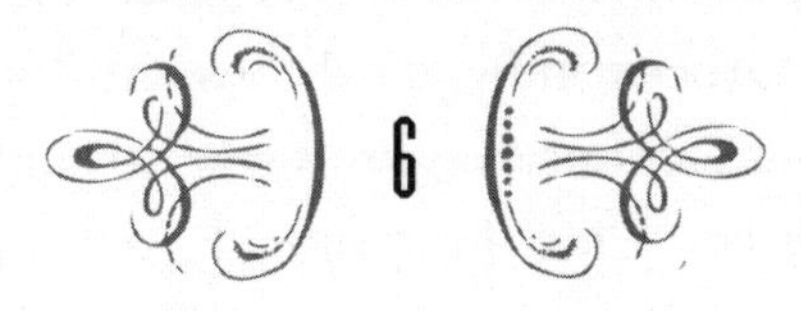

6

miles, revisited

Though Fern had been lying in bed for over an hour, she became more alert with each minute that passed. Blythe and Lee had taunted her for about an hour, calling her every vile name imaginable, but sleep finally overcame them around eleven o'clock. Rhythmic snorts pulsed from the double bed they shared. For a brief moment, Fern smiled, amused at the thought that Blythe and Lee were snorers. She never would have guessed it from their designer outfits and hundred-dollar haircuts. But, Fern supposed, the one time people can't control their appearance is while sleeping. Fortunately for Fern, Candace Tutter was also fast asleep, on the other side of the double bed she and Fern occupied. Had Candace been awake, Fern knew she could never sneak out of bed without being followed or questioned or both.

One floor below in room 629, Sam tossed and turned. He thought about his sister. Ever since she'd been pronounced an Otherworldly, she'd constantly been in harm's way as various factions sought to take advantage of her or even destroy her. This time, though, she was knowingly risking her safety by using her teleporting power to strike out on her own. Earlier, he'd convinced himself that Fern needed to discover the meaning of the strange dreams she was having. He reasoned that if there really were ten other Unusuals out there like his sister, Fern probably did have a responsibility to them. But what if he was wrong? What if it was a trap somehow and he'd encouraged Fern for all the wrong reasons? Maybe, Sam thought, he was more anxious to get answers about his sister's past and future than she was. His curiosity might kill Fern—and if that happened, Sam knew he would never get over it. Reaching to the side table, Sam set the hotel room's Casio clock radio, its face glowing red on the nightstand, for 12:31 a.m.

One floor farther down, room 524 had its own restless occupant. The Spit card tournament had been postponed because of Alexa's cold, and though Lindsey Lin tried to think of anything but Fern, she was failing miserably. She imagined her friend in some horribly dank, foul room, with all sorts of ominous creaks and strange murmurs emanating from the walls. Amid it all, there were the faint cries of a trapped boy. Each time she closed her eyes and momentarily drifted off, Lindsey would see her imagination's version of the boy's anguished face. The fear would cause her eyes to pop open as her heart raced and she gasped for breath. Slowly her heart rate would return to normal. After this cycle repeated itself several times, she turned over and saw her room's Casio clock radio, identical to the one in Sam's room.

11:59 p.m.

Fern would be teleporting momentarily.

Meanwhile, at the same instant, Fern was also staring at the clock radio on her nightstand. Trying not to disturb Candace, Fern put her palms flat against the covers, lifted them slightly, and slipped out of the bed, silently anchoring her feet on the floor. Candace didn't stir. Blythe and Lee remained snoring lumps on the adjacent bed.

Fern tiptoed through the dark.

She reached the dim bathroom and shut the door. Then she took a towel from the rack above the toilet and stuffed it into the crack underneath the door. When she flipped on the light switch, white flashed in her eyes, leaving colored spots that faded once her eyes adjusted. Dropping to the floor, Fern found the pair of shoes and jacket she'd stowed in the cupboard under the sink. She knew that if she had to clamber through the darkened room groping for shoes, one of the girls was sure to wake up. The last thing she wanted, though, was to arrive in Miles Zapo's squalid chamber barefoot, clad only in her pajamas.

After dressing, Fern lowered the lid of the toilet and sat down. Cradling her head with her hands, she shut her eyes and began to think of Miles Zapo. She remembered his thick-framed glasses, his smooth brown skin, and the metal cage imprisoning him. In her mind, she visualized the cold concrete walls and the stacks of equipment they enclosed. Fern's hands tingled. Sensing she was close to disappearing, she doubled her concentration. She recalled the crate with NATIONAL ZOOLOGICAL PARK stamped on its side. She envisioned the pile of bamboo and the shovels. She could hear the orange light buzzing overhead.

Less than a second after that, the bathroom was empty.

Fern was gone.

Scrambling to her feet, Fern oriented herself as quickly as possible. She was used to the blackouts now—each time she teleported, things went black and it took her a few moments to recover. What she would never get used to was the disorienting feeling of a sudden arrival in completely new surroundings. Once her eyes began functioning, she immediately recognized the pair of rooms where Miles had appeared in her dreams. Fern took a moment to collect her thoughts. She had successfully teleported. Part of her was excited. Her dreams weren't dreams at all—she was seeing real places. Or at least, *this* place was real. Even so, part of her was frightened. If this was a reality, then it meant that poor Miles Zapo was or had been imprisoned here.

Directly above her, the orange light she remembered hummed. To her left, cages were stacked almost to the ceiling. Fern glanced at her watch. In twenty-nine minutes, she was supposed to call Lindsey's and Sam's respective rooms and hang up after two rings.

She had no time to spare.

Scrambling over the pile of bamboo on her hands and knees, Fern maneuvered to the doorway in the corner that led to the room where she'd seen Miles before. As her eyes adjusted to the dimmer light in the second, smaller room, Fern used the right wall as a guide. There, in the corner, she could make out a large cage. A small boy was huddled in the back. The cereal boxes and banana peels were in the same place she remembered them. Fern approached the cage, looking around the room to make certain there was no one else present. Craning her neck, she peered up at the ceiling grate, which was slightly askew, above the cage.

Fern mentally gave herself the all-clear signal.

When she pressed her face against the cage, this time she could actually feel the chill of the metal bars on each side of her head. Miles Zapo was sleeping. Now his shoes were completely off, revealing a pair of white socks turned brown with dirt on the bottoms. A soiled, oversize Minnesota Twins cap with a torn brim covered his head. Unlike Lee or Blythe, he was barely emitting any sound. Fern could hear his quiet breath flow in and out. In spite of his dire circumstances, he looked peaceful. Fern almost didn't want to wake him.

"Miles," Fern whispered. He did not move. "Miles, wake up."

Miles whimpered softly. He stretched out his body,

opened first one eye, and then the other. He rubbed his eyes by twisting his fists, like a small child would. In many ways, he *was* a small child. His skin clung to his high cheekbones, and he had a little round nose and large eyes. As Fern peered into Miles's eyes, she was glad she'd decided to come. Miles Zapo seemed helpless, and there was something about him that she inherently trusted.

Miles slowly regained his bearings. He yawned, exposing his large white teeth, smiling as he focused on Fern. Though the boy wasn't as pale as Fern, his olive eyes had a similar faded quality.

"Fern McAllister. You came!" Miles said. He adjusted his torn-brim hat so that it was facing forward. He straightened up and pulled down his ripped sweatshirt.

"Are you okay?" Fern said. There were a million questions she wanted to ask him, but that was the first to pop out.

"I'm all right," Miles said, "except for the whole stuck-in-a-cage thing." He smiled convincingly, but Fern recognized the distress on Miles's face. At least he was much more lucid than the last time they'd talked, Fern thought.

She almost didn't know where to begin.

"How do you know who I am?" Fern asked. She regretted the question as soon as she asked it. Here was Miles Zapo, imprisoned in a rusty cage in a foul basement, put there by what was clearly some evil force, and Fern was asking questions about herself. "Actually, first tell me how you got here. . . . Where is the person who's keeping you here? Where are we?"

"The man keeping me here has a silver tooth, a beard, and gray eyes . . . but I don't know who he is," Miles said at a frantic pace. His wild, uneasy eyes looked Fern up and down. "He took me from my house in Minnesota." Miles stopped for a moment, still wide-eyed, and scooted toward Fern. "Aunt Chan said he was coming for me, and Aunt Chan is hardly ever wrong. Which is why I can't forget to give you the picture this time."

"Who is Aunt Chan? What picture?"

"I live with her. She's one of us," Miles said plainly. He lifted his Twins cap off for a brief moment to rub his head and then tugged it back over his ears. Though she'd seen his hair before in her dream, Fern was still surprised to see a mop of large black curls underneath his cap. Miles's fine features in combination with his wild hair were striking.

Fern had no idea where to go from here. Her questions were like weeds—once she picked one, four more sprang up.

Time was wasting away, but Fern was stuck.

"We need to get you out of here. Where does the man who took you keep the key to this cage?" Fern held the large padlock hanging from the cage door in her hands. It was heavy and obviously very sturdy. She scanned the room, but there were no keys anywhere. Then she looked up at the half-open grate.

"Thank you for coming," Miles said. "I knew you would."

Fern frowned at Miles. Why wasn't he able to answer her questions in any kind of useful way?

"You look confused," Miles said.

"I have so many questions I want to ask you," Fern admitted. "But we've got to get out of this place first. Do you have any ideas? Or know why you're here?" she asked. Truth be told, what Fern really couldn't understand was what *she* herself was doing here. Five minutes had ticked by and she'd made no progress with the boy.

"Rod Carew stole home seven times in one season for the Twins." Miles said. His eyes blinked several times behind his oversize hipster glasses.

"Um, okay . . ." Fern said, trying not to sound frustrated. Why wasn't Miles Zapo more concerned with being rescued? Had he lost it here in his darkened cage?

"See, stealing home is one of the least possible and most impressive feats in baseball," Miles began, speaking so quickly that his sentences ran together like falling dominoes. "Players steal second all the time. But it's approximately one hundred twenty-seven feet away from the catcher, so it's easy to take a big lead off first if the pitcher isn't holding the runner close. Third's a little harder, but nothing's like stealing home. With home plate, the catcher is always there blocking it, no matter what. The pitcher's mound is only sixty feet, six inches away, and the ball travels there so many times a game—every time the ball is pitched. Runners reach third less frequently than first or second. Stealing home scores a run. Runs, of course, are what win games." Miles looked intently at Fern.

"Miles," Fern said, flabbergasted and growing more frantic. "I appreciate the baseball lesson, but we *need* to figure out how to get you out of here." She'd stopped making an effort to sound patient. *Perhaps coming here to visit Miles was a mistake*, she thought.

"No, no," Miles said, shaking his head as if forcing himself to wake up. "You don't understand. Aunt Chan said this was going to happen. She said when you came, we would want to steal home, right away. She told me, though it would be difficult, that I had to be careful to make sure you knew *everything* or we couldn't pull it off. It's like she said: You're trying to steal home right now, but we have to get on base first. Then we have to get to second and third. *Then* we can steal home." Miles said it as if he had just delivered a profound thought.

Fern thought she heard a rustling noise coming from the other room. She whipped her head around and peered through the doorway into the orange-lighted space.

"Please don't worry. We have time. The man has two monsters, Howling Quetzals, and they leave each night for a few hours," Miles said, noticing Fern's uneasy glances at the doorway. "Besides, they don't come from there," he said, pointing through the bars of his cage at the doorway. "They come from up there." He moved his extended finger and pointed up at the grate. Fern wanted reassurance, but other than the fact that a few of them were monsters and one had a silver tooth and strange gray eyes, she had no idea who "they" were. Her belief in Miles Zapo was beginning to fade.

"Okay," she said, clutching the bars of the cage tensely, deciding she had no choice but to play along with Miles's baseball analogy. "What do I need to know to get us on base?" Fern was apprehensive and annoyed, but looking at Miles amid the filth, banana peels, and cereal boxes in the cage, she was shocked that he hadn't crumbled from distress. Maybe the Minnesota Twins talk was the only way he could survive—his aunt Chan had turned it into a game to make it less terrifying. Focusing on what a man capable of locking a child in a dark cage was planning to do was enough to drive anyone mad. The Twins talk was a way for Miles to survive.

But why hadn't this Aunt Chan woman tried to stop Miles from being taken? Why would she let her nephew go through an ordeal like this one?

Miles scuttled a few more feet forward until he was almost flush up against the inside of the cage's door. Looking squarely at Fern through his black-framed glasses, he began his story. Fern concentrated on every detail, wondering which ones would turn out to be important.

According to Miles Zapo, he was born in the small town of Punta Gorda in the southern part of Belize in Central America. He didn't remember exactly when, but according to his aunt Chan, she took him to live with her in Minnesota the day he turned one year old, March 10, Fern's own birthday. He had been living with his aunt for the past twelve years.

Miles continued speaking about how he never knew his parents, but that his aunt had told him they'd died trying to protect him when he was a small child. His aunt had let him know from a very young age, that he was a member of an especially talented group called Otherworldlies. He said Aunt Chan waited until he was eight years old to tell him about his special birth and the Omphalos prophecy, and that he was an Unusual. Miles stopped speaking for a moment.

"When did you find out?" he asked, looking at Fern.

"Only a few months ago. I've been raised by Normals."

"Normals?" Miles questioned, arching an eyebrow.

"You know . . . normal people. Humans who aren't Otherworldlies."

"Aunt Chan said you might have different names to explain things," Miles said.

"Wait a second," Fern said as a thought occurred to her. "If you're an Unusual, why haven't you *teleported* out of here?" Her excitement grew. "We'll both teleport someplace and then decide what to do. . . . There's no reason to stay here!"

Miles's head sunk onto his chest.

"Believe me, I thought of that the moment Silver Tooth put me here."

"Silver Tooth?" Fern asked.

"Sorry . . . in my head that's what I call the man who took me. The only things I can remember about him are the silver tooth in the center of his mouth, his black beard, and his gray eyes—they're like the color of wet clay. I've never seen eyes like them before." Miles shivered as he recalled the man in his mind.

"So why haven't you teleported then?"

"I can't teleport right now," Miles said.

"Why not?" Fern questioned. Though her power had caused her anxiety and pain, she couldn't imagine losing the ability to teleport. She worried about what she would do if Miles's disability was permanent. There had to be some way to get him out of here, but Fern wasn't equipped to break into an iron cage, and there didn't seem to be any helpful tools around.

"It's got something to do with the Howling Quetzals," Miles explained. "Their low howl puts me in a trance. . . . I don't even know how long I've been down here. I think their chant must drain my power. I tried *so hard* to reach you, like before." Miles stopped and hung his head. "But I couldn't. . . . I can't do anything I used to be able to do."

Fern could see wells of tears collecting on the ridges of Miles's lower eyelids. He quickly wiped them away and looked up at Fern once again.

"You will be able to as soon as we get you out of here," Fern responded. She could see that Miles needed to be reassured, but she wasn't positive she was up to the task. Her heart went out to Miles. He was putting on a brave front, but it was clear he was petrified and anxious about everything. Fern had only been in this room for a little over twenty minutes, and she was already feeling its dreadful effect. Her heart began to beat more quickly.

Fern knew what it felt like to be terror-stricken. When she'd first heard the rumors that her birth mother was a Blout—the evil kind of Otherworldly—she was horrified by the idea that Blout blood coursed through her veins. Then, during the time that Vlad was after her, she was never sure when she woke up each day if it would be her last.

A life ruled by fear wasn't a life at all.

She had to save Miles Zapo, a fellow Unusual, from this place . . . and from the howling monsters. Fern looked down at her watch. She had five minutes left.

"Miles, look at me," Fern commanded. Miles turned his tear-filled, frightened eyes to her. "I swear I'm going to get you out of here. But first you need to tell me everything you know about the Quetzals."

Miles wiped his eyes and took a breath, trying to calm himself. After a moment, he began. "A normal quetzal is a fluorescent green bird that's sacred to my ancestors, the Mayans. But Howling Quetzals are giant horrible versions of them."

"What do you mean?" Fern asked.

"Howling Quetzals are more like scary giant green beasts. Silver Tooth has two of them with him. Always. They're ugly and they make this high-pitched, droning wail that you can't get out of your head until everything goes blank. I hear them, pass out, and when I finally wake up, they're gone. The bottom half of their bodies is covered in giant oil-slick colored feathers with these claw-legs, and their top half is covered with hand-size, slimy, pulsing scales, and they have these black-hole eyes and when they look at you . . ." Miles's voice drifted off. He began to shudder uncontrollably.

"Miles." Fern snapped her fingers in Miles's face again. She could hear the clock ticking in her head. He stopped shuddering. It was clear to Fern that Miles was barely keeping it together as the memory of what he'd been through seized him. "Miles, do you know what Silver Tooth is after? Why he took you?"

Fern reached into the cage and put her hand on Miles's shoulder.

"Look at me," she said, trying to make her voice as even as a recently paved road. "When I leave, I'm going to get the entire Alliance to help me break you out of here. You only need to sit tight for a little longer."

"No! Aunt Chan says there is no real Alliance," Miles insisted, referencing the group the Rollens had formed to fight the evil Blouts.

"I've been to the headquarters and it's real," Fern argued, remembering her visit to New Tartarus. "It's very real, and they'll help you."

"You don't understand . . . we can't *trust* them. Aunt Chan says it's like any power-hungry organization—they're more interested in gaining control than doing what's right. Silver Tooth could be from the Alliance, for all we know! You *can't* tell them," Miles said, panic in his voice.

"Okay. I won't. I'll deal with it myself."

"Promise me."

"I promise," Fern said, sensing Miles's desperation.

A sound thundered through the small room. It was as if a large boulder had landed on the air-conditioning duct directly above Fern and Miles. They both became silent instantly, waiting. The noise was moving from the far end of the room toward them. Someone was above them.

"Oh no! They're here. I have to give you the picture," Miles urged.

Miles removed his Minnesota Twins hat quickly, revealing his curly shock of hair once more. He reached inside the cap itself and peeled off a picture that had been carefully taped to the inside of the dome. He pushed the picture at Fern through the bars. She grabbed it.

Clomp. Clomp. Clomp!

"Teleport there!" Miles whispered urgently, pointing to the picture. "As soon as you can!"

The clomps turned into pounding thuds. Fern looked up and was sure someone (or something) was moving toward the grate.

"Get out of here!" he insisted. "Silver Tooth is back. . . . He'll trap you here! Then we'll both be lost!"

Fern's mind raced. She didn't want to leave Miles at the mercy of Silver Tooth, whoever he was. But if she stayed, the man might disable her in the same way he'd controlled Miles.

She closed her eyes and visualized the hotel bathroom she'd just left. The pounding grew louder.

"Go!" Miles screamed, the terror in his voice boiling over.

Fern, clutching the picture, closed her eyes and tried to block out the thundering crashes above her. She hoped she hadn't waited too long.

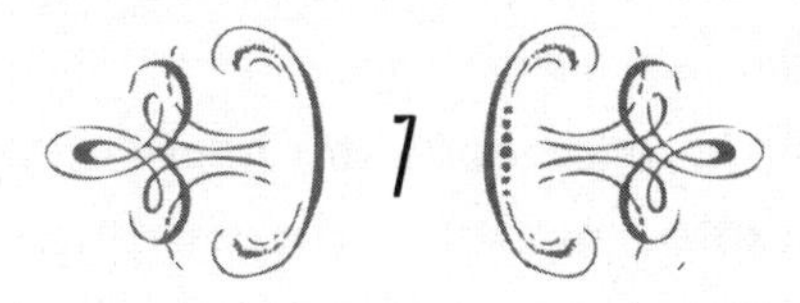

7
the washington monument

When the clock flashed 12:28 a.m., Sam snuck into the bathroom. Before he left, he carefully turned the alarm off and put a pillow over the phone. He made sure that Preston was sound asleep. Taylor Kushner and Greg Daniels were motionless in the adjacent queen-size bed. Sam took his wristwatch into the bathroom, where he could safely hear the prearranged two-ring signal on the bathroom extension phone. To keep himself from pacing, he lay down on the cold tile floor. He tried to think of something besides Fern struggling and alone in a dark basement somewhere, dealing with who-knows-what.

Although he tried to banish it from his mind, Sam wondered if this would be his life from now on. Waiting in uncomfortable places, worried to distraction about his sister. He knew it wasn't fair to be jealous of her, especially when she had suffered so much because of her special powers, but that didn't stop him from feeling resentment building inside.

Why hadn't he been born an Otherworldly? In many ways, Fern wasn't equipped to cope with the cards she'd been dealt. Sometimes he was certain he could have handled it better—the good and the bad.

He looked down at his watch.

12:31 a.m.

Fern was a minute late. Sam, barefoot, opened the bathroom door and crept out of his room into the hotel hallway. He eased the door closed so it barely made a sound. The hall was empty, and Sam headed to the elevator.

A floor below him, Lindsey Lin decided she didn't have a second to lose. She'd been watching the red numbers change on her clock for the last ten minutes.

When 12:31 appeared, she was certain that something had happened to Fern. She rolled out of bed and stumbled to the door. Lindsey didn't care if her roommates heard her. Convinced that Fern was in serious trouble, Lindsey pushed the door open and went to the room three doors down from hers. She had to reach her parents—and soon.

The moment she opened the door into the hall, she let out a gasp. Lindsey let the door swing closed behind her.

Directly in front of her, Sam sat cross-legged on the hall floor. He stood up in front of Lindsey, his blond hair sticking out every which way. Lindsey wondered how long Sam had been sitting there, waiting for her.

"What are you doing here?" Lindsey said angrily.

"You can't tell your parents Fern is missing," Sam said, somehow knowing exactly where Lindsey was going.

"Why not?"

"Wait a few minutes . . . that's all," Sam said, trying to remain calm. He spoke more softly than normal, conscious of the fact that if they were caught in the hallway at this hour, both of them would be in hot water.

"We should have told my parents as soon as Fern started having the dreams!" Lindsey argued.

"Fern's never been good at keeping track of time. She'll call. I know she will." Sam couldn't explain to Lindsey why he didn't want to involve her parents, but he was convinced that Fern would be better off without their help. "Please. Eddie always says there's actual time and then there's Fern time—she's always five minutes late everywhere. Give her a few more minutes."

"Get out of my way," Lindsey snarled, "or I will *move* you out of my way."

"Hold on!" Sam said. "Shhh!"

Lindsey and Sam had both heard it. From inside Lindsey's hotel room, the phone rang once. Then again. Then it stopped ringing.

Lindsey glowered at Sam. Without a word, she pivoted and turned away from him. She opened the door to her room with her magnetic card and let it close in his face.

But Sam didn't care. Fern was safe.

When Fern finally arrived back in her hotel bathroom,

everything was as she had left it: The towel was stuffed into the crack under the door, the lid of the toilet seat was down, and the cupboard where she'd stored her shoes was ajar. Yet, on a different level entirely, Fern felt as though everything had changed. She'd confirmed it for herself. There was another Unusual out there—someone just like her, born at the very same time, who'd lost his parents too—and he was in terrible danger. For the second time, Fern wondered if forces stronger than coincidence had brought her to Miles.

"It's up to me to save Miles Zapo," she said softly to herself, still clutching the picture Miles had given her mere minutes ago.

Fern fell asleep at three in the morning, and when she woke up to Blythe's blaring alarm three hours later, the last thing she felt like doing was getting ready to stand in line to ride the elevator to the top of the Washington Monument. Blythe and Lee had commandeered the bathroom, taking with them bags of makeup and a variety of state-of-the-art hairstyling appliances unlike any Fern had ever seen. The most annoying part, however, was that all access to the bathroom was blocked. Neither Fern nor Candace even had a chance to brush their teeth.

"Where did you go last night?" Candace asked as she layered on clothing. Fern had already seen her put on tights, thick corduroy pants, wool socks, and a long-sleeved T-shirt. She placed a down jacket and thick gloves on a nearby chair.

"Go?" Fern asked, yawning.

"At twelve twenty-three a.m. I registered the time in my notebook. You weren't in bed."

"I was probably in the bathroom or something," Fern said casually, searching through her suitcase for something to wear.

Candace Tutter was about to ask a follow-up question that would most likely poke a hole in Fern's excuse when she became distracted by Fern's outfit and its lack of warmth—jeans and a T-shirt.

"The wind chill is supposed to be severe this morning." Candace said, looking at Fern.

"So?" Fern said.

"So a wind chill causes the body to lose heat due to the evaporative cooling and convection effects of the cold air. If the velocity is severe enough, frostbite is a possibility. I think you should wear your warmest clothing."

"Thanks, Mom," Fern said. She put on her jacket and, when Candace wasn't looking, stuffed her scarf and gloves into the pockets, just to be safe.

At 6:26 a.m. Candace tagged along with Fern down the elevator to the lobby. All students were supposed to meet their chaperones in their groups by six thirty in the lobby, and Fern was guessing that Lee and Blythe were going to be late—they were still primping in the bathroom. The rules never seemed to apply to them somehow, but Fern wasn't sure if they were truly well-liked or if everyone was simply intimidated by them. In addition to cultivating bad-girl personas (Fern had seen both of them smoking cigarettes behind the PE building more than a few times), they also threw the kinds of parties everyone at St. Gregory's wanted to attend, so no one dared cross them.

In the lobby, Fern spotted the Commander first and immediately averted her eyes. She didn't want her own gaze to meet her mother's. Fern could tell by the way the Commander was standing that she wanted to check on Fern. The Commander was peering at the side of Fern's face, where a bruise had formed because of her bus face-plant. Fern could feel the burn of her mother's eyes as she crossed the lobby, but she focused straight ahead—her mother's concern wouldn't solve any of her immediate problems. Straight ahead, Mrs. Phillips, sporting a jacket with a fur-trimmed hood, held up Lincoln. Fern headed toward Abe's floating head with Candace trailing.

"Did you know that Abraham Lincoln's mother died from milk sickness?" Candace said, striding rapidly to keep up with Fern's quickening pace. "It's very rare now, but it was quite common in the nineteenth century. That's why when Mother tries to tell me that a little milk won't kill me, I tell her it just might!" Candace giggled. But Fern hadn't heard Candace's last comment (not that she would have laughed at Candace's attempt at humor if she had).

As soon as Fern's eyes locked with Sam's, she tuned everything else out. Sam gave her a big smile. Fern couldn't help but smile back. Her twin brother mingled with the rest of his Washington group. When Sam gave her a thumbs-up from across the hotel lobby, Fern gave one right back. Much to Fern's surprise, Lindsey was on the opposite side of the group, as far away from Sam as possible. Fern tried to catch her eye, but Lindsey seemed oblivious.

Before long, the Washington, Jefferson, Madison, and Lincoln groups were climbing into the bus. Though the tours for the Washington Monument did not begin until nine in the morning, the line for tickets usually formed by seven.

The Jefferson group was the last to board. Fern searched for Lindsey at the back of the bus. She found her, but she also found Mary Eileen sitting next to Lindsey. Fern was shocked. Lindsey hadn't saved her a seat. Fern felt a sharp sting of rejection. Lindsey was avoiding her for some reason.

"This seat's open."

Fern looked down. Candace Tutter beckoned her by patting the adjacent seat. Unfortunately, Candace had put herself in the first row right behind the chaperone section of the bus. Fern didn't have the energy to look further and risk a repeat of yesterday. She collapsed in the seat next to Candace and closed her eyes as the bus rolled out of the Marriott parking lot.

Not surprisingly, Candace was correct about the wind chill. After nearly two hours standing in a line that circled the Washington Monument, Fern could no longer feel her fingers, even though she had put her gloves on and shoved her hands deep into the pockets of her jacket. Her scarf was now wrapped tightly around her head. The dozens of flags encircling the pointed white tower whipped in the frosty wind. The Tidal Basin to the south of the monument, famously lined with blossoming cherry trees in the spring, glittered with the reflection of the morning sun. Its dull warmth, though, wasn't enough to defeat the chill in the spring air.

To the north, Fern could make out the manicured lawn of the White House. She had to admit that it was all very beautiful—but it was also near freezing. The bus had pulled up to the Mall parking lot at seven a.m., and each student had been given a stale bagel and a boxed orange juice for breakfast while standing in line. In the next hour, the line tripled in length, winding around the monument several times.

As they waited, Candace peppered Fern with obscure facts about the Washington Monument. Fern now knew that it was the world's tallest stone structure as well as world's tallest obelisk (whatever that was—Fern was sure Candace knew, but she didn't have the strength to sit through the answer).

"See the difference in colors between the marble stones," Candace said, pointing up at the structure. It was true; about a third of the way up, there was a clear line where the stones were suddenly creamier.

"Well, because of the Civil War, America didn't have the

funds to complete it, so construction stopped. When they did finish it more than thirty years later, after the war, they used different marble," Candace stated. Fern was pretty sure that if she kept standing next to Candace she would know most of Washington's history in a matter of hours. She wondered why history-conscious Headmaster Mooney didn't just turn the entire tour over to St. Gregory's most precocious student.

Unable to wait any longer to talk to Lindsey and Sam about last night, Fern turned to Candace. Students were supposed to stay with their groups, but Mrs. Phillips, the Lincon chaperone, was busy flirting with another chaperone, Mr. Billing.

"I've got to go talk to Sam for a second. Hold my place, will you?"

"But we're supposed to notify our chaperone if we want to leave the line," Candace insisted, citing Rule Twelve of the St. Gregory's Spring Break Trip Regulations.

"It'll only be a second, Candace," Fern explained. "Besides, I don't think that Mrs. Phillips is very concerned with us." Almost on cue, Mrs. Phillips playfully grabbed Mr. Billing's shoulder. She had her back turned to the line.

"Oh, all right," Candace said. "I'll say you went to the bathroom if anyone asks. Seems like you frequently do that at all times of the day or night," she finished, arching an eyebrow.

"Thanks, Candace!" Fern said, jumping over the silver metal chain that was keeping the line orderly. She ran to the front of the St. Gregory's students. Sam's towhead was sticking above the cluster of boys around him. He was on the opposite side of the monument from the Lincoln group. Preston was with him, and the two were laughing at some inside joke. Fern tapped Sam on the shoulder, motioning him out of line. Sam ducked under the chain and joined his sister as Preston waved to her.

"I've been waiting for you to come find me," Sam said.

"We've got to get Lindsey."

Sam and Fern walked along the outside of the chain toward Lindsey. Lindsey had a large group of girls around her, including her roommates Olivia, Mary Eileen, and Alexa, and was telling a story that was making them all laugh. She took breaks every so often to blow into her hands to keep them warm.

"Pssst," Sam said. He motioned with his head for Lindsey to pop out of line.

Lindsey hesitated, looking at her parents.

"C'mon, Linds. We've got a lot to talk about."

After a moment, Lindsey told her attentive listeners that she'd be right back. Then her eyes moved toward her parents once more. When she was sure they weren't looking, she slipped under the chain. Moving quickly and quietly, Sam, Lindsey, and Fern trotted in the direction of the World War II Memorial and the Reflecting Pool. They found a barren cherry tree off to the side of the monument. Though it was late March and spring had arrived, the cherry trees had not begun to blossom. In the distance, they could hear the large World War II monument fountain bubbling. The St. Gregory's students and chaperones were nothing more than little figures standing in the distance.

"So what happened?" Sam asked anxiously. "Did you get there?"

Fern started from the beginning. She told them how the basement area was real; described the crate with the same National Zoological Park lettering she'd seen in her dream; and explained how Miles was imprisoned in the cage. She told them about the Howling Quetzals that caused Miles to lose his powers and how Silver Tooth had been returning right as she teleported back to the hotel. She said she was sure if she'd waited another few moments, Silver Tooth would have seen her. In truth, Fern wasn't positive that whatever or whoever was making noise hadn't spotted her before she left Miles—but she didn't want to worry Sam or Lindsey.

After she'd recounted the whole story, she produced the picture that Miles had handed her through the bars of his cage.

"Miles begged me to teleport here," Fern said, handing the picture to Sam. Before he could get a good look at it, Lindsey took the picture out of Sam's hands and held it close to her face.

"Hey! I wasn't done looking at that."

"Oh, get over it," Lindsey said.

"What's gotten into you two?" Fern said, grabbing the

photo from Lindsey and putting it back into her pocket.

"Lindsey's jealous of you, Fern, because you're more powerful than she is. She doesn't want to help you anymore," Sam said cruelly.

Lindsey took a step toward Sam, with steel in her eyes, and with one motion, delivered a swift punch to his gut.

Sam crumpled to the grass under the tree and groaned.

"Lindsey!" Fern said, shocked that her friend had punched her brother. As she looked at Lindsey, she noticed a strange look on her friend's face. It was as if Lindsey was staring at something far off on the horizon, even though she was looking right at Fern. Sam got to his feet, holding his stomach, his face red with pain and anger.

"What's wrong with you?" Fern asked, puzzled. She couldn't believe that she was refereeing a fight between Lindsey and Sam when Miles was trapped in a cage somewhere, his life in danger.

"And Sam," Fern said, turning to her brother. "That's a horrible thing to say! Lindsey's helped me so much, I stopped keeping track." Fern crossed her arms. "I want you both to apologize to each other."

Sam and Lindsey glared at each other for a few seconds.

"Now!" Fern insisted.

"I shouldn't have said that about you," Sam said flatly. "I'm sorry, Lindsey."

"I'm sorry too," Lindsey said. Her voice wavered. Fern could hardly believe her ears. Lindsey was always calm and rarely lost her cool.

"What's going on with you?" Fern asked, peering at her friend.

"I just . . ." Lindsey trailed off. "I think I'm on edge," Lindsey said. She scowled at Sam briefly, and then her eyes returned to Fern.

"What is it?"

"I've been keeping something from you both," Lindsey began. "Last week someone stole *The Undead Sea Scroll* from our house. My parents thought maybe someone was trying to find out more about you, Fern. They made me promise to tell them about anything strange involving you so they could keep an eye out for any threats. . . . I really think we need to tell them about your dreams. Sam doesn't agree with me."

"The theft may have nothing to do with Fern," Sam offered. "Maybe it was a burglar."

"*The Undead Sea Scroll* was the only thing taken from the house. Besides you two," Lindsey said, frowning at Sam once more, "no one even knows where we keep it." Fern remembered how *The Undead Sea Scroll* at the Lins' house had been cleverly concealed inside a hollowed-out copy of *Moby-Dick*.

"I get where you're coming from," Fern said, taking her hands and resting them on her friend's shoulders. "I really do . . . and I think your parents can help, but Miles specifically asked me not to tell anyone from the Alliance. And I'm not going to—at least not until I go here and figure out what Miles wanted me to see." Fern took the photo out of her pocket once more.

The three of them huddled around the photo and examined it. The photo was a standard five-by-seven glossy print showing a block of houses. The center house was a Victorian row house painted white, bright blue, and lime green. Every inch of wooden trim looked like it had been enameled with the utmost care. The neighboring houses weren't brightly colored, and they weren't as meticulously adorned. The picture had been taken on a cloudless afternoon, and the sky was a shade of dark blue not often seen in Fern's hometown of San Juan Capistrano due to the always present California smog.

"You don't even know where this is . . . or who lives there! It could be a trap," Lindsey insisted. "Besides, Alliance or not, we can trust my parents."

"I know we can, Lindsey," Fern said, "but Miles wouldn't send me somewhere dangerous."

"How do you know? He could be dangerous himself. You don't really know him."

"I know he's an Unusual. I can't explain it exactly, but I trust him," Fern responded. Fern loved her Normal family and Lindsey—they would always be part of her future life. Still, she couldn't help but think that Miles Zapo and his Unusual status was a key to figuring out her past—specifically more about her birth parents.

"When are you planning on going?" Sam said in his most bolstering tone. If Lindsey was going to question Fern every step of the way, Sam wanted his sister to know that she had his full support.

"I'll go tonight. It's the only time I can get away without anyone noticing. This time, though, I'm not going to give myself a time limit. I'll go as quick as I can and I'll call you when I'm back safe."

As Fern was reassuring both Lindsey and Sam, a pair of uniformed Capitol police officers was walking toward the threesome. Lindsey was the first to notice them.

"Maybe we should walk away," Sam whispered. All three were on edge. The officers were making a beeline toward them.

"That'll only make us look more suspicious," Lindsey replied.

Fern could hear the feedback from the radios on their belts. Apprehension gripped her.

Their dark blue uniforms stood out in the morning sunlight.

"Is one of you Fern McAllister?" the officer on the left asked. His tone was calm but authoritative.

"That's me," Fern said nervously.

"Come with us, please," the other officer said, motioning Fern forward with his gloved hand.

"Where are your parents?" the same officer asked Sam and Lindsey as Fern stepped forward.

"Over there," Sam said, pointing to the line wrapped around the Washington Monument.

"Well then, I suggest you both get back over there before you cause any more trouble," the officer said sternly.

With that, both officers turned their backs on Lindsey and Sam.

They watched in shock as the police wedged Fern squarely in between them and led her away. Fern had only been in Washington for a little more than twenty-four hours, and already she was in the custody of the DC police.

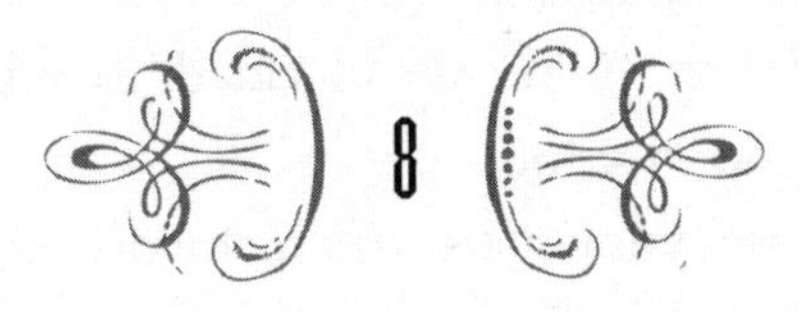

8

the monumental embarrassment

The two uniformed Capitol policemen didn't utter a word to Fern as they escorted her back in the direction of the Washington Monument. Fern weighed the things she might say to the officers and decided to get straight to the point.

"Am I in trouble?"

"That's not really for us to decide," the officer to her left said. She looked up at his name tag. OFFICER HALLET. Officer Hallet had a bushy brown mustache and topaz eyes.

"Do you wander off frequently?" Officer Hallet questioned.

"I don't think so," Fern responded. Talking to a uniformed officer of the law made her nervous.

The policeman laughed.

“Maybe that’s the problem. You don’t realize when you’re actually wandering off.”

“Maybe,” Fern said. She decided to regard Officer Hallet as friend, not foe.

“In any case, your sister was real worried about you,” Officer Hallet said. He put his hand on Fern’s shoulder and directed her toward the side of the Washington Monument where the Lincoln group was standing.

Sister?

“There she is,” Officer Hallet said. “See her pointing at us? She noticed you were missing and she was very upset.”

Fern looked at the line around the monument. She spotted Candace, and then Mrs. Phillips, her blond locks radiant in the sun, then Lee, and finally Blythe . . . who was the one pointing. Fern took a moment to thank her lucky stars that Blythe wasn’t really her sister.

The closer the two officers and Fern got to the rest of the St. Gregory’s students clumped together in line, the more she could feel eyes focused on her. By the time they were a few feet away from Mrs. Phillips, students were actually hopping over the fence to get a better view of Fern between the officers.

“I think we found your sister,” Officer Hallet said, now an arm’s length away from Blythe, Lee, and Mrs. Phillips. The chain was all that separated them.

“Oh, I meant that she was *like* a sister to me,” Blythe said, smiling sweetly at Officer Hallet. “We’re not, like, actual sisters.”

"It's always nice to have friends. Now, ma'am," Officer Hallet said, tipping his police hat at Mrs. Phillips. "I believe we've found what you were looking for."

"Oh, you have!" Mrs. Phillips said, putting both hands to her cheeks, feigning relief.

"She was by the World War II Memorial. Not to worry, though, I don't think she was up to any mischief," Officer Hallet stated.

"Thank you so much, Officer," Mrs. Phillips said, putting out her hand. The officer took Mrs. Phillips's hand in his own and shook it once.

"Well, Fern McAllister," Officer Hallet said, nudging Fern forward, "try not to meander off again." He winked at Fern. Out of the corner of her eye, Fern saw Headmaster Mooney storming toward her as the policeman retreated with his silent partner. Though Fern knew she was in deep trouble, she hoped she was the only casualty—Sam and Lindsey may have been able to slip back in line unnoticed. Surely Lindsey's tight group of girlfriends would cover for her, as would Preston for Sam. Headmaster Mooney was at the head of the St. Gregory's section of the line. Because Fern and the Lincoln group were bringing up the rear, it took him a few moments to reach the back. He was wearing an oversize down jacket and a beanie with I ♥ DC embroidered on it. A large camera dangled from his neck. Fern had never seen him move so quickly. He motioned for both Mrs. Phillips and Fern to step out of line.

"What was Fern doing with the police?" Headmaster

Mooney began. His mustache danced up and down as he spoke.

"I went to—"

"Excuse me, Fern, but I think Headmaster Mooney was asking *me*, not you." Mrs. Phillips gave Headmaster Mooney a flirtatious smile.

"That's right, Mrs. Phillips. I'm sure you have everything under control. But I would like to know what was going on."

"Well, Fern snuck out of line and went off by herself. Fortunately, Blythe noticed and notified the friendly police officers nearby that she was missing." Fern looked toward the front of the line. Every single student had turned around to look at the Mooney-Phillips powwow. Blythe and Lee were beaming with pride. A group of eighth-grade boys were laughing with them. By leaving the line, Fern had managed to give Blythe and Lee more than enough ammunition to exact their promised revenge, as well as time to gather an audience. Worse still, Fern saw the Commander marching toward them. Her mother would probably only make bad matters worse, despite her good intentions.

"Fortunate, indeed!" Headmaster Mooney smiled at Mrs. Phillips. "Well, thank you for taking care of the situation. I'm glad that Fern had such a vigilant chaperone." Mooney then stared down at Fern.

"I'd like to speak to you privately," he said, backing away from the line.

After Headmaster Mooney had put about twenty feet between the monument line and himself, he turned to face Fern.

"Where exactly did you sneak off to?" Headmaster Mooney demanded.

"I wasn't sneaking. I only wanted a better look at the World War II Memorial," Fern said. "It wasn't that far away!" She knew she was stretching the truth, but she wanted to get this whole ordeal over with as quickly as possible.

"Either way, that was in direct violation of the rules of the trip!" Mooney said. Moisture had gathered on his mustache. He flicked it off angrily with one of his hands. Fern was shivering, both because she was frightened of the punishment Headmaster Mooney might dole out and also because she was now far enough from the monument that nothing shielded her from the whipping wind.

"Do you realize that you've embarrassed St. Gregory's once again? Why, you're nothing but a bane on the school, Fern McAllister!" Headmaster Mooney's face was now red as he gasped for more breath. "You're a disgrace! Getting the police involved! If your mother hadn't volunteered to be a chaperone on this trip, I swear I'd have you on a plane so quickly, it would make your head—"

"I guess then, Headmaster Mooney, Fern's pretty lucky I *am* a chaperone on this trip."

The Commander had stalked up behind the headmaster a few moments before. By the time she was close enough to interject, she'd heard quite enough of his diatribe. Dressed in slacks and a pinstriped collared shirt, her flaxen hair was gathered in an understated bun. The Commander was fuming, but collected.

"As for Fern making a foolish, but innocent, mistake, I won't disagree with you there," the Commander said, glowering at her daughter, "but perhaps it would be best if you didn't discipline her in front of such a public audience." Headmaster Mooney's face turned bright red, much as it had when he and Clownface—a teacher nicknamed by the students for her overuse of makeup—faced off with the Commander after Fern's initial Pirate Cove teleporting incident. Fern thought he would have learned by now that he was no match for her mother.

Still, although Fern *was* embarrassed by the fact that Headmaster Mooney was chastising her in front of everyone, she was mortified by the fact that her mother had come to her defense. It had only made her more of a spectacle.

"Fine," Headmaster Mooney conceded grudgingly. "She will not go unpunished for this, though."

"I'm not suggesting that. What I am suggesting is that you keep the scene to a minimum."

"Thank you for your input, Mary Lou. You can go ahead and go back to the Madison group. I'll take it from here." Headmaster Mooney gave Mrs. McAllister a wide, saccharine smile. "Fern, come with me."

"Where exactly are you planning on taking Fern?"

"Fern has lost the privilege of traveling with the rest of

the school to the top of the monument. I plan on sitting with her while her classmates enjoy the spectacular view they've been waiting patiently in rule-abiding fashion to see."

Mrs. McAllister imagined her daughter being cruelly berated by Headmaster Mooney for the next forty-five minutes. She'd probably already overstepped chaperone boundaries by leaving the Madison group to intervene on her daughter's behalf, and she could sense that Fern didn't welcome her involvement, but it wasn't in her nature to stand by while Fern was ridiculed by a buffoon like Ralph Mooney. Why had she left the line? Mary Lou McAllister recognized that Fern had an uphill climb when it came to being accepted by her classmates. Sometimes, though, she honestly thought her daughter only made it harder on herself.

"I'll stay with her and get May Lin to watch the Madison group—there's no reason you should be deprived of the opportunity to go to the top." The Commander smiled sweetly at Headmaster Mooney.

Headmaster Mooney looked at the McAllister girl and then her mother. He wanted as little to do with them as possible. Finally the barrel-chested headmaster shrugged his shoulders at them both and told them to follow him. He led the McAllisters to the front of the Washington Monument where the white building that housed the monument bookstore stood, enclosing the entrance to the elevator that took tourists to the top. Concrete surrounded the base of the building, but beyond that, there was a wide expanse of grass. Headmaster Mooney stalked up to the spot where the concrete slab met the grass.

"You will sit here," he said, pointing at a small, dewy plot of grass. "While your classmates ride up to see the panoramic views of our nation's capital, you will not move from this spot. You will stay here until every single student has gone up in the elevator and come down. Please make sure that your daughter does not walk off in the future. Okay?"

Headmaster Mooney had turned red again.

"Fern will sit here silently, I assure you," the Commander said sternly. Headmaster Mooney nodded once firmly and stalked off to rejoin the line. Once he was a safe distance away, the Commander kneeled next to her daughter.

"Why did you wander off?" she asked Fern.

"I wanted to see the World War II Memorial," Fern said, folding her arms. Mary Lou McAllister looked at the bruise under Fern's eye. She leaned in to get a closer look, but Fern turned away.

"Was it Lee and Blythe? Were they teasing you?"

"No. Seriously, Mom, there wasn't anything else going on," Fern said, almost angry. She realized that everyone was staring at her.

"You can tell me what's wrong, Fern. I want to help."

"If you wanted to help, you should have left me alone," Fern said, directing an angry glare at the Commander. "I have a hard enough time making friends as is without my mom following me around like I'm a baby while everyone watches."

Mary Lou closed her eyes and took a deep breath, trying not to show any injured feelings in her expression. She thought about her best friend, Fern's birth mother, Phoebe Merriam. Phoebe was the most stubborn person Mary Lou had ever met, but Mary Lou loved her all the more for it. Fern was growing more and more like Phoebe every day. Mary Lou wished there was something she could say to her daughter—something that might stem the tide of stubbornness and resentment that she felt was beginning to engulf Fern. And yet, Mary Lou had no idea how to even conceptualize what her daughter was going through. In the last few months, Fern had found out that Mary Lou had been lying to her, that her twin brother wasn't her actual twin, and that she was at the center of a centuries-old battle between good and evil vampires. The Commander wouldn't have believed any of it if she hadn't lived it with Fern.

Since Mary Lou's revelation about Phoebe, when Fern thought no one was looking, she would grow quiet as a sad and distressed look clouded her face—like she'd lost something very important and had no hope of getting it back. The few times Mary Lou had seen this look on Fern's face, she could feel her heart breaking for her adoptive daughter. *What if*, Mary Lou asked herself, *I lose Fern like I lost Phoebe*? She quickly banished such thoughts from her mind.

Mary Lou realized Fern's teeth were chattering.

"Are you cold?" the Commander said, feeling despondent as she thought of Fern's face during those quiet moments.

"No," Fern said coldly.

"Well, I'm going to run into the gift shop and get you another layer just in case," the Commander said sympathetically.

"I *really* don't need anything. . . ." Fern's voice trailed off. The Commander pretended she hadn't heard Fern as she trotted off in the direction of the Washington Monument's entrance.

The fact that the Commander was being so nice to her only made Fern want to distance herself further from her mother. The Commander was trying, maybe, but she didn't have any clue what was going on with Fern anymore. Then again, how could she?

After a few minutes of being alone, Fern spotted Sam entering the white stone building. He saw her in her damp exile and mouthed *Sorry* before disappearing through the security checkpoint. Lindsey separated from her roommates for a moment and gave Fern a small wave.

Before long, everyone from St. Gregory's had entered the building to ride up to the top of the monument, and the Commander hadn't returned. Fern was still alone on the wet patch of grass. But not for long.

"It's pretty cloudy out anyway. You're not missing much."

Fern looked up. Sam's best friend, Preston Buss, was standing in front of her. Preston played volleyball and basketball with Sam and hung out behind the outdoor stage with the other popular kids in school. Preston was a few inches taller than Sam, with a lanky frame, and the two boys had a friendly rivalry in most things. Today he was wearing skinny jeans, a Burton snowboarding jacket, and a skullcap. The hair poking out from under his hat was black, and his olive skin seemed out of place in the cold Washington weather.

"What?" Fern asked, confused.

"The view. On a clear day, you can see all of DC. And I'm not going to lie. It's pretty cool, but it's cloudy today," Preston said, sitting down next to her and blowing a bubble with his chewing gum. "So you're not missing much."

"You've been here before?" Fern asked.

"My dad's a pilot. We go lots of places," Preston said. His eyes were the color of copper and were perfectly suited to his face.

"You may want to get up," Fern said. "The grass is soaking wet."

"Too late," Preston said, smiling at Fern. She was getting the distinct feeling that he was *trying* to be nice to her, but she couldn't decide why.

"Aren't you supposed to be with your group?"

"Nah. They'll lose track of everyone up there. I'll sneak back to my group when they come down."

Preston peered into Fern's eyes in a way that made her heart jump. The two sat on the grass, craning their necks up toward the capstone of the monument. Fern scanned the horizon nervously, expecting the Commander to reappear at any second.

"So what'd you do?" Preston asked, this time not looking at Fern.

"Didn't you see everything? I thought everyone did. . . ."

"I mean, I saw Mooney chew you out and I saw you get dropped off by the police, but no one really knows what you did. Blythe Conrad is telling everyone you were trying to score cigarettes from tourists all over the Mall."

"Oh, great," Fern said, her blood boiling. "I wandered off for a second and Blythe Conrad told the police I was 'missing.'"

"That girl sucks," Preston said with a smile.

"I thought you were friends with her."

"Um, no." Preston turned his body toward Fern. "No one wants to be on her bad side because there's no telling what she might do, but I'm not sure anyone *actually* likes her."

Fern could sense that Preston Buss was trying to be sympathetic, but that almost angered her more. She didn't need charity. She liked it better when she was ignored.

Preston nervously pulled blades of grass out of the ground, depositing them in a pile as they sat cross-legged, facing each other. He reached into his jacket and pulled out a shiny metallic object the size of a large pack of gum.

He cupped it and brought it to his mouth. His cheeks expanded like he was a puffer fish as musical notes began.

It took Fern a few seconds to realize that Preston was playing a harmonica. She recognized the first few bars of the most basic blues riff. He repeated it. *Da-na-na-na-na.* Preston tapped his foot on the wet ground in front of him. Fern couldn't tell if she was more nervous because of Preston's presence or because the Commander would be back at any moment with a cheesy sweatshirt.

"Fern was sittin' in the soakin' grass," he sang, trying to make his voice sound husky. *Da-na-na-na-na.* "Feelin' kinda down 'n low." *Da-na-na-na-na.* "Preston Buss weren't very much help." *Da-na-na-na-na.* "Till he gave his harmonica a blow." Preston's voice dipped as low as it could go for the final lyric of his impromptu song. He ended by blowing a fast pattern of notes out of his harmonica. His hand opened and closed and his lips moved up and down the harmonica's comb. The music flowed from Preston. He was obviously fairly skilled.

Fern grinned at Preston, amazed he didn't seem to care at all about who was watching him—he had a goofiness that she'd never noticed when she hung around Sam and him together. A few people in line had leaned over the chain to get a better look at the source of the music.

"Where'd you learn to do that?"

"My older brother is in a band. I only fool around, mostly."

"You're not bad," Fern said earnestly.

"Yeah, well, at least you don't look so depressed anymore. Better get in position to jump back in with my group. Don't want to pull a Fern McAllister and wind up in custody," he teased, smiling at Fern as he bounded up and ran toward the monument's entrance.

Finally alone in the bathroom of her room after the monument benching and the rest of the day's scheduled events, Fern put both hands flat on the sink basin and leaned forward. Inches from the mirror, she raised a finger and touched the patch of black and blue, puffy skin. Fern winced but didn't mind the pain. It momentarily took her mind off what she was about to do. Blythe and Lee would surely be elated once they saw Fern's black eye. Perhaps they might even leave her alone, satisfied with their revenge—now that they had publicly humiliated her with the Capitol police stunt, the underwear caper, and the bus face-plant incident.

For this trip, Fern hadn't given Sam or Lindsey any time parameters. She'd simply told them that she was going to teleport to the house in the picture once Lee, Blythe, and Candace had fallen asleep. She was exhausted from a day of sightseeing—everyone in the St. Gregory's contingent had walked all around the Tidal Basin, the Jefferson Memorial, and the Mall. After a late-afternoon box lunch that included a dried-out sandwich and a seriously questionable orange, the students were given two hours to wander through the National Museum of Natural History. Fern estimated the students had covered at least five miles in touring.

Though most of her classmates stared at Fern from a distance as rumors continued to swirl that she had snuck out of line to purchase contraband or participate in other nefarious illegal activities, Candace dogged Fern. She hung at Fern's side the entire day, rattling off a potpourri of arcane facts and figures about the memorials and other landmarks. Lindsey and Sam had offered to hang out with Fern for the rest of the day, but she'd dismissed them both, figuring they couldn't actually talk about anything of significance with Candace around. She spotted her brother and best friend throughout the day, surrounded by groups of four or more, laughing and goofing around as they dashed from one attraction to the next. Fern couldn't remember the last time she'd spent time with more than two people at once by choice (unless you included Eddie, but he was her brother, so he didn't count). She was beginning to recognize that, as an outsider, she had more in common with Candace than with Sam or Lindsey.

Also, Fern couldn't help but be impressed by Candace's command of facts as they wandered through the exhibits in the Museum of Natural History.

"Hey!" Lindsey Lin called out to Fern. "Come here for a sec." Lindsey was motioning for Fern to join her in the corner of one of the exhibit halls.

"I'll be right back, Candace," Fern said, before trotting over to Lindsey. "Stay put."

"See that man over there?" Lindsey said, pointing to

the far end of the hall. Fern spotted a white-haired man in glasses wearing a nicely tailored suit. He had a dozen people around him, all listening intently to him as he gestured toward a skeleton encased in glass behind him.

"Yeah," Fern said, wondering why Lindsey had called her over to point out a tour guide.

"That's Dr. Grundfest! He's a professor as well as a curator at the Smithsonian. But he's also one of the most famous Rollens around and a renowned scholar—he's kind of like the vampire version of Indiana Jones. He's a really big deal in the Alliance," Lindsey said, awestruck as if she were in the presence of greatness or, at the very least, a major rock 'n' roll star. "He's a contributor to *The Undead Sea Scroll* and specializes in Otherworldly history and artifacts. Cool, huh?"

Fern nodded at Lindsey but couldn't really muster up the excitement to match her friend's. Lindsey had been raised a Rollen and had a reverence for the Alliance and all its head honchos, but Fern hadn't learned of the Rollen Alliance until a few months ago. It was hard for her to be either impressed or intimidated by a man in a suit, no matter who he was in the Alliance. Fern did, however, appreciate Lindsey's attempts to bring her up to speed on the varied aspects of vampire culture.

"It just goes to show you, the Alliance is everywhere," Lindsey added.

"It sure does," Fern said, curious about whether or not the group surrounding Dr. Grundfest was also made up of vampires. Before Fern could ask, Lindsey told Fern she'd see her later and darted back to her group.

Fern rejoined a forlorn-looking Candace, and they quickly resumed touring the museum as a twosome. While the dinosaur fossils fascinated Fern, she was especially drawn to the dimly lit insect zoo. She laughed when Candace pointed out the incongruity of Orkin, a pest control company, being the official sponsor of the live insect zoo.

"Only in America," Candace said, laughing. Fern wasn't quite sure what she meant but laughed anyway. A sense of camaraderie, even if it was with Candace Tutter, felt good to Fern. She had wanted to skip the Hall of Geology, Gems and Minerals (even the name of the hall put Fern to sleep), but Candace insisted they see the Hope Diamond.

"It's the one from *Titanic*," Candace said. Fern had never seen *Titanic*. The Commander's strict policy limiting television hadn't permitted it. Though Sam and Fern snuck a few hours of television watching in when the Commander wasn't home, they'd never gotten around to watching *Titanic*, mostly because Sam insisted it was too girlie for him.

The Hope Diamond was certainly spectacular. Sitting by itself in its own glass enclosure, it was the largest gem Fern had ever seen. It had its own spotlight and rested on a black velvet pillow. The plaque next to it detailed its actual size, 45.52 karats.

"It's blue to the naked eye because its crystallized

structure contains boron," Candace stated. Fern was tempted to ask what boron was but knew that would start Candace on a tangent providing more gemological information than Fern ever wanted to know. Instead Candace talked about the legend behind the diamond. "The legend specifies that the Hope Diamond was stolen from a temple long ago. In ancient times, it used to be one of the eyes of a famous sculpture. Now it is supposed to bring bad luck to whoever possesses it."

"Well, it definitely is beautiful. But we better move on before we catch its bad luck," Fern said, anxious to leave the Hall of Geology for greener (and less boring) pastures.

"That's just a legend," Candace said.

Fern chuckled to herself. She had experienced too many instances in her short life where things discounted as "just legends" turned out to be completely true. In fact, sometimes it seemed like her whole existence had come to be defined by legends come to life.

Fern's favorite stop of the day, by far, was the Lincoln Memorial. Candace informed Fern that the white columned structure that housed the huge Lincoln statue was modeled after a Greek Doric temple. Fern bent down to feel the worn grooves in the marble steps that led up to the large temple structure with its thirty-six gleaming white columns. She imagined the millions of footsteps that had preceded hers. Fern was impressed by the size of the imposing seated figure of Lincoln—with nearly every other statue she'd seen, the subject was standing. As Fern looked up at him, she felt the effects of her late-night visit with Miles. She had a strong urge to climb up Lincoln's marble legs and curl up in his oversize lap for a nap. The sixteenth president's face looked so calm and serene. The inscription above Lincoln's head was perfect too.

IN THIS TEMPLE
AS IN THE HEARTS OF THE PEOPLE
FOR WHOM HE SAVED THE UNION
THE MEMORY OF ABRAHAM LINCOLN
IS ENSHRINED FOREVER

Lincoln was a hero for the ages, presiding over a nation in turmoil. He could have stood by while the states divided, but instead he took the more difficult, righteous path, abolishing slavery and fighting to preserve the nation. Fern's thoughts about Lincoln's courage unexpectedly returned her to the present, and guilt and anxiety swept over her. She didn't aspire to the sort of accomplishments Lincoln had achieved, but she did feel a growing responsibility because of her special talents. There were few certainties about Fern's status as an Unusual, but she knew she shared a connection with Miles. She also felt sure that if she were in a cage in a concrete cavern, Miles would do everything he could to help her.

Snapping back to the task at hand as she stood in the bathroom, Fern put on her jacket and shoes, which she'd stowed in the same place as the night before. She concentrated on the row house in Miles's photograph. With the image burned into her brain, she closed her eyes. She zeroed in on the pastel colors and the wooden steps leading up to the house.

The prickling sensation began in Fern's fingertips and moved up her arms. Taking a deep breath, she knew she'd be gone in a few moments.

"Fern?" a voice said. "What are you doing in there?"

It was Candace. Though she racked her brain, Fern couldn't remember if she'd locked the bathroom door. She tried to open her eyes to see if Candace had entered the bathroom, but all she saw was darkness.

Fern was already on her way.

Fern always preferred to arrive standing up. In fact, if there was one part of her teleporting skill set that needed refining, it was the landing. This trip, she thankfully reached her destination upright. The street was quiet, and except for the smattering of porch lights, it was dark.

Fern still clutched the photograph. Her eyes danced around in the dimness from the picture to the actual house. Every detail was identical. The colorful trim was muted by the night, but there was no doubt she was looking at the house in the photo. Almost immediately, Fern felt the chill in the air. Washington was very cold in March, but this place was freezing. Fern wished she had followed Candace's "layering" plan.

She tried to see if she could determine her location from

her surroundings. The street sign was in English. DEL LANE. There was no city or other information on it. Fern looked at the address, in golden numbers, nailed to the front of the house: 12101.

12101 Del Lane. Fern knew she could be anywhere. But she reassured herself with the thought that Miles would not send her somewhere dangerous. Another thought nagged at her, though: What if the situation had changed inside this house since Miles had been taken? What if he was unaware of some danger now lurking inside?

Gripping the railing, Fern climbed up to the porch of the house. There was no playbook to go by here, nor did she know exactly what she would say to whoever was inside. Nevertheless, her instincts told her to ring the doorbell.

She gulped and heard a faint scuttling inside. Would she introduce herself? Ask if the person who answered knew Miles Zapo? As the seconds ticked by, Fern wondered if the doorbell would be answered at all.

Fern tensed as the door slowly creaked open. From within, a voice sounded.

"I've been expecting you, Fern."

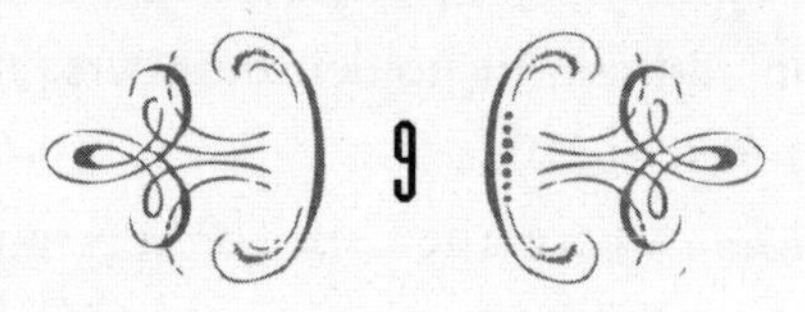

9

the house with all the mirrors

Flarge might not have looked like a skilled sleuth, but after many decades of spying on and ultimately assassinating a number of high-profile Rollens, he had trained himself to become nearly invisible. Though, among Blouts, he was widely recognized for his undercover skills, even Flarge was impressed when he saw Fern McAllister appear on the porch of the house he'd been staking out in Mound, Minnesota. With the three-hour flight to Minnesota from DC, he had needed to move very quickly in order to arrive before the girl did.

After parking his rental car down the street, he'd hidden behind the hedge that separated the house from the neighbor's. Flarge marveled when McAllister appeared out of nowhere on the porch. He knew she'd arrived instantly, most likely from her hotel room in Washington, DC.

For her part, once she'd appeared, Fern studied the partially open front door of the house. She shored up her resolve. Though she was apprehensive, she hadn't teleported in the middle of the night just to stand out in the cold and freeze. Besides, Lindsey and Sam would worry if she was gone too long. She inched inside the open door. The lighting was a little brighter inside, but it still took Fern's eyes a moment to adjust. She was standing in a long hallway lined with different-size mirrors on each side. Some of the mirrors were rounded, ornate gilded frames enclosed some, and others bubbled out. On the far side of the hallway, bits of reflective glass had been glued to the wall at odd angles, forming a mirror mosaic. The whole effect reminded Fern of an artsy fun house. On the floor, piles of Oriental rugs were stacked, one overlapping the other, creating a patchwork of faded colors and designs. Though she expected to find the owner of the voice she'd heard moments ago, the hallway was empty. The only light came from the room at the end of the corridor. A small figure appeared there briefly before vanishing into the adjoining room.

"In here." The same voice that had beckoned her from the porch now drifted down the hallway. The voice sounded worn-out and weathered like an old woman's. "Now is not the time to be shy. We haven't a moment to lose." As Fern quickened her pace, the floor underneath the rugs creaked.

The first thing she noticed as she reached the doorway

to the adjacent room was the large chandelier suspended from the ceiling. There must have been two dozen flickering candles resting on it. Melted wax dripped from its glass structure like creamy icicles. The octagonal room had more mirrors than the hallway. Every inch of wall was covered with some kind of reflective glass. Some of the mirrors were tarnished, but everywhere she looked, Fern saw distorted versions of herself. In the clearer images, she noticed her developing black eye.

"A fluorescent light may be best for illuminating surfaces," the woman said, observing the direction of Fern's gaze toward the dozens of candles floating above her. "But candlelight illuminates the soul. I can discern a person's character more accurately in candlelight than with any newfangled technologies. For Miles's sake, I wish I was more sure about yours." Fern suddenly felt exposed. She looked toward the woman. She ahd not expected her to be so challenging.

As distracting as the flickering light from the chandelier and the mirrors was, as soon as her eyes fixed on the woman, Fern was unable to concentrate on anything else. The woman sat with her arms folded on a table covered with a red tablecloth. Her face was the color of cinnamon, and except for a few deep creases on her forehead and around her mouth, her skin was smooth. Her caramel eyes shone in the flickering brightness of the candles. A multicolored scarf was wrapped around her head, like a radiant cloth beehive. There was a frantic glint to her eyes, though, that made her look frenzied.

Fern peered at the woman, trying to guess her age. It was an impossible task—the woman could've been anywhere between thirty and eighty years old. Fern had never seen anyone like her.

"Sit," the woman commanded, motioning to a seat across from her.

Fern was nervous but tried not to show it. She pulled a velvet-covered armchair out from the table and settled on the edge of the seat.

"I must know . . . is he okay?" the woman asked, a mixture of anger and concern seeping into her voice.

"Is *who* okay?" Fern responded.

"Miles." The woman's clear eyes stared at Fern. "That's why you're here!" The woman pounded the table once with her gnarled hand. "This is not a game, child."

Fern tensed, wondering if teleporting here had been a mistake. This woman was angry and not necessarily on Fern's side.

"I'm here," Fern said, backing her chair up slightly, "because Miles told me to come here. But I don't know who you are."

"*Tell me* about Miles," the woman barked as if she were barely in control of her emotions. To Fern, her voice teetered on the edge of something—as if she was either going to attack Fern or burst into tears.

"I don't mean to be rude," Fern said, tiring of being the only one answering questions, "but . . . before I tell you anything, why don't you tell me something: Who are you? Where am I?"

The woman looked down and traced the tablecloth's fabric with her finger. Fern noticed her hands for the first time. Her nails were long, like Mrs. Phillips's, but each nail was painted a different color. Fern couldn't decide if this woman was some kind of witch or merely eccentric.

"Have you been foolish enough to bring someone with you?" The woman's voice was cold now and most certainly adversarial.

"Bring someone *with* me?"

"I sense someone else here. . . ." The woman trailed off, closing her eyes. Several feet away, having snuck into the hallway, Flarge paused, ready to attack at a moment's notice if discovered.

The woman's eyes popped open at once and she leaned across the table, shoving her long index finger in Fern's face. "The gray in your soul, Fern McAllister, has been known to me for some time. So if you are lying to me, I promise you, there will be consequences. . . ."

Fern pushed back the armchair and stood up to leave. As much as she wanted to help Miles, she was now most concerned about her own safety.

"I came by myself, and I'm here to help Miles. He's alone and he's scared and he's being held in a cage, but if you want to accuse me instead of answering my questions, I think I should go."

The woman cleared her throat.

She paused a moment to steady her voice. “My profound apologies,” the woman began. “I’ve been so anxious over the last few days . . . waiting for you to arrive. I didn’t fully realize the depth of my anguish. Even though I am known as a gifted augur, I’m afraid I was unprepared for how deeply I have felt the boy’s absence.” The woman no longer seemed to be talking to Fern, but to herself. She suddenly looked old in the glinting light of the dozens of tiny flames. “I’ve seen so much destruction, so much needless death, outlived so many I’ve cared for. Despite my best instincts and intentions when he was entrusted to my care, I’ve grown quite attached to the boy. Though I knew it would happen, when he was taken from here, I . . .” She drifted off and looked up, as if trying to see the scarf curled around her head. With a single shudder, the woman’s eyes focused back on Fern.

“I’m Miles’s Aunt Chan.”

“Oh!” Fern said with disbelief. It was hard for her to imagine that this anxious and nearly unhinged woman was Miles’s aunt. “So I’m in Minnesota? In Mound, where Miles is from?”

Aunt Chan looked puzzled. “Didn’t Miles tell you that?”

“We were interrupted. He handed me the photo and told me to come here, but I wasn’t sure why.”

A draft moved through the room and dimmed the candles for a moment before they flared up again. Fern caught a whiff of something that smelled like tree sap. In the corner, she saw a smoking stick.

"*Pom* . . . incense from the copal tree. It helps sharpen my visions," Aunt Chan said, following Fern's gaze. The scent tingled the inside of Fern's nose. She feared she was wasting valuable time.

"Why did Miles tell me to come here?" she asked.

"Because I have always known you would need my help if you had any hope of keeping him, and yourself, alive." Aunt Chan's eyes flickered in the candlelight.

Fern took a deep breath to stem her rising anxiety.

"You have a connection to him, do you not?" Aunt Chan said, her eyes kinder than they'd been previously. Fern couldn't possibly explain why, since she'd first dreamed of Miles, she felt more in sync with him than with her own family who loved her. Perhaps it was because Miles was a part of the prophecy too, or that he had secrets of his own.

"From this point on, child, both your life and Miles's will be marked by extraordinary difficulties," Aunt Chan said, as if she were responding to Fern's inner thoughts. "I have pledged to help you in any way I can. But you first need to tell me what you know of Miles's situation and captors."

Fern didn't fully comprehend how much she *did* know until she began recounting her story. She described the first time she'd seen Miles in a dream. When she was finished, Aunt Chan folded her hands once more on the table.

"So you really came here without knowing your actual destination or who you were coming to see?"

"Miles told me to come to the house in the picture."

"And you trust Miles?" Aunt Chan arched one of her dark eyebrows.

"Well." Fern paused. "He's an Unusual, like me."

"Never lose your instinct to trust people, Fern. Soon you will be tested more than you can currently fathom. You will be tempted to cast hope aside, like your mother did, but *resist.* With all your heart, *resist.*"

"You—you knew—my mother?" Fern stammered. The mere mention of Phoebe caused a spring of emotions to rise within Fern. She instinctively felt for the one letter of Phoebe's she had placed into her inside zippered jacket pocket. As soon as she felt it crinkle slightly under the pressure of her hand, she calmed down. She thought of all she had learned about Phoebe from the letters. Fern wanted to know everything about her mother, but at the same time, she was also terrified that the information Aunt Chan possessed would be disturbing. Sometimes she longed for the days when she knew nothing of Phoebe Merriam—when the Commander had been the only mother she knew.

Aunt Chan's eyes clouded over. Her face turned stone-like. She was absolutely motionless. A minute passed before Fern spoke.

"Aunt Chan . . . are you okay?"

Aunt Chan shook her head as if trying to shoo an

annoying fly that had landed on her head scarf.

Flarge, still standing in the hallway, again got himself in the best position to strike.

"I had a brief phantasm. It was nothing," Aunt Chan said, scrutinizing Fern.

Fern looked at her watch. She suspected Lindsey and Sam were beginning to worry by now, and she was still haunted by the sound of Candace's voice as she left the bathroom. What if Candace had begun looking for Fern? She felt as if she hadn't made any progress.

"How can you help me? What kind of Otherworldly are you?"

"A name is what you make of it, I suppose. I am what some call a Bacab. Not only can I determine which will be fortunate years for my people and which will not, but I have certain types of knowledge about the future. Not infallible knowledge, mind you. In your case, I hope it's not infallible." Worry lines appeared on Aunt Chan's face. "Miles, like you, was born under special circumstances. Since his birth, I've had visions about his possible abduction. But I never knew by whom. I prepared for the day, training Miles, making him strong in mind and heart."

As the time ticked by, Fern was beginning to lose hope that Aunt Chan had any answers.

"Why didn't you try to stop it from happening in the first place?"

"I don't think you are fully grasping the nature of my talent, dear. I can see what will happen, yet I am powerless to stop it. That is not my province."

Aunt Chan scooted her chair backward and hopped down. Fern was shocked by her diminutive size. Gasping inaudibly, Fern stared at the old woman's short legs. Aunt Chan was several inches shorter than Fern, even counting her towering head scarf. Fern hadn't noticed how tiny her arms and feet were. She almost looked like a doll, barely able to see over the table, now that she was standing and not elevated in her chair. How could this woman help her rescue Miles?

Aunt Chan walked through the nearby doorway, leaving Fern all alone in the candlelit room. Almost instantly, Aunt Chan was back, with a tall ladder in her hand. Propping the metal ladder against the wall opposite Fern, she began to climb until her colorful head wrap grazed the ceiling. With one swift move, Aunt Chan dislodged a section of the ceiling. A large book crashed to the floor. From Fern's perspective, it seemed to appear out of nowhere, but there was now a book-size hole in the ceiling. The volume had been disguised as a part of the ceiling itself. Fern had to admit, it was a clever hiding place.

As Aunt Chan climbed down from the ladder, Fern examined the book. It was leather-bound and as large as three encyclopedias fastened together. Its pages had ragged, uneven edges. Aunt Chan, now back on solid ground, took the book in her arms and heaved it onto the table in front of Fern. She pushed her chair toward Fern and with a single movement, hopped up to her seat.

Because she was closer, Fern could detect dozens of small wrinkles on Aunt Chan's face that she hadn't previously noticed. Aunt Chan dusted off the cover of the large tome, revealing the words POPOL VUH.

"The Popol Vuh—the most sacred text we have. It's one account of my people's history. I have been its keeper for the last two centuries." Aunt Chan flipped the book open. There were detailed drawings of beasts and thin cursive writing on every page in a language Fern couldn't decipher. The early pages had a rough texture to them, like they were made of thinly pressed tree bark. Near the back of the volume, the pages were made from more traditional paper. Aunt Chan began searching through the book until she found what she was looking for—a crude drawing.

At first Fern thought the black-and-white drawing was a large snake of some kind. But then she noticed that it had large, talonlike feet and its bottom half was decorated with feathers. The creature's eyes were completely black.

"Is that a Howling Quetzal?"

"Exactly," Aunt Chan said. "They are extraordinarily rare, though their powers are exceptional, as you have heard from Miles. When it howls, those special descendents of Itzamná are rendered powerless under its spell."

"Special descendents of Itzamná?" Fern questioned.

"What your people call Otherworldlies," Aunt Chan explained. "Otherworldlies permeate all cultures and all people. Your view of them may have been unnecessarily narrow before now. Surely your people have a similar volume, recording their story?"

"*The Undead Sea Scroll,*" Fern offered.

"The Popol Vuh, or your *Undead Sea Scroll.* These are our best accounts of that which we do not understand. But they are still mere interpretation, constantly being revised by experience."

"It'll help me figure out how to rescue Miles, then?" Fern asked, still unable to determine why she'd come to Mound in the first place.

"The Popol Vuh is nothing more than a collection of tales. Its stories help us understand . . . to make sense of things that seem incomprehensible," Aunt Chan said, her voice impassioned. "With every myth about the beginning of something, every legend . . . we try to understand life. Human existence would be unbearable otherwise. You must use and integrate what we already know with your own knowledge to save Miles."

Fern's head began to spin.

Aunt Chan began flipping the pages of the great volume, muttering to herself things like "That's not it," and "It can't be that he's after." Fern ticked the minutes off in her head, peering at the pages of the large book. All kinds of strange drawings of bizarre creatures popped out at her.

"Aha!" Aunt Chan raised her arm in the air and pointed toward the ceiling.

"What?" Fern said, trying to follow Aunt Chan's gaze with her own.

"Whoever this Silver Tooth is," Aunt Chan said, "why would he have gone through the process of taming the Howling Quetzal—which would have taken many years—unless he was planning to make the Ah Puch Potation!"

Aunt Chan pointed to a string of pictures on the page before her. The first was a picture of a large green feather.

As she pointed to the picture, in the neighboring hallway, Flarge took out a single scrap of paper and began writing on it. *She knows about the potion*, he wrote. *Calls you Silver Tooth.*

Fern peered at one of the pictures Aunt Chan had pointed to. There was a drawing of an angry man, with five arms, holding golden weapons. The last two pictures in the row were of a large blue diamond and a woman's cartoonlike face with tears rolling down her cheeks. Below the tears was a single crescent moon. The woman's head was adorned with a fanciful headdress, complete with horns and feathers.

Fern was confused and growing more concerned about the time it was taking to piece together any useful information.

"What does any of this have to do with Miles?"

"The Ah Puch Potation is legend—said to give he who drinks it immortality, along with the ability to subdue Otherworldlies, much like the Quetzals do," Aunt Chan said. She turned to face Fern and pointed down to the Popol Vuh. "What you're looking at, child, are the ingredients to be used in the Potation, according to the legend."

Aunt Chan explained. The first component was something Fern quickly recognized: a single feather from a Howling Quetzal. Quetzals were very protective of their feathers and fought to the death to preserve them, unless, of course, the Quetzal had been tamed. The second element was one of Chac's golden arrows. Chac was the Mayan god of rain, who threw his golden arrows toward Earth from the heavens, forming the lightning that mortals saw crash to Earth. Fern stared at the picture in the large book. Chac had many arms and dark menacing eyes, and in each one of his hands he held what looked like a long golden nail, spiked at the end.

The third ingredient was the essence of Ix Chel, the Mayan goddess of birth, weaving, and the moon. According to myths about Ix Chel recorded in the Popol Vuh, Ix Chel's tears had formed the moon and other planets. The last component also originated with the same Mayan goddess: Aunt Chan called it the Stone Eye of Ix Chel. She explained that, according to the Popol Vuh, the Stone Eye had been stolen from a famous Mayan statue of Ix Chel centuries ago and was presumed lost forever. The drawing of a crying Ix Chel with a crescent moon beneath her fascinated Fern.

"No one is entirely sure what the earthly manifestations of each of these ingredients are, if they indeed exist at all, or where they might be located. An ancient rumor has it that powerful members of the Mayan council protected these items by hiding them in plain sight, making them available should it ever be necessary to assemble the components and create the potion. Its power is overwhelming, and in the hands of someone with evil intentions . . ." Aunt Chan let her voice trail off as she imagined what kind of monster would imprison Miles in a cage and the consequences of that monster successfully formulating the potion.

Of course, Aunt Chan didn't know that one of the monsters who had helped imprison Miles, Flarge, was no more than a few feet away from her. At that very moment, in fact, he was in the midst of recording what was said so Laffar would better know exactly when to kill Fern McAllister.

As Flarge listened on, Fern peered closely at the last picture of the stone in the book—the stolen Stone Eye of Ix Chel. She'd seen something exactly like it before.

Then it came to her.

"The Hope Diamond!" Fern blurted.

"What?" Aunt Chan asked, wrinkling her face.

"That stone. It's in the Natural History Museum. I saw it today. The Hope Diamond. It's really famous and looks exactly like that."

Fern took a closer look at the book. She was sure of it. The shape and color were an exact match.

Aunt Chan put her hand over her heart.

"My word," she said in amazement, as if she had seen a shooting star unexpectedly light up the sky. "That is it, then. The man who took Miles . . . is planning to use his talents to steal the stone." Aunt Chan's eyes turned a golden yellow color. She grabbed Fern's arm and squeezed it tightly. "I have helped you as much as I possibly can. You must stop this!" Aunt Chan implored.

In order to appease Aunt Chan, Fern nodded her head in agreement, but she had no idea what she was actually agreeing to do.

Suddenly Aunt Chan and Fern turned around toward the hallway. The front door had slammed shut, creating a draft so strong, most of the candles in the dining room blew out.

"You may not have brought anyone here," Aunt Chan said in the near darkness, "but someone came nonetheless, without being invited."

Fern didn't have any time left to posit guesses as to who had snuck into the Zapo house. Lindsey and Sam would be waiting for her call, and there was still the potential problem of Candace to deal with. Aunt Chan rattled off more details Fern would need to help Miles, insisting she show Fern one last thing before she departed. Fern, distracted with thoughts of who might have been spying on them, tried to take in all that Aunt Chan had to show her. After a few more minutes, Fern declared she had to leave. Meanwhile, Flarge sped to the airport, intent on planning the final demise of Fern McAllister.

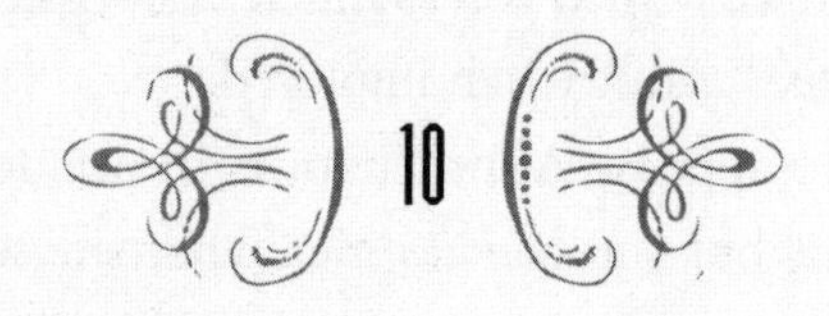

10
the disappearing acts

The conclusion of Fern's visit with Aunt Chan was far more satisfactory than its beginning. Aunt Chan finally revealed a few things Fern was anxious to know—including the nature of Miles's Unusual talent.

According to Aunt Chan, Miles shared certain traits with a famous Mayan hero. The hero, Ixbalanqué, or "Little Jaguar," was one of the divine twins from the Mayan creation story, known for his trickery. As an Unusual, Miles had inherited one of Ixbalanqué's best characteristics.

Though at first Fern was somewhat skeptical about Miles's talent, she soon came to realize that it was one of the best powers a kid (or perhaps anyone) could possess. Specifically, when Miles rubbed his hands together, he secreted a special kind of sweatlike liquid. This liquid, however gross it seemed at first, could do something incredible.

It could make Miles invisible.

Perhaps even more astonishing, if Miles touched any object with the secretion, the object immediately turned invisible too. Aunt Chan said that Miles called it his "magic water."

Both she and Aunt Chan were fully convinced that Silver Tooth was after the ingredients of the potion and was going to use Miles and his Unusual talent to steal them. They also suspected that all the necessary items were hidden in plain sight somewhere in Washington, DC. Why else would Silver Tooth be keeping Miles there? The ingredients couldn't be better protected than in the nation's capital, with its 24/7 security—it was the perfect place for them.

"I want to show you one last thing," Aunt Chan said as she hopped off her chair once more, bidding Fern to follow her. Though Fern tried to impress on Aunt Chan that she had limited time, she would not be rushed.

The older woman led Fern up a rickety wooden staircase, illuminated with candles. Her legs had to stretch for each step until they reached a dark corridor. Inching her hand against the wall for guidance, Fern followed Aunt Chan until they came to a door.

Aunt Chan pushed it open. She flipped on a light switch and stepped in, with Fern close behind her. Fern, acclimated to the flickering candlelight of the rest of the house, shielded her eyes from the sudden brightness. After a few seconds, her eyes adjusted and she removed her hand with only slight lingering stinging.

Minnesota Twins memorabilia filled every inch of the room. Miles had papered the walls with pennants, posters, and pictures of all things Twins. The greats were all there—Harmon Killebrew, Rod Carew, Kent Hrbek, Kirby Puckett, Joe Nathan, Joe Mauer. Miles even had bobble-head dolls of Twins players, an authentic Twins batting helmet, and several signed jerseys. His bedspread was a pattern of the Twins logo and baseball bats.

There was no other way of putting it: The kid was obsessed.

Fern had to smile, though, as she thought of her new friend. It was easy to forget that she'd only met him a few days before. Fern felt as if she had a fairly complete picture of him—Miles Zapo was so confident about his identity. He was comfortable with his status as an Otherworldly and an Unusual. And more than anything, he loved the Minnesota Twins.

Aunt Chan walked toward the opposite side of the room, which had a desk, a light, and a corkboard displaying a school schedule, a few reminders, and a charcoal drawing.

"He drew this picture after he saw you in his dream," Aunt Chan said. Fern walked over to get a better look. In large block letters, Miles had written her name, "Fern!" at the bottom of the drawing. He had done a pretty good job capturing her likeness. Fern was standing on a beach, and in the background a man appeared to be either dead or unconscious. Fern recognized the man's goatee and black tails immediately. It was Vlad, frozen on the beach. The only color in the drawing was green splotches within Fern's eyes.

"Miles was the voice you heard in the water that day you defeated Vlad. I told Miles that if he was seeing you, you would soon see him. It was the hardest thing I've ever done," Aunt Chan said, her voice quaking with emotion, "telling Miles that he would be taken. I was only able to bear it because I knew you would appear to help him. I told him that he shouldn't be frightened." Aunt Chan's voice wavered. Her eyes pooled with tears.

"And here you are, Fern McAllister. As I envisioned you would be. I'm only sorry that you had to meet Miles under these circumstances."

Fern felt a lump in her throat. She wasn't exactly sure why she was so emotional, but with Aunt Chan's trembling voice and Miles's drawing, somehow her connection to Miles had a particularity to it. His plight had become terrifyingly personal to Fern now that she was in his room, staring into the eyes of someone who cared about him so deeply.

Fern swallowed the lump. Determination shaded her face.

"He'll be back here before you know it," she said. The words flowed with such conviction, Fern almost believed them herself.

Fern's landing wasn't as smooth on her return trip to her hotel bathroom in Washington, DC, as it had been when she arrived in Mound, Minnesota. She wound up reappearing in the fetal position on the top of the bathroom sink. She blinked her eyes and wiggled her toes until feeling returned to them. Swinging her legs down, she stopped herself short of tumbling off the sink to the tiled floor. The bathroom door was ajar. In the midst of her curious visit with Aunt Chan, Fern had forgotten all about Candace's intrusion into the bathroom right as she was teleporting to Miles's house.

She quickly scanned the bathroom. Curled up in the corner, Candace Tutter slept peacefully. She must have been there since Fern disappeared from the bathroom—waiting for her return.

Fern decided to sneak out of the bathroom and leave Candace slumbering. She would convince her in the morning that she'd had a bad dream while sleepwalking. Fern gently put one foot on the ground, then the other. She tiptoed nervously toward the slightly open door, reaching for the handle.

"You're back," Candace said, her eyes popping open. She rubbed them with an open palm. Fern shut the door to the bathroom as quickly as she could without making any noise.

"What?" Fern said, trying to turn the tables on Candace. "Did you fall asleep in here? I was about to use the bathroom."

"Who are you?"

"Candace, it's me, Fern."

"I know . . . but who are you? *What* are you?"

"Candace, you're talking like a crazy person. Unless you want to wake Blythe and Lee with your groggy rambling, we should both go to bed."

Gambling that Candace wouldn't talk once the door was open, Fern pressed down on the handle and slipped out of the bathroom. She was right—Fern didn't hear another peep from Candace, who didn't want Blythe or Lee awake and grousing any more than Fern did.

Candace's soft footsteps followed Fern's back to bed. Fern breathed a little easier, knowing that she would have until the morning before she had to confront what were sure to be impossible questions, along with more "Fern" entries in Candace's maddening journal.

Fortunately for Fern, the next morning Candace didn't have the opportunity to grill her about her bathroom disappearing act, because before she was able to corner Fern, the Commander arrived.

Candace, Fern, Lee, and Blythe departed from the room together. Blythe and Lee insisted that Candace and Fern take a separate elevator down to the lobby.

"We don't want to be trapped in an elevator with the two biggest freaks at St. Gregory's," Lee hissed.

The doors closed on the blond girls and Fern's nerves perked up—Candace and Fern were now alone in the hallway on the seventh floor. Just as Candace was on the brink of subjecting Fern to the third degree, the Commander strode down the hallway, eliminating any chance for probing questions. Fern took a deep breath of recycled hotel air. The threesome rode down to the hotel's first floor in silence.

The Commander noticed the dark circles under her daughter's eyes, one of which additionally bore the mark from her fall in the bus. She wondered if Fern wasn't sleeping again but banished the thought from her mind, determined to give her daughter the space she'd requested, and trying not to feel helpless.

In the lobby, Mr. Lin was passing out bags of fresh bagels to each of the four group chaperones. Most of the students in the groups, however, were huddled around a flat-screen in the lobby by the Marriott's check-in counter. The TV was tuned to CNN, showing a news reporter with a cropped haircut and a gray trench coat standing outside the steps of the Museum of Natural History. A large headline crawled at the bottom of the screen:

HOPE DIAMOND STOLEN FROM DC MUSEUM

"I'm live in Washington, DC, where there are reports that the world's most famous gemstone, the Hope Diamond, has been stolen. Some estimates put the stone's worth at around a quarter of a billion dollars—it is said to be the most perfect blue diamond in the world, and this could be the largest heist in the history of the Smithsonian. There is no information currently available as to how such a stunning crime was accomplished or if officials have any suspects in custody. We'll keep you updated, of course, as we learn more about this breaking story."

The whole lobby buzzed with the news. Nearly every St. Gregory's student had seen the diamond the day before, secure in its glass cage.

"It's a good thing I forced you to see the Hope Diamond before it disappeared, huh?" Candace Tutter, in her stealthy way, had snuck up behind Fern.

"Good thing," Fern repeated, but her mind was somewhere else entirely. She clutched the piece of paper she'd taken with her from Miles's house, moving away from Candace and toward the fringe of the growing group gathered around the TV.

Fern pulled the piece of paper out of her pocket. On it, she'd painstakingly copied every picture from the Popol Vuh and written a description underneath. When she'd asked Aunt Chan if she could rip out the relevant page, Aunt Chan was horrified. She told Fern that the Popol Vuh was thousands of years old and could not be desecrated in such a way. So, although not much of an artist, Fern did her best to re-create the information on the page. She'd copied the Quetzal feather; the drawing of the Mayan rain god Chac, flexing with his golden spearlike arrows; Ix Chel's stolen Stone Eye; and a picture of the Mayan goddess crying with the crescent moon beneath her. Fern had also written a list below the drawings:

AH PUCH POTATION
-Quetzal feather (probably already in possession)
-Chac's golden arrow
-Ix Chel's Stone Eye (Hope Diamond???)
-Ix Chel's essence
-All items hidden, protected in plain sight

If Fern was correct, then Silver Tooth had used Miles to steal the Hope Diamond, which was, in fact, Ix Chel's Stone Eye. This meant that Silver Tooth had two of the four ingredients already, leaving only the essence of Ix Chel and Chac's golden arrow needed to complete the potion.

Something nagged at Fern—she wondered if she was completely crazy to think any of this was even possible. It all sounded so ridiculous. The only thing Fern was absolutely sure of was that Miles Zapo was trapped in a cage and she had to help him. Anxious to talk to Sam and Lindsey about everything she'd learned the previous night, Fern tried to calm herself. Surely those two would help her understand.

Fern knew she would have to wait to show the list to Sam and Lindsey until they could sneak off unnoticed during the day's jam-packed schedule. Though she hadn't had time to scrutinize all the events for the day, she remembered the first stop was Arlington National Cemetery. Fern would corral Sam and Lindsey for a conference as soon as she could.

"I really could just about kill you right now."

Fern whipped around, recognizing her twin brother's voice immediately. Sam and Lindsey were both standing behind her, their arms folded across their chests, angry expressions on their faces. Fern smiled at both of them, figuring Sam couldn't possibly be serious.

"What's up?" she said casually.

"Candace, would you mind leaving us alone for a second?" Lindsey said calmly.

"Okay," Candace said, beginning to walk across the lobby toward the blaring TV.

Sam shot a poison-laced glance directly at Fern. He was glowering. Lindsey shook her head in disgust.

"What in the world is wrong with you two?" Fern racked her brain. What could she have done to warrant such reactions from her best friend and her brother? Sam took a step toward his sister.

"You really are unbelievable, you know that, Fern? All you care about is yourself."

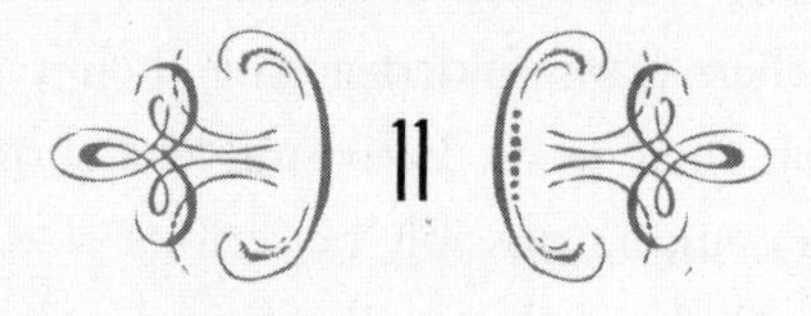

the return of the voices

"I don't understand," Fern said. "What's the matter?"

"You forgot to call last night, Fern. *Either one* of us," Lindsey said, her voice icy.

"Did you tell your parents?" Fern asked Lindsey.

"Of course that's your first concern. . . . Well, you'll be happy to know that Sam and I decided to respect your request not to tell my parents. Though I wish I had."

"You didn't even think to call us," Sam said.

Fern took a step backward. After the encounter with Candace, it had completely slipped her mind to call. But she hadn't done it on purpose.

"I'm really, *really* sorry, guys," she said.

"Lindsey and I were up all night, wondering if we should tell someone, planning what we were going to do if you never showed up. Then, this morning you come strolling into the lobby with your new friend like you don't have a care in the world."

"She's not my friend! You don't understand. . . . Candace was in the bathroom when I got back." Fern felt the pace of her voice quicken. "I couldn't use the bathroom phone to call."

"You couldn't have snuck back in later?" Sam asked skeptically.

"Well, I mean, I guess I could have waited for her to fall asleep or something, but I forgot."

"Whatever," Sam said, turning to leave. Fern reached out to grab her brother.

"Wait!" Fern fumbled with the piece of paper in her pocket. "I think I found out what the man who kidnapped Miles is after!" she said, holding the list of potion components, as if it would somehow change their minds. "I know why he's keeping Miles at the zoo and what Miles's power is!" Fern spoke as loudly as she thought possible without the other St. Gregory's students overhearing.

"You can't ask for help, Fern, and then only play by your rules. The world doesn't work like that," Sam replied before pivoting all the way around and turning his back on Fern. Sam walked across the lobby, toward Mrs. Lin, who was valiantly waving George Washington's head, even though every member of the Washington group was still glued to the televised Hope Diamond news broadcast on the other side of the lobby. Lindsey walked next to Sam, matching him stride for stride.

Fern stood in shock, watching her brother and her best friend walk away. Hot tears formed on her lower eyelids and stung as she wiped them away. Her life, Fern thought, as she fought back the flood of sobs, was not supposed to be like this.

At that moment in time, if Fern could have traded in all her special talents for a normal life, she would have done so in a heartbeat. Being an Otherworldly and an Unusual only separated her from those she loved. Her powers came at a price that was too steep for anyone to pay. Fern watched Sam's blond head bob up and down across the lobby and then caught the reflection of her own dark mane in a mirror across the room. The contrast between the two colors reminded her of the fact that they weren't even genuine twins. Fern was different enough without focusing on the fact that she didn't really even belong to the McAllister family—but it was becoming increasingly impossible to ignore.

At the end of the day, she was alone.

The ride to Arlington National Cemetery took St. Gregory's busload of students across DC and into northern Virginia. They rode past the Jefferson Memorial and over the Arlington Memorial Bridge. Fern hadn't even tried to sit next to Lindsey, taking a seat next to Candace instead. Candace looked concerned when she saw Fern's puffy eyes, but she didn't ask Fern any personal questions. Instead she spouted facts at Fern the whole ride.

"The bridge is of the neoclassical style," Candace began

as Fern stared out the window at the tourists who were walking or biking across the generous beige sidewalks on each side of the six-lane bridge. "The Memorial Bridge crosses the Potomac, which used to be one of the most polluted rivers in the whole country."

"Would you mind shutting up for once, please, Candace?"

Fern glanced over at Candace. The sharp words had clearly wounded her, but Fern was beyond caring at this point. She had her own seemingly insurmountable problems to confront and now, apparently, she had to do it without any help.

Several times during the remainder of the ride, Candace started to speak. Each time, she stopped herself. Fern had to admit that at least Candace was trying.

When Fern got off the bus, she picked Sam and Lindsey out of the Washington group, but they didn't even glance back at her. In the Visitors' Center, where each group leader received a map of the sprawling 624 acres, Fern tried to catch either Sam's or Lindsey's attention. But when their eyes met, it was as if each was looking right through her. Headmaster Mooney looked more ridiculous today than he had yesterday. He was wearing a blue sweatshirt and matching blue sweatpants, all the while keeping a close eye on Fern. Fern tried not to stare at him and shifted her view to the opposite end of the parking lot. She saw Blythe and Lee gathered with a group of eighth-grade boys who were known troublemakers. When they all looked at her from across the parking lot, Fern shuddered. She would have given anything to have one day where not a single person stared at her.

Though Fern was preoccupied with her own thoughts, when she stepped through the gates to Arlington National Cemetery, she quickly forgot her predicament, overwhelmed by the magnitude of the place. The students walked over the hilly ridges of the cemetery grounds. Row upon row of white gravestones, as far as the eye could see, lined the grassy hills. It was still early in the morning, and mist zigzagged alongside the white grave markers. Small American flags stuck out of the still dewy ground next to each gravestone.

"There are over three hundred thousand American war heroes buried here," Candace said, her voice hushed and respectful. This time, Fern didn't tell her to be quiet. Every member of the St. Gregory's contingent gathered on the hill, in absolute silence.

A bugler played "Taps" in the distance. It struck Fern as the most beautiful and saddest music she'd ever heard. "A soldier is being buried right now," Candace whispered to Fern.

The first stop was the Tomb of the Unknowns, at the crest of a grassy hill. The entire group was quieter than they'd been at any time on the trip. They stopped in front of the tomb, where a small crowd of tourists had already formed. The tomb itself rested on a concrete platform, and a wreath of beautiful red, white, and blue flowers stood on a stand in front of the glistening marble square, which was about twice Fern's height. Behind the tomb, there was a panoramic view of Washington emerging through the diminishing morning mist. The front side was engraved with an inscription: HERE RESTS IN HONORED GLORY AN AMERICAN SOLDIER KNOWN BUT TO GOD.

The tomb was dedicated to all the soldiers who had died without being identified. A few feet in front of the grave, a soldier from the Army's Third U.S. Infantry Regiment paced. According to the informational plaque, the Old Guard kept watch here twenty-four hours a day, seven days a week, even when the cemetery was closed to visitors. The uniformed soldier, carrying a large rifle, marched across the platform, pivoted perfectly in front of the tomb, and marched back. Fern began counting the steps of his march. Twenty-one steps in each direction. One step for each shot in the twenty-one-gun salute. Mesmerized by the guard's steady stride and the sharp clicks of his heels at each turn, Fern lost her thoughts in the cadence of footsteps, pivots, and clacks. Lost, that is, until she heard her name, as if it was being whispered to her. Fern surreptitiously cupped a hand to her ear.

Fern began hearing the Voices a few months ago. That's when she'd named them "the Voices," simply because she didn't know what else to call them. Usually she was performing some kind of task, minding her own business, when suddenly she began to hear different voices, as clearly as if someone was talking into her ear. The only catch was, of course, there was never anyone around. Fern eventually learned that, as part of her Otherworldly talents, she could overhear conversations occurring miles away—if they involved her. In legends throughout history, vampires were known to have exceptional hearing, and Fern was no exception. Sometimes she wouldn't have any idea who was speaking or where they were. This time, though, Fern was absolutely sure who was talking.

Fern spotted Mr. and Mrs. Lin in the distance, completely separated from the St. Gregory's group.

Though they were at least half a mile away, standing on the slope below the grassy hillside that led to the Tomb of the Unknowns, Fern could hear every word they spoke to each other very clearly inside her head. After all, the words were about her.

"We can't ignore all this," Mr. Lin said. "We have to act immediately."

"Fern's safely back from her adventure last night, Mike," Mrs. Lin said, referring to her husband by his first name. "This is not something that needs to be solved in the next minute. I'm not suggesting we ignore it. I'm suggesting we inform Alistair and get a team together so we can appropriately handle the situation. The girl can't do this all on her own. We should talk to her, find out what she learned from her visit to that house last night, then formulate a plan from there."

"You heard what Lindsey told us," Mr. Lin insisted. "The man's description is an exact match. And those beasts that the boy says are keeping him captive? You and I both know they sound *exactly* like Sirens."

"What is your point?" Mrs. Lin asked with urgency in her voice.

"My point is," Mr. Lin said, "that only one person in existence knows how to tame a Howling Siren. If it is him . . . if he is back, we need to get the boy out of his clutches. I can handle this. We can't expose Fern. We're lucky he hasn't realized she's been so close to him all this time."

There was silence. Fern looked over at the Lins, who were silhouetted against the far horizon. Fern thought that she'd lost their signal, but then she heard Mrs. Lin's voice echoing in her head once more.

"Fine. Go to the zoo to investigate. I'll tell Headmaster Mooney you had business to attend to. But if you don't turn anything up by this afternoon, you must return. I'll be monitoring you. In the meantime, I'll try to gather all the information I can from Fern."

"Fern won't talk to you," Mr. Lin said.

"Maybe not . . . but she'll talk to Lindsey."

"You always were more devious than me," Mr. Lin said. "I'll be back by this afternoon." He bid his wife good-bye.

Fern squinted in order to get a better view of the Lins. As Mr. Lin started walking away, Mrs. Lin reached out to him, and they clasped hands one final time.

"Mike," Mrs. Lin implored. "Please be careful. If he is back, it is no doubt with some evil plan in mind. Remember Phoebe. He'll stop at nothing."

Fern's ears had been ringing all morning. Her mind was full of questions. But one name was foremost in her mind again.

Phoebe.

Fern didn't know all that much about her birth mother, except that she'd been best friends with the Commander as a girl and that, later in life, Phoebe had fallen in with a "rough crowd" (at least that's how the Commander put it), and she'd died during childbirth.

After Fern learned of her adoption, the Commander had given Fern the box of letters that she'd received from Phoebe throughout the years. Though Fern hadn't wanted to read them at first, afraid of what she might discover about her birth mother, after she'd read one, she devoured the rest in one sitting. Fern had returned to the letters many times since then, having memorized most of them.

Because of Blythe and Lee's earlier intrusion into her suitcase, Fern had her favorite of Phoebe's letters—one of her Amulets—in her jacket pocket next to the Ziploc bag of soil from her backyard.

Truthfully, though she'd devoured them, the whole batch of letters gave Fern very little insight. Phoebe seemed to have had wildly shifting moods. Sometimes she was funny, describing the many adventures she had after she left San Juan Capistrano. Sometimes she was in the depths of despair, telling Mary Lou how much she missed home and wanted to return. Some of the letters read like giddy schoolgirl confessions. In less happy ones, Phoebe wrote about how much she had hated her life in San Juan and how she was happy to have escaped it. She often ended by saying that she might never write again, because things were different between them now and Mary Lou would never understand her. These particular letters generated mixed emotions in Fern. She could imagine how reading her best friend's words must have wounded someone as loyal and faithful as the Commander, yet Fern was dying to know what, exactly, had made Phoebe write such things. Was Phoebe, like Fern, tired of being different? Was she sick of being tormented by Normals who didn't understand her? Had she found a group of Otherworldlies like herself?

The St. Gregory's tour group trekked across the cemetery throughout the morning. The final stop was JFK's gravesite, and the John F. Kennedy Eternal Flame. All sixty students encircled the single flame, which burned from an opening in the ground. A simple stone circle surrounded the flame, and then a patchwork of cobbled stones surrounded the circle. Grass grew around the edges of each of the different-size stones. Across the way, Fern saw Preston and Sam together, laughing as one showed the other something in a guidebook Sam had pulled out. Not wanting to see anything else that reminded her of how alone she felt, Fern turned away.

The Eternal Flame was more understated than the Tomb of the Unknowns but as strikingly sad. Fern thought briefly about President Kennedy, buried underneath the flickering flame. Without realizing it, she began to wander toward the rear of the group of students. She unthinkingly reached into the inside zippered pocket of her jacket, pulled out Phoebe's letter, and sat down on a bench on the perimeter of the gravesite.

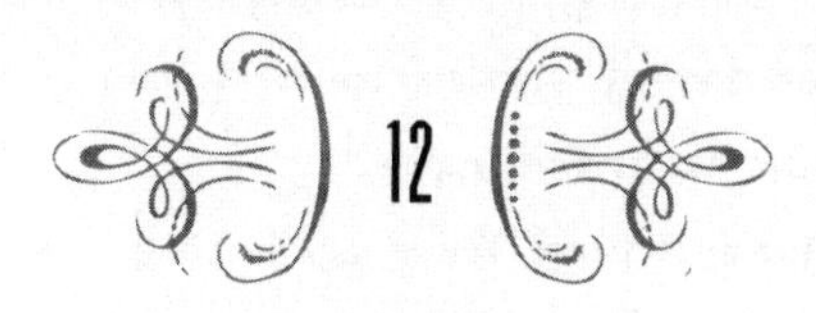

12 phoebe's letter

Fern looked fondly at the wrinkled letter she'd slipped out of its original envelope and flattened it against one knee. Phoebe Merriam never wrote in cursive. Instead she had used tiny, neat printing. Realizing that she had very little time before the presidential groups assembled and left the Eternal Flame, Fern began reading the letter she'd read dozens of times before.

Dearest ML,

It has been TOO long since I wrote you last and I'm sorry about that. But I have some news! This spring I hitched from Tucson to Portland and then train hopped my way down to San Francisco. Train hopping is pretty crazy. There are all these people who hop on and off when a freight train is moving, and it's the biggest rush

I've ever experienced. Anyway, now that I'm in San Francisco, I can't imagine ever leaving a place this beautiful. You can see the bay sparkle from every part of the city. It's impossible not to feel inspired.

Have you ever been? You've got to come! I bet we could even scrape enough money together to get a place in the Mission or Haight or something. You can play your guitar and I can paint and we could be true bohemians! I don't know how else to say it, but things are really happening here. I've been selling some of my artwork down by Fisherman's Wharf and it's going pretty well, if I do say so myself! I actually sold TWO pastels yesterday. You're the only one who's ever believed in me, ML. Everyone else thinks I'm a huge screwup. I'll make sure to thank you when they award me the Oscar for painting, or whatever it's called.

The other big news . . . I met someone! His name is Haryle (you pronounce it Hair-uh-Lee, okay, so I don't want you messing it up when you meet him). I guess it's Greek or something. Anyhoo, he's just like me, ML! In every single way. He thinks like me, he feels things like me, we get along perfectly, and he says that I could be great someday. The best part is that he's crazier than I am.

He's a scientist. But not a nerdy scientist—he's dreamy, ML! He's got this dark hair and these piercing eyes the color of the ocean in the morning. You can't imagine the adventures he thinks of. His latest plan is to steal the moon! Well, not the entire moon, but a part of it—he's got this experiment going. Anyway, he'd get mad at me for telling you, he acts like everything's SO top secret, but it's going to be fun, I can tell you that much.

You should come up here and stay with me! We can conquer the world together . . . everything's more fun with you. It's about time you ditched that sad-sack town anyway. You know, there's a reason the swallows never stay for more than a season.

Miss you like crazy.

XOXO,

PM

Fern looked up and saw the crowd around President Kennedy's grave beginning to move. Quickly folding the letter and returning it to its envelope and then to the inside pocket of her jacket, Fern hopped up from the bench and joined the group once more—yet her thoughts lingered on the letter's contents. According to the date on the postmark, Phoebe was twenty-two years old when it was written (as was Mary Lou).

There were several reasons why Fern had chosen that particular letter to carry with her. First, it was one that demonstrated the enduring friendship that Mary Lou and Phoebe shared. In addition, it was one of Phoebe's most upbeat letters, and her carefree attitude was infectious. Fern liked to imagine that the woman who had given birth to her and the woman who was raising her had the kind of close relationship that other girls envied. She loved thinking they had plans to move to the city and to be free and bohemian together.

But there was another reason Fern kept the letter so close and read it so often. It was the only real clue she had about her father. Fern wasn't even sure the man Phoebe mentioned *was* her father. But it seemed likely—Fern was born not very long after the letter was written.

Perhaps the most important reason Fern treasured that letter was that it was the last one in which Phoebe had seemed at all happy. Reading it made Fern forget the handful of unhappy letters that had followed. In those, Phoebe spent most of her time lashing out at Mary Lou for abandoning her or ranting about how everyone was out to get her. Then the letters stopped.

After Fern had read all of them the first time, she understood why Mary Lou got a pained look on her face each time Phoebe was brought up. It must have been excruciating to witness her best friend's distress and be helpless to do anything about it. Sometimes, though, Fern wondered what Mary Lou had written in response to Phoebe. Had the Commander tried to help Phoebe?

Fern had been mindlessly following the horde of St. Gregory students. They'd reached the bus and were lining up to board it. Candace had found Fern again and was now alongside her.

"What were you reading?" Candace asked. Fern rolled her eyes as she realized that Candace was now her official shadow. As soon as she thought it, she was reminded of Sam. Anytime someone said he forgot something he'd said or done earlier, Sam would tell the person that he needed to hire a shadow. Sam would go on to explain that when Albert Einstein was at Princeton, the university hired a student to shadow the genius physicist wherever he went, in case Einstein uttered something brilliant and then forgot it later.

Fern frowned as she clambered up into the bus. She spotted her brother sitting near the back, next to Preston and Lindsey, and decided right then that she needed to make things right with the two of them—she didn't know if she could rescue Miles alone, and, more importantly, she didn't want to even try.

In any event, Fern was sure that even Sam would agree, if he ever spoke to her again, that Candace Tutter was the most annoying shadow in the history of shadows.

"I read lots of things, Candace, so you're going to have to be more specific," Fern said. The bus lurched forward. Most of the St. Gregory's students began buzzing about the next stop in their day. Fern had no idea where they were off to next. She no longer cared.

"On the bench. By the Eternal Flame," Candace said. "Whatever it was you were reading made you look really sad. I noted it in my study." She dug into her backpack and produced the spiral-bound notebook filled with her observations. She began reading: "'Eleven thirty-four a.m. Fern McAllister has wandered off by herself again. She looks like she's reading a sad story. Must inquire further when given the opportunity.'"

"I really don't know what you're talking about," Fern said, angry at herself for not picking a less conspicuous place to read her letter. "Maybe your powers of observation aren't so good anymore. You may have worn them out."

"Fern," Candace said, taking a pause from her rapid-fire approach to speaking. "Do you know what the word *Schadenfreude* means?"

"Shah-den-what?"

"Schadenfreude . . . it means to be happy because another person is sad or upset or has bad luck. See, Mother is a psychologist, and she says that Schadenfreude is very common among middle schoolers. She says that's one of the reasons I don't have many friends. . . . People our age are insecure, and Schadenfreude explains the complex emotions that are a result of trying to feel better about oneself by taking joy in the misery of another."

"Thanks for sharing," Fern said sarcastically. "Really good stuff to know." She decided that it was no surprise that Candace's mother was a shrink. Candace scanned the chaperones and students sitting around the two girls, trying to see if anyone was paying attention to their conversation.

"My point, Fern, is that I'm not like Blythe and Lee and everyone else. Don't you see that this *isn't* about Schadenfreude. I'm not trying to make you miserable," Candace said, looking up at Fern with earnestness.

"What are you trying to do then?"

"I'm trying to *understand* you. Mother says that's the basic building block of friendship." Candace reached into her bag once more. She pulled out a folded sheet of paper and placed it on her lap. "But I can't determine what's going on with you. That's never happened to me before . . . you simply get more and more confusing. Nothing adds up."

"I'm not a lab rat, Candace," Fern said, growing more annoyed.

Candace lifted the piece of paper from her lap and placed it on Fern's.

Sighing, Fern lifted the paper and unfolded it—why Candace felt the need to chatter constantly and pass her notes at the same time was confounding. But then she looked at the handwriting on the piece of paper. It was hers. In fact, it was the Ah Puch Potion list with the drawings she'd made at Aunt Chan's house.

"Where did you get this?" Fern demanded, turning toward Candace.

"It fell out of your jacket after you got into that fight with your brother and Lindsey Lin, right after you waved it in their faces. You dropped it."

"You took it, didn't you, Candace?" Fern growled, inching her face closer to Candace's.

"Your behavior does not comport with that of a girl who tested into the gifted class, Fern McAllister. In fact, you are acting like an idiot!" Candace hadn't backed up an inch. Fern paused for a minute, wondering how Candace had gotten the note. Was she telling the truth?

Fern thought about it again. Why was she really upset? Was Candace the reason she was angry, or was it the fact that Sam wasn't speaking to her? Or perhaps it was that

Lindsey had gone against their express pact and told her parents everything about her dream and visit with Miles. Candace, Fern realized, wasn't the actual root of the problem. It was her friends and family.

If Candace had stolen the list, Fern reasoned, why would she be returning it now? In fact, if Candace was out to expose her, she could have told everyone about Fern disappearing and reappearing in the bathroom. More than likely no one at St. Gregory's would have believed her, but it would have certainly started tongues wagging about Fern again.

Fern stared down at the piece of paper, feeling like she was slowly losing her mind. Not everyone was out to get her, after all, and she couldn't live the rest of her life trusting no one. Fern looked around. Though both girls had raised their voices, no one was paying them any attention.

"I'm sorry, Candace. . . . I shouldn't have accused you of stealing it. Thank you for returning it."

"That's more like it," Candace said, smiling her goofy smile. "See, Mother was correct. We're finally starting to understand each other!"

"Sure," Fern said, unable to stifle the smile forming on her own face. Fern might be an Unusual, but Candace Tutter was just plain strange.

"By the way, is that slip of paper for some game you're playing? It's like a puzzle or a scavenger hunt, right? Because if so, I think I know what Chac's arrow is!"

"What?" Fern marveled.

"Chac's arrow? The drawing you made on your paper . . . it looks *exactly* like the Golden Spike."

"Say that again?" Fern said, trying to remain calm.

"Father is a train enthusiast," Candace said, resuming her breakneck-speed speech. "I know it is a bit strange, but railroads are actually quite interesting if you give them a chance. Last summer, for Father's birthday, Mother planned this trip duplicating the original path of the First Transcontinental Railroad."

"What does that have to do with the drawing of the arrow?" Fern asked, growing impatient.

"Well, it's just that when the two railroads were connected, they had a ceremony, and the final spike that joined the rails was called the Golden Spike, and it looks exactly like your drawing. Anyway, the Golden Spike is displayed at the California State Railroad Museum in Sacramento, which was the last stop on our trip. The museum is kind of boring, actually . . . wouldn't recommend it. And Sacramento kind of smells like cows, you know?"

Fern pulled out the list again and placed it in front of Candace.

"You're sure it looks exactly like this?" Fern said, pointing to the drawing of Chac's arrow.

"My visual memory scores are in the top fraction of the top percentage of people tested. That's it, all right. Of course, good luck trying to see it now. I read it was stolen about a month after we visited it. They nearly caught the thief, apparently, as he was taking it. I guess it's rumored to have mystical powers because it was made from Mayan gold or something. Hey!" Candace said, putting her finger to her chin. "I've never thought about this before, but maybe I'm bad luck for museums. First the Golden Spike and now the Hope Diamond!" She began laughing uproariously as if she'd just told a very funny joke. She felt she'd made real progress communicating with Fern in the last few minutes and was loosening up.

Fern, on the other hand, felt sick. If Candace was right about the Golden Spike, then Silver Tooth only had one thing left to obtain before he had every item he needed to make the potion. She focused on the list, still unfolded in front of her. *Ix Chel's Essence.* Though Fern didn't know what that component was, one thing was certain: She'd better find some answers soon if she planned on stopping Miles's kidnapper.

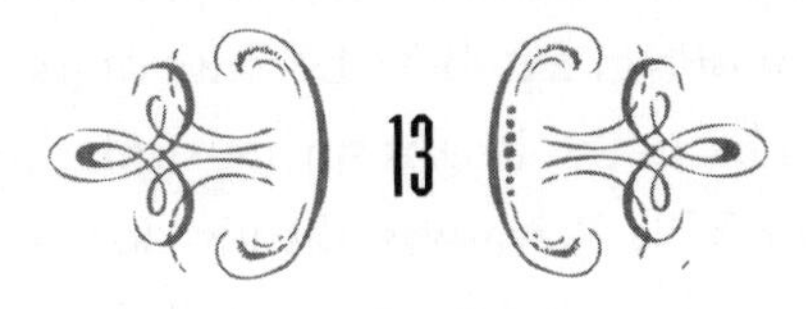

13
the mall

The food court at the Pentagon City Mall in Arlington, Virginia, had seen its fair share of class trips. Usually, after students had visited one of northern Virginia's tourist hot spots (like the Pentagon, Arlington National Cemetery, or the Steven F. Udvar-Hazy Space Center near Dulles Airport), the group would head directly to the Pentagon City Mall, where the kids could blow off steam and eat at one of the myriad of food court restaurants.

The students on the St. Gregory's trip had been allowed to select whatever they wanted to eat but were instructed that they could not leave the food court area under any circumstances. The chaperones sat bunched around one of the tables, keeping a nervous eye on their charges.

The Pentagon City Mall was a hexagon-shaped building, with an open atrium in the center, white-trimmed escalators wrapped around each end, and clear glass sidings protecting the walkways. It was four stories tall and reminded Fern of a greenhouse because of its see-through ceiling, which let in the bright spring sunlight.

The line for Villa Pizza was already dozens of students long, so Fern opted for Panda Express. Not surprisingly, Candace was right behind her. Fern looked around the bustling food court and realized there were other large groups of students from other schools there as well—some of them were in school uniforms. Fern was glad that St. Gregory's had not required students to wear their tartan-themed uniforms on this trip. They would have looked ridiculous.

Once Fern and Candace had picked up their Panda Bowls on cafeteria trays, they searched for open seats among the rows of white picnic and circular tables scattered on the mall's first floor. The circular tables in the middle of the food court were all occupied, but there were some empty seats at one end of a picnic table near the outside cluster of tables. Hungrier than she'd realized, Fern dug in as soon as they sat down, scooping up rice and sauce-lathered broccoli into her mouth. The combination was delicious.

"Fern?" Candace looked across the white table at Fern. She had raised her voice, shouting over the hundreds of other middle schoolers now eating lunch in the food court. "Are you ever going to tell me how you disappeared from the bathroom last night?" Candace asked, meticulously sorting her vegetables into different piles. Fern considered how to respond.

"I wish you would drop that, Candace, because I really don't know what you're talking about. Maybe you're into conspiracy theories, but I'm *telling* you, you were sleep-walking or something." Fern thought she sounded convincing.

Still, a growing part of her wanted to tell Candace. Everything. She was sure Candace would think she was crazy, but lately Fern had the undeniable urge to tell one unbiased person her story, from her own perspective only, without interference. Fern thought about how good it would feel to confide in someone again—to be able to talk about the burden of being different, an Unusual. She trusted Candace, if only because Candace seemed to trust her.

"Candace, if I tell you something, will you promise not to tell anyone, no matter how crazy it sounds?"

Candace's eyes bulged out of her head. She dropped her plastic take-out fork.

"Ooh—trust!"

"Huh?" Fern responded.

"Mother says that if someone trusts you, they tell you things and ask you not to tell anyone else. That this is what friends do! We're friends!"

"Okay . . ." Fern said, unsure of how to interpret Candace's reaction to her request.

"So you trust me!" Candace leaned across the rectangular table.

"I guess that's what I'm asking. If I tell you something,

you have to promise not to go blabbing all over school. *To anyone.* Even your mother." Fern was growing so nervous at the thought of what she was about to tell Candace that the feeling was close to exhilaration.

Candace held up her right hand, right next to her face.

"I, Candace Tutter, do solemnly swear not to tell a single soul—"

"Ewwwwwww!" Candace stopped abruptly as she and Fern shrieked simultaneously.

As she was finishing her truth pledge, a huge gob of hot KFC mashed potatoes landed on both Candace's and Fern's heads, with giant plops. The steaming, gooey potatoes were now running down Fern's face, into her eyes and mouth. They were burning her forehead and cheeks. She scraped them away from her eyes, looking frantically for the source of the attack. She could feel residual grease from the butter on her forehead.

The walkway around the second level of the mall overhung the picnic table where Candace and Fern were sitting. Someone could have easily dropped the potatoes on them from above, with enough time to take aim and then flee.

Whoever did it had made a direct hit. Fern tried to pull the buttery potatoes out of her hair, but ended up smearing them. Rage began to permeate her entire body, making its way up her throat and into her head.

When Fern had cleared enough of the mushy white potatoes from her eyes to see more clearly, she spotted Lee and Blythe. Sure enough, they were running down the stairs from the second level toward the food court. As soon as Fern spied them, they squealed with laughter and gave each other a high five.

Other kids began to point and laugh at Fern and Candace. Candace looked like she was about to cry as she tried in vain to remove potato clumps from her bangs.

"Look! A pair of potato heads!" a student from another school shouted. Fern was enraged. She imagined walking up to Lee and Blythe and punching each of them.

Fern caught a glimpse of Sam. He was staring at Fern, almost with a blank expression. Fern squinted through the potatoes and realized that he looked like he was ashamed of Fern. Perhaps he was tired of his sister being such an easy target. Lindsey sat across the table from Sam. She looked disgusted.

Sadness mingled with anger in Fern's mind.

They had watched Fern being humiliated, and they didn't even care. This realization hurt more than anything Blythe and Lee could have possibly done. It wasn't so long ago that they would have come to her defense in the span of a single heartbeat. In fact, it was only yesterday. Things could change so quickly in middle school.

Suddenly the energy in the food court shifted, almost as if someone had released a large electric charge into the open space.

Someone yelled at the top of his lungs, "FOOOOOOD FIIIIIIIIGHT!"

Once the universal battle cry for a culinary war had sounded, hundreds of individual armies were instantly on the move. First, one lone sandwich flew through the air. Then someone's full Coke took wing, as an explosion of ice cubes lit up the food court sky. The pace of flying food quickened at an astonishing rate until dozens of food missiles were whizzing in every direction. Soon the bottom floor of the Pentagon City Mall became a scene of complete chaos.

One cluster of students decided to man a post behind a large trash can, hurling Johnny Rockets fries across the length of the entire food court. Big Macs, Five-Dollar Footlongs, gorditas, and KFC fried chicken soared through the atmosphere, creating a blurred cloud of fast food hovering over the food court.

Before long, it was raining pizza slices, Pik-a-Pitas, and Dippin' Dots. From behind the protection of his red cafeteria tray, a chubby sixth grader launched an entire peach-mango smoothie high into space, generating a momentary beautiful creamy orange rainbow, which quickly collapsed on a dozen students and Headmaster Mooney himself. The St. Gregory chaperone's normally bald head was now dripping in peach-mango goodness.

A few chaperones from the various schools dining at the food court stood up in the middle of the hexagonal food battlefield, with their hands raised like desperate traffic cops. But as soon as they stood, they were bombarded with a barrage of Cajun sandwiches and pad Thai noodles and were forced to retreat to a protected position. Screams and shrieks rose four stories in the air, echoing off the mall's store walls.

Fern and Candace were hiding under their white picnic table. From their position on the perimeter, they could see the conflagration unfolding. Candace was smiling now, delighting in the complete pandemonium. She nudged Fern, pointing to their left. Blythe and Lee had taken refuge behind a condiment station, where they were laughing at the anarchy they'd instigated. Fern saw that Candace was pointing to a spot slightly beyond the evil blond duo.

"Oh my . . . ," Fern whispered to Candace. Immediately beyond the wicked girls' position, Lindsey and Sam slowly snuck up on Lee and Blythe from behind. Sam was cradling a whole tub of mayonnaise in his arms. Lindsey had a ketchup dispenser in hers. They'd pirated them from an as yet unscathed condiment station on the other side of the area and unscrewed the pump tops from each jug.

Candace and Fern watched excitedly from their position under the table as Lindsey and Sam got closer and closer to their targets. Sam counted to Lindsey silently with his fingers.

One. Two.

Both raised the large plastic tubs over the heads of Lee and Blythe.

Three.

Sam and Lindsey flipped the jugs over in one deft move and began shaking them down on Blythe and Lee with a vengeance. Waves of red and white cascaded on the girls, covering their upper bodies in a matter of moments. They howled, temporarily blinded by the gobs of mayo and ketchup running down their faces.

Fern smiled from ear to ear.

"I know!" Candace said, matching Fern's wide smile with one of her own. "That was amazing!" Candace still had tiny flecks of mashed potato in her hair. Fern could only imagine what she must look like herself.

It no longer mattered, though. Sam and Lindsey had staged a retaliatory attack on her behalf! They may have been ignoring her, but they still had Fern's back. If Fern hadn't thought she'd be hit by a volley of flying burritos en route, she would have run over and hugged both her brother and Lindsey.

"Stop this immediately," a blaring voice commanded from the loudspeaker. "Stop immediately. Those who are caught throwing food from this point forward will be prosecuted."

Slowly, partially dazed, the chaperones stood up from their hiding places. An errant final hot dog whizzed by, but the food fight was over as quickly as it had begun.

Headmaster Mooney was intent on finding someone to punish. Earlier, security had informed him that the food fight had originated from within the cluster of the St. Gregory's students and spread from there. Every kid in the food court had been rounded up and cleared out. Those in the St. Gregory's group were ordered to stand in single-file lines behind their chaperones in Auxiliary Section C of the parking lot behind the mall. Headmaster Mooney walked up and down the lines of silent students with his hands clasped behind his back, like a drill sergeant about to chastise his new recruits, glaring at each student as he walked by.

"We can stand here all afternoon, for all I care," the headmaster yelled, pacing back and forth. The hooded sweatshirt and fanny pack he'd been wearing were ruined, covered in now sticky orange ooze. "Until I find out who's responsible for the *disgrace* that has just occurred, we are not moving. Most students find the Air and Space Museum to be one of their favorite stops . . . but we'll miss it entirely if I don't learn *who started the food fight.* There is always an instigator. *Always.*" Fern, who had been on the receiving end of her fair share of angry Mooney tirades, had never seen Headmaster Mooney seethe to the extent he was seething now.

The extraordinary thing about food fights, of course, is that it's nearly impossible to pin the mayhem on a single offender. Likewise, it is also difficult to punish every participant, because the best food fights involve everyone in some capacity. Besides, there's something undeniably thrilling about winging a McNugget through the air.

All of this was certainly the case with the Pentagon City Mall food fight—which, according to mall security, was the worst food fight in the mall's twenty-plus-year history. Not only was every kid at St. Gregory's implicated, but students from the other four schools eating there had also participated.

It was what Headmaster Mooney referred to as a disciplinary nightmare.

Fern noticed Candace shivering. She'd taken her mashed-potato-covered jacket off, which meant she had only three layers on—far too few for her thin frame. Fern had little doubt that Mooney would keep them out there until the sun went down and they all froze solid, in order to force someone to confess. Without any waffling, Candace took a step forward and raised her hand

"Headmaster Mooney." Her normally squeaky voice was now shaking. The headmaster's head whipped around. When he saw that it was the strange girl genius who had stepped forward, he couldn't hide his shock.

"Yes," he said, moving toward Candace. "What is it?"

"The food fight," she said, shuffling her feet. "See, the food fight began . . ." She was speaking with none of her usual confidence. Every single St. Gregory's student, including Fern, was on edge, wondering what Candace was about to reveal.

"The food fight began when Blythe Conrad and Lee Phillips dumped mashed potatoes on me and Fern McAllister."

Fern winced as soon as she heard her name announced to both Headmaster Mooney and the entire St. Gregory's contingent.

"LIAR!" Blythe Conrad shouted from behind Candace,

jumping out of line. Her hair was greasy from the mayonnaise and her clothing was stained with red drippings. She looked positively crazed. Mrs. Phillips stepped toward Headmaster Mooney from her position at the head of the line.

"I hardly think we should believe the accusations of one jealous little girl," she said, looking worriedly at her own daughter, the accused Lee Phillips.

Headmaster Mooney swiveled his head, turning his gaze from Mrs. Phillips to Candace to Lee and Blythe as he considered the situation. The Tutter girl had a perfect disciplinary record up until this point, and he was unable to conjure up a reason why she would lie.

"Candace, is there anyone who can substantiate your claim?" Headmaster Mooney asked.

Candace's pleading eyes turned to Fern. Fern trembled. She wanted to back up Candace, but that meant becoming a rat. It would be yet another label, another nasty thing all the kids at school would call her. Blythe and Lee would redouble their efforts to torment her. If she didn't support Candace, though, Candace would surely be crucified, both by Mooney and the rest of her grade. In the back of her mind, she remembered how overjoyed she'd been when Sam and Lindsey came to her defense during the food fight. Candace deserved that kind of support from her. As Fern was about to step forward, someone else spoke.

"I saw Lee and Blythe dump the mashed potatoes."

The voice came from the Washington group. Fern whipped around.

It was Lindsey Lin. A few of her fellow eighth graders gasped. Lindsey Lin was the last person at St. Gregory's anyone would suspect for a rat. She was aligned with nearly every popular person in school, precisely because she never told anybody anything. In addition, Lee and Blythe were the unofficial mean girls of the school. No one dared cross them. Until now.

Headmaster Mooney stalked over to Lindsey.

"You're sure?" he inquired.

"Positive," Lindsey said, holding her head up with a defiant gleam in her eye.

"I saw it too," Sam said, standing right behind Lindsey. There were more gasps. If there was anyone less likely to turn narc than Lindsey, it was Sam.

"So did I, Headmaster Mooney." Mary Eileen moved forward from the line, taking a place next to Sam.

"I'm sure I saw it too," Preston Buss said.

Soon dozens of students at a time were volunteering; all confirming that Lee and Blythe had dumped mashed potatoes on Fern's and Candace's heads. Lindsey Lin had made it acceptable for every single student who harbored a grudge against Lee and Blythe to step forward. Their popularity was a house of cards—built on an unstable foundation of intimidation and cruelty. Once someone as well-regarded as Lindsey stood up to them, their whole empire crumbled.

Candace beamed.

She felt she'd fomented a mutiny in the Pentagon City

Mall's auxiliary parking lot. The evil queens of St. Gregory had been dethroned. Candace clenched her fist symbolically and thrust it in the air. *It was a coup!*

"Psssst. Candace," Fern whispered, "put your stupid hand down before anyone notices." Candace obeyed, but her joy had not been dampened in the slightest. None of the hundreds of adventure books she'd read had ever made her feel quite this exhilarated. The thrill was positively electrifying!

"Enough," Headmaster Mooney said, trying to silence the chatter that had erupted as soon as both the seventh and eighth grades had turned on Lee and Blythe.

"Lee, Blythe, you two please come over here," Headmaster Mooney summoned.

Both girls, with their greasy, mayonnaise-covered hair and ketchup-splattered clothing, wore steely expressions. They didn't look remorseful in the least. Fern knew Headmaster Mooney would find a way to make them so.

"Everyone else, please board the bus in an orderly fashion. The Washington group will board first and so on from there."

Headmaster Mooney motioned to Mrs. Phillips, and the two adults moved to the side and began speaking in angry voices to Lee and Blythe. In the past, Fern would have wanted to overhear exactly what Headmaster Mooney was saying to the girls, delighting in their unhappiness. But she didn't care anymore, sure that irreparable damage to their stranglehold over St. Gregory would ensue.

As always, the Lincoln group was the last to board the bus. When Fern finally climbed on, she was reminded of the scene in *The Wizard of Oz* where Dorothy's house had just landed on the Wicked Witch of the East and the Munchkins are celebrating her demise. Only in this case, of course, there were two Wicked Witches, Lee and Blythe, and the Munchkins were the carousing students on the bus covered in small chunks of assorted fast foods.

Fern slumped into the seat next to Candace. She hadn't even looked to see if there was a seat next to Lindsey Lin, figuring she would have time to catch up with her and Sam about everything at their next museum stop.

"That was a gutsy thing you did," Fern said, looking at Candace and wondering if she looked as greasy as Candace did.

"There's nothing that brave about telling the truth," Candace replied matter-of-factly.

"You may be a genius and everything, Candace, but you are totally wrong on this one," Fern said. "Sometimes telling the truth is the bravest thing anyone can do."

Candace smiled brightly. "What do you think's happening to Lee and Blythe?" she asked.

"With any luck, they're being sent home." Fern paused.

She knew she wouldn't be completely relieved until she got something off her chest. "Candace . . . I want you to know that I would have backed you up, out there in the parking lot. Lindsey beat me to it."

If she was being completely honest with herself, Fern wasn't completely sure she would have supported Candace's assertions—but Candace was turning out to be a very loyal friend.

"It's okay, Fern," Candace said. "You're just slow. But I know you would have eventually corroborated my story, just like I know you'll eventually tell me how and why you disappeared from the bathroom. When you're ready." With that, Candace reached into her backpack, which had somehow remained mashed potato free, and pulled out her spiral notebook. No doubt, Fern thought, Candace would document the entire food court incident, from start to finish, with the discerning and impartial eye of an apprentice social scientist.

Candace's last statement had started Fern's mind reeling. She closed her eyes. For the last hour, she hadn't thought once about being an Otherworldly. She hadn't thought about Miles in his cage or how she would rescue him and stop Silver Tooth. For a short time, she was a normal seventh grader who had been in a gigantic food fight, who had seen her two best friends jump to her defense with jugs of mayonnaise and ketchup, and who had witnessed her two blond nemeses toppled by the testimony of a new pint-size friend. The drama had a simplicity to it. Regardless of whether Fern ended up telling Candace her whole story, she knew her craving for a normal life would remain just that—a craving, never to be satisfied.

As thoughts of Miles and Silver Tooth consumed Fern,

Candace Tutter, meanwhile, began the day's journal entry in a rather remarkable way. Abandoning her neutral scientific perspective, the words flowed from Candace's pen in a manner unlike any she had used previously.

Today, Candace wrote, her handwriting messier than usual due to the leftover adrenaline in her body, *was the BEST day ever.*

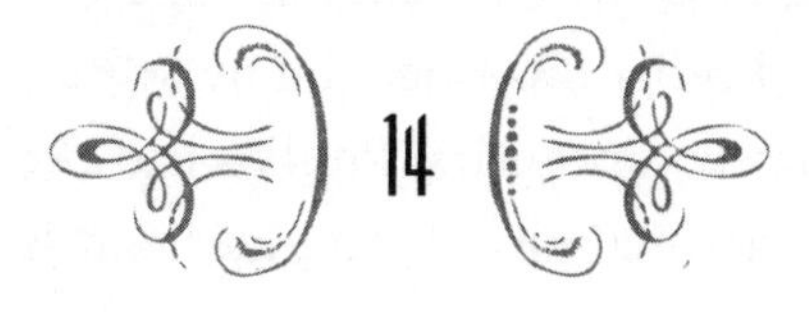

14

air & space & admissions

Fern thought Headmaster Mooney was probably exaggerating for effect when he claimed the National Air and Space Museum was many students' favorite stop during their DC trips. But after a half hour of exploring, she was convinced he was right. Outside the museum stood a large shiny silver pole with what appeared to be stars hovering around it. The museum itself was divided up into four cubelike structures.

Because of the day's earlier fiasco, Headmaster Mooney had instituted a new policy where each student chose a buddy, and all buddy pairs were required to remain within view of their designated chaperone. None of the St. Gregory's students had completely succeeded in wiping off the chunks of food and residue of mustard, mayonnaise, ranch dressing, and grease stains from his or her clothing. This meant any gathering of St. Gregory's students was met with stares and confused sniffs as stale cafeteria aromas wafted toward other unsuspecting museum visitors.

Unfortunately, since Mrs. Phillips had been dispatched to deal with her delinquent daughter and her daughter's friend (who Fern was still hoping were being sent home), Headmaster Mooney himself had taken charge of the Lincoln group. Fern hadn't been implicated in starting the food fight, but judging by the way Headmaster Mooney was monitoring her, she might as well have been.

Even so, it was nearly impossible for Headmaster Mooney to diminish the experience of Air and Space. Candace and Fern had chosen each other as buddies, and now with Lee and Blythe absent from the Lincoln group, they didn't worry about being bullied. They both agreed that it was a huge relief. For the first time in months, Fern wasn't glancing behind her, afraid of what kind of torment Lee and Blythe were dreaming up.

Fern's favorite exhibit was the Wright Brothers & the Invention of the Aerial Age. There was something inspiring about the simple plane, the *Flyer*, which was basically two flat pieces of wood held together with perpendicular sticks, and the story of Orville and Wilbur. Though many people said they could never do it, the brothers used pieces of giant spruce wood and, after several tries, completed the *Flyer* in 1903. The first flight lasted only twelve seconds, which left Candace unimpressed, but Fern imagined how excited the brothers must have been to be the first in the world to accomplish manned flight. Fern recognized the irony for one who had recently teleported across the country to be so impressed with a twelve-second flight of forty yards.

For her part, Candace wasn't able to pick a favorite exhibit. She loved the Cessna 150 cockpit—she sat in it and performed flight experiments as if she were actually in control of the plane, hollering with delight as she rolled the plane upside down. Fern had to admit that it did seem realistic. Candace also loved the Albert Einstein Planetarium. The Sky Vision projection system in the planetarium, with accompanying sounds, made both the girls feel like they were floating in space.

There was also a moon rock that visitors could stand in line to touch. Though Fern and Candace both waited in line (a plaque touted the fact that it was the only moon rock that people could actually feel with their bare hands), they were both somewhat disappointed. It felt like any other rock. There was also a vial of moon dust on display, taken directly from the moon's surface by one of the Apollo astronauts—which by all accounts was pretty cool.

The St. Gregory's groups had been separated from one another—supposedly because Headmaster Mooney reasoned that if all the students were together, another mutiny like that of the Pentagon City Mall food court was more likely. Eventually, the Lincoln group did wind up running into the Washington group in the gallery. There, Lindsey and Sam were participating in the museum's paper airplane contest, which was being judged by older kids. Fern casually strolled by Sam and Lindsey.

"Meet up in the gift shop. Third level," Lindsey said under her breath. Fern kept moving, hoping that Headmaster Mooney's suspicions had not been aroused. Fern would have to lose Candace, but she knew that with some artful maneuvering, it wouldn't be that hard to do.

The Air and Space Museum's amazing gift shop was constructed on three levels, jam-packed with items that certainly could not be found anywhere in San Juan Capistrano. There were model planes and model moons, books of every sort on flight and space exploration, Albert Einstein bobble-heads, and walls and walls of space-related toys. The Washington, Jefferson, Madison, and Lincoln groups were all scheduled to conclude their visit to the museum with a half hour at the gift shop, where students could buy souvenirs. Most students went straight for the freeze-dried astronaut food. The line for the cashiers snaked around the entire first level of the shop, and the chaperones gathered outside the exit on a cluster of benches, exhausted from trying to keep track of their student charges all afternoon in the bustling museum.

As Fern and Candace wandered into the gift shop, hundreds of kids were running wildly around the three levels, which were connected by open staircases. Students chased one another down the aisles with toy stun guns, shouted and fought over who would get the last Saturn V Rocket

Replica in the store, and modeled the Air Force One bathrobes that were for sale.

"If we want astronaut ice cream, we'd better get in line now," Candace said, tracing the ever-growing line with her eyes until she finally found its end. "I think it will take at least a half hour before we reach the register."

"Will you buy some for me?" Fern dug in her pocket and handed Candace her only twenty-dollar bill. It was what the Commander had deemed an acceptable souvenir allowance for the week. Fern knew the sum was nonnegotiable.

"Where are you going?"

"I have to use the bathroom," Fern said. Without waiting to see if Candace had any follow-up questions, Fern wheeled around and moved toward the first staircase. She felt a twinge of guilt for leaving her new friend without a better explanation, but she'd been waiting all day to talk to Lindsey and Sam, and her thoughts had returned to Miles's predicament in the last few hours. He was still all alone in that dark, horrible place.

Taking the steps two at a time, Fern quickly reached the second floor, which was even more crowded than the first, then raced to the third floor, as she groped in her jacket pocket for the list she'd made while she was at Aunt Chan's house. She hoped that Lindsey and Sam hadn't been delayed.

The third floor was mostly apparel, making it the least popular. Fern wondered if Lindsey had known that—it really was the best place in the entire gift shop to hold a clandestine meeting. Besides a few kids trying on bomber jackets, and a couple of boys deciding whether or not to buy their dads solar system ties, the floor was more or less deserted. Fern crept along the rows of T-shirts, finally spotting Sam's blond head sticking up above a rack of clothing in the far corner. She ran toward her brother's head. She looked at the solar system clock on the far wall. She'd have only twenty minutes to confer with Sam and Lindsey.

Deciding she'd have a little fun of her own, Fern stooped and eased into the adjacent row of clothing. She planned on slipping in between two T-shirts and trying to scare Lindsey and Sam by suddenly popping out of the clothing rack. She climbed through a hanging rack until a thick T-shirt forest surrounded her. Separating two of the hanging shirts, she peeked out, then made the gap between the T-shirts bigger, to better see Lindsey and Sam. She also spotted a third person, Lindsey's height, with Lindsey's same hair color, but Fern didn't know who it was. Both Lindsey and the other person had their backs to Fern.

"Fern?" Sam had spotted his sister's pale green eyes staring out from the rack of T-shirts and sweatshirts. "Is that you?"

Sam stepped forward and moved two hangers as far apart as he could, bunching the T-shirts on each end of the rack. Fern, still crouching, smiled awkwardly.

"What are you doing in there?" Sam asked, looking down at his twin sister.

"I was trying to surprise you." Normally, Fern thought, Sam would have laughed at Fern's sad attempt at a joke. But his face was ashen and joyless.

"What's the matter, Sam?" Fern said, moving out from under the hanging shirts.

Sam stepped aside, revealing Lindsey and the person next to her, who were both now facing Fern.

"Mrs. Lin?"

Lindsey's mother looked sorrowfully at Fern. Fern's eyes jumped to Lindsey. Tear trails streaked down her face.

"What's going on? What's wrong?"

Fern was now fully in the aisle, with Sam to her left and Lindsey and her mother to her right. She looked around. No one else was within earshot of the foursome, now gathered in the adult men's clothing aisle.

Mrs. Lin, trying to maintain her composure, wiped her eyes before speaking. Lindsey took one look at Fern and began to cry again. Fern had never seen Lindsey cry before. The sight of her friend in tears and Mrs. Lin close to it was unsettling. It was almost as if by climbing through the clothing racks she'd wandered into an alternate universe that no longer made sense. Panic took hold.

"Sam," Fern said, realizing that neither Mrs. Lin nor her daughter was capable of communicating clearly then. "What is it?"

"Mrs. Lin has been looking for you," Sam answered solemnly. "She needs to tell you something."

Mrs. Lin stepped forward. She was dressed in fashionable jeans and a pink cashmere cardigan. She had on pearl earrings, and the gold locket she always wore was around her neck. Her kind eyes locked on Fern's. She put a hand on Fern's shoulder and lowered her head.

"Fern, Mr. Lin . . . has been taken."

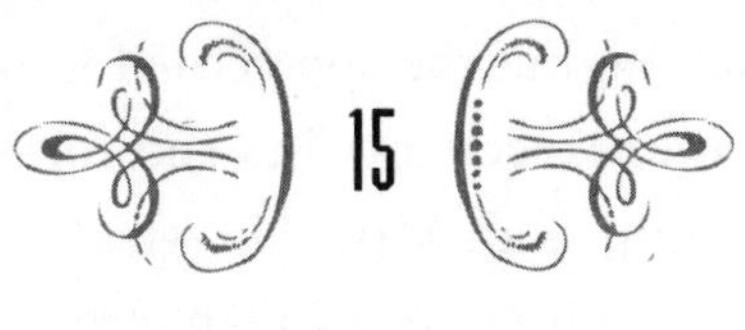

15
a familiar name

If Fern were to make a list of her favorite adults, Mrs. Lin would be at or near the top. It was true that Lindsey complained about her mother's strictness sometimes, but Mrs. Lin was always so friendly and kind. She made the most delicious food with strange names Fern had never heard of, and, perhaps most importantly, she talked to Fern like she was a real person. In fact, she was the only adult besides the Commander who didn't talk to Fern like there was something wrong with her. Fern's special talents brought her special responsibilities, and Mrs. Lin seemed to be the only adult who recognized that.

The first time Fern had visited Lindsey's immaculate house, Fern hadn't really known the extent of her own powers or that she was an Unusual. Mrs. Lin pulled Fern aside and told her that she was in for some rough times, but that if she ever needed help, the Lins would be there for her. At the time, Fern didn't know what to make of the earnest declaration, but she appreciated it more and more as her life took unexpected twists and turns. The Lins—Lindsey, Mr. Lin, and Mrs. Lin—had supported her, refusing to turn their backs on Fern, even when the Alliance had turned against her and tried to use her as bait to trap the evil Vlad.

"Taken? Taken where?" Fern asked, unable to comprehend what she was hearing. She recalled the conversation she'd overheard Mrs. and Mr. Lin having that morning. Mr. Lin had said he was going to try to find Miles Zapo. Apparently, the only thing he'd found was someone who'd captured him.

Lindsey stepped forward.

"Last night," she began, her voice shaking, "when you never called, I got scared . . . and I . . ." Lindsey struggled to find the words. Fern wondered if she should reveal that she knew Mr. Lin had gone in search of Miles, but something stopped her. Though they didn't have much time, she figured it might be important for Lindsey to get the admission off her chest. She looked at the solar system clock again. She had fifteen minutes left. Candace was probably already searching for her.

"I thought something had happened to you, so I told my parents about Miles and your visit. I told them you were going to a house last night. I told them everything," Lindsey said. "But I made them swear they wouldn't tell anyone from the Alliance. I promise, Fern! I know you told me not to tell them, but I thought something might have happened to you!" Lindsey turned to Sam. "Sam, I'm sorry I didn't tell you, either. But I thought I was doing what was best for Fern."

Fern's heart ached for Lindsey Lin. Whatever anger she harbored toward her best friend for leaking information to her parents dissipated with one look at the anguish on Lindsey's face.

"It's *okay*, Lindsey," Fern said, wanting to reach out and wrap her arms around her friend. "I know you were only doing what you thought you needed to do."

"Yeah, it's okay," Sam said, unable to hold a grudge when Lindsey was so worried about her missing father.

"Fern, can you tell me exactly what happened last night?" Mrs. Lin asked. "We *will* get Mr. Lin and Miles back, but I need to know everything."

Fern reached into her jacket pocket and pulled out the list. There was so much to tell. About the Hope Diamond, and the Golden Spike. About the Howling Quetzals and what Aunt Chan had revealed about the Alliance. There were thirteen minutes left by Fern's count. So she wasted no time and started at the beginning, with her landing on Aunt Chan's porch, talking more quickly than she ever had before.

Mrs. Lin, Sam, and Lindsey hung on Fern's every word. They peppered her with questions about Aunt Chan, the

Mayans, Miles's invisibility powers, Ix Chel, the Popol Vuh, and the potion itself. When she was done talking, Fern realized many questions still remained.

"Do you mind if we back up for a second?" Fern asked timidly. She didn't want to further upset Mrs. Lin and Lindsey, but after sharing all her own secrets she felt she deserved to know what they knew as well. The clock was near twenty-five past the hour. They had only five minutes left.

"Are you sure that Mr. Lin was taken? Maybe he's on his way back right now. . . . How can we be sure he's missing?" Part of Fern was obstinately hopeful simply because she knew if Mr. Lin had been taken, Miles's situation had gone from bad to worse. Mr. Lin was a powerful Otherworldly and one of the most respected investigators in the entire Alliance. If he had been taken only a few hours into his search for Miles, Fern wondered how *she* would fare against such powerful forces.

Mrs. Lin reached around the back of her neck and unhooked her locket. She held it out to Fern. Fern thought it had been made of gold, but on closer inspection, she realized that it was made from gold-hued, carved wood. It was the size of a half-dollar coin, and as Mrs. Lin rubbed her thumb on the top, it popped open.

"Do you know what a Sagebrush of Hyperion is?"

"Of course." Fern had seen Lindsey Lin manipulate such a Sagebrush many times. By coaxing the silvery plant with her hands, Lindsey could conjure an image of something that was happening elsewhere in the world. All she needed was to expose the plant to something connected to the person or thing she wanted to view. The Lins were some of the best Otherworldlies in existence when it came to monitoring people and events oceans away with Sagebrushes.

"When Mike and I were married, he fashioned this locket out of a Sagebrush as a gift to me, mixing it with his own blood so that whenever I opened it, it would reveal exactly where he was."

Fern peered into the open halves of the locket. There were no floating images like those that normally occurred when an actual Sagebrush was awakened. She saw only plain wood.

"I can't see anything," Fern said.

"This afternoon, for the first time since we were married over a century ago," Mrs. Lin said, swallowing her sadness, "Mike's image disappeared."

"What do you mean it *disappeared*?" Fern asked, looking at Sam and Lindsey to see if they understood Mrs. Lin's meaning.

After closing the locket, Mrs. Lin put it back around her neck, hooked it, and let it fall to its natural resting point between her collarbones.

"Fern, I am telling you all this because I need your help. I want you to listen to me carefully." Mrs. Lin's tone was calm, but her brown eyes had desperation in them that Fern had never seen before. "Mike . . . Mr. Lin . . . ," she began. "Mr. Lin was at the zoo. I saw him there in my locket. I was monitoring him to make sure he was all right. He had just proceeded down a dark corridor in the Employees Only section of the zoo. . . . I think he was trying to find out if there was some kind of entrance to the underground area where Miles is being kept. Then I saw two strange beasts emerge from the shadows of the corridor. I could hear them emit this horrible sound, and Mr. Lin dropped to the ground almost instantly. Soon after that, the image in the locket disappeared. I opened it and closed it several times more, but there's been nothing."

"The Quetzals," Fern said, having told the Lins and Sam all about what Aunt Chan had revealed about them.

"Exactly," Mrs. Lin agreed. "This Chan woman may have called them that, but these howling beasts go by another name as well. If I saw what I think I saw, then Mr. Lin is now under the spell of two Sirens."

"Aunt Chan said there would be different names for things," Fern interjected.

"It's certainly possible," Mrs. Lin conceded. "Lindsey mentioned to you that our *Undead Sea Scroll* had been stolen, correct?"

"Do you think that's somehow connected to Mr. Lin's disappearance and the Quetzals?" Fern asked.

"That doesn't make any sense," Sam insisted. "What does the Scroll have to do with any of this?"

"I only mention it because since the robbery, I'm unable to verify my recollections with *The Undead Sea Scroll* itself, but I believe that very few people are capable of taming the

Sirens, or Quetzals. Whoever it is that has tamed them must be using them to guard Miles to subdue him so that he cannot escape. I believe that Mr. Lin is now being kept there as well. It will be nearly impossible to reach them with the Sirens standing by. . . . A few moments with them and we will all be rendered completely powerless." Mrs. Lin suddenly perked up. "But, if I'm remembering correctly, Sirens do have vulnerabilities of their own."

"Like what?"

"Music," Sam said.

"That's exactly right," Mrs. Lin said, giving the boy a curious look. "If someone plays music, they no longer wail but instead fall into a peaceful sleep themselves."

Fern racked her brain. They had two minutes before all the chaperones and students were to meet in the lobby.

"Would a harmonica work?" she asked.

"Yes, any instrument should work, in theory," Mrs. Lin said. "Fern, tonight I want you to accompany me to search for Mr. Lin and Miles Zapo."

"But we know where they are and I can teleport there," Fern explained. "Miles told me that the Quetzals and Silver Tooth leave him alone for at least a half hour around midnight. That's when I talked to him the last time."

"I can't let you go alone. We'll have to get there on foot," Mrs. Lin insisted. "You must have some backup."

Fern wasn't sure how to handle the situation. Mrs. Lin talked to her like she was an adult, but Fern knew she still viewed her as a child. Any adult in Mrs. Lin's shoes would feel they needed to accompany Fern into such a dangerous situation, but Mrs. Lin would only be in the way. If it was dangerous, Fern could disappear in an instant. Mrs. Lin, however, could not.

"I'll teleport right back if I think there's any trouble."

"Fern," Mrs. Lin appealed. "I simply can't let you go there by yourself. . . . There's something else you don't know."

"What?" The solar system clock had already reached the half-hour mark. They were out of time. But no one in the group was budging.

Mrs. Lin paused before continuing. "Before the image disappeared from my Sagebrush locket, I caught a glimpse of the man who has tamed the Sirens and took Mr. Lin."

"Silver Tooth?" Sam asked.

"Lindsey's father and I have a history with this man. I recognized him. His name is Haryle Laffar."

Fern felt as if she'd been sucker punched. That name. Haryle. It was the name from Phoebe Merriam's letter. *Hair-uh-Lee.*

Fern knew at once.

"He's my father." Fern stated it as a fact, not a question.

Sam's and Lindsey's jaws dropped open.

Mrs. Lin sighed slightly and closed her eyes for a few moments. She could hear her own heart beating. The discussion she was about to have with Fern was going to be difficult and would provoke more questions than it would answer—she knew that much. She also knew that, at some point, this discussion was inevitable. Still, as Mrs. Lin sat looking into the frightened eyes of Phoebe Merriam's only daughter, she would've given everything to have been able to postpone this moment until the girl was older. It would be hard for anyone to hear, yet alone a girl who was barely on the cusp of her teenage years.

"Yes, Fern," Mrs. Lin said gravely, "I believe he is."

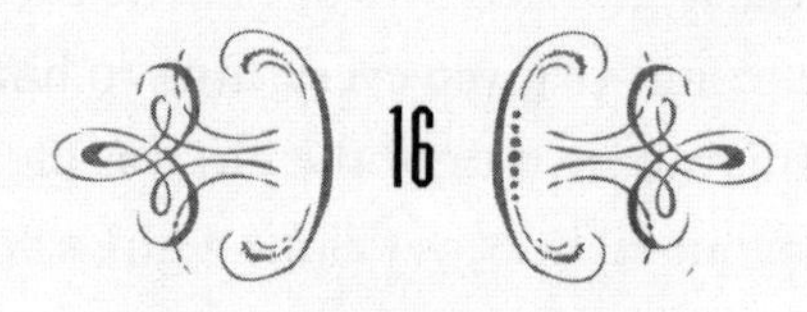

16

learning to play

Shocking didn't begin to describe it. It was the blockbuster revelation of a lifetime. Silver Tooth was Fern's father. Fern had only found out about her real birth mother a few months before, and since then, she'd constantly wondered about her father. Specifically, she'd speculated about what kind of influence he had on Phoebe. She'd heard that Phoebe changed near the end of her life, and Fern often questioned whether or not this was her mysterious father's doing. No one ever spoke of him. Not once. Now, though, he had a name. Haryle Laffar. The Lins knew this man.

Fern was confused. Her first instinct was to mentally skim through Phoebe's letters in her head and search for clues she'd missed when she'd read them so many times before that might help explain things. What about Haryle had made Phoebe abandon her friends and family? Surely,

Fern thought, there had to be something worthwhile about him.

But the cold, hard facts were hard to ignore. This man had caused her mother to abandon her family. He was also the one keeping Miles Zapo in a cage. Those facts were hard to rationalize, and as she thought of them, her blood began to boil. Most kids had a chance to know their fathers at least a little before beginning to resent them. Fern's progression of feelings, like everything else in her life, seemed compressed and out of order. She'd only known about this man for less than a minute, and she'd been unable to stop herself from hating him.

Fern was also angry at the Commander. How many times had Fern asked her mother if she knew anything about her father? The Commander always said she had no idea who he was, but Fern suspected that wasn't true.

As soon as Mrs. Lin confirmed Fern's guess that Silver Tooth was her father, with the words "I believe he is," dozens of questions flooded Fern's mind. She no longer cared that they were late for the scheduled gathering in the lobby. She wanted to stay on the third level of the gift shop until she got some answers.

"Here you are!" Candace Tutter exclaimed as she approached the group. The first thing Candace noticed was Lindsey Lin's tear-streaked face. Candace had never before exchanged a word with the popular eighth grader. The two were, in Candace's own words, in "different social strata." However, standing there witnessing Lindsey Lin's obvious distress made her feel incredibly awkward. Lindsey had backed up Candace when she needed it most after the food fight. Was that a signal that they were friends now? If so, did that mean Candace should say something encouraging? Not knowing what else to do, Candace self-consciously looked down at the zigzag-patterned carpet.

"Hello," Mrs. Lin said. "I was doing one last sweep in order to corral any stragglers still in the gift shop. We should all head downstairs."

Mrs. Lin put her arm on Fern's back, guiding her toward the staircase that led down to the first floor.

"Fern," Mrs. Lin said as Candace, Sam, and Lindsey looked on, "we'll discuss your interest in an independent trip to the Portrait Gallery later, perhaps at dinner."

"Okay," Fern said.

Candace thought Fern seemed to be in a trance. She couldn't wait to get alone with her friend and find out what was the matter. And why Lindsey Lin was crying.

As they were racing down the stairs, with Mrs. Lin close behind, Sam tapped his sister on the shoulder.

"We'll figure everything out. Don't worry . . . okay?" He whispered it, but Candace was a well-practiced eavesdropper and heard every word. Candace was sure something important had just happened, but she hadn't a clue what it was. The next entry in her journal must await additional information.

When they reached the lobby of the Air and Space Museum, Headmaster Mooney tapped his watch with his index finger at Mrs. Lin and the group. They were the last to arrive. The Commander raised her eyebrows curiously when she saw Mrs. Lin, Sam, Lindsey, and Candace all together. She shot Fern a puzzled glance, but Fern pretended not to see it.

"Sorry, Ralph. We had a little accident, but everything's under control," Mrs. Lin explained. Candace was puzzled. Accident? She had discovered the four of them talking calmly. The Commander tried to inch closer to Fern to see if she could overhear anything.

"I understand, May. I hope you realize, though, that when a group's chaperone is not here at the appointed time, I have more than a dozen kids milling around with no supervision. It's very hard to stay organized under those conditions."

"Of course," Mrs. Lin responded. She restrained herself from lashing out at Ralph Mooney. The events of the day had left her nerves frazzled. She and Mike had been through trying times in their years together, but she'd never been forced to rely on a mere child for help—even if that child was as extraordinary as Fern McAllister. Mrs. Lin realized it was the only way, but she felt a tremendous sense of responsibility and doubt. If anything should happen to the girl . . . she would never be able to forgive herself. Ultimately, Ralph Mooney wasn't worth wasting her energy. Especially when there were so many real problems to confront.

"My apologies," Mrs. Lin added, feigning politeness.

"It won't happen again."

Headmaster Mooney smiled. He silently wished that every parent chaperone was as cooperative as May Lin. Mary Lou McAllister, for instance, was often disrespectful, and nothing but a problem. But what did he expect from someone who had produced the second most troublesome student in St. Gregory's history, Fern McAllister? Although he had to admit that day by day, Fern was gaining on Tucker Snude for the number one spot.

Candace and Fern didn't have to look far for their group when they reached the lobby. Headmaster Mooney was still their replacement chaperone, taking the place of Mrs. Phillips, who had been left behind to deal with her misbehaving daughter. They got in line behind him with the rest of the Lincoln students.

"What was that about, Fern?" Candace asked.

"What?" Fern said.

"Why were you talking with Mrs. Lin? Had Lindsey been crying?"

"Hold on a sec. . . ."

Fern, taking advantage of the fact that Headmaster Mooney's back was turned, darted over to the Washington group. Preston Buss was near the back, showing Taylor something on his cell phone.

"Hey," Fern said. Normally, especially in light of their last interaction, Fern would have been nervous talking to Preston. She didn't have time to be nervous, though. "Will you save a seat for me?"

"Um, sure," Preston Buss said, confused. Fern began to run back toward her group. Out of the corner of her eye, she saw Taylor elbow Preston playfully with raised eyebrows. Preston smiled sheepishly.

Candace scrutinized Fern the whole time and when Fern rejoined her, she waited a moment, considering what question to pose first. She decided the more general the better.

"Why are you acting so strangely?" Candace asked. If Fern hadn't been too preoccupied to notice the vulnerability Candace wore on her face, she might have hesitated before answering.

"I'm going to sit with Preston on the way back to the hotel," Fern said quickly.

Candace looked at Fern, shocked. She thought that their bond had been permanent. Clearly, she'd been a fool.

"Oh. Okay." Candace replied meekly. She tried to keep from showing her disappointment. She was silent as she and Fern waited in line to board the bus. Maybe, Candace thought, she'd misread the classic signs of friendship. Had she become biased by her own desires? If so, it was certainly an amateur mistake.

As she watched Fern bob and weave, making her way to the back of the bus where Preston was sitting, Candace thought about how quickly she and Fern had become friends. Now the friendship seemed to be slipping away just as quickly.

Candace scooted into her customary seat directly behind

the last row of chaperones, reminding herself that she'd made it this far in school without a real friend. The logical part of her told her she'd be fine if Fern McAllister never returned to sit next to her again. But the rest of her—the emotional part that she had less control over—told her she wouldn't.

In Candace's mind, there was only one solution. She had to find out what Fern was hiding. The sooner the better.

"Do you still have your harmonica with you?" Fern felt like she was shouting at a concert. Headmaster Mooney normally made sure the decibels inside the bus didn't rise above a reasonable level, but the day was winding down, and all that was left for Headmaster Mooney was to make sure the sixty-four St. Gregory's students got fed before he could retreat to his Marriott suite, so he instructed the bus driver to turn up the music and closed his eyes.

Preston reached into his Burton jacket. He waved the harmonica in Fern's face.

"Can you teach me to play it?"

This wasn't how Preston had imagined things going between himself and Fern McAllister. Though he'd been secretly excited by the fact that Fern had asked to sit next to him, she was confusing him with her businesslike demeanor.

Fern, on the other hand, wasn't confused at all. In fact, as time passed, she'd become increasingly single-minded.

It was how she was learning to deal with the constant dramatic turns in her life. If she blocked everything else out except the task at hand, it was less overwhelming.

And right now, her task was to get her hands on a musical instrument and learn how to play it.

"Now?" Preston said, looking around nervously at the other students on the bus. No one was paying attention to them, but with all the noise around him, he could hardly hear himself think.

"Why not?" Fern said, smiling at Preston. He smiled back.

"Well, it's not rocket science or anything. But people do say that the harmonica is the easiest musical instrument to learn and the hardest to get really good at."

"Then we'd better start with something easy," Fern said.

Preston put the harmonica to his lips and played a chord. He then held the side with the ten holes in it up for Fern to see.

"The easiest thing to do is play a chord," Preston said. "If you hold your thumb over a few of the holes, and then blow, you get a certain sound."

Preston showed Fern how a chord was played. The harmonica, which had seemed so loud as Preston and Fern sat on the bench in front of the Washington Monument, was muted here among the boisterous students and pumped-up music on the bus speakers. The first time he handed it to Fern, she was tempted to wipe it off before lifting it to her own mouth but decided that Preston might take it the wrong way and be terribly insulted.

Fern hadn't realized that blowing and sucking on the harmonica produced different sounds—or that sucking in was allowed at all. Preston patiently taught her a few chords and notes, and Fern practiced them. It was harder than it looked. Finally she felt like she got the hang of the few notes that Preston had taught her—carefully remembering which holes to blow into and when to suck in air.

Satisfied, Preston grabbed the instrument back. "Now you put it all together." Preston put the harmonica to his lips and closed his eyes. The song started slowly, but Fern recognized the tune immediately, watching Preston's mouth move up and down the instrument as his hand fluttered on the other side.

When Preston started over, Fern began to sing along. "Amazing grace, how sweet the sound, that saved a wretch like me."

Preston stopped playing. "Your voice isn't half bad."

"It isn't half good, either." Fern grinned and Preston laughed.

"We could go on tour," he said. "And be mediocre together."

"Can I borrow your harmonica for the night?" Fern asked.

Preston paused. "Well, I mean . . . I don't see why not."

"I want to practice," Fern explained. She grew nervous at the thought of Preston getting suspicious. "I'll give it back tomorrow."

Preston considered the proposition—it would mean that Fern would have a reason to come see him the next day, in order to return it.

"Patience isn't a strength of yours, is it?" Preston said. His tone was playful, and Fern instantly relaxed.

"My mom says that I was born without any."

"Patience is way overrated anyway," Preston said. He stuck his hand out in front of him and opened it. Fern grabbed the harmonica and carefully put it in the pocket of her coat.

"I expect you to have 'Amazing Grace' down pat by tomorrow."

"Don't hold your breath," Fern said, thinking that she had to know only a few bars.

"Same goes for you. It's very hard to play the harmonica that way."

Mrs. Lin had used the bus ride back to the Marriott to figure out how she could talk to Fern out of earshot of the rest of the group. She decided that she'd have to come up with a cover story for Headmaster Mooney and anyone else who asked. Lying had never really been her strong suit, though, so she devised a different plan. As the platters of beef, chicken, and vegetarian tacos were being set up in one of the Marriott's banquet rooms, the St. Gregory's students jockeyed for the best table position. Lindsey wound up sitting with her three roommates, and Sam sat with his. The round tables comfortably seated six, but there were more than enough tables, so most had only four students. A much more formal technology conference had taken place in the same room, before the St. Gregory's dinner, and floor-length black tablecloths remained from that event.

Fern and Candace occupied the only table where there were just two students. Candace was happy to have Fern back at her side again and thrilled that Blythe and Lee were still nowhere to be found, but she still couldn't dispel the notion that it was only temporary. Fern had seemed utterly distracted as they got their food, hovering around the salsa and guacamole station, eyeing the chaperone table. Candace couldn't figure exactly what Fern was staring at.

"Fern, I've designated you to help me clean up after everyone heads upstairs to their rooms for the night." Mrs. Lin was right behind Candace. Candace turned around in her chair.

"Okay," Fern said, barely able to contain her excitement.

"I'll stay too, Mrs. Lin," Candace added.

"That's very nice of you to offer, Candace, but it won't be necessary. Sam and Lindsey have already been assigned to help as well. You can go on up to your room when you're done."

Fern chomped on her taco. There was no mistaking the bland Washington, DC, variety of Mexican food for the kind she got at home in San Juan Capistrano.

"So what did you talk to Preston Buss about on the way home?" Candace said. The forty-five-minute trip in the rush hour traffic had been a lonely ride for her.

"I asked him if I could borrow his harmonica," Fern said. She reached into her pocket and pulled out the shiny silver instrument. Candace picked it up and held it close to her face to examine it.

"What are you going to do with it?"

"Oh, I don't know . . . practice a little. I figure if Blythe and Lee haven't been sent home, we can drive them crazy with it all night."

Candace smiled brightly. Fern had used the word "we." Fern McAllister and she were a *we* again. This fact didn't diminish her resolve to execute the plan she'd just concocted.

"Did you know that music authorities say that though the harmonica is the easiest musical instrument to learn, it's the hardest musical instrument to master?"

"Preston told me that on the bus."

"Do you like him?"

"Who?"

"Preston."

"Sure, he's nice," Fern replied.

"But do you *like* like him?"

Fern thought about it. She definitely got nervous around him. Still, she didn't really have time to *like* like him. She didn't have time to *like* like anyone.

"I don't think so."

Candace and Fern continued to make small talk until most of the room had emptied as students finished their meals and returned to their rooms. With the early six thirty a.m. roll call each day, most of the seventh and eighth graders couldn't wait for their heads to hit the pillows.

But Fern felt like her day was just beginning.

"So I'll see you upstairs?" Fern said, trying to nudge Candace out of the way so she could get to the part of the evening she'd been anticipating.

"Yeah, okay," Candace said, getting up from the table. "Don't forget the harmonica." Candace pointed down at the musical instrument.

"Thanks."

Candace walked toward the lobby in the direction of the elevator bank. She didn't look back once, in case Fern was watching her leave. But when she got to the doorway, she slid past it and pressed herself up against the wall of the hallway outside the banquet room. Slowly she bent her neck around so she could barely scan the room. Fern had gotten up and was taking her paper plate to the trash can at the opposite end of the large banquet room. Candace quickly decided on the best table location, made a mad dash toward her chosen spot, and slipped under the long tablecloth.

It was dark. But the black tablecloth insured that no one would see her and she'd be able to hear everything. All she had to do now was wait.

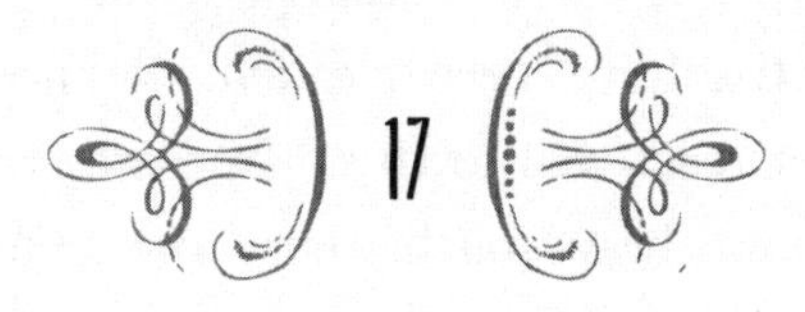

17

hard to say and harder to hear

"It wouldn't be any trouble," Mrs. Lin said, looking concerned. "Are you sure you don't want me to call her down here?" As much as May Lin wanted to respect Fern's wishes, she felt that Mary Lou McAllister, as Fern's guardian, needed to hear what she was about to tell Fern.

Fern shook her head. "If we get my mom involved, she'll stop me from going back to the zoo. She's already super worried, and Sam and I can tell her later, after we rescue Miles and Mr. Lin."

Mrs. Lin flinched—Fern's words served as a reminder that her hopes of seeing her husband unharmed rested on the shoulders of the thirteen-year-old girl in front of her. Would Mary Lou, in fact, try to interfere? Normals never did understand what was at risk when it came to any Rollen-Blout dispute—their peaceful coexistence with Otherworldlies was at stake, after all.

"Please, Mrs. Lin," Fern pleaded. "I know my mom and she won't react well to this." In truth, Fern was still confused about how much the Commander actually already knew and had kept to herself about Haryle Laffar. What's more, during the trip, things had been awkward between her and her mother—Fern didn't want to feel the Commander's pitying eyes on her as Mrs. Lin explained about her birth father.

Finally Mrs. Lin agreed to keep the group as it was.

Mrs. Lin sat in the chair at the table closest to the buffet tables. Sam, Lindsey, and Fern gathered in the seats around her. Except for them (and the stowaway curled up underneath their table—Candace had chosen well), the banquet room was empty. Mrs. Lin and the three St. Gregory's students had picked up all the leftover plates and cups and disposed of them in the trash containers.

From her position underneath the table, Candace could sense Fern's nervous energy—Fern's Vans-clad left foot was bouncing up and down so quickly, Candace couldn't look at it without feeling dizzy. She also noticed that Sam and Lindsey were perched on the edge of their seats.

Mrs. Lin began. "You will, no doubt, have questions. And I will try to answer them as best I can . . . but I ask that you let me finish what I have to say first. I'm not sure how much time we'll have."

Looking down in front of her, Fern traced a pattern on the dark tablecloth with her index finger.

"Fern?" Sam said. He tried to figure out where she was looking.

Mrs. Lin peered at Fern. "Are you ready?" As soon as she said it, Mrs. Lin realized it was an unfair question. Fern would never be ready for what she was about to hear.

"I'm not sure what Mary Lou has told you about your mother, " Mrs. Lin began, "but you probably know that Phoebe grew up in San Juan Capistrano and went to St. Gregory's, just like you. She was, by all accounts, a free spirit . . . made restless by our quiet town. She left when she turned eighteen and traveled the country for a number of years. Along the way she met your father, Haryle, and supposedly fell in love with him. You must know, though, that your mother was raised a Rollen—she was raised to respect Normals and the powers she was given—but when she was with Haryle Laffar, I'm afraid all of that changed.

"I don't know how else to say this except that Haryle Laffar is the worst kind of Otherworldly. He's ruthless, he's brutal, and he's killed many, all in the name of adding to his power and increasing his following. When a group of Rollens nearly killed him to stop him from destroying those who opposed him, he disappeared for some time. But he reemerged, shortly before he took up with your mother.

"The Merriams were quiet and decent people. They didn't live far from us in San Juan. One morning, they came to our house after receiving word that their daughter was living with Haryle. They begged for our help to talk some sense into her . . . to see if we couldn't snap her out of whatever spell she was under. I agreed to try, with another Otherworldly, who used to be friends with Phoebe—Alistair Kimble.

"We found Phoebe living with Haryle in a sprawling compound called the Outlands, north of San Francisco—in a town named Sausalito. Haryle had assembled a terrifying mix of Otherworldly criminals and sociopaths there with promises of building a Blout empire. One of those people was his brother, Vlad."

Fern let out an audible gasp but remembered her pledge not to talk and let Mrs. Lin continue.

"The Laffar brothers were constantly at odds because they disagreed on methods to defeat the Rollens. But Phoebe never belonged there at all—to this day I don't believe she was there of her own free will. Much like Vlad, Haryle Laffar can control minds, and no one was ever sure what he'd done to Phoebe to convince her to live with those people.

"Alistair and I waited until we had an opportunity to talk to Phoebe alone. We finally found her wandering in the woods around the Outlands one afternoon, and she was clearly very upset. She kept saying she had to leave . . . that things had changed. We suggested that she come with us, that we would protect her, but her reasoning had become clouded and she no longer trusted us. She ran back to the Outlands and the very next day, we learned she was missing.

"Of course, Haryle was not used to losing what he viewed as his 'property.' He searched for your mother far and wide. He wanted her back. Phoebe knew he would not rest until he found her again. Eventually, Haryle did find your mother. He tracked her to an artichoke farm near El Centro in the southern part of California. Your mother was living there peacefully with a family who had befriended her.

"And when he found her"—Mrs. Lin paused for a moment—"he killed her."

Mrs. Lin's eyes pooled, and it was clear that she spoke the words with great difficulty. She reached across the table and took the trembling hand of Fern McAllister in her own. Fern let out a small, muffled howl. Sam looked at his sister. The pain in her eyes spread to his own. He wanted to cover her ears. Actually, he wanted to reach inside them and pull out what had just been said so that she could unhear it.

"Fern," Mrs. Lin said, taking Fern's other hand. "Your mother left the compound because she learned she was pregnant with you. When she learned she was pregnant, something inside her snapped back into place . . . she realized she had to leave Haryle. When she sensed that Haryle was close to finding her, she gave you to Alistair Kimble, the one person on earth she trusted at the time, and told him that she wanted Mary Lou to have you. Phoebe began protecting you from the moment she knew you existed—

before you were even born."

Mrs. Lin paused. She took a deep breath. Lindsey, Sam, and Fern were too shocked to speak.

"No one should have to hear such things about her father. But your father is one man and only one small part of you. The most important parts—what makes you *you*—are the people who love you. You must always remember that your mother died protecting you. Because Phoebe hid you from him, Laffar doesn't know he has a daughter. And what he has done has *nothing* to do with you. Even in the short time you've lived, you have been responsible for inspiring such love. You *are* loved. By Phoebe, by Mary Lou, and—"

"By us." Lindsey looked at Sam expectantly. He nodded his head in agreement. He was at the age where he was embarrassed to say such things out loud, especially to his twin sister. But he was glad that Lindsey had said it for him. Lindsey tried to steady her voice and say something else, but as she thought of her missing father, the tears returned.

Under the table, Candace squirmed. She wished that she had not left her notebook upstairs in her backpack. What she had heard was shocking, dramatic, and—if the words hadn't come from the trustworthy Mrs. Lin's own lips—unbelievable. As soon as Candace got back to room 723, she would write everything down. Then she would work on figuring out what in heaven's name an Otherworldly was.

In the limited time they had left before the hotel staff

came in to rearrange the banquet room, Mrs. Lin explained that she could not possibly allow Fern to go unaccompanied to the place where Mr. Lin and Miles were imprisoned. She underscored the fact that should Haryle Laffar find out that Fern was his child, he might try to kidnap or harm her. She would need assistance.

Fern nodded her head, showing agreement with Mrs. Lin's plan, though in truth, as soon as she'd heard the full story about her birth mother and this man, Haryle Laffar, she made up her mind differently. Something in her snapped into place—her father had killed her mother and planned on killing Miles. The idea that stopping Haryle Laffar was her destiny stirred deep within her. If she focused on stopping him, Fern could block out the horrible fact that this evil man was her father.

Mrs. Lin wanted to go with Fern to provide protection. But Fern had learned in the past few months that she had to protect herself. Tonight, she resolved, she would teleport to Miles.

Alone.

Today was different. Miles had spent an unusual amount of time fully conscious, hearing no wails from the Quetzals. Silver Tooth had been underground for most of the day, and Miles was finally getting a chance to study the man's face and demeanor.

He didn't like what he was seeing.

"Why didn't your little friend come visit you last night?"

Haryle Laffar had both his hands wrapped around the bars of Miles Zapo's cage. His hands and face were dirty with soot, and he had black crud underneath his fingernails. Miles was finally conscious enough to notice that his captor was wearing a dark blue bandanna over his shoulder-length hair. Now that he'd gotten a closer look at Silver Tooth, Miles realized that he looked a lot like what he imagined a Hell's Angel might look like—except scarier.

"I—I don't know what you're talking about," Miles said, straightening his glasses. His ripped Minnesota Twins cap was askew on his head and he didn't bother fixing it.

"Look, kid," Laffar said, "either you start leveling with me or I bring my slimy friends in here and start them howling." Laffar poked his finger through the bars and snarled at Miles. Miles backed up as far as he could in his cage. His whole body was shaking.

"So far, I've only cranked up the volume halfway, but if I really encourage their wailing, the effect on you will be permanent. You don't want to be a vegetable for the rest of your life, do you?"

Miles Zapo had no idea whether or not Silver Tooth was lying. From what he'd seen so far, though, he figured the man was capable of anything. Miles had listened as Laffar ruthlessly interrogated a man imprisoned in the next room, beating him until the man could no longer answer his questions. Though Miles could not see what had happened from his vantage point in the other room, he was sure that Laffar had rendered the man unconscious. Every so often, the man would moan and Laffar would get up from his chair in the corner of the room, where he seemed to be studying a map of some kind, and go into the outer room. There would be a loud *whap*, which was what Miles could only assume was Laffar's fist hitting the man's skull, and then the moaning would stop.

Once more Laffar addressed Miles. "I'm not going to ask you again, kid. When is your friend coming back?"

"I told her to stay away from here after she came the first time. . . . I said that you were going to kill her if she came back to help me." The fear in Miles's voice was real, even if he wasn't telling the truth.

Laffar rubbed his beard as his eyes blazed. "I'm not sure why you would go ahead and tell her something as stupid as that."

Laffar pushed himself away from the cage with both arms. He began pacing, his steel-toed boots clicking on the cement floor with every step. When he was about ten feet away, he whirled quickly back toward the cage. Rushing forward, Laffar reached an all-out sprint before slamming into the cage. He rattled the bars with all his might, cackling like a possessed maniac.

Miles Zapo cowered in the back corner of the cage. Laffar's single Silver Tooth flashed in the dim orange light of the underground prison. The rattling of the cage echoed off the bare concrete walls as noise thundered throughout the cell.

Defenseless against the man's terrorizing aggression, Miles curled up in a ball with his hands and arms covering his head. He was sure that he was about to meet his end.

Then, as suddenly as Haryle Laffar had morphed into a madman, he changed once again. He released the cage from his grip and took a step back. A kind of calm overtook his face. Reaching into his leather jacket, he took out a pack of Marlboros and a lighter. He held the lighter to the cigarette and inhaled, and then exhaled a slow smoky breath.

"No matter, kid. Because I got this feeling that your friend is going to come back and rescue you real soon. Seems to me like she's the meddling superhero-complex sort, not likely to abandon you in your time of need. If she don't, that's fine too. Because in about a day, we'll have gotten the very last thing we need. Then I'll have all the time in the world to track the girl who tried to kill my brother. Flarge is already doing it right now."

"What?" Miles said, lowering his arms from his head.

"You heard me. Normally I don't concern myself with children, except in two cases." Laffar raised his cigarette to his mouth and inhaled. The tip began to glow a fiery orange color. "The first case, of course, is when those brats can be very helpful to me, like yourself. And the second case is when some brat tries to kill my brother."

Neither Haryle Laffar nor Miles Zapo knew that the brat in the second case just referred to was Laffar's own daughter.

Laffar narrowed his gray eyes and stared at Miles. "You understand how it is with family, don't you, kid? Like if I were to tell you that something happened to that old woman of yours . . . Aunt Chan . . . that would be pretty upsetting to you, now wouldn't it?" Laffar smiled fiendishly.

"If you do anything to hurt her, I swear I'll—"

"You'll what?" Laffar demanded, laughing at the boy's threat. "Turn yourself invisible and scare me? Now calm down . . . . Getting worked up ain't going to do any good. In fact, you better get your rest now. Tomorrow night's showtime."

Laffar took another drag of his cigarette and then whistled. Miles heard something slamming against the metal ducts above them. In no time, the Quetzals would be back to start their incessant wailing. For Miles, everything would go blank and terror would return.

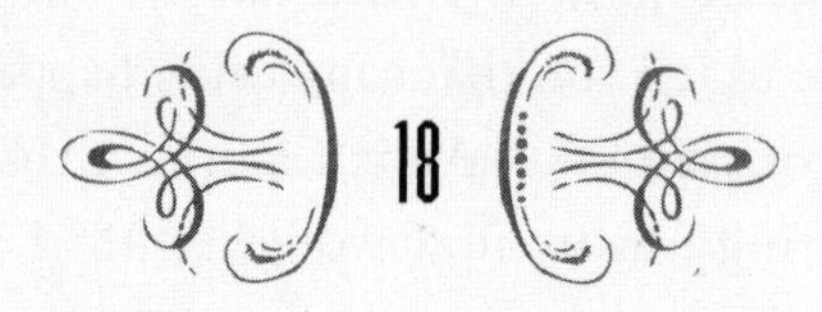

18

the prep and the plan

The scene in room 723 was very different from previous nights.

Fern sat on the chair by the window and practiced "Amazing Grace" on the harmonica. It was eight o'clock p.m., and in the last hour she'd made some progress. Now she could play the first few bars of the song without mistakes. Candace, sprawled on one of the double beds, watched Fern curiously out of the corner of her eye, while writing in her notebook. Lee and Blythe, who had not been sent home after all, but merely suspended from the day's activities, glanced suspiciously at Fern from time to time as they quietly watched a movie on a laptop in their corner of the room. It was hard to believe, but it almost seemed like the tormenting blond duo had been humiliated into submission. Instead of telling Fern to stop playing the harmonica so they could hear the movie, they donned headphones without objection.

Fern dropped the harmonica from her lips. She stared out the seventh-floor window of the Marriott. There wasn't much activity around the front of the hotel. Her thoughts turned to the evening's plan.

For now, Fern put the knowledge that the monster holding Miles Zapo prisoner was her father in its own separate airtight compartment. Fern had lots of these compartments: one for the fact that the Commander hadn't told her she was adopted until she was twelve years old; one for the implications of being a member of the Unusual Eleven as foretold by the Omphalos prophecy; one for her birth mother's questionable status as a Blout; one for the worry that her fangs might come in at any time; and one for the growing certainty that her Otherworldly status was constantly endangering everyone she loved. If she thought about any one of the realities in each closed-off compartment for too long, she knew that she'd wind up tearful, depressed, and immobilized.

Instead she focused on how she would teleport back to Miles before Mrs. Lin (as well as Lindsey and Sam) were able to implement their own plans to accompany her. Sam and Lindsey had informed Mrs. Lin that Miles was most likely to be left alone around midnight, as he was when Fern visited him the last time. While they were in the Marriott's banquet room, the foursome had made a plan to meet in the lobby at 11:40 p.m. and walk the mile from the Marriott to the zoo. Once there, they would retrace Mr. Lin's steps at the zoo and locate the two prisoners. Mrs. Lin assured them that she had watched Mr. Lin's progress by using the locket Sagebrush until he had disappeared.

Lindsey and Sam were to stand guard outside while Mrs. Lin and Fern made their way to the underground bunker where Miles and Mr. Lin were captive. If they ran into trouble, Mrs. Lin would call Lindsey on her phone, and she was to get in touch with Alistair Kimble immediately. Mrs. Lin was fairly certain that they would not be in any danger, because Laffar was not expecting them. In that regard, of course, she was wrong.

Fern knew she'd be able to teleport to the bunker before anyone realized she was gone. The problem, though, was that the Lins and Sam would realize something was amiss when Fern didn't appear at their meeting in the lobby. Sam would probably figure it out first—that Fern had decided to teleport to Miles's location herself. Then they would inevitably go after her. That, Fern knew, would be the worst of all scenarios. She didn't want to have to worry about her brother and the Lins getting in trouble while searching for her, but ultimately, Fern knew there was no escaping it unless she had some method of letting Sam, Lindsey, and Mrs. Lin know that she'd made her way to the bunker herself and they were not to follow her. She turned away from the window. Her eyes met Candace's.

"I need to talk to you."

Candace perked up.

"About what?"

Fern looked at Lee and Blythe. They seemed to be reveling in *Mean Girls*, but she didn't want to take any chances.

"Come with me."

Fern led Candace into the bathroom and locked the door. Normally, Blythe or Lee would have made some kind of snarky comment about the girls heading to the bathroom together, but they ignored Fern and Candace.

Fern started the sink running.

"I need you to do something for me," Fern said as both girls stood in the middle of the bathroom.

"Fern, what's an Otherworldly?" Candace's high-pitched voice did not waver as she asked the question that had been on her mind for several hours now. Fern was stunned.

"How do you know that word?" Fern interrogated.

"I don't want to lie to you, but until you start telling me the truth, I'm not sure why I should volunteer any information."

"Tell the truth about what?"

"About who you *are*. About why you disappeared from the bathroom."

"Candace, I'm asking you a favor . . . that's it. If you do this for me, I promise I'll tell you everything after it's over. I can't tell you right now." Fern was tired of making up excuses.

"Why not? I don't know what happened to you that made you so secretive about everything," Candace said.

My life happened, Fern wanted to respond.

"It's not so hard . . . telling the truth. Look, I'll go first: I saw you move the towel in the exercise room. And earlier tonight, when you talked to Mrs. Lin, I was hiding under the table and I heard everything."

Fern took a step backward, fighting the instinct to pounce on Candace.

"You had NO right! Is that what you've been writing about in your stupid notebook?" Candace's admission had caused the compartment containing the facts surrounding Haryle Laffar to burst open. Fern began to visualize the man who had killed her birth mother. She wondered how he did it . . . whether Phoebe had been taken by surprise. The image of the killer's gleaming silver tooth burned in Fern's mind.

Candace's voice snapped Fern back into the reality of the bathroom.

"This isn't about my stupid journal anymore, Fern. Don't you understand? No matter if you tell me or not, I'll do whatever you want," Candace said. Fern had never seen her roommate put so much emotion into her words. "Because I know you wouldn't be asking for help unless you really needed it. I'm worried that you're in real danger. But I know I can *help* you if you tell me what's going on."

Candace put her hands on her diminutive hips. She'd braided her hair, which had the effect of making her look even younger than she was. She could easily pass for an eight-year-old. Fern began to pace the length of the bathroom.

"Maybe you only see me as some geek who you were forced to room with. . . . But being a geek has its advantages. I may not be able to perform telekinesis, but I can recite the periodic table forward and backward, I can complete geometric proofs that even Mr. Billing doesn't understand, I can memorize ten pages of information in about five minutes, and," Candace said, taking a moment to catch her breath in the midst of her impassioned speech, "I'm betting I can probably help you come up with a way to stop your father from doing whatever it is he's planning."

Fern seriously considered telling Candace the truth. She knew she would feel relieved to tell another person. But she'd realized it wasn't fair to Candace. It would be selfish.

"Even if I told you, Candace, you wouldn't believe me. No one would."

Candace's smirk morphed into a smile. "I think you're forgetting a key fact about me. . . . Sometimes the most important prejudice a scientist can overcome is her perception that reality has boundaries. All the greatest scientists in history have shared one single belief: that at any given moment, anything is possible." Candace's voice had never been more emphatic.

"Who originally said that?" Fern asked.

"I did, Fern," Candace responded. "It's like I've been *telling* you . . . I'm pretty smart. And you can either use that to your advantage or you can keep lying and get yourself in worse trouble than I suspect you're already in."

"Well . . . all right," Fern said hesitantly, even as she looked at Candace's triumphant face. "You may want to sit down for all this, especially if we're going to start at the beginning."

By the end of Fern's story, Candace Tutter was completely befuddled.

"So . . . you're . . . a vampire?" Candace asked.

"That's one word for it, yes."

"There are so many books and movies about them, but I never actually thought they existed. . . . To think I was getting kind of sick of them!"

"Imagine how I feel," Fern said, smiling for the first time since she'd found out about Haryle Laffar's true identity.

Candace swore she would help Fern by stopping Lindsey, Mrs. Lin, and Sam from trying to follow Fern into the den where Miles was imprisoned.

Fern had complete confidence in Candace's abilities to figure out a way to do just that.

After all, the girl was a genius.

Fern waited until her watch read 11:40 p.m. She clutched two objects in her hands, and she only hoped that when the time came, she'd be able to use them. Blythe and Lee were long asleep, and a few minutes before, Candace had set out for the lobby, ready to stop the Lins and Sam from trying to follow Fern.

The whole thing had been Candace's idea.

After Fern explained every detail to her new confidante, including a description of the concrete bunker where Miles, and probably Mr. Lin, were being held, Candace took several moments to ponder. Fern wondered if she was deciding whether or not to believe the strange tale. Fern had to admit that the whole thing sounded utterly preposterous, and she realized Candace would have a million follow-up questions. Fern would need to cut Candace off at some point in order to prepare for her teleportation to the zoo.

The question Candace finally did ask completely surprised Fern.

"So there was a padlock on Miles Zapo's cage?"

"Yes."

"How big?" Candace had the details of Fern's predicament firmly in mind and was already speaking like an authority on the subject. Fern figured she just might be.

"I don't know. I guess it was pretty big."

"Do you think you could break it with your bare hands?"

"Not likely."

"Well, when you get there, how do plan on breaking him out?"

"Well . . . I . . . I guess I hadn't really thought about

that. I figured something would come to me," Fern said. It was true that in her excitement she hadn't given much thought to her next move once she'd found Miles and Mr. Lin.

"Goodness, Fern. You're about as good at planning as Bonnie and Clyde."

"Who and who?"

"Bonnie Parker and Clyde Barrow? The famous outlaws during the Great Depression?" Candace raised her eyebrows. The flowing water from the sink had turned hot and started to fog up the mirrors.

"Never heard of them."

"Well, Bonnie and Clyde were these legendary bank robbers, except they would have been a lot *more* legendary if they ever made an actual plan before they went in and robbed a bank. They charged in with a gun. That was about all the thinking they did."

"What's your point?" Fern asked.

"My point is that you don't even have a gun. Let alone a plan."

"And I suppose *you* have one?"

"As a matter of fact, I do," Candace said, smiling. "Follow me."

There was a spring in her step as she turned the faucet off and opened the door to the room. She made a beeline for her suitcase and began throwing clothing out of it into a pile on the side of her double bed. She dug until finally she produced a combination lock the size of her small fist.

After displaying it proudly to Fern, she zipped up her suitcase and put the lock through the holes atop the zippers, which were now neatly aligned.

"I'm not sure locking your suitcase really gets us any closer to figuring out how to get Miles out of his cage," Fern whispered, turning around to see if Lee and Blythe were paying any attention. They seemed to still be completely focused on the adventures of Lindsay Lohan and Rachel McAdams.

The suitcase was half Candace's size, and she looked like she was in danger of toppling over as she lifted it upright. Candace began wheeling the suitcase toward the door, and Fern followed her into the hallway.

"Moving out?" Lee called after them hopefully. The door shut. Candace marched ahead, wheeling her now-locked suitcase behind her.

"Where are we *going*?" Fern whispered anxiously. It was now well past the St. Gregory's nine p.m. curfew. If they were caught out in the hallway—with a *suitcase*, no less—they would be in serious trouble. Candace traveled all the way around the corner and down the hallway of the eastern bank of rooms. She waited a moment in front of Room 754. Then she knocked.

"What are you doing?" Fern said, dumbfounded, her eyes so wide, she thought that her eyeballs might fall right out. "This is my mom's ro—"

The door opened.

"Hello Mrs. McAllister." Candace smiled cheerfully at

Mary Lou McAllister, who gave Candace a reserved smile in return.

"Are you ladies going somewhere?" The Commander was wearing fleece pants and a St. Gregory's sweatshirt. Her blond hair was up in a bun. She was clearly ready for bed.

"I'm so sorry to disturb you, but someone seems to have put a lock on my suitcase, and I need the medication I keep in it before I go to bed. Fern said you might know what to do."

The Commander's eyes darted from Candace to Fern, and then back to Candace. She raised an eyebrow. Bending forward, she took a look at the suitcase, giving the lock a tug.

"Did Lee or Blythe put this on your suitcase?"

Candace got an anxious look on her face. "I'm not here to get anyone in trouble, Mrs. McAllister, see, I just want to take my medicine."

The Commander's face softened. "Of course, sweetheart." She bent down so that she was at the same eye level as Candace. "Why don't we go downstairs and see if someone can help you with that?"

Mrs. McAllister, Fern, and Candace rode down in the elevator. The Commander had taken charge of wheeling Candace's suitcase. They arrived in the lobby, and after the Commander described the situation to the concierge, they were led down the hall to a locked blue door.

"When he opens the door," Candace whispered in

Fern's ear, pulling her back from the adults, "you need to get a very good look at the inside of the lock. Try to memorize it in your mind, okay?"

"Why?" Fern said, utterly confused. She was starting to believe that Candace's plan was completely idiotic.

"Just do it," Candace said, before the Commander looked back at the two girls. The concierge unlocked the door, revealing a janitor's closet full of mops and brooms. A red tool chest with many drawers sat in the back corner. He whistled as he searched through the chest, finally pulling out a long tool. Fern thought it was a pair of pliers at first, but then realized it was a bolt cutter.

Candace nudged Fern into the room with the back of her knee. Once she was halfway in, Fern stretched her neck around the door so she could see its other side. There was a knob and then, above that, a dead bolt that one of the concierge's keys had just unlocked. Fern didn't know what else she was supposed to memorize, but she remembered the color, gold, as well as the two screws that held the bolt and the circular gold plate in place above the knob.

Meanwhile, Candace prattled on, keeping both the Commander and the concierge engaged in conversation so that Fern could observe the inside of the door without anyone noticing. Candace talked about how she had a thyroid condition and her medicine was very important; she asked the concierge how he knew how to work bolt cutters; she asked how often people locked their suitcases accidentally.

The concierge made short work of the lock on the suitcase. He snapped the bolt cutters closed once, and the metal shackle of the lock was cut in half.

Candace acted overjoyed, rushing to open the suitcase. Sure enough, she produced a bottle of pills from one of the inside pockets.

"Thank you so, so much, Mrs. McAllister," Candace said, beaming as they walked out of the elevator once it had reached the seventh floor.

"If those girls are harassing either of you," the Commander said with motherly concern as she watched Fern and Candace walk down the hallway to their room, "let me know."

"We most certainly will," Candace responded. "Good night."

"Good night, ladies," the Commander added, anxiously trying to make eye contact with Fern, who was actively avoiding it. "Sleep tight."

Fern wondered if they'd be sleeping at all that night.

The Commander turned back down her hallway. Fern was about to ask Candace one of the dozens of questions on her mind when Candace grabbed Fern's wrist and put an index finger to her lips, signaling for Fern to shush.

As if she was waiting for something, Candace stood frozen in the hallway. Finally both girls heard the click of Mrs. McAllister's door shutting.

"Candace, I don't mean to be rude or anything, but *what* are we doing?"

A smile crept over Candace's face. "Did you take a look at the inside of the door?"

"Yes. But what's the plan?"

Candace moved back down the hallway toward the elevator.

"Where are we going?" Fern asked, her frustration level reaching new highs.

Candace pushed the down button and whipped around. "If you're planning on a jailbreak, you're going to need some bolt cutters, aren't you?"

"We can't ask the concierge for them again—he'll know we're up to something."

"That's why," Candace said, getting up on her tiptoes and putting her hand on Fern's shoulder, "we're going to steal them."

On the elevator down to the lobby, Candace explained that if Fern really could move things with her mind, then if she thought about the dead bolt moving from the locked position to the open position, they could break into the closet and get the bolt cutters.

"But I've never moved something I couldn't see before," Fern explained, as the girls stealthily made their way past the lobby to the hallway with the janitor's closet.

"Yes, but you've never *not* moved something you couldn't see before either, have you?"

Candace, as usual, was confusing Fern. They were now

outside the blue door of the janitor's closet.

"Moment of truth!" Candace said, clasping her hands together with excitement. Fern closed her eyes. She imagined the bolt she had seen on the other side of the door a few minutes before. Candace watched Fern's eyes flutter open and closed. Fern turned white. Fern visualized the bolt moving like the hand of a clock around the circular gold plate, from ten o'clock to two o'clock.

CLICK.

Candace eagerly clutched the knob and turned it. She pushed on the door.

It opened.

Fern realized that although she possessed freakish powers that were the envy of others, Candace Tutter had some pretty amazing mental powers of her own.

Before closing her eyes, Fern took a moment to review the plan she and Candace had devised. In one hand, she grasped the harmonica, which fit easily into her palm. If she heard the Quetzals, she would immediately start playing it and hope she put them to sleep before they did the same to her. If she felt faint or dizzy at all, she was going to teleport back to the hotel immediately. If she heard any noise besides the Quetzals, Fern would hide and wait it out. Miles told her that Laffar always left him alone and conscious around midnight, and she was counting on Laffar maintaining this routine.

In her other hand, Fern held the rubber grips of the

bolt cutters. They were locked in the closed position, but Fern had to spread her thumb out wide to hold them in one hand. Taking a deep breath, she closed her eyes. She imagined the dim orange light, the piles of dried-out bamboo, and the crate marked NATIONAL ZOOLOGICAL PARK.

The blackness took hold.

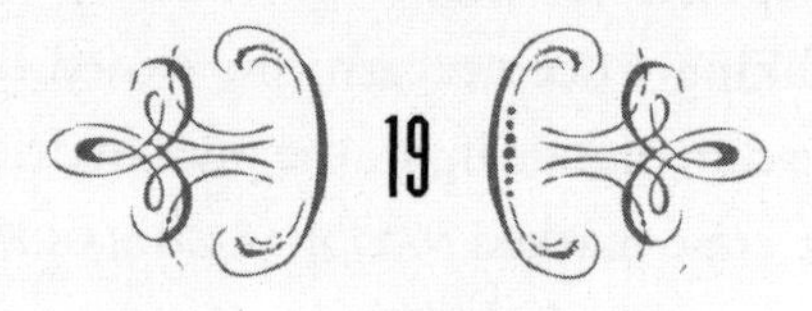

19

the return visit

Blinking her eyes until they worked again, Fern bent low to the ground, putting the harmonica to her lips, ready to blow.

Everything was quiet. Fern's eyes gradually adjusted to the darkness of the room. She took stock of her surroundings. The bamboo was right in front of her, and to the left was the doorway that led to the smaller room holding Miles in his cage. There was no sign of the Sirens.

The stack of cages in this larger room had been toppled and was now scattered on the right side of the room. With the harmonica still pressed to her mouth, Fern bent even lower. She scanned the area more carefully, then crept silently toward the cages. She noticed a dark object in one. She tiptoed closer and then closer still. Finally she could make out a pair of shoes and legs attached to them.

There was no doubt—a person was trapped in one of the collapsed cages. Haryle Laffar had added to his prisoner count. Fern's eyes moved up to the door of the newly occupied cage—it was padlocked. As she got closer, her suspicions were confirmed. The limp-bodied prisoner was Mr. Lin.

"Mr. Lin?" Fern whispered. He didn't answer. He was curled up in a ball, so Fern couldn't fully see his face.

"Mr. Lin? It's Fern. Are you okay?" She didn't dare raise her voice above a whisper. She caught sight of Mr. Lin's left hand, splayed out before her. It was bruised and bloodied. Whatever it was that Laffar had done to Mr. Lin, he was clearly unable to answer. Before she moved on to find Miles, Fern figured she'd try her hand at cutting the padlock, in case they had to make a quick escape. She wished she didn't have to use the bolt cutters at all—but since she couldn't see the inner workings of the lock, she knew she wouldn't be able to open it with her mind.

With her elbows jutting out from both sides like spreading wings, Fern fit the bolt-cutting blades over the lock's U-shaped metal bar. She let out a small grunt as she snapped the cutter shut with all her might. Almost like magic, the lock broke in two and fell to the ground with a loud clang. Fern cringed as she heard the noise echoing off the ground. Nervously she spun around, trying to ensure that the noise hadn't awakened a sleeping Siren.

Everything was still quiet.

"Fern?"

Though Fern could barely make out the voice, she knew instantly that it belonged to Miles.

"Fern?" the voice repeated. "Is that you?"

As she scrambled over the bamboo lying in the doorway between rooms, Fern hoped that Miles was in better shape than Mr. Lin.

She put her head through the doorway first, examining the small room. The grate above Miles's cage was half open. If Miles couldn't teleport out of there with her, the grate might be their only escape route.

Miles was sitting upright against the back metal bars of his cage. Fern hooked the bolt cutters through a belt loop in her jeans and ran to Miles's cage.

"It *is* you. . . ." Miles yawned and blinked his eyes as if he was waking up from a long nap. He removed his glasses and rubbed his eyes. His hat was askew, and he adjusted its torn brim.

"Hey," Miles said, displaying his crooked smile. He seemed genuinely happy to see Fern, who peered at him curiously.

"Are you all right?" Fern asked.

"Oh sure," Miles said, yawning once more. It was almost as if he was unaware that he was being kept prisoner by a maniac in an underground bunker.

Fern pressed herself against the door of the cage.

"Did they just leave?" She asked, taking the bolt cutters from her belt loop and fitting the blades over the padlock.

Miles looked as though he was about to doze off. With one swift move, Fern brought the blades together, and the lock snapped in half and dropped to the floor.

Fern congratulated herself for becoming pretty adept with the bolt cutters. Although she wasn't destined for a life of crime, knowing how to cut bolts was turning out to be a useful skill so far. Fern dashed back to the doorway and stashed the bolt cutters under the bamboo pile. Then she returned to Miles.

Fern opened the cage door. She had to duck a little to make her way into the cage as she closed in on Miles.

"What are you doing, Fern?" Miles said, growing confused. He pushed his glasses up the bridge of his nose.

"We're getting you out of here!" Fern didn't know how much time she had before the Sirens or Laffar would return, and she still had to find a way to rescue both Mr. Lin and Miles. She was growing more anxious by the second.

"Out of where?" Miles said dreamily. Fern was now next to him in his cage. She grabbed Miles's arm and gave it a firm shake.

"Miles . . . do you know where you are?" Fern spoke slowly and deliberately. "You're in Washington, DC."

"What's your favorite part of the city . . . what's your favorite monument?" Miles's eyes kept opening and shutting.

"Can you stand up by yourself?" Fern asked, and Miles muttered something unintelligible. Clearly he was still feeling the effects of the Sirens—they must have recently departed. Which meant that they were still close by.

Fern knew what she had to do. If it meant carrying Miles out on her back, she would do so to get him out of that cage and bunker. Fern put Miles's arm around her neck. He smelled like a locker room mixed with the breakfast aisle of a supermarket.

"Miles," she said, "I'm going to lift you up on three, okay?"

"I'm scared, Fern," Miles said, beginning to cry with his eyes still closed. "Silver Tooth made me steal the diamond."

"It's going to be all right. . . . We're going to get you out of here, right now." Fern was now squatting. She tried to get as firm a footing as possible, ready to explode upward, hopefully taking Miles with her.

"Let's keep chatting, okay, Miles? Keep listening to me. I need you to stay awake." Aunt Chan had made sure to tell Fern before she left that if she could slowly bring Miles out of his Siren-induced stupor, he was more likely to be able to regain his powers of teleportation. Still, Fern had no idea how long the effects lasted once the Sirens stopped wailing.

"My favorite monument by far was the Lincoln Memorial," Fern said, struggling to stand up as she tried to hoist Miles up with her. She leaned against the back of the cage, slowly rising to her feet, straining under the added weight. She gripped him around the waist. She was thankful he was fairly light. She could feel his hip bones protruding.

He probably hadn't had a real meal in a week. "Have you been there, Miles?" Miles's head hung so that his chin was flush against his chest. He shook his head from side to side, without looking up. "Well, you should go. He's in this big chair, and it makes you want to climb up into his lap." Fern thought of all the facts Candace Tutter had enumerated as they stood in front of the large marble Lincoln. As she brought Miles to his feet, she couldn't remember one of them. She could only remember thinking that she wanted to take a nap curled up in Lincoln's large lap.

Fern was now standing up straight. "All right, Miles, now we're going to take three big steps forward and get out of this cage."

Miles's eyes popped open. He looked at Fern as if he was seeing her for the very first time. It was as if he was finally out of his trance.

"You have to leave!" he exclaimed, almost screaming.

"Miles, keep your voice lower. He's going to hear you."

Miles pushed Fern's arm from his shoulder. "Get out of here! Now! Silver Tooth's going to kill you. He told me! He *knows* you're coming back."

Fern tried not to panic. "Do you think you can teleport? Can you teleport back to your house?"

"NO! I've tried. Fern, get out of here!" Miles's face flooded with dread.

"I'm not leaving you. Come on!" Fern motioned to the open cage door. She heard pounding in the ducts above the room. Someone was approaching the grate.

"He's going to make me steal one more thing tomorrow night and then he's going to let me go . . . I promise."

"No, Miles!"

"Teleport now! He's GOING TO KILL YOU."

Reaching into her jacket pocket, Fern fumbled for the harmonica. She signaled for Miles to be quiet, then held the harmonica close to her lips and began to play the first few bars of "Amazing Grace." The thumping from above got louder, drowning out the warbling tune coming from the harmonica. Something moved the grate above Miles's cage until the entire opening was uncovered. Fern's hands trembled as she clutched the harmonica. But she kept playing.

A pair of denim-enclosed legs appeared first. Someone was lowering himself through the opening where the grate had been. Fern couldn't tell if she was shaking from her own fear or because of Miles's trembling body next to her. She kept playing, trying to think of what to do. She couldn't just leave Miles.

A man dropped from the ceiling, landing with a thud as his steel-toed boots hit the concrete floor. Fern eyed him, staring out over the top of the harmonica. He wore dirty jeans, a leather jacket, and a bandanna around his head. He had a short beard and a weathered tan face.

The man smiled, revealing a silver tooth, as soon as he saw Fern and Miles huddled together in the cage. He put his rugged hands on his hips, shaking his head in disbelief.

It was definitely Silver Tooth. Which meant that the man

standing before Fern was her own father, and the same man who had killed Phoebe Merriam—Haryle Laffar.

"Teleport *now*," Miles whispered. "Before it's too late."

Laffar strutted toward the open cage door. Moving swiftly, he slammed the door shut and latched it. Then he reached inside the cage, ripped the harmonica from Fern's grip, and tossed it across the room.

Fern watched it slide across the concrete floor until it hit the opposite wall.

"Well, well, well . . . sometimes things fall right into place, now don't they?" Laffar spoke with a slight twang and sounded as though he had gravel in his lungs.

Fern felt simultaneous bursts of anger and panic suddenly overtake her.

"Why are you keeping Miles here?" Fern demanded.

"The legendary Fern McAllister, as I live and breathe. Somehow, I thought you'd be a bit taller . . . but I guess they say that's always the case with famous people," Laffar said sarcastically, revealing his silver-accented smirk once again.

"I don't know what you're taking about," Fern retorted.

"Oh, now surely you must know that Otherworldlies far and wide are calling you the Dracula Destroyer. I mean, when a little girl causes a ruckus on a beach that results in the capture of an infamous and violent vampire, it starts people buzzing."

Laffar looked the girl over. Rollens, he thought, were so predictable. Always trying to be heroic. Fern McAllister might be the latest edition of the breed, but she was no different.

"There are people coming to look for me. They'll find us, and they'll catch you!" Fern screamed.

Laffar shook his head and laughed, gripping two of the bars to the door of the cage. Fern focused on the harmonica in the corner and began imagining it moving across the room.

"Well, aren't you a feisty little thing!" Laffar chuckled again. He looked at Fern, realizing that she wasn't looking at him, and followed her gaze.

At first all he could do was stare at the harmonica, floating across the room toward the girl. It took him a few seconds to react; then he snatched it cleanly out of the air.

"If my brother made one mistake . . . it was underestimating you," Laffar snarled. "*I'm* not going to do that."

Putting his thumb and index finger to his mouth, Laffar whistled. Almost immediately, something was thundering in the ducts again, and soon Fern heard a high-pitched whine.

Her arms and legs felt heavy, like they were turning into lead. She couldn't keep her head up, and her mind filled with dark clouds. *No!* she thought. It was the Siren's cry. She didn't have much time. She screamed but suspected she could only be heard inside her own head.

Fern tried to think of a place where she could teleport. Her mind drew only blanks. She couldn't focus on anything. Yet she must.

She had to imagine going somewhere. Someplace other than the cage.

Nothing came to her.

She bumped into Miles before slumping to the ground.

"What do you mean, Fern's sick?" Mrs. Lin demanded, trying to remain calm even though thoughts of her missing husband made this a difficult task.

Mrs. Lin, Sam, and Lindsey were gathered in the far corner of the lobby, all fully dressed. At first, when Candace Tutter approached them, they assumed that the girl had snuck out ahead of Fern, fulfilling her role as self-appointed shadow. They had no idea that Candace was about to claim to be Fern's official messenger.

Candace had arranged her flaxen hair in two braids and was wearing a matching flannel pajama set that pictured different kinds of breakfast food—pancakes, eggs sunny-side up, and strips of bacon. She'd almost brought Morris, the small stuffed otter she'd gotten when she was six years old on a visit to the Monterey Bay Aquarium, but decided that bringing him along might be overselling it. She was trying to look as if she'd been asleep for the past few hours instead of burglarizing janitors' closets and hatching rescue plans with Fern in the bathroom.

"Fern said for me to tell you that she's very sorry, but you're going to have to wait a little while longer. She should be okay in a couple of hours. She'll call one of you when she feels better."

"But the Sirens will be back by then!" Lindsey was less able than her mother to control her anxiety over her father. "We can't wait."

"The *what* will be back?" Candace asked, cocking her head to the side, faking confusion. Of course, in reality, Candace Tutter knew as much about the Sirens as any of them did.

Mrs. Lin peered at the small girl in her breakfast pajamas. Would Fern actually send this child to talk to them? From what she knew of the McAllister girl, there was nothing that would keep her from trying to save Mr. Lin and Miles. With anyone else, Mrs. Lin would have chalked the no-show up to fear. But she'd seen Fern McAllister in action.

She was fearless.

"I suppose your natural inclination will be to want to check on Fern," Candace said to Mrs. Lin. "I've read a lot about maternal instincts. But I would not recommend it. Are you aware that gastroenteritis kills between five and eight million people a year? It is highly contagious and, of course, I'm no expert, but I believe that the proper diagnosis for Fern is that she has been hit by the norovirus, which is about as infectious as a virus can be. In fact, I may already be a carrier. I suggest you take a few steps away from me."

Candace put her hand up, signaling for Lindsey, Mrs. Lin, and Sam to back away. She read the confusion on their faces, so she plowed on.

"Of course, it could be salmonella—we all know how unreliable hotel food is. I mean, I saw a *Dateline* episode recently where they had these hidden cameras installed in the kitchen of a hotel, and the cooks were actually using dirty plates and linens to prepare the food. If that doesn't have salmonella written all over it, I don't know what does!"

Mrs. Lin's head was spinning. The little chatterbox had her completely flummoxed. She tried to collect her thoughts. They could certainly attempt going without Fern, but it would be dangerous for any of them to descend into the bunker with no one able to teleport out and get help if danger arose.

"Is Fern throwing up?" she asked.

"Big-time. When I left, her, the count was up to six. She may even break my record of eleven times in twenty-four hours," Candace said, pausing to take a breath. "You know, it's nice that you're taking some of the students on a night tour of Washington, Mrs. Lin. Though I'm surprised that Headmaster Mooney gave you curfew clearance for such an activity. You must be very persuasive."

"Night tour?" Sam asked.

"Isn't that why you're all gathered down here? Fern said you were all going on a special night tour," Candace responded, upping the ante of her innocent act.

"Oh yes, of course."

The elevator dinged as it reached the lobby level. Someone else had arrived. The doors were only partially open when Mary Lou McAllister stormed between them. She was wearing sweatpants and a St. Gregory's sweatshirt. Clearly she had dressed in a hurry. Her face looked haggard, and she was gripping her cell phone.

"Mom?" Sam queried.

The Commander saw the group of familiar faces gathered in the corner of the lobby and let out a large breath.

"So you heard?" Mrs. McAllister questioned, her voice frantic. Worry swamped Sam's thoughts as he looked with trepidation at his mother's face. In his whole life, he'd only seen his mother look that anxious once before.

"Heard about what?" Sam asked.

"Fern!" Mrs. McAllister responded, anguished.

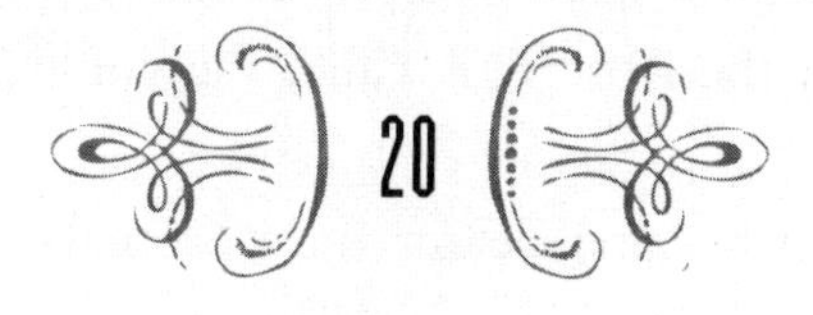

naptime

Fern was being prodded. One sharp jab to the ribs followed another. She wanted to open her eyes, but was unable to. She was very cold—her body was quaking uncontrollably. She heard a voice, faintly, as if it was an echo. As she tried to place it, everything came rushing back to her: stealing the bolt cutters, meeting Haryle Laffar face-to-face for the first time, failing to rescue Miles, and the horrible wailing of the Sirens.

"Wake up!"

Fern listened more carefully to the faraway voice. She expected the gravelly twang of Haryle Laffar. But the voice was different.

"Wake up, please."

The lights around Fern slowly brightened. She began to see the fuzzy outlines of things. She blinked her eyes rapidly, as if willing her sight to return. A large white object came into focus in front of her. She felt another sharp jab to the ribs. This time, she could hear herself groan.

The object became clearer and clearer. Fern realized it was a white marble pillar, with the circumference of a large sequoia tree. She shifted her eyes to the left and saw several white marble columns, all in a row. Had she transported to some kind of temple?

Gathering her wits about her, she realized that she was elevated—on some sort of platform. She looked down and saw more white marble. There was a sharp incline below where her head rested—as though she was perched on the edge of a white marble cliff.

Fern was still shivering.

She flipped her body over, attempting to move away from the ledge. When she saw the huge eyes looking at her, Fern let out a gasp.

She had seen this face hundreds of times before. His beard and elongated countenance remained unchanged. Staring down at her was the famous marble gaze of the sixteenth president—Abraham Lincoln. She reassessed her surroundings and realized that somehow she had teleported right onto the lap of Honest Abe in the Lincoln Memorial.

Fern was shocked by how high she was, suspended on the legs of the supersize Lincoln. "Are you okay?" a voice below her said. "How did you get up there?" Fern peered over Lincoln's knees. Standing at the base of the president's magnificent chair, a uniformed policeman looked up at Fern. He'd stretched his arm toward her but could barely reach her, even with his baton fully extended above him. That explained the pokes to the ribs, Fern thought. She slowly rose to her knees, carefully maintaining her balance. The last thing she wanted to do was crack her head open as she tumbled out of Lincoln's lap and onto the marble base of the memorial.

"I'm not sure," Fern said, finally responding to the officer.

"Well, let's get you safely down, all right?" Fern sensed the concern in the officer's voice. She knew from watching television that there were two kinds of cops—the aggressive ones who threw people in jail first and asked questions later, and the friendly ones who wanted to help people whenever possible. She only hoped that this one was not the throw-you-in-jail type. She spotted the velvet rope that surrounded the statue and remembered the signs posted everywhere warning tourists not to cross the rope. Though Fern technically had not "crossed" the red velvet rope because she'd teleported there, she was certain this explanation would not satisfy the Capitol police officer beckoning her down from Lincoln's lap.

She was still in a state of disbelief. At the time her mind had gone blank and then black, she'd been trapped in a cage with Miles at the mercy of Laffar. Thoughts of the Lincoln Memorial must have entered her mind at the last possible moment. It wasn't the most convenient spot to land in DC, but it was certainly preferable to listening to the Sirens' cries and being immobilized inside a cage.

She had escaped.

Now she needed to get out of this mess and regroup with Sam and company to figure out how to rescue Miles and Mr. Lin. This time, she'd accept Mrs. Lin's offer to provide some backup. It was now clear to Fern that defeating Laffar was going to be more than a one-Otherworldly job.

Fern took a moment to gaze out at the horizon from her unique vantage point. From her roost in the memorial, she could see across the Reflecting Pool to the Washington Monument. The brightly lit marble obelisk was gleaming white, a sentinel against the District's dark midnight skies.

"I want you to rotate so that your stomach is flat against the statue. Then dangle your legs over the edge and slowly lower yourself down, all right?"

"All right," Fern said.

"I'm going to catch you. Don't be scared," the officer said. Fern almost let out a laugh. Sure, she was precariously balanced on a towering marble statue, but *this* was not scary. Scary was looking your murderous father—a man who didn't know you and wanted to kill you—in the eye for the first time.

Fern lowered herself slowly, gripping Lincoln's smooth marble thighs. She wished Sam had been there to see her.

It was the kind of stunt he would have loved.

She felt the officer's firm grip around her waist. He lowered her slowly to the top of the platform where Lincoln's statue rested. Seamlessly he lifted her body, lowering her to the bottom of the platform, still about five feet from the floor of the memorial. With one more step, Fern and the officer were finally on the main level again.

The officer took Fern by the hand and ducked under the red velvet rope. When they were both safely on the other side, the officer got his first good look at the girl who had miraculously scaled the Lincoln Memorial.

He would have recognized her anywhere. It was the same girl who had wandered off when the rest of her friends and family were standing in line for the Washington Monument. A girl wandering out of line was one thing, but climbing into Lincoln's lap was something that the officer had never seen in twelve years on the force.

"You seem intent on getting yourself into serious trouble, Fern," he said, noticing for the first time the strange color of the girl's eyes. Fern glanced at the man's name tag.

Officer Hallet. She cursed her bad luck.

"Good evening, Officer Hallet," Fern said politely. "So nice to see you again."

Officer Hallet remained puzzled by the girl and her predicament. Normally he loved the night shift around the Capitol. The Mall was usually empty, and Washington was never more beautiful than it was on a crisp, clear night with all the monuments and memorials shimmering under the lights. When he first saw the small dark heap on Lincoln's knees, he thought some careless tourist had launched a bag of trash onto the memorial itself. As he ran up the steps, he was shocked when he realized it wasn't a bag on Lincoln's lap but a human being. Judging by the size of the creature, he reasoned it was a young girl, apparently resting peacefully.

"Would you like to tell me what you're doing here, trespassing on government property, past any reasonable hour for someone your age, I might add, before I call this incident into the station?"

Fern looked into Officer Hallet's eyes. She could tell he was not angry. Just confused. She usually had that effect on adults who weren't aware they were living among Otherworldlies.

"I'm really sorry," Fern said, and she meant it. She was sorry that she was putting Officer Hallet in this fix. But she was afraid that if he "called the incident into the station," she'd be detained and forced to answer dozens more questions by dozens more people, while Miles and Mr. Lin remained in serious danger. What was she going to do? The officer's radio rested on his shoulder, buzzing with static every few seconds.

Fern thought carefully about her dilemma. She'd only had brief practice explaining her peculiarities in ways that Normals could understand. However, if there was one thing Fern had learned, it was that if you gave adults enough general information, they'd fill in the blanks so that everything made sense for them in precisely the way they expected it to.

"I wanted to get away for a little bit . . . so I started walking."

"From where?" Officer Hallet put his hand on Fern's back and they began descending the many steps down to the Mall level.

Fern explained that she'd walked from the Marriott in Woodley Park.

"You walked all that way? That's five miles from here!" Officer Hallet marveled at the fact that a young girl could walk such a distance alone without anyone stopping her.

"I guess that's why I was so tired. . . . I thought I would just rest on his lap," Fern said, referring to the memorial.

Officer Hallet's radio buzzed once more, and he reached up to turn the volume down.

"Does your mom or dad know where you are?" His thick eyebrows bunched together.

"No . . . I didn't want to worry my mom," Fern said with practiced innocence.

"Don't you think she'll be pretty worried when she wakes up and discovers you're missing?"

"Yes . . . but . . . I was so tired of the others making fun of me," Fern said, hanging her head.

Officer Hallet studied the girl. Her dark hair in combination with her striking pale eyes and skin gave her a nymphlike quality. Your typical thirteen-year-old probably didn't take off in the middle of the night for a five-mile stroll around the capital. This girl was different. Which probably meant she was on the receiving end of her fair share of bullying. Officer Hallet was long removed from middle school but not so far that he didn't remember what it was like to feel like an outsider. His urge to protect people like Fern was part of the reason he became a cop—he liked the notion that he would play a role in defending the defenseless.

Fern looked at Officer Hallet's face and knew that he believed her. As she had hoped he would, he had supplied his own backstory and was fully on board with Fern's explanation.

"Look," he said, removing all traces of frustration from his voice, "if we can get your mom down here to come pick you up, then we can avoid taking you to the station. Do you know how to reach her?"

Fern stopped herself from chuckling. The Commander practically slept on top of her cell phone. Given her daughter's recent history, she was clearly smart to do so.

Fern's time for rescue had come. She hesitated for a moment before reciting the Commander's cell phone number. Though she knew she wasn't being entirely rational, she wondered for a brief moment if she might not be better off taking her chances down at the police station. The Commander's questions were likely to be infinitely more difficult than anything a uniformed police officer with no knowledge of Fern's history would ask.

But becoming official Washington, DC, police business would take time, and that was the one thing Fern McAllister was short on.

"Yes, hello?" Officer Hallet said into a phone he'd produced from one of his many pouches. "Hello, Mrs. McAllister, my name is Officer Richard Hallet, and I'm with the Washington, DC, police. It seems your daughter has wandered off, and not to worry, she's perfectly safe, but I was hoping you might be able to come down here and pick her up."

Fern could hear the Commander's frantic voice on the other end of the phone. She sounded both anxious and angry. Fern knew by the time the Commander reached her, the anxiety would have receded, leaving only the anger.

Back inside the Marriott hotel lobby, Mrs. Lin struggled to recover from the news that Fern McAllister was in some kind of danger. She stared at Mary Lou, trying to read her face.

"Is Fern okay?" Mrs. Lin asked, speaking generally about Fern's condition without knowing the facts.

"She won't be when I get through with her," Mrs. McAllister responded, ignoring Sam, Lindsey, and Candace's presence in the hotel lobby.

"Where are you going?" Mrs. Lin asked, nervous that Mrs. McAllister would be suspicious of the unexplained presence of the group in the lobby and connect them to Fern's disappearance.

"I'm going to pick her up," Mrs. McAllister responded.

"Would you like company?" Mrs. Lin offered.

"No, thank you. . . . I'm going to hop in a cab. Please make sure they get back up to their rooms," she said, motioning to Sam, Lindsey, and Candace. "Fern's fine . . . but I would like some time alone with her."

Mary Lou considered the idea of asking May Lin, point-blank, what was going on with Fern—but she wasn't sure she could trust the Lins. Mrs. Lin had different priorities. Though Mary Lou realized she didn't know as much about Otherworldly affairs as Lindsey's mother, she did know her daughter, and she knew something was dreadfully wrong. Which was why, without assistance from anyone else, she was going to get to the bottom of it.

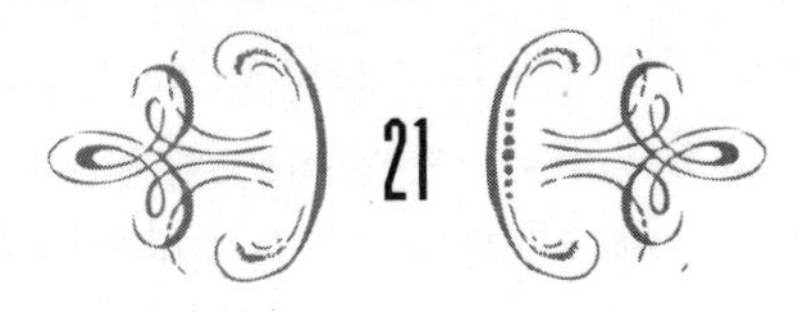

21
the ride home

Mary Lou McAllister's tone was sickeningly sweet. The last time Fern had heard her mother exude this much charm, she was flirting with their new neighbor in San Juan Capistrano, Wallace Summers.

"I can't thank you enough, Officer Hallet," the Commander gushed, taking the policeman's extended hand in both of her own. She brought his hand close to her heart. "I hate to think what might have happened if you hadn't found her!"

"I was just doing my job, ma'am," Officer Hallet responded, letting his hand linger in Mary Lou McAllister's grasp before withdrawing it.

The taxicab Mary Lou had arrived in was waiting for the McAllisters, parked with its engine still running on the side of Constitution Avenue. Mary Lou had told the driver she would be no more than a few minutes.

"Well, I'm relieved to know there are people like you left in the world," Mary Lou said in earnest. She looked over at Fern, a few feet away, shivering with her arms crossed. As usual, her daughter was underdressed.

"I better get Fern out of the cold before she catches one," Mary Lou said, "but thank you so much, again."

"Don't mention it. . . ." Officer Hallet paused. He knew it was a mistake to get any more personally involved than he already was, but the woman in front of him seemed to ooze trustworthiness and he wanted to help her. "Before you go, do you mind if I have a word with you in private?"

Mrs. McAllister looked at him quizzically. "Of course not," she answered, before commanding Fern to go to the cab and wait for her. Fern ran across the lawn that separated Constitution Avenue from the outskirts of the National Mall. Both the officer and the Commander watched Fern get into the red cab and close the door.

"Is this the first time she's run off?" Officer Hallet asked Mary Lou. Mary Lou gave the officer an uneasy smile. Fern never really just "ran off," she thought. She disappeared. Completely and instantly.

"The only reason I ask is because Fern told me she left because she was being bullied. I don't want to pry, but I thought you should be made aware of that fact."

Mary Lou thanked Officer Hallet for the information and made her way to the taxi, suddenly feeling at a loss.

Could it be as simple as normal teenage drama?

As she reached the cab, Mrs. McAllister took two fortifying lungfuls of crisp District air before climbing in next to her daughter.

Fern stared straight ahead.

Mary Lou McAllister told the cabbie to take them back to the hotel. He looked in his rearview mirror and signaled comprehension with a thumbs-up. Then he resumed his muffled conversation with someone over his cell phone earpiece. On her initial ride to the National Mall to retrieve Fern, Mrs. McAllister considered what might be going on with her daughter. She dismissed the possibility that Blythe Conrad and Lee Phillips had gotten under Fern's skin. It was possible, certainly, but Mrs. McAllister was more concerned that Blouts were somehow involved in tonight's misadventure. Had she been wrong?

Without saying a word, Mary Lou let blocks of regal gray stone government buildings zip by the windows of the cab. The downtown streets were empty. She didn't quite know what to say to her daughter.

"You told Officer Hallet you walked, but you teleported, didn't you?" The Commander's voice was flat and cold.

Fern looked out the window opposite the Commander. If only there was a printed guide that explained everything that had happened and was happening to her. Anytime someone had questions, she could hand over the guide and instruct them to read it. Fern was starting to feel like she was going to spend the rest of her life explaining herself to the people who cared about her.

"Yeah," Fern said, figuring it was only a matter of time before the Commander really laid into her.

"Why?"

Perhaps the most frustrating thing, Fern realized, was that lying was fairly useless. The Commander's lie detector was infallible—and she wouldn't stop until she was satisfied.

"If I tell you everything, you're going to get upset and you're going to try to stop me . . . and . . . I won't stop . . . I can't." All at once, Fern felt a lump form in her throat. In her mind, images of a caged Miles and a bruised Mr. Lin flashed. The tears were coming.

She couldn't cry. It would only make everything worse. Fern was convinced she was in for a stern lecture from her mother.

Silence filled the cab. A minute ticked slowly by.

"Can I ask you a question, Fern?"

Fern was puzzled. The Commander had never once asked her permission to pose a question. Wondering what was going through her mother's mind, Fern carefully studied her face. Even in the dim light of the cab, the Commander's eyes looked tired, no doubt from the worry Fern had caused her tonight.

"Sure," Fern responded.

"I know I haven't done everything perfectly, or even close to it, throughout this whole situation, but have I ever been unreasonable when you told me the truth? Have I ever made you doubt that I won't make every effort to try to understand what you're going through?" The Commander paused, and Fern could tell her voice was about to crack. "Since I found out the truth about you being an Otherworldly, have I done a single thing to make you doubt that I have your best interests at heart?"

Fern didn't have to think about it. The Commander had been on her side from the beginning. She never blamed Fern once. Some mothers might have snapped or resented a child like Fern for presenting so many difficulties and challenges. The Commander, though, had shown more patience and understanding than Fern probably deserved.

"No," Fern said, turning away from the window, finally facing her mother. "I think that if I tell you everything, it'll only worry you."

"Fern, I'm already worried!" the Commander insisted. "I only want to know what I should be worried about."

The Commander looked at Fern so sympathetically that her compassion broke the barrier of restraint Fern had built between them. Hot, salty drops fell from Fern's eyes and down her cheeks. She tried to swipe them away with the back of her hands, but the old tears were replaced by new ones as quickly as she could wipe them away.

It wasn't only one thing that had brought on Fern's tears: She was crying for Miles Zapo, her new friend, brutalized and trapped in a cage; she was crying for the female members of the Lin family, who were probably sick with worry; the tears fell for Aunt Chan, who only wanted Miles returned safely to her; they fell at the revelation that her mysterious father had turned out to be a murderer—not only that, but he wanted her dead; and they fell for Fern herself and the weight she now constantly carried on her shoulders.

Mrs. McAllister slid over to the middle seat. She wrapped Fern in her sweat-suited arms.

"Honey, it's going to be all right." Fern let her mother hug her for a few moments and then backed away from the embrace.

"How do you know that?" Fern asked, her voice laden with the rush of emotion.

"I just do, okay? Now why don't you tell me what's going on."

Fern took a few breaths.

"You know the voice I heard when I was in the ocean, when I froze Vlad on the beach?"

"Yes," the Commander answered. She usually preferred to sweep that incident from her thoughts—she hated the idea that her daughter had almost died and that she'd been unable to stop it.

"Well, I was hearing the voice of another Otherworldly. A second Unusual. His name is Miles Zapo."

"Another Unusual?" The Commander glanced up front at the taxi driver. He was still jabbering on his cell phone headset. It was safe to talk openly. "Are you sure?"

"Yeah. . . . I first saw him in a dream. He was locked in

a cage in some basement. I wanted to know more, so three nights ago I teleported to the place from my dream. He was really there."

"Why doesn't he teleport out of there then? Does he have the ability?"

"Yes, but there are these monsters that zap his powers. He's in a daze most of the time."

The Commander's expression was blank. Fern couldn't tell how she was taking it.

"Anyway, last night I went to visit his aunt in Minnesota to find out more about him. He told me to see her. Together we figured out that the man who's keeping Miles locked up is trying to gather all the ingredients for a potion that will give him immortality. . . . He's the one who stole the Hope Diamond."

"But why is he holding this other Unusual child prisoner? What's in it for him?"

"Miles has special talents, like me, beyond teleporting. He can turn objects and himself invisible . . . which, if you think about it, is the perfect talent for stealing valuables from a museum."

"I'll say," the Commander said.

"Mom?" Fern said, gathering strength for her next revelation.

"Yes, honey?"

"The man keeping Miles prisoner . . . who wants to make the potion . . ." Fern paused. "I'm pretty sure he's my father."

"Haryle!" the Commander shouted with a gasp.

"You know his name?" Fern asked, somewhat shocked. *So the Commander had heard of the evil Blout.*

"You're not the only one who's read Phoebe's letters dozens of times." The Commander became more distant. "I've always thought he was responsible for the bad turn Phoebe's life took near the end."

"Why didn't you ever tell me that?" Fern asked accusingly.

"I was never positive. And why would I burden you with information like that when I couldn't be sure?"

Fern thought about the Commander's words. As much as she wanted someone to blame, Fern knew she'd have done the same thing in her mother's position.

"Well, according to Mrs. Lin, he never knew that Phoebe had a daughter. He doesn't know that I exist," Fern added. She left out the part about Haryle Laffar wanting to kill her as revenge for what she had done to his brother Vlad. The Commander already had enough information to digest for one cab ride.

"I'm sorry, Fern. What a horrible thing to discover," she said. "Wait. Mrs. Lin told you?"

Fern winced as she thought about how she'd deliberately kept the Commander out of the conversation with Mrs. Lin. She moved on quickly so she wouldn't have to think about her own guilty feelings.

"He's planning to steal the last ingredient tomorrow, and I think he may hurt Miles after he's done using him."

"Do you know where Haryle Laffar is keeping Miles? Can you get there on foot, without teleporting?" the Commander asked.

"He's keeping him underneath an exhibit at the National Zoo."

"Well we've got to tell the Alliance and get Alistair and some of the others on their way to rescue the boy."

"We can't tell anyone," Fern said in a low voice.

"What do you mean we can't tell anyone? You can't be expected to take care of this on your own!" the Commander insisted. "What about the Lins?"

"Mr. Lin was already captured trying to rescue Miles. He's down there with him," Fern explained.

Mary Lou gasped at this additional disclosure.

"Well, that proves it's far too dangerous to attempt a rescue on your own!" The Commander realized she was shouting. The cabbie glanced up at his rearview mirror, and she smiled at him.

"I *have* to go. If Laffar gets that potion to work, he'll be after every single Unusual, including me."

"Fern, this is insanity. You're thirteen years old, for pete's sake."

"I won't be able to live with myself. . . . I have to at least try to stop him . . . try to rescue Miles. This is what I'm *supposed* to do. Don't you understand?"

Mary Lou McAllister didn't understand at all. She tried, but sometimes she recognized she would never fully comprehend her daughter. How could she? Fern had already experienced things Mary Lou couldn't begin to imagine. She put both her hands to her face and began to rub. She thought of Phoebe's letters. She had read them and reread them countless times. Over the years, Mary Lou had come to realize that the biggest reason her best friend had fled San Juan Capistrano was because she felt alone and isolated—Phoebe believed there was nobody in the world who understood her. Mary Lou was not about to let that happen to her daughter . . . to their daughter.

She forced the words out of her mouth.

"What can I do to help you?"

"You're going to *help* me?"

"Fern," the Commander said earnestly, shifting in her seat so that her knees were touching her daughter's. "We're in uncharted territory here, kiddo." The Commander put her hand on Fern's shoulder. "Believe it or not, there is no parenting book on dealing with a teenager who vampires think is some fulfillment of a centuries-old prophecy, or one who seems to have terrible people looking for her and who has an evil father out there kidnapping children, or one who can disappear and move water with her mind—"

"I forgot to tell you, I can move objects now. Telekinesis."

The Commander opened her mouth. "Really?"

"I'm not sure I can move water anymore, but I kind of moved a full bottle of Coke across the room and dumped it on Blythe and Lee," Fern said sheepishly.

"I'll bet they weren't very happy about that," the Commander said, grinning.

"Not really, no," Fern said.

"Were you responsible for the food fight?" Though the Commander's question sounded like an accusation, Fern could tell by the tone of her mother's voice that it wasn't meant to be one.

"No, Blythe and Lee started it. But Sam and Lindsey did nail them afterward in retaliation. With entire vats of ketchup and mayo."

The Commander brought her hand to her mouth to stifle a laugh. She shook her head in disbelief. "Sam would eat his own hat if it meant saving you pain."

"I know," Fern said.

"We all would, Fern. My point is . . . I want to help you in any way I can. Besides, what else am I going to do? Ground you? You'd just teleport wherever you wanted anyhow."

The Commander was right. Fern had already made up her mind. Tomorrow (which had technically already arrived, since it was now after midnight), she would figure out a way to rescue Mr. Lin and Miles and stop Laffar.

The cab stopped in front of the Woodley Park Marriott. Fern got out first while the Commander paid the fare. The temperature outside was frigid—it had dropped several more degrees since they'd left the Lincoln Memorial. She blew on her hands, which reminded her of playing the harmonica. The memory of it as it floated before being snatched out of the air by Laffar bothered her. She dreaded telling Preston that she'd lost it. Jamming her hands deep into her pockets, her left hand felt something. She pulled it out. It was a folded piece of paper. She unfolded it. Messy handwriting covered the top half.

Meet me in the lobby at six a.m. tomorrow.
I need to show you something.

Fern scrutinized the note for a moment. Out of the corner of her eye, she saw the Commander scooting across the seat toward the cab's open door. Quickly she refolded the note and placed it back in her pocket—she'd revealed enough for the time being.

Still, Fern couldn't stop thinking about the strange message as she and her mother crossed the lobby and rode up in the elevator to their seventh-floor rooms.

When could someone have slipped it in her pocket? Why wasn't it signed? At first she suspected Candace. But Candace roomed with her and could talk to her anytime. Lindsey Lin was the most likely candidate. After all, the last time Fern had received a note like that, it had floated in through the window of her bedroom in San Juan. Lindsey had thrown it there because she wanted to confirm her suspicions that Fern was an Otherworldly, just like Lindsey was herself.

In the back of Fern's mind, an alarm went off. There was the possibility that it was a trap. Maybe Laffar knew where Fern was staying and had slipped the note in Fern's pocket in order to lure her somewhere.

The Commander walked Fern all the way to her room and wrapped her daughter up in a tight hug before saying good night.

As soon as Fern opened the door to her dark room, she could hear the uneven snores of Blythe and Lee. Suddenly the snores were interspersed with the pitter-patter of quick footsteps.

Candace Tutter jumped out of bed and surged toward the opening door. Upon spotting Fern's backlit outline against the light of the hallway, she jumped forward, throwing her arms around her friend.

Both girls tumbled to the floor in a pile. They slammed into the half-open door, closing it with the force of impact.

"You're okay!" Candace whisper-shouted into Fern's ears. Their limbs were tangled together.

"Yeah, Candace, I'm okay." Fern let out a muffled laugh. Only Candace would sneak up on Fern in the darkness and tackle her—all because she was glad her friend was safe.

"What happened? Did you see Laffar? Is Miles okay?"

Fern tried to lift herself up, but Candace's body was on top of her legs.

"Everybody's all right," Fern whispered, untangling herself from Candace and getting up. "But we shouldn't talk now. Lee and Blythe can't know I've been gone."

Candace got to her feet too. She ran back to the bed she

and Fern shared, and Fern followed, collapsing on her side. Candace fell asleep shortly, and Fern could hear the soft breaths as her chest rose and fell in perfect rhythm.

Fern looked at the alarm. Though she set it for five forty-five a.m., she wasn't positive she would keep the appointment with whoever had slipped her that note. Deciding she would make a game-time decision in the morning, she fell into a shallow and restless sleep, waiting for what the morning would bring.

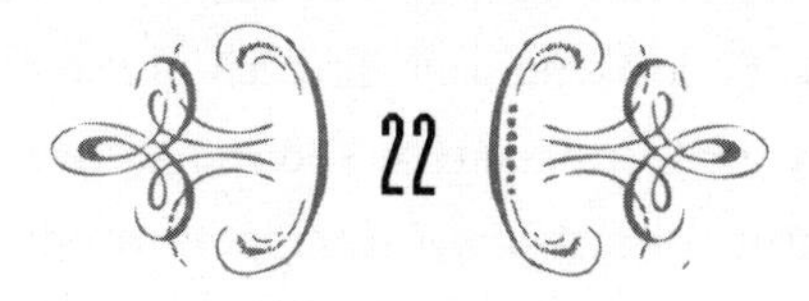

22 answers

As soon as the alarm rang at five forty-five a.m., Fern slammed her wrist on the snooze bar and then turned the alarm off completely.

"I'm gonna take a shower," Fern said to Candace, half-awake. Candace rolled back over, taking Fern at her word.

Fern had fallen asleep in her jeans and jacket and felt listless and dirty. She went into the bathroom and started the shower running. She debated with herself whether or not to meet the note sender in the lobby. The students on the St. Gregory's DC trip had a later start than usual this morning—they weren't due in the lobby, in single-file lines behind their group leaders, until seven thirty a.m.—so there was time. The more she thought about it, the more she knew that there was no way she could resist the temptation. Yes, there was a chance that it was Laffar or some other dangerous person, but the lobby was a very public place. Someone couldn't kidnap her with two hotel desk attendants looking on. She thought about telling Sam, Lindsey, or Candace that she was going down to the lobby, so that if something *did* happen to her, they would know. But if she alerted them, they would only insist on accompanying her.

She stepped out of the bathroom and closed the door. Silently she opened the door to the hallway and guided it shut behind her. Now that her grogginess had worn off, her nervousness reignited. Fern pushed the button for the lobby. She counted each floor as the elevator descended. 6. 5. 4. 3. 2.

The lobby was empty, and Fern crept along the edge of the large space, hoping no one would notice her moving toward the left corner, which offered a vantage point of the entire room.

At first she didn't see a soul. But when she rescanned the room, she noticed someone, sitting in one of the chairs on the right side of the lobby, next to the hotel's large revolving door.

Fern moved quickly toward the chair.

"Sam?"

The towheaded boy stood up and turned around. He was wearing his snow jacket and blue corduroy pants, already dressed for the day. His hair was still damp from a recent shower. He had a backpack, which he swung over his shoulder when he stood up.

"You're early," Sam remarked. "I wasn't watching for you yet . . . because you're never early."

Fern was very relieved it was only her twin brother waiting for her in the Marriott lobby, but she was also surprised.

"Who wrote the note? It's not your handwriting."

"I wrote it with my left hand so you wouldn't know."

"What's with all the secrecy? Why didn't you just tell me that you wanted to talk or something?"

"Believe it or not, Fern, with mini-girl-genius and the Lins constantly around, it's kinda hard to get any alone time with you."

Sam had a point. Whether it was walking home from school or doing their homework, the twins normally spent many hours together, just the two of them. Yet since they'd landed in DC, Fern couldn't recall a single conversation they'd had where someone else wasn't nearby.

"Well, what is it?" Fern asked. Sam wasn't one for drumming up drama with secret meetings.

"We can't talk here," he said, his face darkening. "Follow me."

"Tell me what's going on first," Fern said impatiently, grabbing her brother's arm.

"There's something about the potion you don't know," Sam said. His face contorted into a pained look.

"What are you even *talking* about?" Fern was confused by Sam's odd behavior.

"Fern, if Laffar gets all the ingredients to the potion, he is going to *kill* Miles."

Fern's jaw hung open.

"Are you crazy? How do you even know that?"

"Not here," Sam said, raising his voice and then clenching his teeth. He began walking toward the western wing of the hotel. Unless she wanted to create a scene in front of the two desk clerks, Fern had no choice but to follow her brother.

Fern couldn't take her eyes off the leather-bound volume. It was the most expensive-looking book she'd ever seen. The cover was shiny red, and the title shone in engraved gold letters on both the cover and spine: *The Undead Sea Scroll, 287th ed.*

After Sam finished grilling his sister about her run-in with Haryle Laffar, he had placed the book on the table in front of them.

"Where'd you get this, Sam?"

Fern was sitting next to her twin brother in a padded office chair behind the closed doors of the Woodley Park Marriott's business center. They were alone. The three computers were all in sleep mode.

"On eBay," Sam responded, laughing a bit nervously. Fern still couldn't get over the fact that Sam had produced a copy of *The Undead Sea Scroll* out of his backpack—there were less than a hundred in existence, and it was one of the Rollens' most secretive texts. Supposedly, it detailed what was known and rumored about every fact and myth throughout the history of the Otherworldlies.

It was like an encyclopedia explaining Rollen secrets. It was from *The Undead Sea Scroll* that Fern had first learned about the prophecy surrounding the Unusual Eleven.

"This isn't funny! You stole it from the Lins, didn't you?" Fern accused.

"Lower your voice, Fern. We don't need someone coming in here to check on us." He paused and then began flipping through the large volume. "Who cares where I got it from?"

The print was so tiny, it almost required a magnifying glass to read it. Sam flipped through entries on Giants, Ogres, and Cyclopes. He turned the gold-lined pages until he finally came to the one he wanted.

"If someone finds out that you were the one who took it, you could get in big trouble. They'll send you to—"

"They're not going to send me anywhere, because they're not going to find out!" Sam insisted. "Unless you go telling them."

Fern ignored Sam's passive-aggressive accusation.

"Why didn't you ask to see it, Sam? Stealing isn't like you," Fern said. "The Lins probably would have shown it to you. They are our friends."

Fern was inexplicably saddened by the fact that her brother had stolen the Scroll.

"Lindsey's our friend, sure. But Mr. and Mrs. Lin?" Sam questioned, his voice hardening by the second. "We don't really know much about them. They're your friends *now*, while it's still convenient for them. But beyond that, who knows?"

"Why did you bring it here, to DC? And why steal it at all?"

Sam swiveled his chair to face his sister, stopping his half spin by slamming his arm on the computer desk.

"I did this for *you*, Fern! You have all this pressure on you, and all these people are after you . . . they want to control you, and no one really ever *tells* you anything. Doesn't it drive you crazy?"

Fern nervously bit her lip, checking the glass pane in the middle of the business center door. There was no one there.

"Look, Sam, I want to know everything too, but the world doesn't work like that." She almost felt sorry for her brother. Sure, the uncertainty of her life was maddening. It seemed like one unbelievable revelation followed another and she never knew what crazy thing would happen next. But sneaking into the Lins' house and stealing something that belonged to them, when he had no reason to believe that the Lins were anything but allies, was wrong. It was desperate.

"Well, I'm not going to keep it. I brought it here because I wanted to read the whole thing before I gave it back. And I'm glad I did!" Sam pointed to a bold subject heading in the middle of the page, titled Everlasting Elixir. Fern began to read:

INGREDIENTS: Though not much is known about the Everlasting Elixir, rumors about the magical potion appear to have originated from a southern clan of Otherworldlies, who lived primarily in the Americas. The ingredients have been the subject of much speculation, but the feather of a Siren is believed to be a key ingredient, as well as the golden tip of a famous warrior deity's arrow. Some scholars theorize that the ingredients are being kept in the northeastern part of the Americas.

POTENTIAL EFFECTS: The Everlasting Elixir, if created with the right ingredients, will provide any person who drinks it with immortality. Additionally, some hypothesize that the Elixir, if mixed with the blood of an Unusual, will cause a transference of powers from the Unusual whose blood is taken to the drinker of the potion. The Unusual whose blood is used will, according to most estimates, expire.

Fern's eyes hung on the word "expire." She repeated it out loud.

"You're not misreading it, Fern . . . expire as in dead." Sam closed the book. "Which means that if the Everlasting Elixir is the same thing as the Ah Puch Potion—I think we both know it is—and Laffar knows that the potion can transfer powers, he's probably going to use Miles for his teleportation and invisibility powers; then he's going to use the potion to make himself as powerful as an Unusual.

And he's going to kill Miles in the process."

"When I tried to rescue Miles and Mr. Lin, he closed me in the cage too!" Fern marveled, terrified. "He's going to get the last ingredient tonight, and he was probably hoping he'd be able to transfer *both* our powers."

"And kill you both," Sam added, wide-eyed.

"But how do we know *The Undead Sea Scroll* is right about the potion?" Fern said, her mind doubling back.

"We don't. But wouldn't you rather know it's a possibility than not know anything?"

Fern's empty stomach rumbled. The stakes for stopping Laffar from obtaining the last ingredient of the potion had been raised dramatically. Fern began to panic, wondering what the last ingredient was. *The Undead Sea Scroll* offered no guidance at all.

Sam was the first to hear someone slipping a keycard into the business center's door. He hurriedly grabbed *The Undead Sea Scroll* from the desk and slid it into his open backpack.

Fern spun around. Ralph Mooney stared through the door's glass window at the McAllister twins. He grinned as if he'd just shot his first buck of hunting season.

The door swung open and Headmaster Mooney walked in. He was wearing a fanny pack, Dockers, and a white T-shirt, stretched tightly over his large belly, with FBI written in large block letters. Headmaster Mooney had purchased three of the shirts for ten dollars at a stall in the mall, and Fern thought it might have been better had he sprung for the fifteen-dollar XXL sweatshirt.

"And what, might I ask, are you two doing up at this hour?"

"Nothing," Sam said, clutching his backpack close to him.

"It sure doesn't look like nothing," Headmaster Mooney said, fiddling with the end of his walruslike mustache. The fluorescent lights on the ceiling made the top of the headmaster's bald head shine like a bike reflector.

"Well, it is," Sam said, this time more defiant.

"Did you let anyone know where you were?" Headmaster Mooney asked. The first thing Ralph Mooney thought of when he came upon the McAllister twins in the business center was that he'd caught them breaking curfew. But technically, there was no rule about how early you could wake up for breakfast. Still, he figured they were at least breaking Rule Seven of the St. Gregory's Spring Break Trip Regulations. They had failed to let their group leader know where they were.

"We didn't go anywhere. We came down here to talk before breakfast."

"Now, we both know that's not true. You are expected to remain in your rooms until the appropriate meeting time," Headmaster Mooney said. "It's only six fifteen now, which leaves well over an hour until we're supposed to meet in the lobby."

Headmaster Mooney scrutinized the brother and sister. They were both fully dressed. He began to think that there was something else going on.

"What did you put in your backpack just now?"

"Huh?" Sam said, playing dumb.

"When I came into the room, there was something on the table there," Headmaster Mooney said, pointing to where *The Undead Sea Scroll* had been resting. "Where is it?"

"Where is what?"

"Please give me your backpack."

"What?"

Headmaster Mooney lunged at Sam and yanked the bag out of his hands.

"Hey!" Fern yelled. "You can't take that from him!"

"Oh, really?" Headmaster Mooney said, stepping back toward the door while he reached into the bag. "And why not?"

He pulled out *The Undead Sea Scroll.* Sam's and Fern's eyes bulged out of their sockets.

"What have we here?" Headmaster Mooney palmed the book with one hand. He looked at the binding and figured it had to do with some role-playing game the students at St. Gregory's were enthused about. "I'm afraid that I'm going to have to investigate this a little further." Headmaster Mooney tossed Sam's backpack at him. Sam caught it and stared inside its now empty large compartment.

Fern and Sam were at a loss for words as they watched Headmaster Mooney take the Rollens' most sacred text and casually put it under his arm. As he pulled the door open, he turned around and faced the twins.

"Oh, and you better head directly to your rooms. When everyone meets at seven thirty, I'll deal with you then. But I wouldn't expect to leave this hotel today."

And with that, Headmaster Mooney left the twins sitting alone in stunned silence in the Marriot business center.

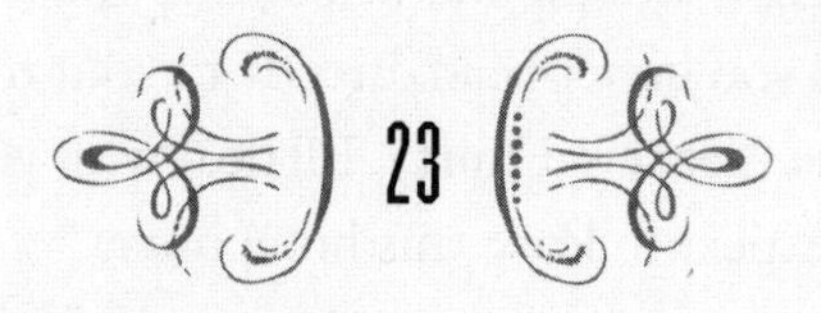

23

fern mcallister's day off

Despite wanting to remain in the business center, Sam and Fern couldn't linger there any longer. Headmaster Mooney was waiting for them outside in order to verify that the McAllister twins were heading back to their rooms. He went so far as to ride the elevator up to the seventh floor with them. When Fern opened the door to room 723, Candace Tutter was waiting for her, sitting cross-legged, clearly sulking. As soon as the door opened, she got up.

"I thought you were going to stop lying to me," Candace reproached her. She scrunched her small eyes and nose together, making an angry face.

"Sorry, Candace. I had to talk to Sam," Fern said, already low on patience after the Mooney debacle.

Candace was tempted to ask a follow-up question, but

she knew Blythe and Lee were only a few feet away, digging through their respective suitcases in search of something to wear.

"Where were you?" Blythe said, craning her neck to look at Fern.

"Out. Don't bother telling Mooney on me," Fern said, blowing past Blythe into the middle of the room. "He already knows."

Blythe and Lee continued to stare at Fern as she rifled through her things to find a clean shirt. A few days ago, the blond twosome would have bullied her into revealing more details, but after the ketchup and mayo shower and their fall from grace, they were feeling decidedly less inclined to test the limits of their power over Fern.

Before long, it was time to gather in the hotel lobby. Fern scrambled to change and splashed some water on her face. Blythe and Lee still refused to ride in the same elevator with their roommates, but this time they opted to let Candace and Fern take the first one. Fern quickly filled Candace in on the recent developments, and Candace responded as she always did . . . with an endless string of questions.

Fern tried to answer them all by the time the twosome reached the lobby, but it was simply impossible.

As they stepped into the lobby, Candace turned to Fern.

"Tonight we have to find a way to rescue Miles before . . . *he* completes the potion." Candace's eyes teared up as she thought of Miles's situation. An outsider would not have guessed that Candace Tutter had never met Miles. Fern was getting used to her new friend's unpredictable empathy.

"We need to know what that last ingredient is," Fern said.

"Is there anything to go on other than what Miles's aunt showed you in that weird book of hers?" Candace asked while searching for Mrs. Phillips so that she and Fern could properly line up.

"No," Fern answered.

"Well, we have all day to brainstorm, right?" Candace said, already beginning to sort through the possibilities in her head.

Headmaster Mooney cleared his throat to announce his presence to the girls.

"Fern, I've thought about it. . . ."

Fern and Candace both whipped around. Headmaster Mooney stood close behind them, with his hands on his hips. He began talking once he realized he had gotten Fern's attention.

"I'm afraid that if I let you and your brother escape any kind of punishment, it would set a horrible precedent."

"A horrible what?"

"A precedent . . . a standard," Headmaster Mooney explained, all the while wondering if a St. Gregory's education was still all it was cracked up to be. "My point is that I'm afraid you and Sam are both suspended from the day's activities. You will not leave your hotel rooms."

"What?" Fern said. "But we weren't even do—"

"I don't want to hear another word. Perhaps next time you'll reconsider when you make a plan to sneak out."

"At least give Sam his book back," Fern insisted.

"*What* book?" Headmaster Mooney asked with counterfeit innocence. Fern could tell Mooney was enjoying messing with her.

"Mr. Billing will be here momentarily to make sure you go straight back to your rooms. At noon, someone will bring you a brown-bag lunch."

Fern shook her head in disgust.

"And Fern," Headmaster Mooney said, resting both hands on his protruding gut, "I'm sure the thought hasn't crossed your mind, but don't even think about leaving your room. There's only one way out of this hotel, and I've instructed all the employees at the front desk to notify me immediately if they spot either you or Sam in the lobby. Now you'll have to excuse me. I have to go deliver the news to your brother."

Candace scowled at the back of Headmaster Mooney's bald head.

"That man has it in for you," she said.

Fern smirked. "It doesn't even take a genius to figure that one out, Candace."

Fern watched her brother's face contort into an expression of anger as Headmaster Mooney told him about their daylong suspension.

Before Mr. Billing came to collect Fern, she handed

Candace the list of ingredients she'd scribbled down while at Aunt Chan's house.

"Find Lindsey and see if you can come up with the missing ingredient. . . . We don't have a lot of time." Candace folded her fingers around the wrinkled piece of paper just as Fern was led off to her hotel room "cell" by Mr. Billing.

Fern awoke with a start. The ringing phone had jolted her out of a shallow slumber. She quickly remembered she was back in room 723, serving her sentence.

When Fern had first gotten back to her hotel room, she'd thought about taking a shower, but as soon as she laid eyes on her unmade hotel bed, she couldn't resist plopping down. The sleepless, teleporting nights were taking their toll.

She tried not to sound groggy as she answered the phone. "Hello?"

"This totally stinks."

It was Sam. Fern laughed and checked the clock. It was eight in the morning. Fern had been asleep for only half an hour.

"Oh, I don't know. I think we picked a good day to sit out. Weren't you complaining about going to the Bureau of Engraving and Printing and the National Museum of the American Indian?"

"Maybe we should try to break into Mooney's room and get my book back!" Sam raised his voice at the thought of a new caper.

"Don't you mean the *Lins'* book?" Fern asked sarcastically. "Anyway, even if Mooney does read it, he'll think it's all a bunch of nonsense."

"Have you figured out what the final ingredient is or where it might be?"

"No. You?"

"No." Sam paused. "You should go back to sleep. Maybe something will come to you after you've had some rest."

"How did you know I've been sleeping?"

"Um, I've lived with you for the last thirteen years, Fern. Your voice sounds like it's got sand in it when you first wake up."

"Oh," Fern said.

"I'll call you in a little while."

Fern hung up the phone and closed her eyes. She knew she should be developing a plan to try to stay one step ahead of Laffar. But lack of sleep soon overcame her thoughts, and she passed into a state of deep slumber.

When she woke up again, she felt cold sweat on her forehead. She'd been dreaming of Haryle Laffar. She'd dreamt she'd been in a room and witnessed Laffar kill her mother. In the dream, Phoebe looked a lot like a grown-up version of Fern herself.

There was a knock at the door. Fern rubbed her eyes and got up. She opened the door.

"Preston?"

Preston Buss stood in front of her. He stuck out a brown bag and smiled at Fern.

"Your lunch, compliments of St. Gregory's."

Preston was wearing dark jeans, an American Apparel hoodie, and a dark corduroy blazer. Fern took one look at him and was immediately self-conscious about her disheveled state.

"What are you doing here?"

"I said I was sick and rode back with Mr. Billing. He said I could deliver your lunch before going back to my room to rest."

Without waiting to be invited in, Preston stepped through the doorway. Fern backed up to give him room.

"For girls, your room is pretty messy," Preston said, looking around. Fern had to agree. It was almost as if a tornado had transported the entire contents of Blythe's and Lee's closets to Washington and then dumped them all over the hotel room. There was little visual evidence that she and Candace even resided here.

"You don't seem sick," Fern said, playfully furrowing her brow.

"Oh, I'm not really."

"Then why did you come back here? Shouldn't you be learning all about how money is printed with the rest of the school?"

Preston put his hand on top of his head and tousled his dark hair. Fern could see his cheeks redden slightly before he answered.

"I guess. I don't know. I heard you were sick so I thought I'd say hi."

Fern felt a surge of guilt.

"Preston, I lost your harmonica," Fern blurted.

"You what?" Preston said. Fern studied his face to see if he was angry.

"I didn't lose it, I mean to say that I left it in my mom's room, so I can't give it back to you right now."

"No problem . . . but that reminds me," Preston said, sticking his hand inside his blazer pocket. He pulled out a shiny object.

It was another harmonica. Preston handed it to Fern. It had WASHINGTON, DC engraved on its top. "I saw this at the souvenir shop and thought you should have one of your own. You can give mine back whenever."

The guilt overwhelmed Fern. She vowed she would recover Preston's harmonica somehow, when she'd freed Miles and Mr. Lin. The worries over whether she'd unearth the last ingredient in time consumed every other thought. Because Laffar was her father, Fern was beginning to feel like stopping him was her responsibility—that fate had designated her the only person who could.

Fern slipped the harmonica into her sweatshirt pocket.

"Thank you," she said. "For the lunch and the harmonica."

"No problem," Preston said. "I better get back to my room. Mr. Billing said he was going to check on me in a few minutes."

"If you're missing, he'll probably think I kidnapped you or something."

Fern stood by the door and listened to Preston's

footsteps fade. She was thankful for his gift because she would need it to silence the Sirens, but she also was no closer to solving the puzzle of the potion. Fern felt her heart sink under the monumental weight of the responsibilities she'd undertaken.

Her last hope was that Candace Tutter had solved the riddle of the potion, a solution that so far had eluded Fern.

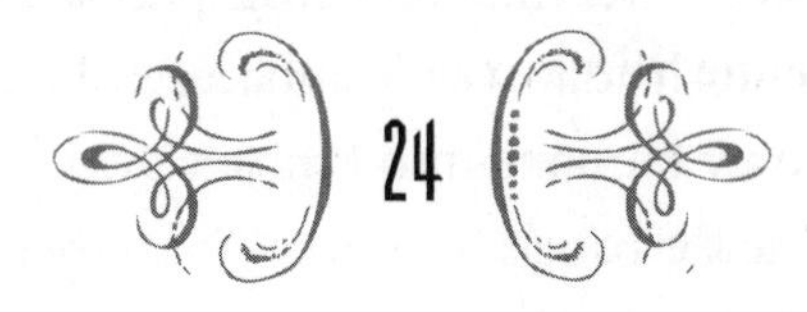

24 the essence of ix chel

Lindsey Lin was close to strangling Candace Tutter. Fern had told Lindsey that morning over the phone that Candace knew everything. Fern was convinced Candace might be able to help in some way. Lindsey couldn't understand why Fern had told Candace about her Unusualness, Miles, the potion, and who-knew-what-else. Revealing one's Otherworldly status was counter to everything Lindsey had been taught. If her mother hadn't been so distraught over her father's absence, Lindsey would have reported the intel leak. May Lin would come *unglued* if she knew that Fern was telling Normal middle schoolers her life story. But Lindsey didn't want to burden her mother further. In truth, though Lindsey wouldn't have ever admitted it, Candace's chatterbox tendencies were a welcome distraction from her own worries over her missing father.

Mary Eileen, Olivia, and Alexa all wondered why Lindsey had insisted after her morning phone call that she needed to spend the day with Candace. At breakfast, Candace and Lindsey bumped into Lindsey's other roommates standing in line for bagels. Candace stood there silently for a minute while Lindsey chatted with her friends, and then she cleared her throat.

"I think we should move on, Lindsey," Candace said. "We've got a lot to discuss."

Lindsey rolled her eyes and whispered to Mary Eileen that she would explain later. Once Lindsey's other friends left, Candace resumed her barrage of factoids.

In the end, Lindsey put up with Candace following her around for the day, yammering about everything under the sun as they took spots in the long line in front of the Bureau of Engraving and Printing. She honestly didn't know how Fern had tolerated Candace as her DC roommate—she was already at her wit's end. Candace had spent breakfast and the bus ride peppering Lindsey with tidbits about money and the bureau itself.

"Did you know that bills aren't made from trees? They are seventy-five percent cotton and twenty-five percent linen."

"Fascinating stuff," Lindsey said, on autopilot. She'd already learned from Candace that in addition to printing money, the Bureau of Engraving and Printing also made postage stamps, treasury bonds, and all the invitations for White House functions. Now, as the line slowly progressed, Candace sensed that Lindsey was tiring of money factoids.

She decided to move on to the more pressing matter. She reached in her jacket pocket and unearthed the slip of paper Fern had given her.

"The essence of Ix Chel," Candace read from the slip of paper. "Now, Fern said that Ix Chel was the Mayan goddess of birth. Birth . . . birth . . . death . . . life . . . Maybe something from the Natural History Museum?"

"Would you lower your voice?" Lindsey said crossly. "People might hear you."

"No one has any idea what we're talking about," Candace said, studying the line in both directions. Candace Tutter had a point. The students in front of Lindsey and Candace were playing the alphabet game and the group of boys behind them were talking about their favorite teams in the upcoming NCAA March Madness basketball tournament.

"Why don't you go back with your group?" Lindsey asked impatiently. Lindsey hoped one of the chaperones would make Candace return to her assigned group, but they all were either distracted or unworried while the students waited in line.

"Because Fern asked me to work with you to unravel the clue to the last component. She thought we would have a better chance of discovering it together."

"I work better on my own," Lindsey said. She wanted to be left alone so she could try to piece things together.

"You don't seem like you really want to solve this mystery at all," Candace said, tired of putting up with Lindsey's negative attitude.

Something inside Lindsey snapped. She grabbed Candace by the shoulders and squared them so the two girls faced each other.

"Now listen here, you little moron," Lindsey said, tightening her grip on Candace. "My father is down there in the hands of that maniac, *all right*? We haven't heard from him in two days and he may be dead for all I know. So don't you dare tell me that I don't want to find the last ingredient! Because it's *all* I think about."

If the St. Gregory's students surrounding Lindsey and Candace hadn't been paying attention to the two girls before, they certainly were now. Lindsey could feel tears forming, so she quickly jumped out of line and headed for the lobby restroom.

Olivia saw her friend streaking across the lobby and followed her. She had no idea what that twerp Candace Tutter could have said, but Lindsey never got upset for no reason.

Candace may have been a genius, but as she watched Lindsey rush to the bathroom, she felt like an idiot. She wanted to apologize immediately, but Lindsey didn't return for several minutes. Her mother had told Candace that one of the important interpersonal skills Candace needed to work on was sensitivity. Candace tried, but sometimes she felt as though people were impossible to predict. Most times, she never quite knew what would be upsetting to others. This time, though, she should have realized that Lindsey Lin's nonchalant attitude was masking her deep-seated fears about her father.

When Lindsey and Olivia stepped back in line, they joined their roommates, who were a dozen or so places ahead of Candace. Candace understood. For Candace Tutter, before this week, when she'd forged a genuine friendship with Fern McAllister, being left by herself was the status quo. She was accustomed to it. So she waited in line alone for the next hour until a tour guide led the St. Gregory's group around the bureau. Walking through the large, warehouselike building, she peered through the windows as color was added to big reams of paper. Her favorite step in the process was the last one—where the sheets of printed bills were cut. She liked watching machines slice the currency up and then bind the cash into stacks.

After the bureau tour came lunch, and Candace sat alone on one of the benches lining the grassy area of the National Mall. She picked at her tuna sandwich, unable to take her mind off offending Lindsey Lin and wondering what Fern might be doing in her room. She saw Lindsey sitting across the grassy area and could tell she was distracted. Candace didn't understand how Lindsey's roommates couldn't notice the distant look on their friend's face.

Her thoughts turned to Fern—Fern was counting on her, she knew, to determine the last ingredient, but she was no closer than when her alarm had sounded that morning. Brainstorming with Lindsey was no longer an option, but if she helped free Mr. Lin, she knew that Lindsey would easily forgive her earlier insensitivity.

The sun was shining and many of the St. Gregory's students had stripped off one of their layers of clothing, basking in the sun's warmth on the Mall's expansive grass. Instead of busing to their next stop, Headmaster Mooney decided to take advantage of the beautiful weather and walk. The students formed a single-file line and marched out, large presidential heads on sticks poking up here and there, garnering puzzled looks from fellow tourists.

The building that housed the National Museum of the American Indian was unlike the other museums they'd visited. It was constructed of sand-colored limestone and had no right angles—only curves. There was a large domed lobby and tall windows many stories high that welcomed the afternoon sun. Headmaster Mooney announced that they would have an hour and a half to wander through the museum on their own until reassembling in the museum store near the welcome desk.

Candace didn't waste any time. She took one of the pamphlets from a holder on the welcome desk and quickly scanned it.

There it was, halfway down the second panel of the brochure, as if meant for her eyes only: *Exploring Mesoamerica: The Mysteries of the Mayan Civilization.*

Candace nearly leapt in the air. She didn't want to get her hopes up, but she began to speculate that something in the exhibit would reveal a clue about the Mayan god Ix Chel.

She had to restrain herself from sprinting up to the fourth level. Now was not the time to draw unwanted attention.

She scanned the map of the fourth floor and pinpointed the location of the temporary exhibits. She raced through rooms of ancient artifacts and a hallway dedicated to Indian cowboys and cowgirls, famous for their rodeo skills. She found the enclave devoted to the mysteries of the Mayans. Each wall exhibition was spotlighted from above, but the enclave itself was dim, adding to its eerie quality. Candace felt her heart race. Her eyes darted from a wall exhibit to a glass case and then back to a booth playing an information video. The room was a treasure trove of Mayan artwork and artifacts. She studied the wall map that explained where the Mayans had lived when the civilization was at its heyday from 300 to 900 a.d. There were over five hundred Mayan cities with a total of fifteen million people inhabiting much of the Yucatán Peninsula.

Candace zoomed across the room, past a small replica of an actual Mayan temple. There were samples of Mayan texts as well as different theories discussing why the Mayan civilization declined. Historians still disagreed about the reason for the disappearance of the Mayan cities.

Candace spotted the exhibit she'd been searching for. In a corner chronicling Mayan spiritual life, there was a glass case dedicated to Mayan gods and goddesses. Candace zeroed in on the display. There were beautiful carvings and paintings of fantastic-looking gods. Under each one of them, a plaque described the god's meaning to the

Mayans and its functions. Candace studied the information, her mind processing even faster than normal as she sensed she was nearing the answer she so fervently hoped to find.

There was Itzamná, the creator god, pictured with an ornate headdress, then Chac, the rain god, and Ah Puch, the god of death. Candace recognized the name immediately—the potion's name was derived from this frightening creature. Jewels jutted from Ah Puch's forehead, and a bony spine extended down his back.

Finally, there was Ix Chel, staring unblinkingly at Candace. Candace leaned on the glass case to examine the Mayan goddess more closely, pressing her hands up against the pane. Her chest tightened. She reminded herself to breathe.

A guard moved behind Candace. He'd been watching the entire time, deciding that she was exactly the type of museum guest who didn't think the rules applied to her. "Please *do not* touch the case. If you do not remove your hand within the next few seconds, an alarm will sound."

Candace recoiled, already on edge. Closing her eyes, she calmed herself.

"Sorry, sir," Candace said, smiling submissively at the guard. Conspicuously placing her hands behind her, she stepped back slightly from the display. Ix Chel was painted in bright colors. Her headdress consisted of dozens of turquoise-colored snakes, all intertwined. Around her neck, she wore a necklace made from different-size bones.

Her eyes were shades of brilliant blue. From a distance, the snakes melted together and the necklace could have been of any composition—Ix Chel was beautiful. Candace read the description beneath the picture.

> Ix Chel, a powerful deity in Mayan culture, had many attributes. She was the goddess of childbirth, weaving, and medicine. Some historians speculate that the Mayans also viewed her as Itzamná's consort. Ix Chel's fundamental qualities and beauty were said to exist in the moon itself.

Below the plaque was a picture of Ix Chel's radiant eyes drawn inside the face of a full moon. Candace's attention converged on two words. "fundamental qualities." She unfolded the list Fern had given her. *Ix Chel's essence.* Quickly glancing back and forth from the plaque to the list, the exceptionally fast wheels inside Candace Tutter's brain began spinning. Her mind recalled all synonyms for "essence" she'd found last night, while trying to figure out what the cryptic clue could mean.

Memorizing the list had taken her only a few minutes: *basic*, *core*, *foundational*, *pivotal*, *essential*, *inherent*, *intrinsic*, and *fundamental.* Ix Chel's luminous blue eyes stared out at Candace from the face of the moon. Candace imagined them penetrating right through her.

Much like the tail end of a solar eclipse, it was as if bright light had emerged from darkness and suddenly illuminated all the pieces to the puzzle. It was so simple.

The moon itself!

The only question that remained for Candace Tutter was how quickly she could find Lindsey Lin.

They had a lot of planning to do.

"How can you be sure that Laffar is after a moon rock?" Lindsey asked doubtfully.

Candace had located Lindsey and her roommates in the gift shop, a few minutes before the St. Gregory's group was to assemble. She'd looked everywhere for her and, just when she was running out of options, found her standing between two rows of authentic Native American crafts, looking somewhat dazed. She'd asked to speak to Lindsey alone, and Lindsey had rolled her eyes and asked her roommates to give her a second.

Candace wasn't surprised by Lindsey's skepticism—she'd expected some resistance. Fortunately, the search had given Candace time to crystallize her theory.

"There's an entire exhibit on Ix Chel upstairs," Candace reported as she started to pace back and forth between the aisles. "Apparently, she's a goddess of the moon. The Mayans believed that they could see her *essence* in the night sky when they looked up at the moon!"

"Okay," Lindsey said, "but that could be a coincidence."

"The probability of all the other factors aligning in this way would be a highly unlikely outcome!" Candace insisted.

"What other factors?" Lindsey asked. She picked up a hand-sculpted clay pot and traced its pattern absentmindedly. Candace could sense that Lindsey *wanted* to be convinced that the last ingredient had finally been identified but needed more proof.

Candace dropped her backpack to the ground and searched inside its main compartment for her spiral notebook. She was sure, given her photographic memory, that she could recite the evidence she'd meticulously compiled by heart, but now was not the time to risk overlooking even the smallest detail. She flipped to the page where she'd detailed her deductive reasoning, cleared her throat, and began.

"First, we know that whatever the final article is, it is most likely located in Washington, DC. We know this because Miles is being held captive here, and Miles indicated that Laffar is going to use him to secure the last item tonight. Secondly, we now know Ix Chel's essence was thought to be the moon itself. A clear manifestation of the moon here on earth is a moon rock." Candace looked up and realized she'd already hooked Lindsey. She was listening intently. Candace continued.

"You may have known all this. But what you probably don't know is that, on Earth, moon rocks are available from only two sources. They either originate from a space mission that transported them here, or they exist in the form of a meteorite that fell to Earth.

"Now, you may be asking yourself why Mr. Laffar

would bother burglarizing a museum to get a moon rock when moon rocks that have fallen as meteorites are for sale on eBay," Candace continued, beginning to pace back and forth across the aisle. "That is a valid question, but if Mr. Laffar has gone to all this trouble acquiring the other elements, then he's going to want to make sure that the moon rock he gets is not a fake—which means one thing: He's got to get one that's verified as completely authentic. Normally, moon rocks are stored in nitrogen to keep them free from moisture. Those would be difficult for Mr. Laffar to obtain and transport for a variety of reasons. But had you been paying careful attention this week, you would have read that there is only one lunar rock in the world the public is allowed to touch. It's a four-billion-year-old sample taken from the moon's surface during the Apollo Seventeen mission in December of 1972, and it is housed at the National Museum of Air and Space." Candace swiveled and turned toward Lindsey.

"I am one hundred percent convinced," Candace concluded dramatically, "that Mr. Laffar is going to strike there tonight, in an attempt to gather a moon rock, the last substance required to formulate the Ah Puch potion!"

Truth be told, Candace Tutter was not 100 percent convinced. After all, she knew that a scientist with integrity was rarely 100 percent sure of anything. But she assured herself that her exaggeration would be forgiven, and she'd deemed the percentage of doubt in her mind to be statistically insignificant.

Though Candace had slowed her rate of speech while expounding her theory for Lindsey (her mother was constantly reminding her that effective speakers paced themselves), Lindsey still needed a moment to process all that she'd heard.

"I don't know why I didn't put it all together before," Candace added, icing the evidence cake she'd baked in front of Lindsey. "It's pretty obvious, now that I think about it."

Lindsey's almond eyes stared intently into Candace's. Perhaps she'd underestimated the girl. In that brief moment, she began to see why Fern had relied on Candace as a keeper of her most precious secret. She had all the qualities of a pint-size consigliere.

"How do you know all that stuff about moon rocks?" Lindsey asked, hoping that this was the moment when things started turning around for the Lins and they began to discover how to rescue her father.

"Space Camp. Last summer." Candace's mother thought that at a place like Space Camp her daughter would make some like-minded friends, but even among the science nerds assembled in Huntsville, Alabama, that summer, Candace Tutter stuck out.

"I'm impressed," Lindsey said.

The residual guilt from their earlier confrontation outside the Bureau of Engraving and Printing resurfaced in Candace's mind.

"I'm sorry I said you didn't care," she said. "I know that's not true."

"It's okay," Lindsey said, looking pensively at Candace. Lindsey preferred not to think too hard about her unstable emotional state when she'd taken Candace by the shoulders.

Candace struggled to fill the expanding emptiness between them, but Lindsey got there first.

"Hey . . . can I ask you a question?" she said.

"Yes," Candace responded, bracing herself.

"Why do *you* care so much about all this?"

"I'm not sure what you mean," Candace responded, put off by Lindsey's sudden earnestness.

"It's funny," Lindsey said. Her expression was both kind and thoughtful. "You'd think that we don't tell Normals about our existence because we don't want Normals knowing our secrets, but I think it's really because we're afraid Normals won't believe any of it. But you . . . you've believed everything Fern told you. You've lied for her, you've stayed up scribbling things in your notebook in order to solve the puzzle of the potion, and today I saw you running around the museum like a crazed beast." Lindsey drew her eyes away from Candace's as if she were embarrassed. "I guess I'm wondering . . . why do it? Why did you even believe Fern in the first place and why put yourself in the middle of something so dangerous? What's in it for you?"

Candace tried not to gawk at Lindsey despite her surprise at Lindsey's willingness to open up to her.

"Fern's a friend," Candace said, letting a hint of defensiveness seep into her voice. "Actually, Fern's my only friend."

Lindsey looked reflectively at Candace Tutter—there was no shame on her face. Instead Lindsey saw fiery integrity within the girl's big chestnut eyes.

"Well, thank you. For helping figure out how to get my dad back."

Lindsey's family was more tolerant than most, but even she'd been raised to mistrust all Normals. All her life, she'd kept them at arm's length. She'd been told that if Normals found out about Otherworldlies, Otherworldlies would be persecuted and perhaps exterminated. But Fern, raised by Normals, didn't harbor any preconceived notions. When Lindsey had been distracted by thoughts of her imprisoned father, Fern relied on this small girl genius. Plus, it wasn't Normals who had taken her father, but an evil Otherworldly.

"And," Lindsey began again, "Fern's lucky to have you on her side too." She smiled at Candace.

Candace had recovered from the excitement of her frenzied race around the museum and now astonishment set in. Here she was, talking to the most popular girl at St. Gregory's, using what she'd learned at Space Camp to help her new friend Fern—a real live superhero—stop her father from carrying out a murderous plot.

Though she knew it was utterly illogical and irrational, and never to be admitted by a true scientist, Candace Tutter was starting to believe in fate.

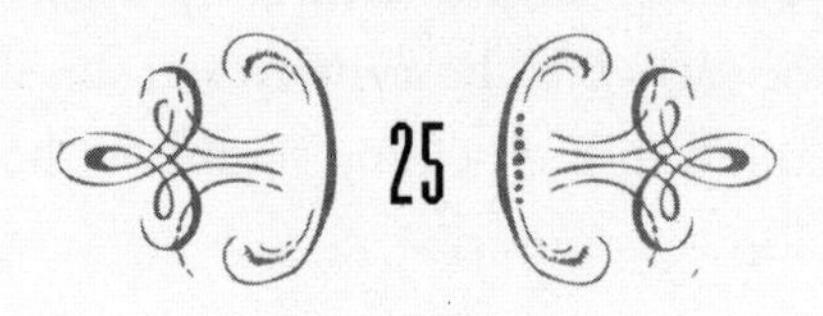

25
two plans

It's impossible to determine whether Haryle Laffar knew the names of each of the unlikely cast of characters assembled in room 754 plotting his demise, but he was certainly aware of Fern McAllister's presence there.

Mrs. McAllister had been selected to host the clandestine post-dinner meeting because her room was in a different wing of the hotel from the rest of the St. Gregory's tour group, thereby making the parade of people filing in less conspicuous. Even so, they had to wait until nine p.m. to meet for fear that an outsider might discover the gathering.

Fern wasn't surprised by the pristine condition of the Commander's room—there were no visible signs that the room had been occupied for the better part of a week. She, Lindsey, and Sam sat on the king-size bed, Mrs. Lin and the Commander took places on opposite sides of the small table by the curtained window, and Candace Tutter balanced cross-legged on a counter in the entryway, leaning against the wall.

When Candace appeared at the door with Lindsey and the McAllister twins, Mrs. Lin made no effort to conceal her displeasure. Her jaw dropped slightly, and she raised her eyebrows at the small girl.

"I'm not sure this is advisable," Mrs. Lin said, trying not to be rude as she eyed her daughter and blocked access so Candace couldn't enter the room.

"It's okay, Mom. She already knows everything, and *she's* the one who figured out the last ingredient," Lindsey said defiantly. "We may need her."

Candace wanted to jump for joy. She couldn't remember a time when she'd been *needed* by anyone.

After Fern read aloud the part of Phoebe's letter that included a description of Haryle Laffar's plan to steal the moon, all those present were convinced that the moon rock was what Laffar sought. Apparently, he'd been pursuing the Ah Puch potion for decades. After years of plotting and planning, he was on the brink of possessing everything he needed.

For the first half hour of the meeting, the six debated how to prevent Laffar from obtaining the moon rock. The first proposal involved intercepting Laffar while he was on his way to steal the rock, but the group ultimately concluded that with the Sirens under his command, Laffar would be far too powerful. It was Candace Tutter, emboldened by her recent deductive triumph, who proposed the ultimate solution.

"What if we steal the moon rock before he does?" Candace suggested from her vantage point on the ledge in the entryway. Anyone larger would have broken the ledge right off the wall, but Candace weighed less than seventy pounds.

"I hardly think grand theft is the solution to our problem," Mrs. Lin said sharply, unafraid to show her mistrust of the Normal. There was no away around it: For Mrs. Lin, Candace's presence was an unwelcome intrusion. The Normals who comprised Fern's family were a different matter, but according to May Lin's way of thinking, Fern's new friend had no business at the meeting. If she hadn't had other things to worry about, Mrs. Lin would have insisted on ejecting the small nuisance from the room. But as it was, she just wanted to get her husband safely back.

"Candace is right," Fern said, sitting upright. "If we steal it before he does, then he can't make the potion."

"You both have a point, but we have no way of knowing when he's going to attempt his theft," the Commander added. She was willing to listen rationally to the assembled teens' ideas, but as the only other adult, she felt she needed to support May Lin. Furthermore, she was not particularly comfortable signing off on a plan that had her daughter committing a federal offense.

"Actually," Candace said, "we do." She hopped off the

counter and waded into her backpack, which she'd placed beneath her. She produced her spiral-bound journal and began flipping through it.

"Yes, here it is. . . . The *Washington Post* reported that the Hope Diamond was stolen right after the shift change of the security guards, at one in the morning. The Air and Space Museum uses the same security detail—Air and Space and the Natural History Museum are all part of the Smithsonian," Candace said, tracing her detailed notes with her index finger. She began pacing as she had when she was connecting the dots for Lindsey Lin in the Museum of the American Indian's gift shop. "Miles told Fern that Laffar leaves him alone around midnight, which means that if Fern were to teleport to Miles and rescue him tonight, we would have approximately a half hour before Laffar came back and realized Miles was missing."

Every eye in the room was on Candace, fascinated by her unflagging precociousness.

"But will he really leave Miles around midnight the night of the heist?" Mrs. Lin asked, still skeptical.

"Yes—he still has to make sure everything at the Air and Space is just as he's planned it," Fern offered, backing Candace up.

"Exactly. So taking into account that I'm no expert in stealing national treasures, I think half an hour should be enough time to get in and out. With Fern and Miles able to teleport and Miles able to turn invisible, it seems like—"

"But wait—Miles won't be able to use his powers because he's been weakened by the Sirens, right?" Lindsey questioned.

"That was my first thought too," Candace said, scribbling something down in her notebook, "but then I realized that if Laffar intends to use Miles to steal the moon rock, then he must have allowed Miles's powers to rejuvenate. Therefore, when Fern reaches him, he should be able to teleport out of there without a problem."

"What's keeping him there right now, then, if he has his powers back for the big burglary in a few hours?" Lindsey interjected. Fern was wondering the same thing, knowing that if Miles could teleport again, he'd be out of that cell in the blink of an eye.

"I know," Mrs. Lin said, having her own "aha" moment. May Lin rose from her seat and walked to a spot right in front of Lindsey, Sam, and Fern, deliberately standing with her back to Candace. "We must not forget that Laffar is a powerful Hermes, able to control minds. I have no doubt he could subdue Miles for at least an hour without the Sirens by putting him in a trance. He is probably planning on leaving him in such a trance while he makes his final preparations for the burglary."

"So can Fern wake him up or something?" Sam asked. "Will he snap out of it?"

"A person must be very careful when awakening someone from a Hermes trance." Mrs. Lin turned to Fern. "The only way to do it is by talking calmly about a familiar subject. He must not be startled awake or he will fall deeper into the trance."

Fern wasn't worried about waking Miles—she knew the exact thing to bring him out of the trance.

May Lin had her husband in her thoughts. She wanted the boy rescued as well, but she had to be her husband's advocate and found herself in the strange position of depending on a thirteen-year-old for help.

"Is there a way to rescue Mike as well?" she asked.

"Oh, I'm planning on waking Mr. Lin up too, and he can escape through the grate. If the Sirens are up there, this time I'll be ready for them. Laffar will be so concerned with finding Miles, I doubt he'll be paying any attention to Mr. Lin," Fern said.

"But if you do succeed in rescuing Miles and Mr. Lin, why steal the moon rock at all? Without Miles, Laffar will no longer be able to get it," the Commander offered, trying to understand why her daughter should put herself in additional danger once Laffar was no longer an immediate threat to Miles or Mr. Lin.

The group considered Mary Lou's point. She appeared to be correct—breaking into one of the most secure places in the world when there was no immediate danger of Laffar getting the moon rock seemed unnecessarily reckless.

The idea of leaving the moon rock was deeply unsettling to Fern.

"No!" she exclaimed. She hadn't meant to yell, but the thought of the moon rock still out there for Laffar to steal shook her to the core. "Are all of you forgetting what we already know about Haryle Laffar? He won't stop until he finds Miles again. He'll never give up until he captures him and steals the rock. Then he'll kill Miles in order to transfer Miles's powers to himself, and then guess what?" Fern was trembling. "I'll be next."

Mary Lou McAllister looked at her quaking daughter. The sight nearly brought tears to her eyes, but with concentrated, forceful blinks, she managed to keep her eyes dry. She thought of the manhunt Laffar had conducted to locate Phoebe, and she remembered the tragic conclusion in that case.

"Miles has already stolen the Hope Diamond. We can do this," Fern insisted with new resolve. "This isn't a choice—we've got to get that rock and then we've got to destroy it."

The room grew silent for a few moments.

"All right," the Commander said finally. She knew, though, that Fern wasn't asking for permission. Fern would go with or without her mother's consent. Sam and Lindsey nodded supportively as she thought of what her father would want her to do.

The group made rapid progress from that point on as all six plotters cobbled together the strategy to rescue Miles and Mike Lin from Laffar's clutches and preemptively steal the rock. Because it was already nine fifteen p.m., they knew they would have to move quickly to be ready by the midnight deadline when Miles would be left alone. Soon every task had been assigned to a specific person and every minute had been carefully planned. At ten p.m., the party finally dispersed to begin the appointed duties.

Candace made straight for the computers in the Marriott business center, hoping to find important security details about the Air and Space Museum online and obtain a picture of the room that housed the moon rock, essential for Fern and Miles to successfully teleport there. Lindsey Lin followed her mother down the hallway with a freshly clipped piece of Fern's hair. Together, they would program a Sagebrush of Hyperion to follow Fern's every movement so she could be constantly monitored.

Mrs. McAllister remained in her room, considering the different excuses she might give the DC police when her daughter was found after hours in the Air and Space Museum.

Meanwhile, Sam grabbed his sister's arm as she headed toward her room. "What if Laffar is expecting you at midnight?"

Fern could see worry lines appear on her brother's tan face.

"He won't be," Fern said, with more confidence than she actually felt.

"He was waiting the last time you teleported to Miles," Sam whispered, scouring the hallway to make sure they were still alone. "He almost had you."

"Which is why he won't expect me to appear again."

"If he captures you, Fern . . ." Though unaware of it, Sam was wringing his hands.

"He's not going to capture me. The only way he could possibly do that would be with the Sirens. I'll have the harmonica, and this time, I'm not going to lose it, okay?"

"I hope you're right," Sam said. Fern had never seen her brother so jumpy. "But if something does happen . . . if he gets the potion together . . . I, well . . ." Sam trailed off.

"What is it?"

"If the worst-case scenario happens," Sam began again, "I have an idea."

"Why didn't you bring it up earlier so everyone could hear?" Her brother puzzled Fern. She could always count on Sam to be straightforward.

"Because I couldn't."

"Well . . . out with it already," Fern said, careful not to let her voice exceed an acceptable decibel level.

Sam breathed in through his nose twice and then revealed the one thing essential to any successful plan: a back-up plan.

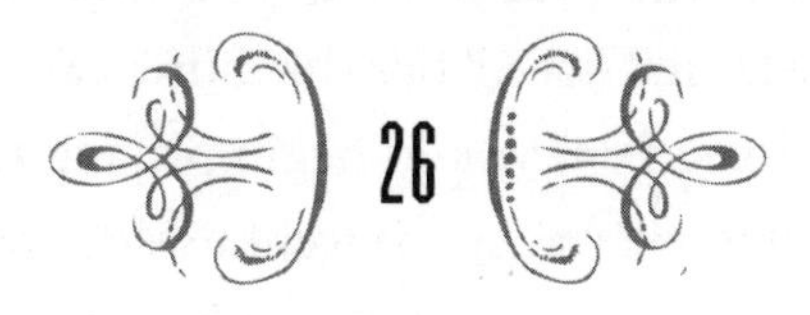

26

going for miles

Fern dutifully waited until 11:59 p.m. before teleporting to the zoo. This time, though, as she stumbled to her feet in the cold darkness of the underground holding cell, she was wary of the unexpected.

With both hands, Fern groped around until she touched something smooth and round, roughly the diameter of a flagpole. It was the bar of a broken cage. When her eyes finally adjusted to the dimness, Fern saw the now familiar crate with NATIONAL ZOOLOGICAL PARK stamped on its side. Moving silently, she crept to the corner of the room where she'd last seen Mr. Lin in his cage. The large rusted cage was there.

But Mr. Lin was not.

Dread swamped Fern's thoughts. If Mr. Lin wasn't there, what other surprises were in store? No longer concerned about making noise, Fern pulled out her Washington, DC, gift harmonica and gripped it tightly. She doubted that she could recall the precise notes and holes in which to blow for "Amazing Grace," but she didn't care. At the first sign of the Sirens, Fern would begin playing the harmonica, continuing until the Sirens went to sleep or she passed out from lack of oxygen—whichever happened first.

As soon as Fern entered the smaller second room, she hunted for Miles. His cage was in the corner . . . and, to her relief, so was he.

Without waiting to see if there was anybody else lurking in the deeply shadowed corners of the backlit room, Fern darted to the door of Miles's cage. Retrieving the bolt cutters from beneath the pile of bamboo where she had left them, Fern attacked the new lock. *CLACK*. The noise reverberated off the walls as the lock clanged on the floor. The grate covering the opening to the duct above Miles's cage had been completely pushed to the side, but Fern didn't bother looking up. There was no time to waste.

What struck Fern first was the tidy state of Miles's cage. The cereal boxes and debris had been removed. As Fern stepped into the enclosure, she noticed that someone had even swept the inside of the cage. It looked as if Laffar was intent on covering his tracks.

Fern directed her gaze to the opposite side of the room, in the direction of a creaking noise. Her eyes narrowed, as she tried to penetrate the darkness. She clasped the harmonica tightly in her palm once more, now unable to hear anything except the pounding of her own heart. Inhaling one sharp breath after another, Fern tried to make peace with her hostile nerves.

She scanned the room again. Other than Miles, there was no one else there.

Slowly Fern sat down on the cage's cold metal floor. The bill of Miles's ripped and dirtied baseball cap covered his eyes. Timidly Fern extended her index finger beneath the brim of Miles's hat and lifted it to reveal his face. His eyes were open, but empty—his pupils had disappeared. It was as if someone had set two blue-tinted glass pieces where his eyes used to be. Fern waved her hand in front of Miles's face. Nothing. She chided herself for not working more quickly, fully aware that every second was precious.

She remembered what Mrs. Lin had said about waking a person up from a Hermes trance, and her voice morphed into a monotone whisper.

"You remember the game on August 19, 2007, don't you, Miles? Santana was on the mound against the Rangers at the Metrodome. It was his thirteenth win that season . . . right? The Twins only got him one run, a homer against Millwood in the second inning. Santana won the Cy Young Award the year before, but you don't happen to recall how many strikeouts he had that day, do you? Miles, I can't remember, but you watched the game, I bet. How many was it?"

Miles's glassy eyes rolled back into his head. Fern panicked. Had she miscalculated the best method of bringing

Miles out of his trance? She began to talk more quickly. "I think it was a franchise record . . . against the Rangers. One strikeout, then another, then another. How many strikeouts did he get that game?"

Miles's head snapped up.

"Seventeen."

Fern covered her mouth so she wouldn't shriek.

"Miles!"

Confusion clouded his face. He looked around and realized where he was. Fern saw his eyes return to their normal color, pupils and all. "Fern? What are you doing here?"

"We've got to get out of here! Miles, can you teleport? Have you seen the Sirens lately?"

"Were you just talking with me about the Minnesota Twins?" Miles said, squinting. He didn't seem to grasp the severity of the situation. "Have you been hiding the fact that you're a fan?"

In truth, Fern had Googled "famous Twins moments" to get all the info she needed. She dug into the other pocket of her jacket and produced a color photograph Candace had found and printed in the business center.

She waved the photograph in front of Miles, who was slowly regaining his senses.

"I need you to try to teleport here," she said, pointing at the photograph. "Can you do that?" Miles craned his neck closer to the photo. With his finger, he traced the metallic tower in front of the National Air and Space Museum.

"Where is that?"

Fern snapped her fingers in front of Miles's face.

"See if you can teleport here, and if you can, I'm going to follow you," Fern said, looking up nervously at the duct opening for the first time.

Fern realized with a jolt that the grate was gone and Laffar could hop down into the room at any moment, close them both in the cage, immobilize them with the Sirens, and follow through with his diabolical plan.

She held the photo inches from Miles's face.

"Is that a spaceship?" Miles asked.

"Yes. Close your eyes and imagine yourself standing in front of the spaceship you see in the picture." It was as if Fern had to reteach Miles to teleport.

Fern looked above the top of the paper. Miles was closing his eyes.

"I so didn't know you were a Twins fan," Miles repeated, his eyes still closed.

"*Now*, Miles!"

Fern peeked over the paper once again in order to see if Miles still had his eyes closed, but she couldn't tell one way or another.

Miles Zapo had disappeared.

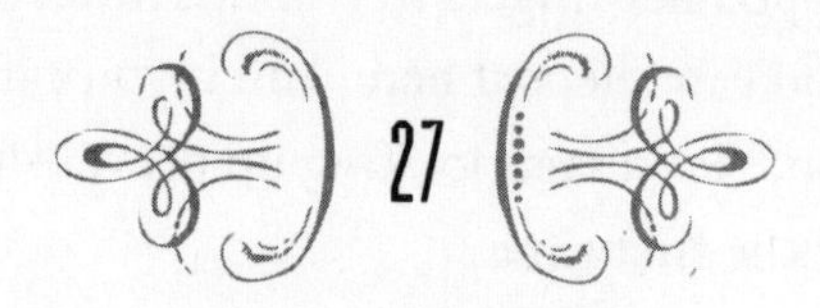

27

meet & greet

Even in the dim midnight light, Candace Tutter would have recognized Miles Zapo anywhere. He had big eyes, and his dark curls were tucked under a dirty baseball cap that was too large for his head, just as Fern had described. Candace was surprised by how small he was—he was only about an inch taller than she was.

"Are you . . . you must be . . . Miles Zapo?"

"Where am I?" Miles Zapo had regained most of his cognitive faculties, and he was beginning to piece together the past few hours of his life. Silver Tooth had come back, but this time without his Quetzals. The last thing he remembered was Silver Tooth telling him that after tonight, Miles could be out of the cage. Miles recalled the strange effect Silver Tooth's words had on him and then, as if his brain had stopped recording, all memory ceased.

Until Fern arrived, that is. At first her voice sounded like she was underwater. He heard her talking about the Twins, and then he revived and she was sitting next to him in his cage, demanding that he teleport to a strange place.

Now he was at that strange place, with a very strange girl peering at him intently.

"Where am I? Who are you?"

Candace smiled at Miles.

"I suppose it's natural to have a lot of questions," she said. "You're outside the National Air and Space Museum in Washington, DC. My name is Candace Tutter, and I am a student at St. Gregory's and a friend of Fern's."

"Where is Fern?"

"She should be arriving momentarily. She wanted to make sure you safely teleported before she followed you." Candace tried to sound official, hoping it might calm Miles down after his journey.

She took a file folder out of her trusty backpack. Then she pulled out several sheets of paper, each with three or four photos printed on them. Before she could show them to Miles, a sound broke the silence.

In the blink of an eye, Fern appeared in front of Candace just as Miles had moments before. Candace found it as awe-inducing as the first time she'd seen Fern disappear from their shared hotel bathroom.

With a bewildered expression, Miles looked at Fern, newly arrived, and then at the looming stone building and the illuminated monuments he'd previously seen only in pictures. The fact that he had escaped from the control of Laffar and the Sirens began to sink in.

"I'm free!" he said, shouting through the biting night air. He extended both his arms out to the side and ran at Candace and Fern, pretending he was about to clothesline them. Instead he wrapped one arm around each of their necks and pulled them to him in a forceful group hug.

Fern thought about calling Mrs. Lin and the Commander, who were monitoring Fern from the makeshift command post at the hotel, armed with cell phones should anything go wrong. But she realized she didn't need to notify Mrs. Lin that her husband was nowhere to be found in the concrete bunker—May Lin would have seen it with her own eyes in the Sagebrush of Hyperion she was using to track Fern.

There was nothing more to be done right now. They would have to turn their attention to rescuing Mr. Lin after completing the impending heist.

"I have to go see Aunt Chan! She's probably so worried about me."

Fern wanted to tell Miles to lower his voice. After all, she had firsthand knowledge of the close watch the Capitol police kept on the buildings and monuments surrounding the National Mall. If Officer Hallet, or his equivalent, were to find her roaming near the Mall again at this hour, they would all be taken into custody on the spot.

"Miles, you can't go see your aunt yet."

"Why not?" he asked defensively.

"Because we have something to do first."

"What?" Miles said, still close to Fern and Candace.

"We're going to steal the moon rock that's inside this building."

"What?" Miles said, confused. "But that's what Silver Tooth wants! He's planning on stealing it tonight. . . . Why do we need it?"

Fern sighed, hating to deliver the ominous news—that Miles would be hunted by Laffar so that he could complete the potion and carry out his plan. But before she found the right words to cushion the blow, Candace spoke.

"Silver Tooth," Candace explained, "is Fern's father, though he doesn't know it. His name is Haryle Laffar, and he's a complete psycho who killed Fern's mother. His actual strategy is to create a potion that will give him immortality, and the last ingredient is the moon rock inside this museum. Then he will add your blood, which will transfer your special powers to him and will most likely kill you." Candace said it in a matter-of-fact way, as if she was reading aloud the label on her favorite breakfast cereal.

"Who are you again?" Miles said, turning his attention to the strange girl with the backpack and the photographs.

"Like I said before, I'm Candace Tutter, grade seven, and I am Fern's friend."

"What can you do?" Miles demanded.

"What can I do? What kind of a question is that?" Candace replied, raising her eyebrow.

"What's your special talent? Why are you here?"

"Oh, I'm not an Otherworldly," Candace said, wondering what Miles was getting at.

"Candace has plenty of other talents that don't exactly fall on the Otherworldly spectrum, believe me, Miles. . . . She's here to help us."

"So what she says is true? If Silver Tooth, er, Laffar, makes the immortality potion, he can also use it to transfer my powers to him? That's why he wants to make it?"

"Yes," Fern said gently, recalling how she'd felt when she first heard this information. "He'll take your blood first, and then mine. Doing so will most likely kill us. Then he'll have the special powers of two Unusuals."

"So how do we stop him?" Miles said, dejection replacing his earlier elation.

"You two have to steal the rock before he does! Then you can destroy it." Candace rarely raised her voice, knowing it was not the most effective way to express rational thought, but Miles and Fern had wasted enough time.

"I know this is a lot to digest, but we don't have much time, Miles." Fern looked at her fellow Unusual compassionately. "You and Laffar committed the first robbery around one a.m., right? We think he'll follow that timing again, which gives us about a half hour before he goes to retrieve you from your cell and discovers you're gone."

"But we need to know exactly what he's after and what it looks like before we can steal it!" Miles said. "We don't know what kind of security there is, what the exact moon rock even looks like so I can teleport there. . . . Before I went in to get the Hope Diamond, Silver, um—I mean Laffar—reviewed the details with me for days."

"We may not have much time to prepare," Fern said, noting Candace busy at work, carefully laying sheets of photos on the bench in front of them. "But just listen."

Candace took that as her cue to explain to Miles all that she'd discovered and memorized about the layout of the museum, the placement of the security cameras and infrared sensors.

"The rotating security cameras at the north and south ends of the gallery containing the moon rock should be no problem because you'll be invisible," Candace said, pointing to a color image of the entire room. "Miles, you don't happen to know if the invisibility coating you apply stops you from emitting black body radiation, do you?"

"What?" Miles said, pushing his glasses up his nose to get a clearer look at Fern's peculiar "friend."

"Never mind. Because we're unsure, you must be careful to avoid all doorways and thresholds. I'm simply not certain if you two will set off the infrared sensors when you're invisible, so it's best to play it safe."

"You *two*?" Miles questioned. "Who else is coming with me?"

Fern stepped forward.

"I am," she declared. "You can make me invisible, can't you?"

Miles felt as though he had unwillingly dragged Fern

McAllister into this whole mess.

"Yeah," he started, "but there's no need for both of us to put ourselves in—"

"Listen, Miles. We got into this together and we're going to get out of it together, all right?"

"Now, once Sam and Lindsey arrive, they'll take their positions at the southern and the eastern entrances to the museum," Candace said, continuing her instructions. Miles considered asking who in the world Sam and Lindsey were but rejected the idea. He was on information overload as it was.

Sam and Lindsey were to follow Fern on foot to the zoo, about a five-minute walk away, in case she needed support. But once they'd been given the all-clear signal, they were to go to the Air and Space in a taxi to act as lookouts. Fern expected them to arrive at any moment.

Candace fished in her backpack once again. She produced a hammer and a flathead screwdriver and laid them on the bench next to her collection of Air and Space Museum printouts. Pointing to a close-up of the moon rock, Candace explained the specific task at hand.

"Miles," she began, "you will teleport to the southern base of the stand that holds the moon rock." She pointed to the south side of the stand in the photo.

"Where's the moon rock?" Miles said, growing confused as he studied the picture. The picture showed a rectangular cube that appeared to be about chest high, without a glass case or even a stand of any kind. It was like the podium for a statue without the statue.

Candace pointed to the sheet of paper closest to the screwdriver and the hammer. It was the only sheet with a single picture on it. Miles and Fern hovered over it.

Fern recognized it immediately, having seen it only two days ago (though it felt like those days had been weeks). Miles, on the other hand, had no idea what he was looking at. The top of the marble rectangular stand was covered with a gray granitelike substance. A small space had been cut into its center. The small triangular-shaped object placed inside the opening was about the size of an arrowhead, slightly darker than the gray material surrounding it.

"That is the moon rock!" Candace revealed.

"*That* is the moon rock? It's so dinky," Miles said.

Candace put her hands on her hips impatiently. "I guess some people are impressed that they're able to touch a four-billion-year-old artifact from space and others are not."

"Well, I think it looks like any old rock," Miles said, returning Candace's volley. He peered more closely at the picture. "It's like someone dug a hole in the granite stand and then cemented it in there. How are we going to remove it?"

Candace moved her hand toward the screwdriver and hammer. "You can turn objects and people invisible, correct?"

"Sure," Miles said, picking up the hammer. "Where did you get these tools?"

"Why does it matter?" replied Candace.

Fern looked at Candace and then at Miles. One thing she had not expected was for them to butt heads.

"If you *must* know," Candace said sharply, "Fern and I gained access to a supply closet at the hotel. We secured them before Fern left to rescue you.

"Now one of you will hold the screwdriver in place, wedged into the crevice where the rock's been glued, and the other will hammer the top of it, which will turn the screwdriver into a forceful lever, enabling you to separate the moon rock from its display."

"How do we know we'll be able to get the moon rock out at all?" Miles demanded, stepping closer to Candace so that their faces were inches apart.

Candace did not back down, instead moving a little closer to Miles. "We know because the Smithsonian officials in charge of the exhibit are not likely to use a corrosive material on a rock that's worth *millions* of dollars. You may have to strike it a few times, but I have little doubt you will be able to pry it loose."

"All right, enough, you two," Fern broke in. "We're all on the same team, okay?"

Two people approached from the north on Independence Avenue. They stopped adjacent to the entrance.

"Get down!" Fern whispered, directing the group toward a covered area behind the bench. Fern, Candace, and Miles all stumbled behind the bench's cover.

Through a crack in the wood-planked back of the

bench, Fern watched the pedestrians. She spotted Lindsey's long dark hair first and felt herself relax.

Sam and Lindsey, dressed in black from head to toe, ran quickly up the steps leading to the entrance of the museum.

Fern emerged from behind the bench as the black-clad duo approached.

"About time you arrived," she said. Sam smiled broadly as he spotted Fern.

"We had a little trouble getting a cab at this time of night," Sam said.

"I didn't see a taxi pull up," Fern said.

"I made him let us off a few blocks away. I didn't want him to get suspicious. Gave him twenty bucks to wait there for us."

Sam was wearing a black beanie, and Lindsey had on a charcoal jacket. There was no other activity on the street in front of the Air and Space Museum. All was quiet in the District.

Realizing that there was no immediate danger, Candace hopped out from behind the bench and grabbed another sheet of paper from her backpack. It was a Google map showing the streets in the surrounding area.

"By the way, Miles, this is my brother, Sam, and our friend Lindsey Lin," Fern said, feeling awkward because they all knew so much about Miles and he knew nothing about them.

"Nice to meet you," Lindsey said, extending her hand. Miles took it in his own and gave it a shake.

Lindsey pulled the hood of her jacket around her head. They all crouched around the map.

"Lindsey, you are going to be watching the museum from here," Candace said, pointing to the intersection of Jefferson Drive and Seventh Street. "I will man my post from the front of the museum, and Sam, you'll take the other side of Jefferson Drive.

"If anything goes wrong, we're going to call your cell phone, Fern. You should both be able to hear it. Remember that you *cannot* answer it—we don't want your voice winding up on a surveillance recording. One ring means we all will meet back out here, near the side of the museum. Two rings means that our lookout positions have been compromised and we will reassemble at the hotel. But either way, if your phone rings, you need to get out of the museum."

Candace pulled out a brochure. At the top, it said WOODLEY PARK MARRIOTT, and inside there were glossy photographs of the hotel. The first was the lobby. Candace pointed to the picture.

"Two rings means you need to teleport back here, Miles. Do not go back to your aunt's house. It may not be safe."

Miles looked at the photograph of the nicely decorated lobby, memorizing the upholstered checkered chairs and the light orange drapes. As an insurance policy, he crammed the brochure in his back pocket.

"Okay," Miles agreed. The group of conspirators stood in a circle and stared blankly at one another for a few moments. They weren't sure what to do next but weren't quite ready to flip the mental switch on and officially embark on the riskiest stunt of their lives.

"Have you gone over everything?" Sam asked.

Candace was clutching her notebook and pencil, making entries on a to-do list. She handed Fern the screwdriver and then Miles the hammer, instructing them to hide the tools in their jackets.

"I believe so," Candace said, checking off the last item on the list.

"What's left then?" Fern asked, so nervous that she could taste the stomach acid in her mouth.

"I guess there's just one thing," Lindsey said, inspecting Miles first, then Fern. "You two need to get invisible."

Other than himself, Miles had turned only one person invisible before. Aunt Chan, who always seemed more interested in investigating the full extent and limits of Miles's power than Miles himself, had insisted that he practice on her, and he was fairly certain he could erase Fern in front of the National Air and Space Museum.

Candace, Sam, Lindsey, and Fern all watched as Miles closed his eyes tightly. He put his hands together as if he were beginning to pray. Then he began rubbing his hands together, slowly at first, then faster and faster until finally no one could tell where one hand ended and the other began.

Fern was the first to notice Miles's fingertips disappear.

She nudged Sam and pointed.

"Whoa," Sam said, incredulous.

Soon Miles's arms vanished, followed by his legs. He was a torso with a head, floating off the ground. His eyes were still closed, and he grimaced. Though no one could see his hands, the frantic swish of Miles rubbing them together filled the night air. Fern began to worry that Miles would rub his skin right off. Only Miles's head, complete with his thick-framed glasses and his Twins cap, was left, magically levitating off the ground.

"Moving things with your mind is pretty cool," Sam said, "but that right there is real magic, Fern." Even Fern had to admit that it was an amazing feat. There was no trace left of Miles.

"Miles?" Candace asked. "Where are you?"

"Are you ready, Fern?" Miles's voice came from a spot directly in front of her. Fern squinted and stared as hard as she could, but there was no trace of Miles—not the thick curls on Miles's head, not his dirty Twins cap, not his torn shirt.

"Yes," Fern said, feeling a surge as every neuron in her head fired.

"All right, put out your palms, facing up," Miles's detached voice commanded. "You're going to feel something wet on them. That's what I'm putting on them. Once you feel the liquid on your hands, rub them together as fast as you can, like you saw me do. It will cause a reaction and turn you invisible."

Fern put her hands out. She felt Miles's hands on her own, and it was as if he'd dipped them in slime. He rubbed the gooey liquid all over her hands. It felt ice-water cold at first. Then it started tingling like Icy Hot.

Fern began to rub. At first she thought she wasn't rubbing fast enough, so she clenched her teeth and moved her hands even faster. Soon both her arms were aching so painfully, she felt like they might fall off. But she continued to rub.

"Whoa," Sam said again. Fern looked down at her hands and arms. She could no longer see them, though she could feel the sharp ache vividly.

It was working! Fern rubbed faster and faster. Soon she could no longer see her legs. Then her torso disappeared. She knew she couldn't rub much longer without completely running out of steam.

"You're gone, Fern! You can stop now."

Fern let her arms drop to her sides. The tingling sensation had overtaken her whole body. It was as if she'd jumped in a huge vat of superstrength Vicks VapoRub.

Fern waved her hand in front of her face. She couldn't see anything.

"You have to quickly touch the screwdriver to make sure it turns invisible too," Miles said. Fern was anxious to ask more questions about Miles's awesome power, but she knew they didn't have time. She followed instructions and rubbed her palms all over the screwdriver.

"You should bottle that stuff and sell it," Sam said,

hoping he was talking in Miles's direction.

Miles's disembodied voice came from behind them. Candace, Lindsey, and Sam turned around. "Yours is going to wear off in about fifteen minutes, Fern. So we don't have time to waste."

Fern felt a bulge inside her jacket. She'd forgotten until her hand brushed up against them, but she was still carrying the bolt cutters. She rubbed them with the palms of her hands. She probably wouldn't need them, and her invisible coat covered them. But it was best to play it as safely as she could. As she was about to check to see if they'd turned invisible, Candace called out to her as she moved back to the bench.

"Come over here, so you can look at the exact place you're supposed to teleport to."

Fern stepped toward the bench when her knee collided with something hard, causing her to topple to the ground. Her kneecap was radiating pain.

She heard Miles let out a low moan too.

"What is it?" Candace said, looking around, speaking to the open air because she was unable to see Fern or Miles.

"We slammed into each other," Miles said. "I think we hit knees."

"They can't do that when they're inside the museum!" Lindsey exclaimed. "They might run into each other and knock something over."

It was a dilemma Candace was ashamed she hadn't

considered. Being able to teleport while invisible was the perfect skill set for a burglar. Having a partner in crime who couldn't be seen, though, was potentially problematic.

"Why don't they talk to each other?"

"It's too risky. There are sound-activated recording devices," Candace said. "We can't leave any record of their voices. They'll have to hold on to each other."

"Fine, fine, let's get this over with," Fern said, as if she were merely waiting to get blood drawn, instead of about to steal a multimillion-dollar item out of a national museum.

"Where are you, Fern?" Miles asked, trying to follow the sound of her voice.

"Right in front of the left side of the bench." Fern felt Miles's hand grab her hip.

"That's not my hand," Fern said, annoyed. She felt for Miles's hand and placed it in her own.

Lindsey and Sam laughed, imagining where Miles's hand might have landed.

"Time to man your positions," Candace announced to Lindsey and Sam.

"Good luck," Sam said, in the direction of the bench where he knew Fern and Miles were standing.

"We'll be waiting for you when you get back," Lindsey added, abandoning the urge to give Fern a hug because she had no idea where Fern's shoulder might be.

"Thanks," Fern said, still gripping Miles's hand. Sam and Lindsey began running in opposite directions, streaking across the landscape in their dark clothing.

"Are you ready? Miles asked.

"Ready," Fern responded.

"Let's go on three," Miles said.

They both looked down at the photo of the podium that held the moon rock, focusing on the exact location for their arrival as Candace had outlined.

"One," they both said.

"Two," they continued counting.

"Three."

Candace thought she felt a slight breeze rush past her face.

"Fern?" she said into the still darkness. "Miles?" Candace knew she was alone.

Though Fern McAllister and Miles Zapo had disappeared from sight several minutes ago, now they were actually gone.

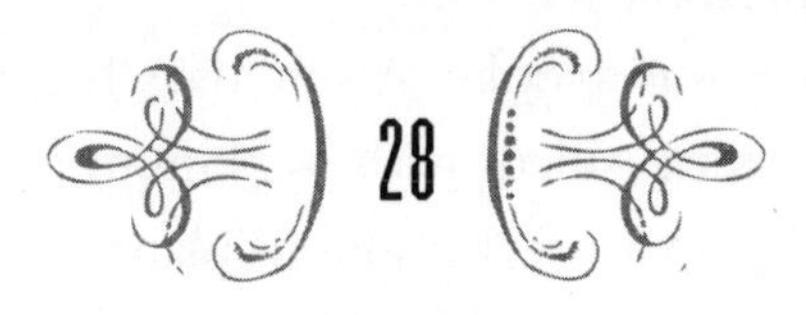

28

the imperfect crime

Fern had arrived standing up, but she was no longer holding Miles's hand. She took a moment to marvel at where she was. Though most of the lights were off in the gallery, each of the room's important exhibits was illuminated with dim spotlights. Fern hadn't realized it before, but the ceiling was made of glass, which let in the capital's ambient light. The windowpanes cast long, subtle shadows on the floor.

Although it was dark, Fern could see out of the Milestones of Flight gallery to the street outside. Hanging above her head was the *North American X-15*, a rocket-powered research aircraft. Fern spotted *SpaceShipOne* floating above the south side of the gallery, gleaming in the darkness with its white rocketlike frame and red-tipped wings. It hung between Charles Lindbergh's *Spirit of St.*

Louis propeller plane and Chuck Yeager's *Bell X-1*, a record-breaking supersonic jet.

The silence was spooky. A few days before, the same gallery had been filled with screaming kids running around gazing up at all the famous planes and spaceships. Now, though, you would be able to hear the tiniest sliver of moon rock hitting the floor.

She looked down at the podium curiously. The moon rock was there. The plaque on the podium, Fern noticed, called it the "Lunar Touchrock." Museums always had a way of expressing things in fancy terms, she thought, making them sound more impressive.

She cautiously felt around the podium for Miles, groping the stand as she circled it. At last she grasped something solid in what appeared to be the empty space in front of her. She wanted to shout his name, but with effort, she adhered to Candace's strict silence warning.

She felt a hand on her wrist. Fern was still flummoxed by the fact that she couldn't see her own hands *or* Miles's. It was more jarring than an out-of-body experience . . . it was a no-body experience.

Miles gripped Fern's wrist tightly as they moved toward the moon rock. With her free hand, Fern reached into her pocket and pulled out the screwdriver. She felt it in her invisible hand, but she couldn't see it. She could hear the soft scratch as the tip of the screwdriver hit the smooth, shiny surface surrounding the small triangular Lunar Touchrock.

As she wedged the screwdriver in the crevice between the moon rock and the shiny surface, Fern realized how unrealistic heist movies were. In the Commander's favorite *To Catch a Thief*, which Fern had been forced to watch a half-dozen times, Cary Grant played a cat burglar stealing jewels while remaining cucumber cool. His hands never shook, his knees didn't knock, he never breathed heavily, and there wasn't the faintest trickle of perspiration on his face.

But in the reality of the dark stillness of the Air and Space Museum, Fern was so nervous she thought she might throw up. She imagined being put in a "national treasure thief" prison. If she was locked up for the rest of her life, she questioned whether the Commander, Sam, and Eddie would even visit her. She might have to teleport out and spend the rest of her life on the lam, like Richard Kimble in *The Fugitive*, another of the Commander's favorites.

Her breathing became shallower until she wasn't sure her lungs contained enough air for her to maintain consciousness. Her heart was thumping so loudly, she thought Miles could probably hear it. Of course, she couldn't ask him. She worried that her shaking knees would give way, causing her to collapse on the floor.

Fern inhaled deeply, guiding Miles's hand to where she held the screwdriver securely in the crevice. She positioned his hand so that he would know where to aim the hammer. Wincing prematurely, imagining that when Miles brought the hammer down blindly, he would hit her hand and not the top of the screwdriver's handle, Fern braced herself.

THWAP!

The metal of the hammer pounded the plastic of the screwdriver handle with force. Fern felt the reverberation shoot through her hand. The moon rock had not budged much, and Fern steadied herself for another blow, wondering how many it would take to pry it out.

THWAP.

The sound of the hammer's second blow echoed off the walls of the Milestones of Flight gallery. Fern glanced around, scanning the edge of the gallery where the glass roof met the walls, seeing if any of the motion detectors, sensors, or alarms had been activated. Through the paned glass of the entrance, she spotted what she assumed was a security guard. The guard put something to his mouth, and Fern could see the momentary orange glow of a cigarette.

Fern's nerves were completely frayed.

Was the man outside the night watchman? Was he supposed to be patrolling inside and had stepped out for a smoke break? Fern wanted more than anything to urge Miles to hurry, but there was no way to communicate with him verbally.

THWAP.

Fern lowered herself so that she was eye level with the triangular piece of stone. The hammering had lifted the rock enough for Fern to wedge her finger in next to the rock. A gooey substance was visible beneath the stone. A few more blows and she could get a good enough grip to pull the rock off with her hand.

Riiiiiiinnnggg!!!

Fern leapt in the air. At first she assumed the hammering had activated the alarm. Then she felt Miles's arm wrap tightly around her bicep, squeezing it with panic.

Miles was terrified too.

Then she recognized the sound—it was her phone. Both burglars knew the signal. One ring and they were to teleport out of the museum back to their meeting place. Two rings and they were to go back to the hotel. Either way, it was a very bad sign. Fern wondered if the night watchman outside had heard the hammering and alerted the police.

Riiiiiiinnnggg!!!

Fern was dripping with sweat. She felt Miles's continuing iron grip around her upper arm. Fern looked down at the moon rock. It was partially dislodged. A few more blows and they would have it. Her mind raced. Should they stay a few seconds longer in a final attempt to dislodge it? They were so close! But then again, most likely, so were the police.

Riiiiiiinnnggg!!!

Fern let out a low gasp. Three rings wasn't part of the established code. There was no three-ring signal. What did it mean? Outside, she saw a flashlight come to life. Whoever was there might not have heard the hammering, but the cell phone had been a dead giveaway. The light was now shining into the museum through the glass entrance, scanning the exhibits for any sign of movement. Fern heard the jingle of keys. Soon the watchman would be inside the gallery with Fern and Miles.

Riiiiiiiinnngggg!!!

Fern jammed the screwdriver back in her jacket and grabbed her phone in her pocket, fumbling to silence a device she couldn't see. Suddenly she no longer felt Miles's grip on her arm. He had teleported. Fern was alone and about to be caught invisible-handed.

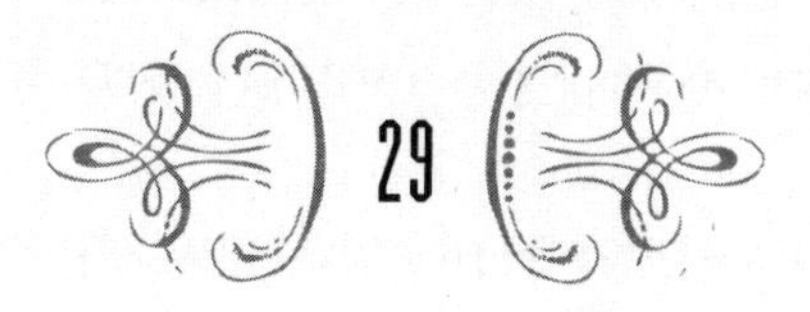

29

the bush ambush

Fern didn't hesitate for even one second. Her most daring instincts took over. A single image dominated her thoughts—the silver-glinted smile of Haryle Laffar. She could not abandon the moon rock, leaving it for him to steal. There simply was no other option.

Minus Miles's hammer, Fern would have to work quickly. She could hear the sound of the dead bolt retreating into the door after the guard slid his key into the slot. The flashlight gleamed near the doorway, advancing at waist level with the security guard.

Quickly Fern grabbed the bolt cutters from beneath her jacket. Aghast when the shiny bolt cutters appeared fully visible before her, Fern realized that she'd not succeeded in turning the bolt cutters invisible. She was relieved, though, that at least her hands still could not be seen. The visibility of the bolt cutters worked to her advantage in one respect, allowing Fern to quickly place the closed blades directly beneath the loosened part of the moon rock. She shoved the metal head as deeply as it would penetrate beneath the rock.

Then, as if on one end of a miniature seesaw attempting to launch an object from the other side, she raised up on her tiptoes and fell on the end of the bolt cutters, pushing with all the force in her on the red handles that extended out past the edge of the Lunar Touchrock podium. She felt a jolt as the head of the bolt cutters jerked violently upward, completely dislodging the moon rock.

The maneuver accomplished exactly what Fern planned, hurling the small lunar arrowhead up in the air. Out of the corner of her eye, she saw the guard, now in the gallery. Just as the moon rock took flight, the guard shone his flashlight on the podium.

"Freeze!" he yelled, though he was unable to see Fern. The blade of the bolt cutters reflected in the flashlight's white light.

Distracted by the guard, Fern had completely lost sight of the rock. Her frantic eyes scanned the air, unable to spot it.

Fern was about to give up until she found the rock in flight, inches below the *Spirit of St. Louis.*

She took off sprinting.

With one hand around the bolt cutters, she looked up, following the flight of the soaring rock like one of baseball's best center fielders chasing a deep fly ball. She extended her hand as the rock plummeted back to earth. Fern quickened her pace, hoping to intercept it before it hit the ground.

She reached it as it tumbled to eye level. Cupping one hand to form a pocket, she felt the smooth rock nestle into her makeshift invisible mitt.

Then came the crash. Fern had been looking up, not forward, and was unable to see that the guard had been tracking the moon rock as well. They collided with a thud.

Fern felt a crack as her skull hit the concrete floor. She wouldn't allow herself to acknowledge the pain. Instead she clutched the bolt cutters in one hand and the moon rock in the other, as if her life depended on it.

At that moment it did. She remembered the unending ring of her cell phone. Something unexpected must have happened—it was the only reason she could think of why Sam, Candace, or Lindsey would've let her phone ring more than twice. Even though everyone might have left the southern entrance by now, her invisibility would allow her to check the area as a precaution before teleporting to safety.

With her skull throbbing on the hard floor of the Milestones of Flight gallery, Fern imagined the southern entrance. Blackness enveloped her. But she had the moon rock. She had triumphed.

Fern knew that a clean landing was unlikely, considering her state of disarray at the moment of her departure from the museum. But sprawling across Candace's planning bench was not the touchdown she'd hoped for. The bolt cutters dug into her side, and she rolled off the bench onto the ground. She stood up, gripping the bolt cutters, quickly determining that there was no sign of Lindsey, Candace, Sam, or Miles. She took the moon rock, which she carried snugly in the palm of her hand, and placed it carefully inside the zippered pocket of her jacket.

As soon as the guard recovered, she knew he would summon the authorities. It was only a matter of time before the Air and Space Museum would be crawling with Capitol police.

When he materialized in front of the bushes, calmly stepping out of the shadows, Fern froze.

Haryle Laffar reached into his worn leather jacket and pulled out a pack of Marlboros and then a match. He stuck a cigarette in his mouth and then struck the match on his gleaming silver tooth. The match sparked. Laffar held it to the end of the cigarette, and the tip burned red, then orange.

"Next time," Laffar said, his eyes focused on the far-off horizon, "you should probably get around to turning everything invisible." His voice was rough and ragged. Paralyzed, Fern studied Laffar. His outfit was the same as before; dirty dark jeans with his steel-tipped boots, sunglasses, and bandanna. Laffar chuckled, each laugh punctuated with gravel and phlegm. "Those bolt cutters almost blew your whole gig, you know?"

Fern looked down at the bolt cutters that she held by

her side. To Laffar, they must have appeared to be floating in air. He advanced toward Fern. She considered dropping the cutters and moving away from them so that Laffar could no longer locate her. In the distance, she heard police sirens.

"I guess you aren't exactly the talkative type, Fern McAllister, which I understand. But I'm gonna ask anyway. I need to know if I have to send the boy in to finish the job. Did you get the lunar rock or not?"

Laffar tapped the steel of his boot against the concrete.

"A yes or no will do just fine."

Laffar waited and Fern stood there, crippled with fear, wondering if Laffar had captured her friends.

Laffar didn't wait for Fern to answer. Instead he dropped his cigarette and lunged toward the floating bolt cutters. His clawlike hand made contact with her throat, squeezing as hard as he could, slamming Fern back against the bench with the force of his charge. Laffar growled like an attacking lion.

He felt for the girl's small windpipe with his strong hands and pressed down with his thumb. Fern could barely breathe. Trying to teleport, she couldn't think of anything except her throbbing head and decreasing air supply. Tears collected in the corners of her eyes as she struggled in his grip as Laffar pressed her tightly against the bench. Her head was bent so far backward, Fern thought it might snap off entirely. As Laffar applied pressure to the blood vessels in her neck, she saw spots forming against the cold night sky. Her thoughts began to float away from her. Fern wondered which would happen first—the stopping of her heart or the crushing of her windpipe.

"I'll make this real simple for you, sweetheart," Laffar purred in Fern's ear. His breath was putrid. The back of the bench cut into the skin above her shoulder blades. "Your friends are all in a trance with my dear friend Flarge, not far from here. You have five minutes to produce the moon rock. If you don't, I'll kill 'em all," he snarled.

With a jolt, Laffar pressed harder against Fern's throat. "And it won't be an easy or pretty death, sweetheart. I can guarantee you that."

Fern tried to speak but could only cough and gasp. Laffar lessened the pressure. When she spoke, she could hardly recognize her own voice.

"I—I—have—it," Fern said, coughing up a mixture of mucus and blood. Laffar smiled. For the first time, Fern saw the chiseled sharp fang in Laffar's mouth, opposite the silver tooth. Laffar's face had a coarseness that made his menacing smile all the more frightening.

Fern couldn't imagine how Haryle could possibly be related to Vlad. Though Vlad was menacing in his own right, he was polished, with a calculated, almost sophisticated appearance.

"Where is it?" Laffar said, unwilling to remove his hand from Fern's throat.

"I want to see that my friends are still alive first," Fern said defiantly with her hoarse voice.

Laffar leaned in again, this time close enough that Fern could see her own reflection in the silver mirror of his tooth. Blood was dripping from her forehead. It was then that Fern realized she was no longer invisible. Miles's magic had worn off.

"Finally, we can see eye to eye. Swell," Laffar said sarcastically. He stared into the girl's eyes and was troubled by a bizarre familiarity. But he dismissed the thought. His repulsive breath made Fern squirm from his grasp.

"I want to see my friends," Fern said, coughing again as she restated her demand.

"I don't have a problem with that, considering that this place is going to be swarming with the police in about three minutes, but let me explain how this is going to work. You try anything and Flarge will break the neck of one of your friends. You teleport, and Flarge will kill one of 'em and I'll ask questions later. I have five in total, so I can afford a few mistakes."

Fern figured he must have Sam, Lindsey, and Candace, but she wondered who the other two were.

"Now walk," Laffar said, finally releasing Fern. She put her hand on what seemed to be permanent indents where his fingers had been.

Though wobbly, Fern followed Laffar down Independence Avenue, away from the Air and Space Museum. Laffar's steel-tipped boots made a *click-clack* noise as he guided Fern, his painful grip on her shoulder. The two walked side by side and Fern's earlier tears returned—she thought how different this scenario was from the way most teenage girls walked with their fathers among the storied monuments of Washington, DC. The real difference, Fern supposed, was that her father happened to be the embodiment of pure evil. The sidewalks on Independence Avenue were wide, and the avenue itself was six lanes across. They passed Seventh Street, and the blare of the police sirens seemed to come from only a couple of blocks away.

"I've got to admit, sweetheart," Laffar rumbled, "that this wasn't exactly the way I pictured it all going down, but I guess I should give you credit for the assist. Fortunately, Flarge has been following you from the get-go. Once I saw your little plan developing, I figured there was no reason for me to bother stealin' the moon rock if you were gonna be doing it for me."

The thought that their brilliant plan had been useful to Haryle Laffar sickened Fern. After passing the Hirshhorn Museum and Sculpture Garden, Laffar steered Fern to the right. They cut through a more heavily wooded area, with nicely manicured shrubs, trees, and spring flowers. To their right was the redbrick Smithsonian building known as the Castle. Laffar shoved Fern into the line of trees. She stumbled over a patch of ivy and fell to the ground. As she fell, she spotted Sam's blond head in the grass. He was unconscious. Though it was dark, she made out Miles's head. Candace and Lindsey sprawled next to him on the ground. Sam's eyes were eerily open, as if he was dead.

Fern stumbled to her feet and ran to him.

"I wouldn't do that if I was you!" Laffar cautioned. "You see, I've put 'em all into a Hermes trance, and if you jar him awake, he won't ever come out of it."

Mr. Lin's was the fifth body in the row. Next to the still bodies Fern spotted two bright green beasts. Their red chests were moving up and down rhythmically, as if they were sleeping. Laffar had probably brought the Quetzals along in case of an emergency, knowing their wails would attract unnecessary attention with the Capitol police on high alert after the incident at Air and Space. The Sirens' yellow Mohawks distinguished them, even in the darkness under the trees. Fern checked to make sure the harmonica was still in her pocket.

After looking around for a moment, Fern realized that this was the perfect place to hide in plain sight. Dense rows of trees and shrubs surrounded about five feet of space. Although pedestrians were unlikely at this hour, anyone using the walkways on either side would be unable to see anything between the plantings.

Flarge emerged from the shadows. He was rotund, with a graying beard and yellow teeth. He wore an eye patch over his left eye.

"Flarge," Laffar said, "meet the famous Fern McAllister." The man glared at Fern with visible hatred. Laffar, still next to Fern, lowered his head so that his mouth was less than an inch away from her ear.

"Bet you're wondering about that eye patch of Flarge's,

aren't ya?" Laffar whispered so Flarge couldn't hear. Though she'd become somewhat desensitized after her harrowing experiences, Fern could still smell the rot and tobacco on his breath. "Well, sweetheart, I pulled his eye out with my own two hands when Flarge lost track of you for a day because he wasn't listenin' to me. Guess what, though? He sure does listen to me now!" Laffar began to laugh maniacally in Fern's ear.

Laffar looked Fern over once more. He believed that Vlad's real mistake had been trying to reason with the girl. His brother thought he could turn the girl against the Rollens so that she would join the Blouts. But Laffar knew better. No, he'd torture the girl a bit first before he used her blood and then disposed of her. He'd make her watch as he killed her friends.

With all the potion ingredients now collected, Laffar would finally make himself immortal and kill the girl whose existence had been a menace since her birth. With the girl and the small boy gone, maybe they'd start calling them the Unusual Nine. He chuckled at his own joke. It didn't really have the same ring to it, though, now did it? If Laffar got his way, it would soon be eight or seven in a declining sequence. His laughter tapered off.

"It's rock-handing-over time," Laffar said, with his hand out, as Flarge loomed large over the bodies of her friends. Fern was running out of options.

"I want to make sure they're conscious and alive first."

Laffar considered Fern's request.

"Flarge," Laffar said. "Wake up the little Normal girl. I know she won't be going anywhere, and I'm not opposed to her watching."

Flarge bent over Candace's limp body and muttered something into her ear. Fern's heart skipped a beat when she saw Candace's hand reach to rub her eyes. Groggily, she sat up in the grass.

"Fern!" Candace exclaimed, her eyes lighting up at the sight of her awake friend.

Flarge grabbed the girl's head between his hairy arms and told her to be quiet or else.

"She's awake. Of course the trance did nothing to cure her annoying personality, but I'm no miracle worker. Now tell me where the rock is."

Fern hesitated a moment, trying to think.

"Look, sweetheart, I can do a variety of things. I can start killing your friends here, or I can wake the Sirens up and put you to sleep and take the rock from you. I'm sure it's somewhere on you."

"If you thought that, you would've already put me in a trance," Fern replied. "You're afraid that I've hidden it somewhere and if you knock me out, you'll never be able to find it."

Laffar let a sly smile slip across his face. The girl was a worthy opponent. He stalked the five feet over to Candace and swept her up in his large arms.

"You tell me where the rock is *right now* or I swear I'll break her neck."

When she saw the genuine terror in Candace's eyes, Fern gagged. She reached into the inside zipped pocket of her jacket and unzipped it. She felt the sharp triangular tip of the moon rock and grabbed it. Fern extended her arm and opened her hand.

Laffar's eyes flashed. He dropped Candace to the ground and stepped over her. He snatched the moon rock from Fern's hand. A devilish, silver-toothed smile overtook his face. Running toward a tree in front of him, Laffar reached up and produced a golden goblet. As if he had no time to waste, he dropped the flat piece of lunar rock into the goblet. It made an Alka-Seltzer fizz as it dropped into the container.

The goblet already contained the Quetzal feather, the Golden Spike, and the Hope Diamond. As soon as the moon rock was completely submerged, something began to happen within the goblet.

Laffar peered inside the glass and his whole face became illuminated. A beam of unearthly light shot up from the golden cup.

"It's ready!" Laffar said. Finally, after decades of searching, he had completed the Everlasting Elixir. Now he must eliminate Fern as a potential threat to his plan. The Normal was less of a problem, but he'd remove the possibility of any interference by putting them both under the Hermes spell.

"Flarge," Laffar shouted, unable to contain his diabolical jubilation, "I'll put the two girls out and you get blood from the boy. We'll be able to use the fresh blood from the girl's forehead."

Flarge lumbered toward Fern. She knew Laffar was about to put her in a Hermes trance and she panicked. If Laffar managed to perform the trance, she was sure she was dead.

They all were.

"Excuse me . . . Mr. Laffar." Candace's uneven voice drifted through the wooded area. "Before you mix the blood, I have information that you may want to hear."

Laffar held the beaming cup of light in both his hands. He lowered it a few inches. Flarge stopped and waited for further instructions.

"Why would *you* have any information that I'd want to hear?"

"Because you're about to make a terrible mistake."

Fern was in shock. "What are you doing, Candace?" she yelled.

"Shut up!" Laffar said, pointing to Fern. "You will let the girl speak or your brother will suffer the consequences."

Laffar was fairly certain the girl was playing some sort of game with him. But nevertheless a tiny, nagging doubt entered his thoughts.

"Why would you help me?" Laffar asked, raising an eyebrow.

"Because I want you to promise that if I do help you, you'll let me go," Candace replied.

Laffar looked at the wide-eyed girl. It was too bad he had to kill her . . . because he was about to teach her an important lesson. He was no longer surprised by the stupidity of Normals. They actually believed that there was inherent goodness in people. Yet without fail, they quickly turned on one another as well. This young girl, Laffar thought, was willing to backstab her friend to save her own life.

"If your information does prove useful, I promise to let you go," Laffar said. It was hard for him not to laugh.

Candace braced herself for the most important scientific speech of her lifetime.

"The fact that you were waiting for us outside the museum tonight leads me to believe you've been gathering information about us," Candace said, steadying her voice. "But we, Mr. Laffar, have also been gathering information about you. We know that you are holding in your hand the completed Everlasting Elixir. We also know that the Elixir, if mixed with an Unusual's blood, will transfer the power of said Unusual to whoever drinks the potion."

"If I needed all this explained to me," Laffar said, impatiently interrupting the girl, "I would have asked."

"Please let me finish, sir," Candace said, mimicking the professorial tone her mother always used when addressing a room full of chauvinistic male doctors. "I believe from what I've witnessed tonight that you plan on mixing both the blood of Fern and the blood of Miles together with the potion in order to transfer their powers to you. But I also believe you have not studied blood the way my father, who is a certified hematologist, has. A hematologist, in case you don't know, is a doctor whose specialty is blood. What you do not know about blood's unique properties is that if you mix two unique specimens, they will blend together and lose their uniqueness. The blood ceases to exist on a molecular level in the way that it does when it is not combined with other specimens."

"What exactly are you getting at?" Laffar asked, beginning to understand the girl's point.

"If you want both Miles's and Fern's powers, you should not corrupt the potion with both of their blood samples at the same time. You will likely get neither person's power this way. Instead, you should do one at a time."

Laffar scrutinized the girl. She certainly *talked* like a hematologist's daughter.

"Another thing you should realize, from a common-sense perspective, of course, is that you will most likely want to keep whoever's blood you use first awake. I can't imagine the drinking of the potion will go well, when it occurs, if the person has none of his or her powers available to transfer because you've put him or her in a trance."

Laffar began to seriously consider keeping the girl alive. Someone with half a brain could be useful. Flarge was good for brawn, but Laffar often wondered if he was the only one among his Blout unit who had any sense at all.

"How have you figured all this out?" he asked, marveling at the young girl's intellect.

"Haven't you heard? I am Candace Tutter, grade seven, and a genius," Candace said, puffing out her chest. If she had to evaluate her scientific presentation, she would've given herself an *A*.

"I'll knock her out and wake the Unusual boy! We'll kill them all at once after I've drunk the potion." This time, Laffar only had to look deeply into Candace's eyes and she was out once more. She slumped back down to the grass.

Laffar moved down the line, rousing Miles from his Hermes trance.

"Fern!" Miles said, seeing his friend for the first time since he'd teleported from the museum. Fern fervently wished he'd teleported to the hotel and not back outside to the museum entrance. She was sure, knowing Miles as she did, that he'd returned to make sure Candace, Sam, and Lindsey were all right. Now he was lying here in the weeds.

"Let's do him first," Laffar said.

"You try to teleport out of here and they are all dead," Flarge said, grabbing Miles and carrying him over to Laffar. Laffar took a switchblade out of his back pocket in order to cut Miles and get some of his blood.

Fern could've teleported at that moment. She was not being carefully watched. But she knew that as soon as Laffar noticed she was gone, he would certainly kill one of those who remained in retribution.

"Wait!" Fern screamed.

"What is it?" Laffar said, grabbing Fern's ear.

"Take my blood first!" she demanded, tears streaming down her face.

"What's this now?" Laffar asked, partially amused by the fact that he'd managed to turn the heroic Fern McAllister into a sniveling mess.

"I don't want my powers anymore. They've brought me nothing but horrible pain! I just want to be a Normal. I never asked for any of this. I can't stand it a second longer."

Fern continued to plead with Laffar.

"Please, I'm begging you. Just do it."

Laffar looked at Fern McAllister with disgust. She wasn't a hero, she was a coward. She was also a disgrace to every Otherworldly—Rollen or Blout—alive. She was willing to hand over her powers without a fight? She wanted to give up the one thing that separated her from the chaff of mankind? It was revolting. But he didn't want to hear her sniveling for the next few minutes while he dealt with the boy. Blood was still flowing from the wound on her forehead. He took his finger and wiped Fern's blood with his fingertip.

Then, rather unceremoniously, he dunked his finger into the golden goblet, which was still glowing with white light.

Laffar raised the goblet to his red lips with both his hands.

"Nooooooo!" Miles shrieked at the top of his lungs, sobbing. Flarge placed his hand over Miles's mouth, preventing him from either moving or making more noise.

Haryle Laffar looked at Fern, still alive, over the brim of the golden goblet. "No one trifles with a Laffar brother without paying the ultimate price," he said, smiling as the white light made his silver tooth positively sparkle. "Night, sweetheart."

Laffar gulped the liquid of the potion down until all that remained in the cup was the moon rock, the Golden Spike, the feather, and the diamond.

Almost instantly, he fell to his knees. Fern collapsed on the ground at the same time, as both man and girl cried out in unbearable pain.

the transfer

Laffar hadn't anticipated that the transfer of Fern's powers would be such a painful process. Still, as he writhed on the ground, the pain slowly abating, he figured it was a small price to pay for immortality and the ability to teleport.

Fern rocked to her feet. Her pain was diminishing as well. Flarge still restrained Miles.

Laffar tried to stand, but he couldn't. He felt so weak, he could barely move his arms. He was flat on his back, lying in the ivy under the first row of leafy trees.

Flarge stood back, holding Miles, unsure of what to do next.

"What have you *done* to me?" Laffar panted, unable to raise his voice above a whisper.

"I'm afraid you've done it to yourself," Fern said, leaning over Laffar's body. "Don't you recognize my eyes?"

Laffar had no choice but to look directly into them.

"Your brother said that I was the spitting image of my mother, Phoebe Merriam." Anger boiled within Fern. "Vlad never told you that, did he? Otherwise you would have pieced it all together . . . and realized that the eyes you've been staring into belong to your own daughter."

"No," Laffar whimpered. "It's im-impossible."

"If you'd known that, I'm guessing you know enough about Otherworldlies to figure out that breaking one of the most sacred Otherworldly tenets—desecrating your own flesh and blood in any way—carries a severe consequence. An Otherworldly loses all his strength, and becomes as weak as he was on the day he was born. When you drank your own daughter's blood, you violated the oldest rule in *The Undead Sea Scroll*."

Laffar let out a pitiful whimper. Painstakingly bringing his hand to his mouth, Laffar began to whistle. Fern realized he was testing her theory, trying to see if he still had the power to summon the wails of the Sirens, thereby incapacitating her.

But Fern was confident.

Sam's backup plan had worked.

Laffar wouldn't be able to control the Sirens any longer, now that he had lost his Hermes powers. It might even take him time to learn to walk again.

The Sirens did awaken to the sound of Laffar's weak whistle and stood upright, straightening their giant legs. Fern watched as the two large, beautiful creatures extended what looked to be enormous green wings. They began flapping furiously. Fern took out Preston's gifted harmonica, bracing for the wails that she was sure were coming. Instead the Sirens lifted off the ground, rustling the trees and bushes much as a helicopter takeoff might.

Soon the Sirens were hundreds of feet up, gliding through the air, their beautiful green bodies creating a luminous line across the District sky.

Laffar had nowhere to look but up and began to mutter as he saw his prized Sirens fly off. They were no longer under his control.

Fern picked up the knife that Laffar had dropped to the ground. For the briefest of moments, she considered driving the knife into Laffar's chest. She would never have to worry about him again.

But she wasn't a killer like her father was. Instead she took the bolt cutters from her jacket and wiped them off and placed them next to Laffar, just out of reach. Turning around, she waved the knife at Flarge.

"Let him go!" she said. Flarge released Miles, who darted next to Fern. Flarge looked at the two Unusuals standing together, a united front against the Blouts. Before Flarge's eyes, the original promise of the Unusual Eleven was being realized. The prophecy was correct.

"If you leave right now," Fern said, "I'll let you go before I call the police."

"Don't leave me, Flarge," Laffar rasped.

Flarge took a long look at Laffar. He figured his best bet was to mimic the Sirens and cut his losses. Flarge took off, running as fast as his legs would carry him across the National Mall and toward the National Gallery of Art.

Meanwhile Fern and Miles whispered in the ears of Candace, Sam, Lindsey, and Mr. Lin, who remained slumbering in the grass. One by one, they came to.

"Are you sure we should've let Flarge go?" Miles asked, as anxious for revenge as Fern was after his long stint in the cage.

"I don't think he's going to get very far," Fern said.

In actuality, Flarge would get as far as Henry Park before a Capitol police officer stopped him for questioning and ultimately placed him under arrest.

Fern pulled out her phone. She dialed the Commander. Even Miles could hear the happy squeal of Mary Lou McAllister on the other line, asking if Fern was all right.

"I'm fine. I can't talk now. You need to call the police and tell them to come to the walkway outside the Castle. Tell them there is a suspicious man here, on the ground, acting strangely."

Fern hung up the phone. Covering her hands with the lining of her jacket, she dumped out the remaining contents of the goblet. She picked up the Golden Spike and the diamond and placed them in Laffar's jacket pocket. As she watched the diamond slide out of sight into his pocket, she remembered what Candace had said about the stone bringing bad luck to its possessor. Another legend proving its truth.

"Why aren't you picking those up with your hands?" Miles asked, squatting next to Fern.

"In a few minutes, when the police find Laffar still

here, with not one, but two national treasures stuffed in his jacket pocket, I don't want my prints on either one."

"Of course," Miles said. Behind the two Unusuals, Mr. Lin was now fully awake. His first sight was of his daughter, slowly regaining her senses. He rushed toward Lindsey, picking her up off the ground.

"You're okay," she cried, hugging him back tightly.

"What about the moon rock?" Miles asked.

"That's got my prints all over it already, so I think I'll hang on to it for now." She slipped the smooth gray rock into her jacket. The truth of the matter was, Fern could wipe her prints from the rock, but she wanted to ensure that no one could ever assemble the ingredients of the Everlasting Elixir again.

The group retreated out of sight in the shadows, wanting to make sure that Laffar was apprehended by the police. The police found Laffar lying beside a pair of bolt cutters, and soon after, they discovered what looked suspiciously like the Hope Diamond in his jacket pocket. Lindsey, Fern, Mr. Lin, Sam, Candace, and Miles watched as two uniformed officers lifted Laffar up and shoved him into the back of their squad car, warning him politely not to bump his head and letting him know he had the right to remain silent. Fern recognized one of the policemen immediately. It was Officer Hallet. He was having another busy night.

But then again, so was Fern.

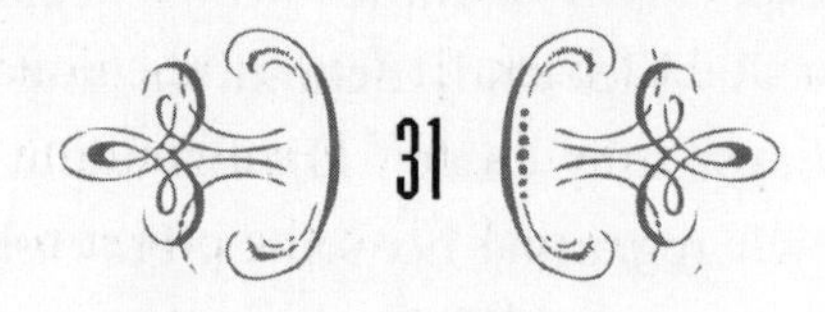

31 the ghost bandit

Fern felt a sharp jab to the ribs and jumped up out of her seat at Ford's Theatre.

"Time to wake up, Fern," Sam said. "The presentation's over."

"What happened?"

"What always happens," Preston Buss said, leaning over and smiling at Fern. "Lincoln got shot by some crazy actor."

When Preston had insisted on taking a seat next to Fern, both Sam and Candace Tutter were visibly annoyed. All they wanted to do was talk about last night's events, but with Preston there, they couldn't. Fern smiled in response to Preston's tired joke, and Candace and Sam both had to repress the urge to punch Fern in the shoulder.

Sam had realized the night before that his sister had a crush on his best friend. He figured it out when, after

Laffar's arrest, Fern insisted on teleporting to the cages where Miles had been held—all in the hopes of getting Preston's harmonica back. It was a ridiculous mission in light of the night's events, but Fern wouldn't take no for an answer and no one really had the power to stop her.

Still, when Fern fell asleep on Preston's shoulder during the reenactment of Lincoln's assassination at Ford's Theatre, Sam almost lost his lunch, even though they hadn't had lunch yet. When Preston refused to wake her, Sam felt like yelling at his friend to stop coddling his sister.

Ford's Theatre wasn't the only place Fern fell asleep that day. The week's physical toll finally caught up with her. Headmaster Mooney thought he'd saved the best of the itinerary for the last day of the St. Gregory's trip. After the long-awaited trip to the zoo, the group was to travel to Ford's Theatre, then take a scheduled tour of the White House, followed by a late lunch at the famous wood-paneled Old Ebbitt Grill. Exhaustion overcame Fern while she stood in the White House's State Dining Room. The guide was telling the group that Chelsea Clinton had thrown pizza parties in the famous room, and Fern began snoring standing up.

Candace nudged her that time, but not before several heads turned, including Mrs. McAllister's. Headmaster Mooney, delighted that he could see the light at the end of the spring trip tunnel, didn't let it bother him. The nightmare that was the St. Gregory's 2011 Spring Break DC Trip would be over soon enough. The one-of-a-kind group of presidential heads could mercifully be returned to the storage shed for two more years.

As for the rest of the crowd, no one dared make fun of Fern. In truth, her newfound narcolepsy was only adding to her mysterious reputation. Rumors had spread (mostly through Blythe Conrad and Lee Phillips) that Fern had been sneaking out of her room every night, exploring the city on her own. No one knew quite what to make of the girl with the pale lime eyes.

When the group arrived at the Old Ebbitt Grill, the seat jockeying began immediately.

"Can I sit with you?" Preston asked, moving close to Fern as the students from St. Gregory's filed into the historic restaurant.

"Our table's full, Preston," Sam said even though they hadn't found a table yet. "We don't have room for anyone else."

Sam looked expectantly at Fern. He wanted her to back him up. Fern was divided. She did like Preston. But she was also dying to talk to Sam, Candace, and Lindsey about last night.

There was no way to do both.

Fern wondered if her life would be a series of these kinds of decisions—the choice between living her life like everyone else or giving in to her differences.

"Preston," she said, looking into his deep brown eyes, "how about we hang out when we're touring the Capitol after lunch?"

She could tell she'd wounded him, if only slightly. To soothe his hurt feelings, she pulled his recovered harmonica from her pocket and played a few barely recognizable bars of "Amazing Grace" before handing it back to him. Preston walked away half smiling, in search of his other roommates.

In all honesty, Fern didn't think about him for long.

"I've secured a booth!" Candace yelled, waving her hand in the air. Candace had managed to find them the best of all the booths, tucked away in the corner of the restaurant, where the high wooden benches had backs at least six feet tall. It was as close to private as they could get. If Miles hadn't had to return home to his aunt the night before, things would have been totally perfect.

Candace and Lindsey sat on one side of the table, and Fern and Sam sat on the other. They grabbed their menus and set them aside, all four exuding happy exhilaration over last night's triumph. A few of the other St. Gregory's students stared at the grouping curiously from afar, wondering what Candace Tutter, the biggest nerd in the seventh grade, was doing sitting with Sam McAllister and Lindsey Lin. But the foursome was too involved in conversation to notice.

"Do you know they're calling Laffar the Ghost Bandit?" Candace offered in her high-pitched voice.

"Really?" Lindsey asked.

"I saw the news this morning," Candace prattled. "The Smithsonian released the surveillance footage and it's kind of grainy, but you can see the bolt cutters appear out of nowhere over the lunar rock. Then all of a sudden, you see the cutters move on their own like a catapult, launching the rock in the air. A guard comes into the picture with a flashlight to check out the commotion, and then, BOOM! He gets knocked out by the floating bolt cutters and the rock disappears."

"So they think that Laffar's a ghost?"

"They still can't figure out how he didn't appear in the security film," Candace responded.

"You actually knocked the security guard out?"

The voice came from behind them. All at once, the foursome turned their heads around.

"Miles!" Candace was the first to shout. Miles's brown skin was scrubbed clean, and he was wearing a freshly pressed Joe Mauer jersey that was at least seven sizes too big for him. Fern laughed as she noted that Miles still had on his ripped Twins cap. His large-framed glasses nearly swallowed his face. He pulled up a chair at the end of the table.

"I can only stay for an hour," he explained. "Aunt Chan's become a worrywart since the whole kidnapping thing." He let his wide smile wash over the group. *It is so good to see Miles again,* Fern thought.

"How did you know where we were?" Sam asked.

"Aunt Chan," Miles said. "She knew you'd be here."

The conversation among the five flowed easily, sharing as they did the common bond of last night's traumatic events.

"What was really weird," Sam said, as they began to go through all the proceedings of the prior evening, "was that Laffar used the Sirens' cries to subdue Lindsey, and the wails worked on me, too, when the wails aren't supposed to affect Normals."

"Maybe you're an Otherworldly and you don't know it!" Candace exclaimed.

"Or you were having sympathy Siren pains," Lindsey teased.

"I'm telling you, I fell into a trance," Sam insisted defensively.

"What *I* still can't figure out is how you knew about the Otherworldly punishment for desecrating next of kin," Lindsey said, referring to Sam's vital backup plan, which had been fully exposed now that it had worked.

In the hallway the night before, Sam had explained that if worse came to worst, Fern should make sure that Laffar drank the potion with her blood in it first. He reasoned that Laffar wouldn't know that he was drinking his own daughter's blood, which would render the Otherworldly completely mortal. The potion in this case would have the opposite of its intended effect.

What Fern knew already, and what Sam couldn't tell Lindsey, was that he'd learned the fact from *The Undead Sea Scroll*, which he'd stolen from the Lins' home the week before. Sam shot Fern a knowing look. Fern had promised Sam she wouldn't betray him as long as he returned the book. They'd decided to ask their mother to get the book back from pilfering Mooney. Fern had no doubt that the task would be easy for the Commander to accomplish. The Commander seemed to be the only person Mooney genuinely feared.

"I'd heard it from Alistair Kimble," Sam lied, "when he was first explaining how important family is to Otherworldlies and the power kin has in the culture—for both Rollens and Blouts." Although Fern had shared Sam's backup plan with Candace before the mission began, even Candace didn't know where the information had actually originated.

Fern looked around at the assembled group. She realized that there wasn't anything she wouldn't do for any one of them, and they for her. Whatever other people called them didn't matter. They were her family.

Fern tried to change the subject away from Sam's backup plan.

"I'm just glad your father is a hematologist so you knew all that stuff about the blood," she said, looking at Candace. "If he'd taken Miles's blood first, we all would have been done for."

"Oh, my father's not a hematologist," Candace said with a smirk.

"He's not?" Miles said, stunned.

"I made all that up. See, I was trying to think of a reason why Laffar should feel he needed to use Fern's blood first. It was the first idea that popped into my head."

"How did you know he would believe you?" Lindsey asked, her jaw still agape.

"I've learned that once people think you're smarter than they are, they'll pretty much believe anything you tell them—it's the two *C*s, credentials and credibility."

The other four members grinned and shook their heads at Candace Tutter. She was turning out to be a real piece of work.

Miles turned to Fern. "I had a dream about another one of us," he whispered to Fern while the others discussed what they would eat.

"Really?"

"I think she's Austrian or German or something." His eyes widened with the buzz of discovery. "Guess what? She shoots fire *from her hands*!"

Miles stopped as the others' conversation died down. Soon the waitress arrived. They asked for five grilled cheese sandwiches, five orders of fries, and five Cokes. The five perfect sandwiches arrived—piping hot, with gooey melted cheese leaking out the sides. Candace gave Miles, who had the appetite of a boy twice his size, half her sandwich. Fern looked at him in his ripped Twins cap, gobbling his third half sandwich down. She took strange comfort in the fact that she'd now found another person like herself. Miles also had to shoulder the weight of a prophecy he had never chosen to be a part of.

In the dim light of the old restaurant, the unlikely group feasted on fries. The cheese spread into dangling lines connecting the bread to the bites in their mouths. Fern washed a large mouthful of buttery bread and cheese down with a gulp of fizzy Coke. Nothing had ever tasted more delicious.

In a few more minutes, it would be time for Miles Zapo to return to his aunt in Mound, Minnesota, and resume his status as the world's number one Minnesota Twins fan. Fern would be sad to see him go. But she took comfort in another prophecy that was all but assured of coming true.

Miles Zapo and Fern McAllister would cross paths again very soon. Whatever the future held, Fern knew they would tackle it together.

acknowledgments

First and foremost, I want to thank John and Clare Kogler, the best first readers a girl could ask for. Bradford Lyman and Marnie Podos had tremendously helpful things to say during the writing of this book. Thanks to Jan Wilhelm for lending her attentive eyes to later drafts. More generally, John Hurlbut has been a constant source of sage advice and encouragement. I am so grateful, as well, to Joel McIntyre, who, as my very wise and very underpaid consigliere, always manages to say exactly the right thing when I need it most. Under the steady and imaginative hand of my editor Sarah Sevier, these characters have flourished—with her help, it all seems easy. Finally, thank you to Faye Bender, who makes dreams come true.